ONE BABY DADDY

A DATING BY NUMBERS NOVEL

USA TODAY BESTSELLING AUTHOR

MEGHAN QUINN

CHAPTER ONE

HAYDEN

"Do you have any regrets about that fight with Marcus Miller?"

"No."

Flashes of light repeatedly go off, the clicks a sound I've become accustomed to.

A sound I hate.

Sip my water.

Look around the room.

Cameras point in my direction, stage lights blare from above, the bill of my hat being the only protection from the onslaught of light. I adjust it, curving down the sides as reporters raise their hands for the next question.

I know what they want to prove, what they want to get at, but I'm not taking the blame.

"So you don't think the fight cost you advancement in the playoffs?"

Of course he would ask that question.

Bob, I think his name is.

He's a dick. He makes it his mission to turn any story into

1

something completely fabricated for more reads on his news site. I'll never understand why the Brawlers still let him in the media room.

"The shots O'Reilly deflected cost us our advancement. He played a hell of a game and shut down our offense."

"You were tied heading into the last five minutes of the game, right before you were sent to the penalty box, leaving your team short a man. You don't think that has anything to do with the loss?"

I cap my water bottle and clear my throat. Pinching the microphone with my fingers, I lean in and look directly at the smarmy reporter with yellow teeth, sporting a brown suit and a cue ball of a head. "Tell me, Bob, if someone came up to you and slapped a hockey stick across the back of your legs, would you bend over and ask for another? Or would you have retaliated?" He's about to answer, but I cut him off. "From the look of it"—I eye him up and down—"*you* would have bent over, but that's not how I handle things. Miller deserved to be brought down to the ice, and I won't apologize for my actions." I grip the table's edge and look around, ready to stand. "Unless you have any other questions about the actual game, I'm done for the night."

Questions fly but I don't listen, I zone out and stand from the table, taking my water with me.

Gripping the curve in the bill of my hat, I walk down the steps of the podium and head out of the media room, my publicist hot on my heels.

"Could have handled that better," he says, trotting next to me to keep up with my pace.

"Well, we just lost our chance at fighting for the championship, so excuse me for being fucking pissed."

"Steinman is not going to be happy about that comment."

Greg Steinman is the owner of the Philadelphia Brawlers, and the controlling nitwit sure as hell won't be happy with that comment, but he can deal with the repercussions. I'm allowed to be pissed. I answered their questions, I played the media game, but I don't deal well with being blamed for the loss. There are a lot of factors that went into that game, resulting in us being knocked out of the playoffs. We are a team. Everyone contributes to every aspect of the game, for fuck's sake.

Do I regret cracking Marcus Miller's jaw with one solid punch to his face? Fuck no. That dickhead had been on my ass the whole series taking cheap shots with his stick. Today was the only time I lost my cool, which is rare for me. It takes a lot for me to shuck my gloves and fight on the ice.

And maybe the Renegades will be going to the championship, but Marcus won't be playing. I made sure of it when my fists connected with him over and over.

I squeeze my hand, pain searing through my bruised and swollen knuckles.

"I'll deal with Steinman," I huff out. Turning the corner to the locker room, the space is silent, my teammates either quietly packing up or already gone after Coach's speech.

Next year, we will train harder. We will study harder. That championship will be ours.

It's the same damn thing you hear after every hockey season. I might be a rookie in professional hockey, but I've heard my fair share of end-of-year speeches and this one is no exception. Did I think we would win the championship my rookie season? No, but fuck, it would have been awesome.

"Are we not meeting?" James asks, looking so goddamn put together it's pissing me off. One hair out of place would have been nice, one button undone, one showing of how upsetting our loss was would be fucking comforting at the moment.

"Does it look like I want to meet with you right now?" I toss my water bottle into my locker and shift around my gear, pulling my wallet and keys from the locked box. My phone is already in my pocket, and the suit I'm supposed to be wearing is hanging from the coat hook. Fuck that shit. I'm walking out of here in a T-shirt and athletic pants. "Can't you tell now is not a good time?"

"When will be a good time?"

Head turned down, my hand gripping the back of my neck, I answer, "When I'm fucking ready."

Doesn't he get it? The last things I want to talk about right now are endorsement deals and positive publicity during the off-season. Let me fucking mourn my loss for a day. He should know this. Working with athletes, we take a loss hard, let alone a loss that ends the season.

Shifting behind me, his shoes rubbing against the short carpet of the locker, he says, "I'll call you tomorrow."

Tossing an almost empty roll of tape across the room, I spin on my heel, suit hooked in my finger and hanging over my shoulder, I say, "Don't bother. I'm heading to Binghamton for a few weeks, clear my head. I'll call you."

"Hayden." He walks next to me as I make my way to the parking lot. "We have some important matters to discuss. You have business meetings you have to attend."

I ignore him and continue on my path.

"What about the power drink deal? They have a promotional photo shoot scheduled."

"I'll be there; send me the information."

"I really think we need to talk about this."

Halting, I come within inches to James's face, bending at the knees to meet his shorter height. My voice is menacing when I speak, my jaw tight with each syllable uttered. "If you want to keep your job, I suggest you leave me the alone for now. Give me fucking space, man."

Startled, James backs up, hopefully well aware of the kind of damage I can cause despite my usual sunny and outgoing temperament.

I'm a fucking fun guy, easygoing, but when it comes to my sport, my job, I take it seriously and expect nothing but the best from myself. When I lose, I need time to regroup.

Succumbing to my request, James backs off and leaves me to walk alone to my black Porsche Cayenne, one of three cars still left in the parking lot.

Unlock. Toss the suit in the back.

Everything feels so . . . robotic.

Sitting behind the wheel, I let out a long breath and press my forehead against the cool leather.

The season is over. "Fuck," I whisper and push the start button, the car coming to life.

The windshield is glistening, the leather seats chilly, and since I'm only wearing a T-shirt, my entire body stiffens, aches. I know I should have showered. I know I should have worked out the lactic acid currently burning my muscles. I know what I should be doing as an elite athlete.

But I welcome the chill.

Philadelphia in spring isn't pretty and isn't easy on you. It's chilly and dreary, which is perfect because that's how I'm feeling right about now.

Letting my car warm up for a few minutes, I take my phone from my pocket and let out a long sigh.

After the game text messages are either fun to read or fucking dreadful. Tonight's round of messages are going to fall under the category of torture, especially when I get to my dad's text. I know it's there, and I can tell you what it's going to say before I even read it.

Call me.

Two simple words that hold so much weight I dread seeing them come from him. I might be an adult now, twenty-three to be exact, an old rookie in hockey years, but I still fear the wrath of my dad, the lecture I get whenever I get in a fight.

I taught you better than that.

True men don't fight on the ice; they prove their point with their footwork.

Do you enjoy upsetting your mother?

It's the same thing every time, and frankly, even though I'm grateful for the time my dad has put into getting me to where I am today, I'm not up for the lecture.

Bringing my phone to life, I press on the green text message button.

Ten. *Christ.*

Scrolling through, I see a few from Calder, one of my best friends, telling me to call him when I'm done with the press. Some from my friend Racer congratulating me on a stiff right hook—I chuckle at that one—one from my publicist—insert eye-roll—a few from my mom, *and* the infamous text from my dad.

I can deal with the text from my dad when I'm in a better headspace, so I call Calder.

"Where are you?" he answers.

"In my car, in the player's parking lot." My car starting to warm up.

"Rachel made some bread pudding and I have some beer chilled. Come over."

I strap my seatbelt on. "Does the bread pudding have raisins in it?"

"No."

"Be there in twenty."

~

My keys fall against the marble countertop as I take a seat at the kitchen island of Calder's house. One of our defensemen, Calder Weiss, knows exactly how to sulk. In private with beer and sweets.

When I joined the Brawlers, Calder took me under his wing, and through the season we grew incredibly close, relying on each other for the good and the bad. This being the bad.

"Saw your interview." Calder hands me a beer and chuckles. "Steinman is going to have your ass."

"Tell me something I don't know."

He chuckles some more. "But the guys are worshipping you for finally telling that piranha off. Bend over . . ." Calder sips his beer a smile on his face. "Man, that was great."

Taking a gulp of beer, I feel the faint tug of a smile on my lips. "I'm not sorry."

"Evidently."

Rachel strolls into the kitchen wearing an apron, looking domestic and right at home. A month ago, Calder met Rachel at a noodles and donuts restaurant . . . outside of the bathroom. Romantic, right? The best part, Calder was dressed up for his little girl, Shea, as a fairy, so he was decked out in fairy wings and a tiara looking like a real man-lady. For some reason, Rachel couldn't say no to giving him her phone number.

That's some game right there.

They've been together ever since and I have to admit, I adore Rachel. She's perfect for Calder and has really taken on the role of a female figure in Shea's life. You can tell Rachel loves that little girl.

"Are we ready for bread pudding, or do you need more time to drink your manly beer?"

Calder takes the seat next to me. "Bread pudding."

I nod in agreement. "Bread pudding."

"You got it."

Making her way around the kitchen, she pulls a few plates from the cabinets, some spoons, and dishes out three heaping helpings of her banana bread pudding. She tops them with some melted caramel and a little scoop of vanilla ice cream.

God bless this woman.

"Here you go, boys. Sulk away."

"Thanks, babe."

"Yeah, thanks, babe," I mimic. Calder territorially eyes me—a playful warning—and then dives into his dessert.

I do the same, scooping up ice cream, caramel, and bread pudding all in one bite.

Heaven.

"Was this supposed to be a celebration dessert?" I ask, mouth full.

"I figured it could go either way. I did pop the congratulations balloons I'd bought, figuring a congratulations on your loss wasn't appropriate."

"It's appreciated," Calder says.

We sit in silence, enjoying our dessert, no need to speak about what happened on the ice. No need to hash it out. What's done is done; we can't go back.

When I finish my dessert, I take my plate to the sink, rinse it, and then stick it in the dishwasher. "That was really good; thank you, Rachel."

"Anything for the tripod." She winks.

It's what we jokingly call ourselves, a nickname Calder doesn't quite appreciate, being that Rachel and I get along so well that we joke around with Calder more than he wishes.

Calder takes his empty plate along with Rachel's, presses a light kiss across her temple, and then hands me the dishes to take care of. It's hard not to be a tripod when we look like a goddamn old married couple, a weird threesome married couple.

Wrapping Rachel in his arms from behind, Calder asks, "What are you going to do now? Take some time off?"

Propped against the counter, I grip the edge of the marble. "Yeah. I'm sure my parents will want me to stay with them for a few weeks."

"Where do they live?" Rachel asks.

"Scranton." I drag my hand over my face and let out a long breath of air. "Not sure I want to go there though. I know my dad, and he'll want to rehash every angle of the game until I'm blue in the face. And staying here in Philly"—I shake my head—"I don't want to be sequestered to my apartment in fear of running into Brawlers fans."

"They're brutal."

And that's the goddamn truth. Beyond brutal. They've been known to flip cars over because of a loss, and I can only imagine the kind of beating the city is taking tonight.

"Vacation then?" Rachel asks. "I heard Europe is beautiful during the summer."

I chuckle. "Yeah, I wish. As much as I would love to leave the country after tonight's game, I have some obligations keeping me close to Philly and New York City." I push off the counter and snag my keys. "I think I might spend a few weeks visiting my hometown."

"Binghamton, right?" Calder asks.

I nod. "Yeah, my friend Racer lives there. It might be good to play catch-up. Thanks for the dessert and half a beer. I'm going to head out."

"You sure?"

"Yeah, I'll talk to you guys later."

As I'm leaving, Rachel calls out, "For what it's worth, Miller deserved a hell of a lot more than the ass-beating you gave him."

I shut the door with a smile. Rachel is good people. Marcus, the prick, deserved so much more. Reaching into my pocket, I scan through the contacts on my phone and press send.

I turn the car on, and listen to the phone ring on my Bluetooth.

"Dude!" Racer answers. "You dropped that motherfucker so hard."

I pull out onto the street and head to my apartment. "How are you, man?"

"Semi-drunk after watching that game, a little turned on from your right hook, and wondering why you're calling me when most likely your dad is frothing at the mouth to recount your entire game for a good three hours."

Racer is one of few people who know my family well. That's what happens when you grow up together. You end up knowing the ins and outs of each other's lives.

"Haven't called him yet. Kind of waiting on that phone call."

"Smart."

Feeling awkward, I ask, "So, what would you say if I decided to come to Bing for a few weeks?"

He doesn't skip a beat when he asks, "Too afraid to go home?"

I laugh. "Not afraid, more not in the mood."

"Yeah, I would avoid that lecture train for as long as I could."

"Tell me about it."

"Are you asking if you can stay at my house? Because I'm on the hunt for a girl, and I don't want you stealing her away with your brawny athletic body and good looks. It would actually be detrimental to have you around."

Racer is such a nitwit.

"I was going to ask Mr. Lockwood if I could stay at his place for a few weeks; he's offered it up before."

"You fucker. Of course he would offer up his house to you. Let me guess, you leave a few signed hockey sticks around the house and call it even?"

Pretty much.

Racer and I both had Mr. Lockwood as a teacher in high school. He lives on a hill in a little cottage that overlooks the area. He's retired now and spends his summers in the Adirondacks, leaving his cottage up for grabs for any of his friends or former students.

"If I leave a signed jersey for the man, that's between me and him."

"Such bullshit." He huffs and says, "So you're coming to Bing, huh?"

"I think I need to."

"Then let me throw together a welcome home party, but you're paying for it."

I roll my eyes. Of course I am, the cheap fuck.

CHAPTER TWO

HAYDEN

R*ing. Ring.*
"It's about time you gave me a call."

After settling into Mr. Lockwood's cottage, organizing my clothes, putting away food I picked up from Price Chopper, and popping open a much-needed beer, I decided to finally call my dad.

"Sorry about the wait, Dad. I needed some time to cool down."

"I can understand that. So what happened, kiddo?"

Kiddo. I'm twenty-three with a year of professional hockey under my belt, and yet my dad still calls me kiddo. Oddly, it soothes me.

"This is going to sound really immature, but . . . he kept slashing me, Dad."

He chuckles. "Yes, it was quite clear Miller was taking cheap shots, but that doesn't mean you can lose your temper. I taught you better than that."

And he did.

React on the ice with skill not fists. It was ingrained in me from the very beginning, when I would spend countless hours in the driveway with my dad bundled up in pillows, acting as a goalie. He was larger than life in that goal, difficult to get anything past him. But he tested me, pushed me, encouraged me. Memories I'll always hold close to my heart.

"I know, Dad." I exhale and lean back into Mr. Lockwood's brown leather couch. "I'm sorry." It feels weird to apologize, but I know I let him down, not because we lost the game, ending our playoff run, but because I embarrassed him.

"No matter how heated you get, just remember where you came from. We don't solve problems with our fists. I know some fans go to games to see the fights, to see the brutal battle, but hockey is more than that. It's about your footwork, your puck handling, the communication with your teammates. It's about finding the small inches others don't see. That's what makes a great player, don't forget that."

"I won't." No matter how old I get, these lectures will always be a part of my life. "So how's Mom?"

There is a low chuckle from the other end of the phone. "Over talking about the game?"

"Still a little raw, Dad."

"Understandable." There's a smile in his voice. Everyone knows my dad as someone who's kept me in line, who's pushed me to be the best version of myself, but when it comes down to it, he's never pushed me too hard, and it's the reason he's backing off now. He knows I've punished myself enough, no need to harp on it. "Your mom is good. A little upset about the fight, but you know how she is, she'll get over it. I will say this, she was a little shocked from the power you have in that right hook."

"That's professional athletic training for you. She didn't pretend to faint, did she?"

More chuckling. "No, but she did tsk. I caught her looking at replays afterward making a little fist of her own."

"Yeah? Did she wish she could have a little piece of Marcus Miller herself?"

"I think so. You should have heard her during the game yelling louder than me. At one point she threw one of her throw pillows across the room."

"I can see where I get my temper. Calm, cool, and collected until we're pushed a little too far . . ."

"And snap, you two explode."

I chuckle. "Yeah, I definitely get that from Mom."

"The best is when she's in the kitchen cooking, and she forgets an ingredient or something doesn't turn out the way she wants it to. There is always a slam on the pan. It's my indication to boast about the meal and make it seem like it's the best thing she's ever made."

"Smart man. I remember the pound of the pan on the kitchen counter. I would stay in my room and not make myself known until I was called down for dinner."

"You know I can hear you, right?" my mom chimes in. I should have known she was on speakerphone.

"Hey Mom."

"Sweetie, what did we say about fighting?"

Jesus.

With the palm of my hand, I rub my eye.

"Already got the lecture from Dad. Believe me, I get it, you guys aren't happy."

"We taught you better, that's all." She takes pause. "But that Miller boy deserved a good swat to the eye socket in my opinion."

"Marion . . ." my dad warns.

She huffs and then asks, "Are you coming home now? What are your plans?"

They aren't going to be happy I'm in Binghamton instead of visiting with them, but after the long season and brutal loss, I need to be here. I need to step away from reality for a few weeks. I'm hoping they can understand that.

"Uh, not at the moment. I'm actually in Binghamton. I'm staying at Mr. Lockwood's cottage."

"Oh."

Silence.

Fuck.

"Nothing against you guys. I'll be visiting soon. I just wanted some space, you know?"

More silence.

This is what happens when you're close with your parents. They expect you to come home after a long hockey season or during college break, and when you don't, man, oh man, do they lay a heavy guilt trip on you, which I know I'm about to get.

"I'm a grown man, you know." I bite on my bottom lip. Fuck that sounds stupid. "I needed fresh air?" That came out as a question rather than a statement.

"I think he wants to get frisky, and he can't do that in our house, William."

Well, that's true, but not the reason.

"Mom, that's not the truth. If I wanted to get frisky with someone at your house, I would just pay for you two to go out to dinner."

"Hayden Robert!" I laugh. Faintly in the background, I can hear my dad chuckling as well. "Honestly, you men. I'm going to go finish my beef stew. Sweetie, make sure to make time for your parents."

"Will do, Mom. I love you."

"Love you, sweetie."

"I'm going to go too, son. I'm in the middle of carving a chair and my whittling hands are feeling good right now."

Both my parents are retired and happy as can be. For fun, my mom often makes loads and loads of food and invites the neighbors over for dinner. My dad spends a lot of his time in the garage, making handcrafted rocking chairs. They're impeccable. He sells them at a local store in Scranton, and they do very well. He loves doing it and it keeps him sharp.

"Sounds good. I'll let you know when I'm headed your way."

"Don't take too long. Your mom will be nagging me every day until you come see us."

"And we can't have that, can we?"

"Not unless you want to hear from me every day."

Looking at the ceiling, I shake my head. "No, I definitely don't want that. Have a good one, and I'll talk to you guys later."

"Love you, Hayden."

"Love you, Dad."

I hang up and stare at my phone for a few seconds, letting out a long breath. That was easier than I thought it was going to be. Probably because my dad knew I was already upset, he didn't need to go over the entire game in detail. And I was grateful for that.

Pulling up my text messages, I open the last one from Racer.

Racer: *Seven, my house, bring beer . . . and Little Debbie snacks.*

I roll my eyes. Such a fucking sweet tooth. Ever since I've known him, Racer has been obsessed with Little Debbie snacks, and it's only gotten worse since he's become an adult. Maybe because there is no one to stop him from overdosing. *Or maybe because he isn't really an adult . . .*

What time is it now?

Six. Shit, I better get moving, especially if I have to take Racer Little Debbie snacks.

～

"Everyone quiet down, quiet down." Racer is standing on a picnic table in his backyard, hushing the little crowd of people surrounding the fire pit. "The prince of the ice is here, the man with the killer right hook, the one and only Hayden Holmes." He carries out my last name a little longer than necessary while clapping.

"Get the fuck down, you tool," I say as Racer hops to the ground and pulls me into a bear hug, followed by a giant kiss to my cheek.

"God, I missed you." He grips my head with his palms, staring intently at me, his eyes glassed over. Someone is already drunk.

Just for the record, Racer is one of those guys who has no problem making an ass of himself, as you can tell.

"Good to see you too, man." I push at his chest, putting some space between us. Holding up a bag, I hand Racer his "treats." He practically eye fucks it, and in one giant rip, tears open the bag, the boxes of snacks falling to the ground.

Holding a box above his head as if it's baby Simba on Pride Rock, he shouts, "Star Crunch!"

Two other guys cheer as a girl I've never met rolls her eyes.

"Hey, where is everyone?" I ask, not knowing anyone here.

"What do you mean?" Racer rips open the box and the telltale sign of cellophane being opened slices through the cool night air. "I invited my friends. Did you think I was going to invite anyone else? Pssh, the only person from high school I talk to is you."

Of course.

Not that I talk to anyone else beside Racer either, but it would have been nice to at least know one more person. I'm a sociable guy, but there are times I'm not in the mood to make get-to-know-you small talk. There are times I just need to be Holmes, the lanky teen who likes hockey.

Gripping my shoulder, stuffing his mouth full, Racer mumbles, "Let me introduce you." He brings me to the little circle around the fire. "Hayden, this is Tucker and his fiancée, Emma. They like to make out a lot, so look out for that. The big guy over there with the permanent scowl is Aaron, but we all call him Smalls, and there is a pretty brunette floating around here I don't . . . see . . ."

"She's in the bathroom," Emma calls out just as she puts her hand on Tucker's thigh. They're snuggled up really close. They're in love; that's obvious.

"Thanks. The brunette is in the bathroom," Racer repeats, taking another bite of his Star Crunch.

Feeling slightly awkward, I hold my hand in a mock wave. "Nice to meet you all." To Racer I say, "I'm going to put the beer in the fridge. Need anything while I'm there?"

"I'm good to go now that I have these." He nuzzles his Little Debbie snacks.

Some things never change.

I give him a good pat on the back and head toward his house.

I could make my way around Racer's house with my eyes shut, I've been here so many times. When I was younger, during the off-season, I would spend weekends helping Racer and his dad with little projects around the house. My dad would come along too, loving to get his hands on any kind of construction. The log house looks the same, even after the passing of Racer's dad. Fuck, what a shitty day that was.

The familiar scent of wood and leather greets me when I walk through the back door. My second home.

But something is missing . . .

"Where's all the furniture?" I whisper, scanning the area. There is nothing homey about the space. Not that Racer's dad was a big decorator, but there was more in the house than a recliner and dining room table.

The kitchen isn't far from the back door. I make my way to the fridge, pop the beers inside after grabbing one for myself, and turn back around to observe the space. Why has everything gone?

Casually, I make my way around the kitchen to a little built-in shelf near the hallway. There are unopened envelopes stacked high. I give the back door one more glance and pick one up.

Overdue.

In bright red, a giant stamp across the envelope.

I pick up another, and another.

All overdue.

What the fuck?

"Who the hell are you?"

Startled, I drop the envelopes to the ground and splash a little of my beer on the hardwood floors.

"Shit." I pick up the bills, re-stack them, and squat to wipe up the little droplets of beer with my hand.

"Unless your hand is a Downey towel, that is not going to work." The smooth sound of a women's voice echoes through the empty space.

I glance over to find pink painted toenails laced through white flip-flops, and a set of long and lean toned legs in short denim shorts. Moving my eyes up, I take in her tight red shirt, showing off an inch of midriff. Farther up. Full breasts, V-neck shirt with an ample amount of cleavage popping past the low-cut collar. Smooth olive skin, long brown hair curled at the tips. Slender neck, heart-shaped jawline . . .

My eyes scan the last few inches. Full lips, painted in red, high cheekbones . . . and those eyes.

Deep.

A heavenly chocolate.

Sultry with a hint of . . .

Anger?

"Are you done checking me out?"

Clearing my throat, I stand and wipe my hand on my pants. "Sorry, you . . . uh . . . startled me."

She walks to the kitchen and grabs the sponge from the sink. "Maybe because you're snooping where you shouldn't be." Bending in front of me, her head mere inches from my crotch, she wipes up the beer. "Who are you anyway? Does Racer know you're in here? He's a private guy and doesn't really like people in his house."

When she stands, I tilt my head to the side, studying her. "You must be the brunette Racer was talking about."

Tossing the sponge from her position, she lands it directly in the sink. Damn. "Avoiding my question, I see."

"Not avoiding." I stick out my hand. "I'm Hayden, known Racer since we were kids." I nod at the cabinets in the kitchen as she slips her slight hand in mine. "I helped install those on one of the hottest fucking summers of my life."

She quirks her head, a welcoming smile tugging at her lips. "Hayden Holmes? As in the man with the right hook?"

I roll my eyes and pull on the back of my neck. "How much was he talking about the fight?"

"Ever since we got here. He keeps trying to reenact it with everyone. When it was my turn, he told me to flop my tongue out of my mouth when he made fake contact."

"Jesus Christ . . . did you do it?"

She shrugs. "I mean, I had no reason not to."

I chuckle, loving her sense of humor. "So do you have a name, or are you just referred to as the brunette in the bathroom?"

"God, they have no class." Shakes her head. "Brunette in the bathroom is unfortunately my nickname, but I go by Adalyn."

Adalyn. Such a pretty name.

"Nice to meet you, Adalyn."

We smile at each other for a few moments before Racer busts through the back door, chocolate on his face, beer in hand.

"There you are. We thought your ass got stuck in the toilet." Racer comes up behind Adalyn and wraps his arm around her shoulders and pressing a kiss against her temple. "Did you meet my boy, Hayden?"

"I did." She scans me up and down, her little pink tongue barely wetting her lips.

"He didn't give you any problems, did he?"

Still eyeing me, I grow a little nervous wondering if she's going to call me out for snooping in front of Racer. I don't want to embarrass him, so I pray she keeps our little interaction to just us.

"Nah, he did spill some beer on your floor, but I took care of it."

"That's my girl." Racer presses another kiss against her cheek, and I wonder if they're romantically involved. From the stiff set of Adalyn's shoulders I'm going to assume no. Directing his attention to me, Racer says, "Addie Girl is one of my best friends and is untouchable, so don't even think about making a move on her."

"Untouchable, huh?" Adalyn asks, patting Racer on the stomach and pulling away, headed toward the backyard. "When did that happen?"

"When a professional hockey player, who just so happens to be one of my best friends, decided to grace us with his presence, that's when."

"Afraid I'll get caught up in all his muscles?" She's at the threshold of the door, waiting for his answer.

"Terrified."

Laughing, she steps out into the cool night air, heading straight for the fire pit.

When I make eye contact with Racer again, he shakes his head at me. "Off limits, man."

I hold up my hands. "Sure, man, off limits."

CHAPTER THREE

ADALYN

The fire pops as I take a seat next to Emma and Tucker. Their hands are linked, their bodies pressed together. I couldn't be happier for them.

Sort of.

I mean, I'm happy for them, I'm not a shitty friend.

But am I jealous?

Hell yeah, I'm jealous.

Have you seen Tucker? All broody and sexy and passionate about his girl. And I know he's good in bed from Emma's boasting, and when he's with her, he's overly protective. It's sweet, and makes me think maybe I want something like that one day.

One day being the key word.

Right now, I'm still just trying to figure out life after college as a nurse. Hours are long and grueling in hospitals. Patients are moody or downright nasty, and then there is the occasional incredibly sick patient or surprise death. Having to live through the worst of moments with family members takes a toll on you. I've been told you become immune to it at some point, but I have yet to feel numb around death, around bad medical news. I'm still very much affected and wonder every day if I chose the right profession.

"Little Debbie snack?" Emma asks, offering up two different boxes. Racer and his freaking treats. He's ridiculous.

"I'm good. Beer and sweets don't mix well in my stomach." I pat my belly just as Racer and Hayden join the circle on the opposite side from me.

Nudging my shoulder, Emma says, "Did you meet the hockey player? Tucker says he's really good."

At that moment, Tucker takes a second to lean forward and say, "Really good. His puck-handling skills are some of the best I've seen, and he just finished his rookie season. The guy has a huge future in front of him."

"Oh, sounds like he's an all-star. You should go talk to him." Emma is practically bouncing up and down, beyond excited, poking my leg to get me moving.

"Stop being obvious." I swat her hand away.

"You really should go talk to him." Tucker nods with his head toward Hayden who's intently talking to a drunk Racer.

"And say what? Heard you're good at hockey, want to show me your stick?"

Emma nods. "That's a great line."

"It would get my attention," Tucker adds.

"I'm not saying that."

"Why not?" Emma asks as Racer gets up and makes his way to the house, taking Aaron with him as more of a support so he doesn't fall over, leaving Hayden alone. "Oh, he's free, go talk to him."

Emma shoves me right off my seat and into the grass.

"What the fu—"

"Are you okay?" Hayden asks, moving to my side to help me up.

Glaring at a very happy Emma, I say, "Yeah, I'm fine."

Helping me up by the arm, Hayden towers over me, and I'm a little awed how the light of the fire flickers across his face.

"Tucker, will you help me get some more snacks? I'm hungry,"

Emma loudly announces, probably pulling the attention of all surrounding neighbors.

"Wha—" Emma gives him a stern look and recognition lights up in Tucker's eyes. "Oh, yeah, snacks. Boy, I could really use some more." Rubbing his belly, he stands and takes Emma's hand. Leaving me alone with Hayden.

That wasn't obvious at all.

I could kill them.

Looking behind at the retreating couple, Hayden asks, "How long have they been together?"

"Seems like forever," I sigh and take a seat on one of the logs surrounding the fire. Without invitation, Hayden joins me.

"I feel like we started off on the wrong foot."

"Well, you were snooping."

"Yeah." He pulls on the back of his neck, and I take that moment to observe him.

Strong, thick thighs stretch the denim of his jeans. Pulsing, sinew-filled forearms, biceps like boulders straining the sleeves of his T-shirt, and a set of the broadest shoulders I've ever seen, making me feel incredibly small and fragile. His jawline is sharp, caressed in a light brown stubble. And his eyes, shades of brown and gold hooded by dark brown eyebrows and a thick head of styled hair. He's rough and untamed with his scruff, but styled and sophisticated when it comes to his hair.

In fascination, I watch his large hand move back and forth along his neck. Does he have calluses on his hands from holding a hockey stick a good portion of his life? Does he enjoy the scrape of his fingers along his skin?

And his ears, they stick out barely more than others, giving him a boyish charm that warms my heart.

"I'm worried about him," Hayden says, pulling me from my reverie. "His house used to be fully decorated, fully furnished, and he has all those overdue bills. I didn't mean to snoop, I just . . . is he doing okay?"

"He's making things work," I answer honestly, knowing a little bit about Racer's financial struggle from Emma, who heard it from Tucker.

"I would offer to help him, but knowing Racer, he would never accept any kind of help."

"Never."

"So how do you know Racer? You guys seem pretty close." Chuckling, he adds, "Really close. Told me you were off limits."

My eyebrow rises, my head tilting to the side. "That man is infuriating. We're just friends if that's what you're getting at. I met him through Tucker and Emma, and for some reason, he thinks it's his job to protect me from any and all men."

"It's good to have a friend like that, you know, with all the psychos out there. You can never trust just anyone."

"Especially hockey players, right?"

"Oh no." Hayden shakes his head. "Hockey players are very trustworthy. Upstanding citizens. Some of the best people you will ever meet."

"Is that right?" I turn on the log to face him, straddling the wood. Insert your perverted thoughts right here, I know you're having them. "What brings you to Binghamton? Don't you live in Philadelphia?"

Propping his thigh on the log, turning as well, he says, "Needed a little breather. It was a long season, the Brawler fans are ruthless, so I didn't feel like walking around the city being heckled every turn of the corner."

"They do that?"

He nods slowly. "At the beginning of the season, when I was still getting my feet wet, we lost against our rivals. It was a tough loss and wasn't taken very well by the fans. The next day, I couldn't walk ten feet in the city without being booed. They are ruthless."

"Seriously? Wow, I had no idea grown men could be such babies."

"Grown men, women, and children." He chuckles. "So you can understand wanting to get away."

"Makes sense. I'm wondering why Binghamton out of all places. If I were you, I would have gone to some exotic location."

"Thought about it, but I have obligations in the city, sponsorships and whatnot. Figured this would be easier. And I'm staying in a killer cottage up on a hill that looks over the city. It's peaceful, just what I need."

"Sounds relaxing. What I wouldn't do for a little break right about now, which sounds ridiculous because I'm new to the workforce, but still . . ." I shake my head, hating that I have an early shift tomorrow. Seven to seven. It's better than a late night shift, but it's still tiring.

"What do you do?"

"I'm a nurse. It's a challenging job, and the hours are brutal. I work in a hospital so I see a lot of things that weigh heavily on me."

He's silent for a second before saying, "I can't imagine. The medical field is a tough one."

"It is. For the longest time I thought I was going to be a teacher, but somewhere along the way, I switched, deciding to be a nurse. Kind of wish I was grading spelling tests right about now."

Chuckling, he says, "More than assisting with removing forks from eyes and resetting broken legs?"

"Pretty much." I smile softly, studying him. He's engaged, interested with the way his body language points toward me, the lean in of his shoulders, the way his eyes are so intent on mine. He's different from other men I've talked to. Genuine. Real. I like that. And even though Racer can be one of the craziest people I know —regularly—he's also one of the most decent. It doesn't surprise me this man, who expressed *instant* concern for Racer's well-being, has been a friend for years. How he noticed straight away things weren't all sunshine and roses in Racer's world. That sort of friend is rare, and I think I've discovered a rare gem.

"What's going on over here?" Racer asks, stumbling into our little conversation. "What did I tell you, man? She's off limits. Right, Addie Girl?"

"I think you've hit your beer and sugar intake for the night." I pat his rock-hard stomach. How he's able to maintain his physique when downing a box of Little Debbie snacks a day is beyond me. He's one of those annoying people.

"Are you and Aaron in cahoots? He said the same thing." Racer sits behind me and places his chin on my shoulder, wrapping his arms around my waist.

Drunk Racer is turning into touchy-feely Racer. Happens every time.

I pat his arms and say, "Yes, we're in cahoots."

Striking a glance at Hayden, I notice his eyes fixed on Racer's arms intimately wrapped around me. He stiffly smiles and shakes his bottle and says, "I'm going to get a refill."

When he steps away, I elbow Racer in the gut.

"What the hell is wrong with you? Why are you being so possessive over me right now?"

"Possessive? I'm not being possessive."

"Racer, you're practically peeing a circle around me, warding off any guy who comes within ten feet of me."

"I'm not peeing a circle, but I can if you want me to. Just let me drink one more beer—"

"You're done with drinking beer tonight." I shake him off me. "Seriously, what's going on?"

His eyes are glassed over but I can still see a little bit of common sense floating around in that fogged-up head of his.

"I don't want you getting hurt, that's all."

"Well, I'm a big girl, Racer, and I can take care of myself."

"Then how come you let Logan hurt you?"

I let out a heavy sigh and sit on the log next to Racer.

"Logan was a mistake, and I got over that quickly. We're friends now. That's it. Crossing that line with him was stupid."

"Yeah, he sure as hell let you know his opinion on the matter. Who was the one there for you? Whose shoulder did you cry on? Mine, which now gives me the right to be super protective over you, because I don't ever want to see you that upset again, especially over a guy."

There is a time in everyone's life where they look back at a decision they made and think, yeah, I probably shouldn't have done that. Logan was my bad decision.

We were the three musketeers; Emma, Logan, and me. We somehow survived nursing school together and found jobs right out of college. When Emma started becoming serious with Tucker, we saw less of her and more of each other. Dinners led to late nights, which led to a stupid, yet passionate night.

Want to talk about the most awkward morning after ever? It was . . . torture. We sat there, sheets up around our chests, staring at the wall in front of us, wondering what we did, and when Logan's first words were, "That was a mistake," it was hard not to take it personally. That's when I went to Racer and cried it out. I guess you could call that mistake number two, because after a few good cries, we fooled around a little.

I know, I know.

Why is this girl a hussy? That's what you're thinking, right? And to tell you the truth, I don't know why; it's in my blood I guess. I like comfort and seek it from the wrong people. A therapist could have a field day with me.

And now Racer is super protective. And no, we don't like each other like that. We both came to the mutual agreement that we're better off as friends.

So basically, if you're noticing a pattern here, I'm friend-zone material. Maybe it's because I've never really been in a serious relationship. When I was in high school, dating anyone wasn't close to a possibility, having seven brothers. Yes, you read that right, seven brothers. I wasn't allowed to look at a boy without one of my brothers giving me a lecture about how boys only want is sex at that age, it won't be enjoyable, so I best wait until the little squids understand how to please a woman properly.

Which brought me to college. Nursing school is stressful. So much studying, so many late nights, so many parties to help you wind down.

See where this is going?

Without the protection of my brothers, I kind of . . . let loose. That's the *nice* way of putting it.

College was one giant whirlwind of studying, clinicals, and random one-night stands. If I had a good time, then some one-night stands turned into two- or three-night stands, but that was where it ended.

So I have no idea what it takes to be a good girlfriend, what it means to communicate effectively with another human being when it comes to love, and compromise? Sheesh, what's that?

If I were a guy, I would be *that* bachelor with the fancy apartment who's completely clueless when it comes to a girlfriend's needs.

Basically, I'm a total catch . . .

I lean in to Racer and press my head against his shoulder. "I appreciate you trying to prevent pain, Racer, but I'm a big girl and can handle whatever comes my way."

"Can you?" Even in his drunk state, I can see *some* clarity in his eyes. "Because do you see that guy over there?" Racer nods toward the back door to his house. Hayden is walking toward us, his eyes trained on me. "That guy right there has a look in his eyes, a look that says you're in for one hell of a ride if you choose to take the ride. But I don't want you to hop on, because you will get hurt." Having briefly seen him interact with others and particularly from his concern for Racer, yeah, I'm intrigued. *Until this moment.* What surprises me is Racer's reasoning. *What am I missing?*

"Have you actually thought maybe I'm not interested?"

"Pfft." Racer scoffs. "Please. The man is not only a professional hockey player with a bank account to put us all to shame, but he's good-looking, has a heart of gold, and believe me when I say this, he has a big penis."

"What?" I cough, choking on my saliva. "How do you know that?"

"I've known the guy forever. We went to school together, shared a gym class, and you're bound to see each other's junk." He carelessly shrugs. "Just happens. So knowing all of that, you can't tell me you aren't interested. The man is a goddamn catch."

"So if he's a catch, how come you don't want me going out with him?"

"Because, despite him being one of the best guys I know, his schedule, his lifestyle, it's not what you want. You want to slow down, you want to switch to a general practitioner office, and you want a quiet life. That's not what you'd get with him. Guarantee it."

Hayden smiles sweetly and takes a seat near Aaron, striking up a conversation. I study him from a distance. He isn't animated like Racer, but he isn't shy either. He's relaxed, confident. There is an air about him that makes him approachable and fascinating all at the same time.

"Adalyn, I'm fucking serious." Racer's voice drops, seriousness dripping from his tongue. "Don't even think about it." He has a heart of gold, is *extremely* good-looking, is smart and confident. And, thanks to my friend, I know he is packing serious meat.

How could I not?

CHAPTER FOUR

HAYDEN

I don't normally do this, which I'm sure guilty people say all the time, but I'm being completely honest.

I REALLY don't do this.

But after a few days of having dreams about Adalyn every night, I'm desperate. I want to get to know her better, you know, *as friends*.

At least that's what I'm going to tell Racer if he catches us. That's if I can find her.

She seems like a great friend, someone I want on my side, a confidant I not only need in my life but also want in my life. How can Racer be mad about that kind of response?

He can't.

And it's not like I want to take her back to the cottage, bend her over the couch, and fuck her till morning. I mean, that would be amazing, but right now, I just want to get to know her better. I barely spoke with her at the get together the other night. I felt cheated of an opportunity.

That's why I'm visiting my second hospital in the area, hoping to find Adalyn working.

I told you, I'm desperate.

Locking my car, I stroll into the main entrance of the hospital. There's a gift shop to the left chock-full of every occasional greeting card, balloon, and candy bar you can think of. To the right is a small waiting room with two people bent over, scrolling through their phones. It's quiet with a sterile feeling floating through the air. I can see why Adalyn wished she had a different job.

Walls coated in brown and mauve hues, floors off-white, speckled with multiple colors, the entire entryway depressing, the only bright color in the space is the red lipstick on the receptionist sitting at the front desk.

Making my way to the front, I pull her attention away from a crossword puzzle and clear my throat. "Hi, I was wondering if, uh, Adalyn was working today."

"Adalyn?" The girl looks me up and down, suspicion oozing from her. "Adalyn . . . who?"

Shit. I'm pretty sure saying Adalyn with the brown hair and killer legs will not go over well.

I decide to go a different route.

"You don't know Adalyn? The nurse with brown hair and, uh . . . long legs." I wince. "Really sweet and has a friend named Racer."

"Sir, I'm going to have to ask you to leave. Harassing employees is not tolerated."

"I'm not harassing—" I wipe my hand over my face, my shoulders tensing, eyes closed for a brief moment. "I'm trying to find a friend, that's all."

"If you were friends, you'd know more about her than her hair color and leg length. So I'm going to ask you again to leave before I call security to remove you."

"Is this how you treat all of your patrons? What if I needed Adalyn to assist me with a splinter in my hand? Or something like that."

Help me with a splinter? I couldn't have come up with something

31

a little more interesting than that? Something that doesn't affect every five-year-old out there.

"If you do have a splinter that for some off-chance you can't take care of yourself, you are more than welcome to sit in the emergency room for hours only to pay a hefty bill for a nurse to pull it out with tweezers you can get from a drug store for two dollars."

"You know what?" I ask, pointing at her.

"What?"

"You . . . you have an attitude, and it's not a pretty one."

She doesn't flinch, doesn't even bat an eyelash. Stoic, brewing, I'm sure preparing herself for an all-out tongue-lashing on my end. I don't know what's come over me, picking on receptionists because they don't happen to know a nurse by the name of Adalyn in a giant hospital.

She blinks once. Twice. Opens her mouth and—

"Hayden?" I turn my head to see Adalyn walking down the hallway with another female nurse, holding a brown lunch bag to her chest.

"Adalyn." I heave a sigh of relief.

Maybe too much relief because her brow creases as she comes up to me, telling her coworker she'll catch up with her later. "Are you okay?"

"He has a splinter," the receptionist deadpans, going back to her crossword puzzle.

"A splinter?" Adalyn's nose scrunches up. "You came to the hospital because you have a splinter?"

"No." I grumble. "I came to . . ." The receptionist pulls her attention away from her crossword and stares down our little conversation, leaning in. "You're being fucking nosey, don't you think?" My temper is starting to get the best of me.

"You're standing in front of my desk, therefore I'm allowed to listen to anything you're saying."

She has a point.

Stepping to the side and bringing Adalyn with me, I put space between the snarky receptionist and us.

"Where's your splinter?"

"I don't have a splinter. I just said that to . . . to . . . hell." I pull on the back of my neck. "I don't know why I said that."

"Then why are you here? Do you need help finding someone?"

"Well, I did need help finding someone, but I found her." Smile, keep eye contact, make her see how interested you are.

"Are you being corny and implying I'm the one you wanted to find?"

"Are you being lippy when I came all the way out here to bring you . . ." Fuck, I didn't bring her anything. I reach into my pocket, rooting around and pull out my ChapStick. "To bring you this ChapStick. Jesus, how fucking rude."

Eyes focused on the ChapStick and then back to mine. "You brought me ChapStick? Is that because you think I need it? Do you think I need ChapStick that bad that you came all the way to my place of work to give me some? Are my lips really so horrible to look at that not another minute could go by without bringing me some lubrication?"

I hold back the smile that wants to beam brightly. "Did I say ChapStick?" I shake my head and reach into my back pocket. I pull out my wallet, shuffle through it and grab the only piece of cash I have.

A one-dollar bill.

Perfect.

That was sarcasm in case you didn't get it.

"A dollar? You brought me a dollar?"

I've dug my grave, might as well lie in it. "Yup." I hand it to her. "Go crazy."

She presses the dollar between her fingers, not buying it, but still playing along. "You're so kind. I don't think anyone has ever come to my place of work just to give me a dollar."

"Sweet, right?" I rock on my heels, hands in my pockets now.

She chuckles and shakes her head. "The absolute sweetest."

"Does that mean if I ask you out on a date, you're more likely to say yes now rather than no . . . thanks to the dollar?"

Okay, not the best way to pick up a girl, bribing her with a one-dollar bill and used ChapStick, but I'm a little out of touch here. Hockey has consumed me for as long as I can remember, not granting me much time to date. I'm slightly rusty, a little awkward, and a whole lot of nervous.

"You want to take me out on a date?"

I nod. "Would love to."

"And if I say no, do I have to give the dollar back?" The smallest of smiles tugs at the corner of her lips.

"The dollar is yours regardless. Consider it a friendship dollar. Whatever happens between us, that dollar is yours to do with whatever you want."

"Wow." She brings the dollar close to her chest. "The world is my oyster, think of all the possibilities."

Fuck, she's funny.

"So, is that a yes?"

She tilts her head to the side, the ponytail swaying with her movement, the long strands like a wave of chocolate behind her.

"Did you tell Racer you were doing this?"

"No," I answer immediately.

"He has no clue you came searching for me, harassed a receptionist, and offered me a one-dollar bill?"

"Nope." I shake my head, my lips pressed into a thin line. "If I told him, I would have asked for your last name and the hospital you worked at so I didn't wander around different hospitals looking for a girl named Adalyn with brown hair and killer legs."

"Ooo, killer legs, I like that." She winks at me and stuffs the dollar in her bra strap. "Let's say I were to say yes, what would your date entail?"

Eh, fuck, I haven't thought that far ahead.

"It's a surprise," I answer, feeling smooth.

She shakes her head knowingly. "You have no clue what we would do for a date."

Chuckling, I go for honesty. "Got me there, but I promise it'll be worth it."

Twisting her lips to the side, heavy in thought, she clutches her lunch bag and says, "Racer can't know."

Well, I wasn't expecting that.

"You don't want Racer to know?"

She shakes her head. "No, he'll make a big deal out of nothing, and I'd rather not deal with that. Are you good with keeping this from him?"

Am I? Not really, he's a good friend. But then again, we don't necessary tell each other everything.

But he did tell me to stay away.

But . . . killer legs.

I think the choice is obvious.

"Yeah, I can keep this between us."

"Excellent. Hand me your phone, I'll plug in my number. You're in for one hell of a ride, Hayden."

I can't fucking wait.

$\sim$

Hayden: *How was the rest of your day at work?*

I twiddle my thumbs on the couch, looking around the cottage, unsure of what to do with my time. Normally, I'm working out, or doing drills, or preparing for a game, or squeezing in a few more reps in the weight room. So this free time is throwing me for a loop.

And Mr. Lockwood doesn't believe in the Internet or television besides a collection of mafia movies on VHS, which are stored under his small tube TV.

But there is a variety of playing cards in a drawer along with Boggle, Scrabble, Sudoku, and colorful puzzles. I started one of the puzzles last night, and it's already kicking my ass. I thought the landscape I picked out was going to be easy, but boy, was I wrong. A one-thousand-piece puzzle is no joke. I barely have the border done. But that's also because I can't find two edge pieces, and it's driving me crazy.

So I put the puzzle on hold and started playing Scrabble, player of one.

Let me tell you, I'm really good at playing myself. *HAY*-den is really smart with his moves, and Hay-*DEN* is a free-balling kind of player, goes with the flow, no thought in his moves whatsoever.

Can you guess which Hayden won?

But I can't complain about the peace I've been granted staying in the cottage. It's been comfortable, stress free, besides the constant phone calls from my publicist. I finally told him to email me everything or else I'd let him go because the constant badgering was getting on my nerves.

My phone beeps, drawing my attention away from the rustic-looking ceiling.

Adalyn: *Ugh, not the best end to the day. We had a thirty-year-old patient come in off the ambulance, suffered a massive heart attack, and we couldn't do anything to help him. His wife was still crying in the waiting room when I clocked out for the day.*

Fuck, that's hard. I couldn't imagine having to watch such life changing moments every day. I don't think I'm strong enough.

Hayden: *Shit, I'm sorry, Adalyn. That had to be really difficult to witness.*

Adalyn: *It was. I'm actually sitting in my car in the parking lot of the hospital, taking a few moments to compose myself.*

I sit up and rest my arms on my legs, my phone propped in front of me.

Hayden: *Can I help you take your mind off your shitty day?*
Adalyn: *What did you have in mind?*
Hayden: *Do you know where Roundtop Picnic area is?*
Adalyn: *I can look it up.*
Hayden: *Meet me at the Sunset Pavilion in half an hour.*
Adalyn: *Do I need to bring anything?*
Hayden: *Just your pretty self. I have everything else covered.*
Adalyn: *See you in thirty then.*

Hopping from the couch, I pocket my phone and head to the bathroom. *She said yes.* A guy's got to make sure he looks good . . . As much as I was lying to myself that I only want to *talk* to her, I get the sense that she needs this type of downtime. And I want that . . . with her. She's witty and sarcastic, but I'm thinking also very real. *That's what's been missing for me at times.* The lack of filter. I want real conversation . . . like Calder and Rachel have.

I pull into an almost empty parking lot besides one vehicle. When I look into the driver's side, I spot Adalyn, fingers curling around her ponytail, staring off into the distance. The movement from my end draws her attention and when she recognizes me, a soft smile plays at her lips. I nod toward the grass in front of us and start to get out of my car while she does the same.

I pull out a box, a bag of drinks and utensils, and a blanket.

"Do you need help?" Adalyn asks, walking to my open trunk.

"I think I got it, can you shut the trunk for me?"

"Of course." She goes to grab the hatch when I stop her and nod at the button on the side.

"Just press the button."

She eyes it and sticks her pinky in the air. "Oh fancy."

Laughing, I say, "It's about the only fancy thing I have in my life, so don't go thinking I'm a snob or anything."

Eyeing me, she says, "Nice watch."

Okay, I might have a fancy watch too, but I didn't buy it.

"It's from my team. They gave it to me for my birthday because the one I was wearing was apparently so abhorrent for everyone to look at, especially during press conferences. Makes me think, maybe I should start wearing shitty-looking suits and shoes to score some new apparel as well."

She taps her head. "You would be missing out on an opportunity if you didn't."

We head toward the grass and Adalyn takes the blanket from

under my arm to lay it out over the little field of green. The sun begins to set and the temperature starts to drop, so thankfully I prepared for the occasion. Jogging back to my Porsche, I open the door behind the driver's seat and grab two sweatshirts and another blanket.

I've lived in New York for most of my life, so I know what it's like in June when the sun sets around eight thirty. It gets chilly, and I don't want to have to cut our night short because the temperature drops. We have at least an hour before total darkness, and even then there are little streetlights surrounding the area.

"Here." I hand her one of my Philadelphia Brawlers sweatshirts. "I don't want you to get cold."

Hesitantly she takes the sweatshirt. "Thank you, that was sweet to think of me."

"Didn't think it would be cool to wear a sweatshirt while you're over there freezing." I lift the hoodie over my head and situate it around my waist before sitting next to her and draping the spare blanket over both our legs. Thankfully it's a smaller blanket so I have to scoot closer to her.

"Mmm, your sweatshirt smells good."

Okay, maybe I sprayed a little cologne on it before I left the cottage, but we can keep that between us.

"I hope you like cake." I bring the box to our laps and flip it open, revealing an entire sheet cake. Chocolate and vanilla marble cake with buttercream fudge frosting. Goddamn, my mouth is watering. I haven't had anything like this in a really long time. My nutritionist doesn't allow it for obvious reasons.

"Oh my God. Does that say . . . Hayden is hot?" Adalyn looks closer at the cake.

Pulling out forks, I hand her one. "They asked if I wanted anything written on it, so I figured *why not?*"

"And you went with Hayden is hot?"

"Just to make sure you were aware."

Shakes her head, a smile beautifully spread across her face. "I'm well aware. Thanks for the reminder though."

"Anytime. Dig in."

"No plates?"

"Nah, don't need them." I fork a giant piece of cake and shove it in my mouth, icing spread across my mouth. I chew, letting the sugar soak in and then swallow. So fucking good. I groan and go for another bite while Adalyn just stares at me. "Do you not like cake?"

"I do, it's just . . . fascinating watching you eat. It's like you've been starved for months."

"Starved of sugar. During playoffs, mainly, we're on a strict diet, which means no sugar."

"Seriously?" She takes a bite and closes her eyes for a brief second, truly tasting the cake. Wegman's makes the best sheet cakes. "How could you live without sugar?"

"It's hard, especially since I have an addiction to caramel and cheddar popcorn."

"Gah!" Adalyn turns toward me, completely serious. "Garrett's popcorn!"

My eyes widen in shock. "You've tried it?"

"Uh yeah. Whenever I go to New York City, I always stop by their little shop and grab the biggest tin they have. It's my favorite. My brothers think it's too greasy, but weirdly enough, I feel a sense of pride after eating ten handfuls having cheese-and-caramel-covered fingers. It's like I truly accomplished something."

"Do you lick your fingers?"

"Of course. That's the best part. It's like experiencing the delight for a second go around."

I hold my heart. "Holy shit, a girl after my own heart."

Growing more intense, she shifts, takes another bite of the cake, and says, "Have you tried Wegman's version?"

"No. Smartfood has a decent version, but it doesn't come close to Garrett's."

"Yeah, it's okay, but honestly, it's trash compared to the real deal. You should try Wegman's. It's a good knockoff. Not entirely as cheesy as one would hope, but it does the job when you're craving."

I reach into the bag of drinks and pull out two waters, handing one to Adalyn. Her fingers graze over mine when she takes the bottle from me, and for a split second, I feel a pulse of electricity bounce between us.

"This was really nice of you and the view is amazing. Who knew cake and a sunset would wash away my worries for the day?"

"So you're telling me I'm impressing you."

Forking a piece of cake in her mouth, she says, "You would have truly impressed me if this cake was red velvet and that water was a cold glass of milk."

"Milk?" I raise my eyebrows.

"Oh yeah. I love milk. And it has to be plain milk, none of this chocolate or strawberry stuff. Give me the real deal."

Hell, I can't stop the smile that sneaks out. "I don't think I've met an adult who loves milk."

She winks. "Does the body good, you know?" She motions up and down from her toes to her head. "You can't tell since I'm all covered up, but milk has treated me very well over my twenty-three years. And these bones?" She knocks on her forearm with her knuckles. "Stronger than steel. There will be no osteoporosis in this body."

Knowing what she looks like in shorts and a tight T-shirt, I say, "Milk *has* treated you well."

Forks in the cake, hands posed for our next bite, we stare at each other, my deep brown eyes to her lighter whiskey-colored ones, my smirk to her grin. Orange and pink hues paint the sky as the sun sets, casting a radiant glow over us.

Adalyn is the first to break the silence when she says, "From the looks of it, it would seem you're an average milk drinker yourself."

"It's the bulging biceps, isn't it?"

With the hand that's not holding her fork, she squeezes one of my arms. Like a total douche, I flex just in time, giving her rock-hard contact.

"Oh, those are bulging, aren't they? Impressive, Holmes."

"What about you, do you have any muscles under your scrubs?"

Lifting her arm, she makes a flexing motion and squints, as if she's really trying to flex her muscles. "Give it a squeeze, but be careful, I'm very muscular."

I pinch her cute little arm with my index finger and thumb, my giant sweatshirt adding a layer of cushion. Just to tease her some more, I pull my hand away and shake it. "Damn, Adalyn. You're a female version of the Hulk."

She dusts off her shoulder. "It's all the IV bags I lift on a daily basis. Patients need their fluid, and thankfully everyone involved benefits from it."

I chuckle. "IV bags, huh? That's all it takes? What the hell am I doing in the gym then?"

"Who knows, come work with me for a day, you'll get a work-out." She places a piece of cake in her mouth and slowly removes the fork, her lips smoothing across the metal tines. Full and plump, decorated in buttercream frosting. Her pink tongue peeks out, licking the tip of her lips, her eyes closed briefly before they open and make contact with mine. Stunned, she shyly smiles and turns her head back to the box of cake as I clear my throat, embarrassed I was caught staring.

"So you said you have brothers?"

She nods. "Seven of them and one sister."

Seven?

Holy shit, that's a lot of testosterone in one household. Her poor mother. Two daughters. Two against seven. *Shit.*

"Seven brothers? How was that?"

"It had its ups and downs. No one messed with me but no one wanted to date me either. I ended up going to my senior prom with my brother, Shane, which can we say was absolutely humiliating, especially when my mom was gushing to take pictures." She sighs. "But they made it special for me. All of them pitched in, got me a beautiful gown, my hair and makeup done professionally, and they all picked out a corsage for me to wear. It was as magical as taking your brother to prom could be."

Hell, I couldn't imagine going to prom with a sibling, that would be . . . devastating.

"Did you at least get to dance with any other guys while at prom?"

"Yup." She places a small piece of cake in her mouth. "With Shane hovering a foot away, arms crossed, making sure there was no *funny business* happening."

I'm trying really hard, but fuck, a chuckle pops out of me. Her eyes laser in on me, and I hold my hand up to apologize. "I'm sorry, I don't mean to laugh. That must have been a total nightmare for you, but comical for someone to watch on the outside."

"I can laugh about it now, but at the time, when word spread Shane wasn't allowing guys any kind of alone time with me, the dance requests slowed down. I ended up kicking my brother in the shin 'accidentally' after that when we were dancing. And I might have done it multiple times."

"Ooo, the shin is a good payback."

"I figured as much. The next day he had black and blue bruises up and down his legs but showed no remorse for what he did. And of course, my other brothers worshipped him and his cock-blocking ways."

"Brutal."

"Do you have any siblings?"

I nod. "Twin brothers. They're in college right now. They both play hockey but clearly aren't as good as me." I smirk.

Picking up on my humor, she says, "Well, is anyone really as good as you?"

"Can't say that I've found anyone."

She points her clean-licked fork at me. "Confident and cocky, I like that."

"Nah, it's all show. Inside I'm just a giant teddy bear looking for someone to spoon me."

A harsh laugh releases from her mouth. "Oh, that is a good line. Do you get a lot of girls to fall for that?"

"Nope, they pretty much have the same response as you."

She places her fork in the cake box and leans back on her hands, looking out to the valley below, the sun barely peeking past the tree line. She grows quiet, just observing.

What's going through that pretty mind of hers? Is she recounting interaction with her patients today? Are they always on her mind? If I were in her position, I think it would be hard to separate my personal life with work. Hell, I have a hard time doing that with hockey. I bring the game into my personal life all the time, letting it affect me, letting it drive me crazy. Does she have the same problem?

"I don't know how you do it," I say, breaking the silence. "Taking on patient after patient, treating them and moving on to the next, staying cognizant enough to help heal people." I shake my head in awe. "It's admirable."

"Thank you." Shifting forward, she moves the cake to the side and snuggles close into my side, draping my arm over her shoulder, her head landing in the crook of my arm.

The fresh scent of her shampoo hits me first, then the faint scent of sugar, followed by the light hum of her content body. It's a small move, innocent really, but for some reason, it feels like an anvil-sized weight was placed on my heart with every little sigh of content she takes.

It's comfortable.

It's easy.

It's new but also feels right.

Adalyn wrapped up in my arms, pressed close against me, like she was made specifically for me.

She is an unexpected surprise that has me wondering how can I make sure to see this girl as many times as possible before the season starts again, before the crazy re-enters my life.

Because just like the other night at Racer's, no part of me feels ready to say goodbye. I simply want to stay.

CHAPTER FIVE

ADALYN

"So who was that guy the other day?" Samantha asks as she sits down in a squeaky chair next to me. Samantha and I are usually on the same nursing rotation, thankfully. It helps to have a good friend to rely on when the emergency room starts to take its toll.

"Uh, that was Hayden." I squint looking at the chart I'm entering into the computer, trying to read Dr. Fallon's handwriting.

"Hayden, huh? Is he someone special?" She leans back in her chair, making the hinges squeak even louder.

"He's a friend," I answer, even though I know we might be more than friends. At least that's where I think we're headed. That's what it feels like, especially after the other night.

Once we finished eating the cake, we didn't spend much more time outside because it was beginning to get cold, and I was totally beat from the day. My yawns hinted at my fatigue. I helped Hayden pack up and offered him his sweatshirt, but he told me to keep it for now. And I did, no argument from me. After a warm hug, Hayden helped me into my car, shut my door, and sent me on my way with a tap to the top of my car. The entire drive home, I pressed my nose to the fabric of his sweat-shirt, taking in his scent, remembering what it was like to be held closely to him. Hard body, strong and powerful, yet soft and gentle when he carefully held me, his thumb stroking along my arm leisurely. It was sweet, a moment I wish I was still in right now, instead of listening to the incessant beeping of machines around me.

And when I woke up at five thirty this morning to get ready for my seven-o'clock shift, I was greeted by a text from him that told me to have a good day.

Simple, yet comforting.

Nursing isn't an easy job, and to see that little text . . . it put a smile on my face before I had to walk through these sterile halls.

"Just a friend?"

I nod, trying to decipher a word on the chart in front of me. What the hell is that? It looks like a W with something scribbled after it. I don't even know where to begin with that. "Just a friend."

"So why is he coming toward us right now with a huge smile on his face and a bag in hand?" My head snaps up to find Hayden striding in our direction, purpose in his every step. Worn jeans clinging to his thick quads, Brawlers T-shirt stretched across his broad pecs, and a New York Yankees baseball cap propped on his head, darkening his eyes way past dangerous.

When he reaches the nurses desk, he places the bag on the counter, and leans forward, his forearms propping him up, hands clasped together.

"Hi, Adalyn." The way my name rolls off his tongue so effort-lessly, so deep and sultry, sends chills down my spine.

Caught off guard, I sit taller and say, "Hayden, hey. What are you doing here?"

He nods at the brown bag next to him. "Brought you some lunch, wasn't sure if you had a few minutes to spare. If not, I'll just leave this here for you to pick at when you get a chance."

"She's about ready for her lunch break actually," Samantha cuts in and holds out her hand in greeting. "Hi. I'm Samantha."

"Samantha, it's a pleasure to meet you. I'm Hayden. So our girl has a little bit of time to spare?"

"Half hour actually." Samantha takes the chart from me and says, "I'll finish this up for you. Why don't you go take your lunch break?"

She bulges her eyes at me as if to say, "If you don't leave now, I will take your place."

Not wanting to mess with Samantha, I thank her and stand, patting down my scrub top. I snag my phone, put it in my pocket, and say, "Do you want to go to the cafeteria?"

"That sounds good to me." Picking up the bag of food, he gestures down the hallway. "Lead the way."

We fall in step together, walking past patient rooms and busy medical staff. When we reach the elevator, I press the down button and turn toward Hayden, arms crossed over my chest. "You didn't have to bring me lunch, you know."

"I wanted to." Smiling, he opens up his arm and says, "Give me a proper hello."

I step into his embrace, and he brings me into his firm chest, his fresh cologne warming me up like a heat wave weaving its way through my veins.

Quietly, I say, "Hey."

The bell dings and the doors part. Logan is leaning against the elevator wall, checking out his phone when he looks up, spotting me snuggled close to Hayden. Straightening, he says, "Hey, Addie." Sizing Hayden up, he gives him a once-over. The two are very similar with their dark hair, broad stature, and domineering presence, but with Hayden, there's a notable softness in his eyes.

"Logan, hey. I didn't know you were working today." I separate myself from our warm embrace and walk into the elevator, holding the door for Hayden.

"Timothy called in sick so I'm covering for him." Glancing at Hayden, who happens to be standing awfully close to me, he asks, "Who's your friend?"

Before I can answer, Hayden leans forward and extends his hand. "Hayden, nice to meet you. Logan, was it?"

"Yeah." They shake hands, their grip tight from what I can tell. "You two going to have lunch?"

Hayden holds up the brown sack of food and says, "Chicken Spiedies."

"Ah, jealous. I love Spiedies. Did you get them from Spiedie and Rib Pit?"

"Is there really anywhere else to get them?" Hayden practically scoffs.

"Nope." The elevator dings and the doors open to the first floor. Logan is the first to exit. "Well, you two have fun. I'm headed to the geriatric wing to collect some urine samples, stopping by the gift shop to get a Milky Way beforehand. It's the only way I'll make it through the next hour. Call me later, Addie. I miss you." With a wink, he takes off, and for some reason, I let out a low, silent breath of air.

Things still might be a little weird with Logan and me.

Immobile for a second, Hayden presses his hand on my lower back and leans down to my ear. "Where to, *Addie?*"

When I give him a pointed look, he just laughs and pulls me into his side again as I walk us toward the cafeteria. We pick a table next to a window in the back to give us some privacy.

"You start unwrapping the sandwiches, I'm going to get some drinks. Anything in particular you would like?"

"Water is good for me."

Giving me the sweetest, sexiest wink, he says, "Be right back."

His retreating backside grabs my attention, pulling me from my task. I study him. Brawny, wide shoulders that taper into his narrow waist. His shoulders blades tent the back of his shirt, his triceps pull on the threads woven into the fabric draped over his body. The hem of his shirt dances loosely with his waistline, every once in a while showing off the waistband of his Calvin Kline boxer briefs. And his ass, lifted and tight, complements an insanely athletic body I've never seen in person.

What would it feel like to grip his ass? To feel it undulate back and forth under my grasp.

What would he feel like on top of me?

Sweaty and driving his strong force into me.

His muscles contracting, his smooth voice draping over me like a warm blanket, his mouth pressed against my burning skin.

"Adalyn, you okay?"

Startled from my little fantasy, I straighten in my chair, hands still posed at the bag of food. Hayden takes a seat across from me, placing the drinks on the table.

"Uh, sorry. I was thinking about something." When I look at him, those dark eyes shadowed by his baseball hat, I'm sure my cheeks flame with a wave of crimson.

I was picturing him naked, pulsing in and out of me, and now I have no idea how to stop that image from playing over and over in my mind.

"You sure? You're all red."

How humiliating.

"Yup, good." I clear my throat and reach into the bag, pulling out two wrapped sandwiches. "Thank you for bringing me lunch. You're really scoring some points with me. Cake and Spiedies. Seems you know the way to my heart."

"Just want to spend more time getting to know you, so I'll take any stolen moment I can get."

I twist my lips to the side, studying him. "Racer was right, you're dangerous. I really should stay away from you."

"Racer doesn't know his head from his ass. Don't listen to him." Hayden unwraps his sandwich and takes a man-size bite, smiling at me as he chews. I bite into my sandwich as well, but I don't take nearly as much of the sandwich as Hayden does. Pretty sure I'd choke if that happened.

Swallowing and taking a sip of water, Hayden asks, "So . . . Logan, you two have some history?"

"Could you tell?"

"It was obvious from the tension in the elevator, which was fun by the way."

I softly chuckle. "Sorry about that."

Before he takes another bite of his Spiedie, he says, "Tell me about him."

"Do you really want to talk about another man on our little lunch date?"

He chews a few beats before answering, "If he was a part of your life, I want to hear about it because it involves you. Spill your guts. What's the dirt with you two?"

Sighing, I glance in the direction that Logan went and turn my attention back to Hayden. "We went through the nursing program together at Binghamton University. It was Logan, Emma—Tucker's fiancée—and me. We relied on each other, were practically dependent upon one another during those four years because nursing school is no joke."

"I believe it." It's so sexy that he truly appreciates my job, like he believes whole-heartedly it's one of the toughest out there, because at times, it feels like it is.

"We were all really close, we still are, but after we graduated, we might have tested the waters with our friendship, and I hooked up with him." I glance up to see Hayden's eyes sharpen, his jaw become tight. Yeah, I didn't think he wanted to hear that.

Looking at his sandwich, he says, "Well, that explains the tension."

"Only a part of the tension." I put my sandwich down and start playing with the cap of my water bottle. No girl wants to talk about her insecurities with a handsome, interested man, but I have a feeling Hayden isn't going to let this go.

"There's more?"

I slowly nod, feeling massively insecure. "The next morning, we woke up and the first thing he said to me was"—I bite the inside of my cheek and take a deep breath—"that was a mistake."

Hayden's hands grip the table, his forearms dangerously flexing. "He said that to you?"

"Unfortunately."

"What a prick." Hayden glances toward the gift shop, but of course by now, Logan is long gone. Thankfully. From the look in Hayden's eyes, I fear what would happen to him.

"It's over now. We're friends, and we keep it that way."

Still tense, Hayden sits back in his seat. "Still, friends don't treat friends like that. It was shitty of him to say something so harsh and immature."

"You don't have to make it sound any worse than it was. Believe me, he isn't your competition." I smile shyly while Hayden interestingly raises his eyebrow, a slow, devilish smile replacing the former scowl.

"Not competition, huh? Is there anyone else I need to worry about?"

I pick at the wrapper to my Spiedie and slowly shake my head. "None."

Leaning forward now, he takes my hand in his large, calloused palm. Those blue eyes peeking out from under the brim of his hat. Seductive, and yet mysterious. I know practically nothing about this man, but even with that, there is this crazy pull I feel when he's near, like I was meant to meet him.

"What are you doing Friday night?"

Turning my hand in his, he weaves our fingers, his palm so warm. "I work until seven, but I don't believe I'm doing anything after that. Why?" I smile, looking through my eyelashes, feeling so freaking shy with the way his thumb is running along the back of my hand. "Did you have something in mind?"

He nods slowly, eyes never leaving mine. "How about I text you with the details later?"

"Do you have to text me later because you don't technically have any plans of what to do?"

The corner of his lips tilt up, his straight white teeth peeking past his lips. "Way to call a guy out."

"Just keeping you on your toes. Can't make you believe I'm an easy catch."

"Nah, we couldn't have that at all, could we? You've got to play hard to get."

"Exactly."

Chuckling, he releases my hand with a quick squeeze and picks up his sandwich. "Well, your secret is safe with me." Winking, he takes a big bite out of his sandwich and casually chews while his eyes study me from across the table. Observant, casual, yet one of the sweetest men I've ever met. Whatever he comes up with Friday, I'm game, which is unusual. By Friday, I will have worked far too many hours, and I know I'll be exhausted and probably prefer a night in to veg in front of Netflix for a few hours. Yet if it means I get to spend more time with this man by accepting a date on Friday night? I'm in. In fact, it's practically all I care about at the moment.

∽

"So, who was the guy?" Logan takes a seat next to me at the nursing station, sitting backward in his chair, arms resting on the seat back.

After lunch, Hayden walked me to the elevators, gave me a warm, comforting hug, his chin resting on the top of my head, and then sent me back to work. I can still feel his strong arms tightly insulating me, giving me a brief reprieve from the stress of my job. When I arrived at the nursing station, there was already a text message from him, waiting to be opened.

Smiling like a fool, I opened it up and read it at least five times before responding.

Hayden: *Thanks for stealing a moment with me. Seeing that smile of yours gave me the energy I needed for the day. Can't wait for Friday. Have a good rest of your day.*

I've been on cloud nine since, and I think it's showing, because I'm not normally this peppy at work.

Typing away, I focus on the computer in front of me, pushing

MEGHAN QUINN

back the giddy smile wanting to take over my controlled and neutral lips.

"Come on," Logan pokes my side. "He looks familiar, do I know him?"

A lot of people know him, especially a little south of Binghamton. I'm surprised we haven't run into any fans yet.

"He's a friend," I answer, being as vague as possible.

"Really? Because he seemed like a lot more than a friend."

Sighing, I turn in my chair and cross my arms. "We're, you know . . . getting to know each other. That's all. Nothing serious."

"And he brought you lunch?" Logan thins his lips and nods, his eyes trained on something above me, not able to look me in the eyes. "He likes you. Not just because he brought you lunch, but I saw the way he stepped closer to you when he saw me in the elevator. I saw the way he looked at you, and he really likes you."

My cheeks heat up, my skin breaks out in a light sweat. It's hard to believe a sweet and caring, not to mention extremely popular, man like Hayden could *like* me. And yet, he keeps coming around, searching me out, making me feel valued. I've never felt this comfortable around a man this quickly before. Even with Logan, I kept my distance until I realized he was a good guy and I could trust him. Maybe because for my entire life my brothers told me I couldn't trust any man. And my sister's life has practically proven that point as well.

"I mean, there might be something more than just friends . . ."

"Yeah?" Logan wiggles his eyebrows at me. "Have you been out on a date?"

I shake my head. Logan isn't going to let up, so I turn completely toward him, one leg crossed over the other now. "But he did ask me out at lunch today."

Logan nods knowingly. "He's totally into you." Chewing on the side of his lip, he looks to the ceiling for a second before asking. "How come I feel like I know him?"

Probably because his face is all over commercials and billboards.

52

"Uh, you might have seen him around. He's Hayden Holmes."

"Hayden Holmes? Who the hell is Hay—?" Realization hits Logan hard as his mouth falls open and his eyes widen. "Hayden Holmes . . . as in the hockey player?" I nod slowly. "Holy shit, Adalyn. Where the hell did you meet him?"

"Racer is good friends with him. They grew up together. I was at Racer's house the other night for a little gathering. He said his childhood friend was coming back home for a few weeks, and it happened to be Hayden. I didn't think we hit it off until Hayden showed up here the other day, looking for me." I chew on the side of my lip and glance at Logan, a wince in my eyes. "Racer told me to stay away, and he also told Hayden to keep his hands off me."

"Which of course only makes you want to get to know each other even more," Logan says.

"Kind of, yeah."

Nodding, Logan tilts his head and asks, "And what happens when his little stint in Binghamton is over?" Leave it to Logan to be the sensible one. "Are you going to continue to date him when he's in Philadelphia? Isn't the hockey season super fucking long, one of the longest out of all the sports? That's a lot of away trips and days on the ice. Are you up for that?"

I twist my lips to the side, never actually thinking that far ahead. "I mean, I guess I never thought about his profession since I don't pay attention to hockey. I only see him for who he is: a sweet, interested, and extremely good-looking man."

A questionable, yet playful brow is raised in my direction. "Extremely good-looking?" Logan asks.

"Uh, yeah. Have you not seen the jaw on that guy? And his eyes." I sigh. "Like a clear windowpane straight to his soul."

"Oh, Jesus." Logan scoffs. "Okay, so you have a crush on the guy."

"How could I not? He's dreamy and thoughtful and . . ." I lean forward and squeeze Logan's arms. "Did you see the forearms? Rock-solid boulders, that's what those were. Every time he shifts, it's like a wave of sinew rolling up and down."

"Okay, so you have a crush on him, and he has muscles. What does that mean about the next few weeks? What happens when he leaves?" I shrug my shoulders, not wanting to think about it. "I want you to be careful, okay, Adalyn? I don't want you to get hurt."

Like you hurt me?

I want to say it, it's on the tip of my tongue, but before I can put those searing words between us, Logan pulls me into him, the rolling chair I'm sitting on making it incredibly easy. Encasing me with his strong embrace, he hugs me tightly to his chest and kisses the top of my head.

"I care about you, Adalyn."

Relenting, I fall into his embrace and say, "I know you do, and I appreciate it. But this is just, you know, a little date. Who knows, we might actually hate each other and not know it yet. Maybe he thinks Zack Morris is more superior than AC Slater?"

Logan chuckles quietly, the rumble in his chest warming me. "That would be a fucking game changer."

"A quick kick to the curb if you ask me."

"Personally, I think you should lead with that question on your date. Who is more superior: Zack or AC? If he answers Zack, you walk right back out that door, you hear me?"

"Oh, believe me, I would hightail it so fast. That is a deal-breaker for sure."

CHAPTER SIX

ADALYN

"Oh, Zack Morris is by far superior," Hayden answers, draining a pot of boiling noodles into a strainer.

"What?" I can feel my eyes bulge out of their sockets, my entire world flipping upside down. How on EARTH does anyone believe Zack is better than AC Slater from *Saved by the Bell*? "How can you possibly think that?" If I wasn't so damn curious as to why he would think such a thing, I would be grabbing my purse and walking out of this quaint little cottage to my car to get as far away from this . . . this . . . anarchist as I can get.

"Well for one, AC's real name is Albert Clifford."

"Not by his choosing."

"Two"—Hayden wiggles two fingers at me while he stirs the aromatic pasta sauce bubbling on the stove—"the dude has a curly mullet."

"That was the style back then. You would have been so lucky to be able to have such luscious locks like AC."

"Three." Hayden pulls the pot from the stove and puts it on a trivet. Staring at me from over the island where I'm sitting, he grips the counter and says, "AC didn't get the girl in the end."

"What are you talking about? He had Jesse."

Eyes shut, a smirk on his face, Hayden slowly shakes his head. "Jesse was a hot mess. She had a drug problem—"

Jabbing my finger into the counter, I can feel myself become far too passionate. "She took caffeine pills! It wasn't like she was shooting up heroin in the girl's bathroom at Bayside. It was caffeine pills."

"That's where it starts, with caffeine pills, then next thing you know, she's doing Molly at Coachella."

"You're ridiculous." I fold my arms over my chest.

Snagging a noodle from the strainer, he pops it in his mouth and says, "I'm right. The girl to get was Kelly. Every guy who ever watched the show will agree with me on this. Kelly was the *it* girl. Hell, even AC wanted to be with her, but who ended up marrying her in the end? Zack. Despite AC trying to throw his jock, macho-man status in Kelly's way, she saw past his shifty veneer and went for the by far SUPERIOR guy." Smiling like a fool and nudging me with his finger, he says, "Come on, you know I'm right."

"You're not." I turn my nose up at him.

"Denial. It's okay, I'll let my logic sink in, because it will. Sooner or later, you will realize I'm right. Kelly was the voice of reason in *Saved by the Bell* and there was only one choice for her to make: the right choice, and she made that with Zack Attack." Hayden pauses for a second and then adds, "Plus, he was one of the first kids ever to have a fucking cellphone . . . soo . . ."

"That 'phone' was a monstrosity."

"That phone was an absolute dream and you know it."

I fiercely press my lips together. "By the time we were old enough to watch the show, we had cellphones that eclipsed that phone in cool status. So frankly, I can't take your word for anything."

With a steady glare in my direction, he slips another noodle into his mouth and says, "I would have traded a Nokia for Zack's phone any day."

"Just goes to show"—I snag a noodle as well, slurping it past my lips—"you don't have very good taste." Hayden's eyes are transfixed on my mouth.

He licking his lips seductively and gives me a full once-over, his eyes blazing a wave of fire up my body. "Pretty sure I have great taste."

A blush creeps over my cheeks from his compliment and heated stare. Unsure of how to answer, I clear my throat and wave my finger over the steaming pots. "So how does this work? Uh, just put the sauce on the pasta?"

Posed, focus still on me, Hayden stares at me for a few beats before chuckling and shaking his head. "Yes, you put the sauce on top of the pasta. It's as if you haven't had pasta before." The way he teases me, it makes me feel that much more comfortable around him, like we've known each other longer than a week. "Here, take the wine, and I'll grab some plates of food." He hands me two wine glasses and a bottle of red. "We're going to eat out on the deck." Winking, he adds, "Meet you out there in a second."

Shakily, I take the wine and the glasses out the sliding glass door to a beautiful refinished deck that expands the length of the house and overlooks the valley below. The sun is setting over the lush-green oak trees surrounding the property, fireflies start to play in the darkened woods, and the sound of crickets chirping a lullaby fill the air. It's the perfect northeast summer evening, even if the air has a small bite to it.

To the right, there is a high-density wood dining set with red placemats, napkins, and silverware already laid out with bright yellow flowers in a short vase decorating the middle of the table.

Well, that's . . . romantic and thoughtful.

Taking a seat, I pop open the wine and pour us both a short glass. I swirl the liquid around, take a small sniff, and then let the wine slip into my mouth, a small taste.

What do the wine gurus have to say about this one? *Herbaceous and spicy with a hint of tartness.*

Damn good.

I go in for another sip as Hayden walks through the door,

holding two plates in one hand a basket of garlic bread in the other. Next to the sliding glass door, he effortlessly flips on a switch, illuminating the deck with large-bulb string lights. The mood immediately switches from playful to romantic, the yellow lighting casting a soft glow over us.

Past the strong and powerful façade of this hockey player is an intimate and romantic man, with a smirk that can kill, and a stare so devastating, I'm not sure if my heart can take any other surprises.

Placing our plates on the table and the basket between us, he sits in his seat and turns toward me, his hand going to a wayward hair of mine, pushing it behind my ear, his hand lingering on my face. "Thanks for coming over tonight. I've been looking forward to it ever since our lunch in the cafeteria."

"Yeah?" I ask like a dweeb, unsure of what to say to this honest and sweet man.

"Yeah." Pressing his thumb against my cheek, his eyes fixed on mine, I feel the breath from my lungs slowly evaporate as our bodies inch closer.

Eyes move from mine to my mouth and up again.

Lips are licked.

Fingers wrap around my neck, gently pressing me forward.

My breath hitches.

My body tingles.

My fingers suddenly feeling numb.

Another glance to my lips.

Another inch forward.

Another lick to his lips.

He's going to kiss me. Hayden Holmes is going to kiss me . . .

Chest rising and falling, the fabric of his shirt stretching over his thick pecs, I await the press of his lips to mine, but just when I think he's going to close in on the final inches keeping us apart, he clears his throat and slowly pulls away leaving me . . . yearning.

Picking up his fork and knife, he stares at his plate and clears his throat again. "Sorry about that."

Sorry? Why the hell is he sorry?

Looking frustrated, he sets his silverware back on the table and plants one of his hands firmly in his hair where he pulls on the messy strands. "There's something about you, Adalyn." Head dipped, he turns slightly to look at me. "You make me a little crazy with those lips of yours, so pink, so goddamn plump. I want to taste them."

"Wh-what's holding you back?" Why am I stuttering? When have I ever been nervous around men? It almost feels like this is the first time I've ever . . . cared about a man, truly cared to get to know him, to be with him.

Hands folded in my lap, I turn my attention to my pasta, nervous about his answer.

With his index finger, he hooks my chin so I'm forced to look him in the eyes. "What's holding me back?" He shakes his head as if he's in disbelief. "Those lips are lethal, Adalyn, and I know the minute I get a taste of them I won't be able to stop myself."

"So . . . it's not because you don't want to?"

His brows pinch together. "You're fucking kidding, right?"

Hating my question and the insecurity that slipped in there, I shrug my shoulders. "Forget that last question." Picking up my fork, I say, "Let's eat this delicious pasta."

Swirling the pasta and sauce together, mixing in the parmesan cheese Hayden grated on top, I fork a few pasta spirals and bring the bite to my lips when I realize Hayden is still staring at me intently.

Fork poised mere inches from my mouth, I ask, "Can I help you?"

"Yeah, you can." Reaching over to my lap, he takes my hand in his and fuses our palms together. Picking up his fork as well, he gathers some pasta and says, "There, that's better."

With the lights above, the sounds of the nightfall surrounding us, we hold hands and eat a meal I don't think I'll ever forget. And it's not only because Hayden made it for me, but because it's one of the first times I've ever felt self-worth from a man who wasn't one of my brothers.

"Who taught you how to cook?" The dishes are in the kitchen, the wine has been consumed, maybe a little more than I expected to drink, and we're now lounging in a glider on the deck, with Hayden setting a light sway with his foot propped against the coffee table in front of us.

"My mom. She made it her mission to make sure her sons knew how to cook before they left for college. So every Sunday and Monday, we were required to make a meal with my mom. At the time, I was kind of annoyed, because I was a teenage boy wanting to do anything but cook a proper spaghetti sauce, but now as I look back on the time I shared with my mom, I cherish those moments."

"That's really sweet." Turned toward him, my feet tucked under me, one of my hands in his, I take a small sip of wine. His fingers dance along my palm occasionally, sending a tingling sensation up and down my spine and a nervous flutter in my stomach.

"I spent so much time with my dad in the driveway, taking shot after shot at him, that the only moments I had with my mom were when I was in the kitchen cooking with her. It was our time."

"And do you still cook with her when you get a chance?"

Small dimples settle in the corner of his lips. "She puts me to work right away whenever I go home for a visit, and she still has the apron she got me when I was in middle school."

"Does she make you wear it?"

He nods. "Of course."

"What does it look like?"

Rolling his eyes dramatically, he says, "I knew you were going to ask."

"Oh, it sounds embarrassing, I need to know what it is now."

He takes the last sip of his wine and sets his empty glass on the coffee table. "It says Chef Hayden and has an embroidered wood-chuck on the front holding a puck."

Like there are two strings slowly pulling at the corner of my mouth, I can't hold back my smile. "A woodchuck?"

With the hand not holding mine, he grabs the back of his neck. "This is really fucking weird and sort of embarrassing, but for some reason, back in middle school, I thought woodchucks were cool. Who knows where it came from, but I had a small collection of woodchuck figurines."

I sit a little taller. "No, you didn't."

Shamefully he nods. "Yeah, it was weird. I might have one or two figurines left I couldn't part with, but the apron, that's still hanging in my parents' kitchen next to my mom's."

"Oh my God, that's so unexpected, slightly weird but really adorable."

He wiggles his eyebrows at me. "Really adorable, huh?"

"Don't push your luck, mister."

Squeezing my hand, he says, "Wouldn't dream of it." I finish off my glass, and he politely takes it from me, setting it on the coffee table next to his. He turns to face me and edges a little closer. "So why did you want to become a nurse?"

Resting the side of my head against the cushion of the glider, the slow rocking lulling me into a very comfortable and relaxed state, I say, "My mom's sister, Aunt Peg, used to live with us when we were growing up. She lived in the basement and helped out with us, especially when my mom was about to lose her mind having so many boys in close succession under one roof. My sister is the eldest, twelve years older than me, but then Mom had six boys, me, then my youngest brother." He looks shocked . . . horrified really. *Can't blame him.* "My sister helped out with lots of chores and was busy a lot of the time. And I grew close to Aunt Peg. I'd go to her room in the basement and play with her nursing gear and play doctor on her. As I got older, I knew taking care of people was what I was meant to do."

Hayden nods. "Well, it's an attractive attribute you possess, wanting to take care of others. You have a compassionate soul. I really like that."

"Thank you." I play with his hand in mine, our fingers seductively gliding over one another. "What about you, did you always think you were going to be a professional hockey player?"

Growing serious, Hayden says, "Well, I didn't know if I was going to be a professional hockey player, but I knew that's what I wanted."

"And if you weren't a hockey player, what would you be doing?"

"Hmm"—he smirks—"good question." Pausing, he really thinks about his answer. "Are you asking, if hockey in general wasn't an option, what would I be? Because if hockey is still on the table, I would probably say coach or scout."

"Hockey is off the table. Pretend hockey doesn't even exist in this scenario."

"That's a sad fucking scenario." He chuckles but then grows serious again. He scratches the side of his jaw, his five o'clock shadow disrupting the peaceful night air. "I guess if hockey wasn't an option on any accord, I would probably have gone to culinary school and hopefully own a restaurant somewhere in the city."

"In the city?"

He winks. "Aim big, baby, never settle."

"Apparently."

"What about you, if you weren't a nurse, what would you be?"

"Is hockey an option in my scenario?"

He arches his eyebrow in question. "Uh, sure."

"Perfect." Casually I pick a piece of lint off my pants. "If I wasn't a nurse then I would totally be a hockey groupie, because I'm liking this whole hockey player persona. Very sexy."

A drawn-out grin plays on his lips. With our connected hands, he pulls me closer until I'm practically sitting on his lap. Talking quietly, his forehead pressed against mine, he says, "Don't let me fool you, I'm the exception. All other hockey players are massive dicks. You got lucky with me."

Chuckling, I say, "Seems like you're trying to distract me from finding myself another piece of man muscle on skates."

His nose gently passes over mine as he talks low. So deep, so seductive. "Is it working?"

Oh God . . . is it working.

~

Pressed up against Hayden's chest, his arm wrapped around me, his fingers playing with my hair, I toy with the buttons on his shirt as we look into the dark abyss in front of us. I have no clue what time it is, but I can feel my eyes starting to get heavy, and yet, I haven't made a move to leave.

I'm too comfortable.

I'm too warm under this fleece blanket with Hayden.

I want to get to know him even more.

I want more time with him.

"What was Racer like growing up?" I ask, holding back the yawn that wants to escape.

"Racer?" Hayden chuckles. "Can you guess what he was like?"

"Hmm . . . a total tool?"

"Pretty much, but it was oddly okay in our group of friends. We knew he was the jokester, the one who pulled pranks, but he was also very sensitive, so we didn't return a lot of his jabs. We let him have his fun."

"He is sensitive, isn't he?"

"Very, and now that he's older, he's very sensitive to people around him, compassionate and understanding when he needs to be. He can read a situation well and knows when he needs to stop joking around and be the incredible friend he is."

"Mmm," I hum in agreement. "That's very true. He was there for me when everything with Logan went down."

"He was?"

I nod against Hayden's chest, his arm growing tighter around me. "Racer is not a fan of Logan, but then again, he doesn't know him like I do, or like Emma does. He's a good guy, and he's been there for both of us from the very beginning."

Hayden grows quiet, and I'm sure Logan isn't one of his favorite topics, especially after the way he reacted when I told him what happened between us.

Not wanting there to be unnecessary beef between Hayden and Logan, I add, "He really is a good guy. I think you guys would actually get along."

"Doubt it," Hayden mutters under his breath.

Lifting off his chest, my hand against his pecs propping me up, I look Hayden in the eyes. Instead of the usual jovial expression he wears, his brow is creased, his jaw hard and set in stone, and his eyes are cast forward.

"You really don't like him, do you?"

"I don't. He treated you like shit during a moment that needed more sensitivity. Doesn't seem like a guy I would get along with."

"It was an awkward moment. I'm sure he handled it the best he knew how to."

Hayden shakes his head and lowers me to his chest. "There are about ten other ways I can think of off the top of my head on how he could of handled that situation. He didn't have to be a dick to you and that's what he was. The dude isn't cool in my book, not sure he'll ever be."

Taking a small breath, I say, "He's still my friend."

Heavily sighing, Hayden presses a kiss against my head but doesn't say anything. Instead, he rocks us back and forth, letting the night we've shared speak for itself. And it's in this moment I appreciate why he and Racer are close. Why he and Racer share their dislike of Logan. They're loyal. One hundred percent loyal toward those they consider theirs. Even in the small amount of time I've known Hayden, I can see if you are considered a friend, that invitation never goes away. And that's possibly more dangerous to my heart than all other amazing attributes thrown together. That's what I learned from my family. *Loyalty and love go hand in hand.*

CHAPTER SEVEN

HAYDEN

I keep my mouth shut because there is no use talking to Adalyn about Logan. She knows what he did, she knows deep down the kind of coward he is; I don't have to point that out. I would rather spend the rest of the evening with this woman snuggled into my side, the scent of her sweet shampoo slowly eating me alive, and her small hand playing with the buttons of my shirt.

No need to dwell on someone who has nothing to do with us.

Yes . . . *us*.

There is no doubt in my mind we are becoming an us, at least I'm hoping we are becoming an us, because with every touch and conversation we share, I'm becoming more and more addicted to this woman.

It isn't only her beauty that has captured me—those golden eyes and luscious lips. It's the way she smiles so innocently when her eyes light up with sin, or the way she beautifully cares for others but easily keeps me on my toes with her wit.

Racer was right to try to protect Adalyn from me because right now, I feel like a wolf, stalking his prey.

Back and forth, back and forth we rock, our breath mixing

together, falling in rhythm. Adalyn's fingers start to slow, her body pressing heavier into mine.

"Hey," I whisper to see if she's awake.

No response.

"Adalyn." I press a kiss against her forehead.

"Mmm . . ."

"Are you sleeping?"

"Maybe," she grumbles.

Knowing how hard she works and how long her shifts are, I don't think twice when I scoop her into my arms and take her inside the house. Her head lulls into my chest. No doubt the wine and long hours conked her out.

I have three options here: I can drive her back to her place and help her get into bed, I can walk her into the guest room and tuck her in, or . . . I can take her to my room and spend the rest of the night wrapped around her lithe body, running my hand over her soft skin, smelling her delicious lavender scent.

I'm a good guy, but I also have my selfish moments and spending the night wrapped around Adalyn is going to be one hell of a selfish moment I'll capitalize on.

Turning the lights off, not worrying about the wine glasses outside, I do a quick lockup and carry Adalyn to the back of the house where I lay her on the bed. As I remove her shoes, her eyes flutter open, lazy and sexy, and she asks, "What's going on?"

"Just getting you ready for bed."

Instead of putting up a fight like I thought she would, she nods and lays her head back down. Chuckling, I finish up with her shoes and head to the bathroom where I brush my teeth, shuck my jeans and shirt, and grab a cup of water and toothbrush for Adalyn.

She's half awake when I offer her the toothbrush, running through the motions of brushing her teeth. But to her credit, she doesn't forget to brush her tongue. She's high-functioning when practically sleeping, her eyes closed the entire time.

When I return from dropping off the spare toothbrush I had, I find her struggling with her jeans, the zipper giving her a run for her money. Okay, not as high-functioning as I thought.

"Do you want your pants off?"

"Mmm," she answers with a sleepy nod.

"Okay." I assess the situation and wonder how I'm going to make this happen when she flops to her back, arms spread, giving me easy access to the button and zipper. "Well, that's one way to do it."

Without trouble, I undo her pants and ease them down her legs, her tight black shirt painted onto her stomach, a few inches higher than the waistline of her . . .

Oh fuck.

She's wearing a thong.

For the love of God, don't flip over. Please don't flip over.

Turning my back to her, I fold her jeans and place them on the bench at the foot of the bed and work my way to my side of the bed. She's going to be covered in blankets. This brilliant idea is not going to turn into a painful one. I know it won't.

I sit on my side of the bed, plug my phone into its charger, take a deep breath, and turn to find Adalyn curled up in a ball, her backside to me, her black lace thong burning a hole straight into my soul.

Her ass . . .

Fuck.

Smooth, round, begging for my hands.

No, you're not going to feel up a woman who's passed out in your bed. Get ahold of yourself.

I glance at her ass one more time and inwardly grown; there goes the snuggling I had planned. There is no way I'm going to press against her when I have a fucking growing hard-on in my boxer briefs. That just spells out creeper.

Grumbling to myself, I flip off the light and turn away from Adalyn. I *try* to erase the images of her ass that's only a foot away from my memory.

This is going to be one long fucking night.

Have you ever had a dream that felt so real? Like it was actually happening in real life?

That's what is happening to me right now.

I'm in some kind of dream haze where my mind is making everything feel so damn real it actually feels like Adalyn is touching me.

Touching me all over.

Her small, thin fingers running under my pecs, scraping my nipples with her fingernails, pressing her palm against my thick chest.

Her nails scraping down my abs, one divot at a time, making me so damn hard that I can feel a sweat break out over my skin.

Her fingers linger back to my chest where they play with my nipple, causing a groan to erupt from my throat.

Her feather-soft hair tickles my chin, her scent so strong, it feels so real.

Scanning, scraping, touching, exploring, her fingers move up and down my torso, my dick growing harder with every touch until her fingers play with the edge of my waistband, my cock inching to be released.

My hips thrust up, begging, pleading, needing to be satisfied.

Fingernails scrape along the waistband, dipping in right near my cock. So close, so goddamn close.

"Fuck," I mutter, the sound loud on my ears.

Eyes fluttering open, I notice the light streaming in through the windows of the small cottage, the white curtains barely blocking the morning sun. My body tightens when I shift to the side. My hand is wrapped around Adalyn, my wrist trapped by a piece of fabric, my hand full of soft, luscious skin.

My cock throbs.

My skin tingles.

My breath is erratic.

My balls tighten as innocent fingers continue to play with my boxer briefs.

Trying to blink away the fog I'm in, I realize I wasn't dreaming. Adalyn *is* in my arms, my hand is gripping her bare ass, her hair is spread across my shoulder and chest, and her hand is inching closer and closer toward my cock.

But when I think she might be awake, doing some early morning exploring, I look down at her beautifully sweet face and notice her eyes are closed. Eyes closed, mouth barely parted, blissful sleep consuming her.

Fuck, she's asleep—*caressing me*—and it's killing me.

Squeezing my eyes shut, I take in a deep breath, willing my body to relax, but when Adalyn's finger grazes the tip of my cock, my eyes shoot open and my balls tighten so goddamn hard that I'm scooting out from under Adalyn before I can stop myself.

Dick hard as a rock, I shuffle to the bathroom, turn on the shower, and keep the bathroom door partly open as the water starts to warm up. From the mirror, I can see Adalyn plain as day. Eyes still shut, she flips to the side and curls into her pillow, the sheets covering that pert ass of hers.

Stripping out of my boxer briefs, I hop in the shower, grab some soap, lather up, and lean against the tile of the wall as I start to work the soap up and down my hardened length.

Hissing between my teeth, I grip the back of my head, my elbow pressing against the cold tile, my legs feeling wobbly. I'm already there, a few seconds from coming, just from some innocent touches, just from the memory of her scent floating past me, of the way her hair felt against my bare chest.

Up and down.

Up and down.

"Fuck," I grunt, squeezing my eyes shut, biting down on my lower lip.

Her lips, those fuckable, kissable, sexy-as-sin lips.

Up . . . and . . . down.

"God . . . shit." My head falls to the tile, my hand relentless on my cock, my forearm burning from the erratic motion. My abs tighten, a euphoric feeling working its way up from my toes to my gut, to my balls.

Up.

Down.

Up . . .

"Goddamn it," I press my head harder into the tile, trying to keep my groans together, the head of my cock ready to burst.

Her smile.

Her laugh.

Her caress.

Those long legs.

That . . . ass.

Inexplicably groaning, my hand pulls on my cock as my orgasm takes over, my vision tunneling, my legs shaking, my grip squeezing so goddamn tight I'm almost positive I'm about to black out.

My hand stilling, my cock throbs in my palm, my come pouring out of me until I don't think I have any left. Spent and partially satisfied, I take a deep breath, the steam of the shower opening my lungs, rejuvenating me.

I might just be able to get through this morning without jumping Adalyn unexpectedly. Because I want to fucking jump her. God, how I want her.

Quickly, I soap up my body, wash my hair and face, then turn off the shower. Peeking past the shower door, I glance into the bedroom to find Adalyn still sleeping. Man, she must have been really tired. That or she's the heaviest sleeper I know.

I towel off, put on a pair of Nike shorts, and head into the bedroom, droplets of water careening from my hair, down my chest. I make sure one last time she's fully asleep, snag my phone, and walk to the kitchen.

What should I make for breakfast?

I rub my hands together and take a look at the time. Eight o'clock. Wow, I never sleep in this late. I must have been extremely comfortable sleeping with Adalyn.

Well, that was until she started skimming her fingers over my cock.

Shaking those thoughts out of my head, not wanting to get excited again, I pick up a box of waffle mix from the pantry and scan the ingredients. Just add water, that's easy.

While I'm searching for a waffle maker, my phone rings in my pocket. I answer without even looking at the caller ID.

"Hello?"

"Hey, man. What are you up to today?" Racer, shit.

"Hey Racer, uh . . . not much. Just making some breakfast."

Where the fuck is the waffle maker? Ah, there it is.

"Breakfast? Dude, it's eight."

"I'm aware. I slept in. I'm allowed to do that when it's the off-season, you know."

Racer tsks into the phone. "Not if you're dedicated to being the best. The best wake up at five every morning for an early morning workout."

"Shut the fuck up." I laugh into the phone. "What do you want?" I plug the waffle iron into an outlet, set the temperature to medium to be safe, and start stirring the mix together with water. I know I have some strawberries in the fridge I can cut up and put on top of the waffle, making me look like a goddamn professional. My mom would be proud.

"I was hoping you might be available for some hard labor later tonight."

"Hard labor? Why would I want to do that?"

"Because I need your help desperately, and I would have to pay anyone else, but I know out of the goodness of your heart, you would help me for free, because you're such a good guy."

"Really trying to pull at the heartstrings, aren't you?" I spray the waffle maker with some PAM, and pour half a cup of batter onto the hot irons.

"Never." He pauses. "Did I ever tell you you're my best friend?"

Rolling my eyes, I turn on the toaster oven and set it to warm so I can store the waffles in some heat when they're done cooking.

"You must be really desperate if you're willing to throw down the best-friend card."

"I can offer you some good tunes, an artfully crafted peanut butter and jelly sandwich for dinner, and some good old-fashioned jokes."

"Damn, how could I ever turn down a night like that?"

"I know, I offer up a good bargain, don't I?"

"Practically irresistible."

"What do you say?" Racer sounds like he's holding his breath, awaiting my answer, as if I say no, it will really put a damper on his evening.

A part of me wants to say no because it's a stolen opportunity I can spend with Adalyn, but from the sound of Racer's voice, I'm going to assume this would mean a lot to him. *He needs me.* Given I'm hanging out with the girl he told me to stay away from, I'm going to need all the good vibes on my side when shit goes down.

"Yeah, I can come help. Just shoot me a text with all the information, and I'll be there."

"Really?" Racer sounds shocked.

"Of course, but you owe me a Little Debbie snack."

"Oooo, cheap shot, man, but I'll allow it. See you tonight."

Hanging up, I put my phone on the counter as the waffle iron beeps. Flipping open the top, I use a pair of tongs to remove the golden-brown waffle and put it directly in the warming toaster oven.

"Perfect," I say to myself, excited to making breakfast for someone else.

"Smells good," a sleepy voice says from behind me.

Spinning around, I find Adalyn leaning against the counter, palm pressed to one of her eyes, hair a beautiful disaster, those long, toned legs completely bare. Not even the slightest bit bashful, she walks toward me in nothing but her thong and T-shirt and circles her arms around my waist, pressing her face against my chest.

Surprised, it takes me a second to realize I should hug her back, but when I do, she snuggles in even closer.

"Thanks for not making me drive home last night. I'm not sure I would have made it. I'm kind of a heavy sleeper."

Yeah, I gathered that from the way she was practically stroking my cock without batting an eyelash.

"It wasn't a problem at all. I liked it."

"Yeah?" She looks up at me, her chin to my chest, a bright smile on her face. Studying me, there is a little pinch in her brow when she asks, "Did we kiss last night?"

"No." I chuckle. "We didn't."

"Hmm, I must have had some dreams about you last night. It felt like we . . . you know . . . fooled around."

I cough, choking on my saliva, remembering the way she innocently explored me in her sleep.

"Uh . . ." I pull on the back of my neck, my flexed bicep pulling her attention. "We didn't fool around, but I woke up this morning to, uh . . . to you feeling me up."

Her mouth drops open, and she presses her hand to her chest in shock. "How dare you accuse me of such a thing. I would never do that."

Shit.

"I didn't mean to offend you," I try to recover. "It's just, your hand was kind of wandering."

"You're ridiculous. I would never." She steps away and folds her arms over her chest, anger clouding those chocolate-stained eyes of hers.

Not wanting her to be mad, I try to backpedal. "I mean, I'm not mad about it, but you asked and I thought I'd let you know, it was . . . fuck, it turned me on." Shit, don't say that. "I mean, it was nice, your fingers were gentle . . . errr, I mean they were . . ." Fucking hell.

Christ, man. Keep digging the grave.

I glance at Adalyn to gauge how mad she really is when I see her giggling to herself, her shoulders shaking, her hand over her mouth. "Why are you laughing?"

"Watching you squirm. It's cute. Of course I remember touching you. I like to do a quick test drive before I actually buy the car, if you know what I mean."

"Sooo, you were awake the entire time when you were running your fingers over my nipples . . . over the tip of my cock."

She nods, a giant smile on her face.

"You're fucking kidding me."

She shakes her head. "And hearing you come in the shower, that was seriously hot. But don't worry, I passed out again shortly after that."

What.

The.

Hell.

The sound of my fingernails scraping over my short scruff fills the silence between us.

Walking past me, her bare ass swaying back and forth catches my attention. "So that means you felt me gripping your ass this morning."

She's looking through the cupboards when she says, "Mm-hmm." Looking over her shoulder, she says, "You have quite an impressive grip on you, young man. It left me intrigued, looking for more."

Perplexed, I drag my hand down my face.

"Aha." She takes a mug from a shelf and goes to the coffee maker where she starts making a pot of coffee. "Don't look so distraught. This is a good thing."

With her back toward me, she scoops coffee grounds into a filter, followed by filling up the coffee maker with water.

This is a good thing?

No, a good thing would have been NOT pretending she was asleep and letting her hands do some more wandering, some seriously dangerous wandering.

Instead, I had to take care of business, and it wasn't nearly as satisfying as the real thing.

Growling under my breath, I walk up behind her and place my hands on her hips, my thumbs tucking under the hem of her shirt.

She gasps and arches her back against my chest. Leaning forward, I murmur into her ear, my lips pressed against the side of her head. "Do you realize how much you drove me crazy with your hands?"

My thumbs move upward over her ribs until I reach her bra.

"Do you realize how impossibly hard you made me with just the light graze of your fingers?"

I pull her closer, her ass hitting my hardening cock.

She gasps, her head falling to my shoulder.

"Do you realize how difficult it was to remove myself from that bed, to remove your warm body away from mine to be the gentleman?"

Without warning, I spin her in my arms, easily pick her up, and place her on the counter. Spreading her legs, I step into her personal space and glide my hands up her silky thighs until they reach her hips where I slip my thumbs under the fabric of her miniscule thong.

Her eyes become heady, her chest rising and falling at a rapid pace.

"Do you realize how incredibly hard I came in the shower, thinking about your touch?" I drop the tone of my voice to a low rumble. "Thinking about the feel of your sweet ass in my palm, or the way you looked last night, under the dim lights of the deck?"

Eyes closed, leaning into my touch, her mouth parted, a light flush stains her cheeks.

"And then you walk out here, wearing nothing but a shirt and thong, tempting me, teasing me." I move my thumbs down, closer to the juncture of her thighs. She hisses through her teeth, her eyes widening, connecting with mine. "Do you think that's fair, Adalyn?"

Shaking her head no, she licks her lips and whispers, "No."

"Yeah, I didn't think so either." I lean in closer, our bodies so damn close, her legs wrapping around me, her core pressing against my cock. She fits so perfectly. The tips of my fingers bury into her round ass, marking her.

Running her hands up my bare chest, she links them together behind my neck, pulling herself closer. She wants to kiss me. She's wetting her lips and her gaze is intense.

Soft and warm. I crave her. I want this. I want to kiss her.

"What do you want?" I ask her, pressing my forehead against hers.

She doesn't skip a beat. "Your lips on mine." Threading her fingers through the soft strands of my hair, she pulls, our lips seconds from touching when I slip out of her grasp and turn away.

"Wh-what are you doing?" she asks, sounding shaken.

Smiling, I turn back around, both hands behind my head, my shorts riding low on my waist, a *very* clear bulge pushing against the fabric. Her eyes roam my entire body from my toes to my lips.

"Giving you a little taste of your own medicine."

Her eyes sharpen as she grips the edge of the counter and propels herself forward toward me. Laughing, I back up until the backs of my legs hit the couch, and I tumble backward.

Taking advantage of the situation, she runs toward me and hops onto my lap, her legs straddling my hips. Placing both her hands on my chest, she leans down.

"Lesson learned. Don't tease Hayden."

I raise my eyebrows in shock. "Really? It was that easy?"

She chuckles and says, "As some misogynistic men like to think, I'm not some 'stubborn female.' I can find fault in my wrongdoings."

"Damn." I chuckle and grip her hips as she grinds down on me, positioning herself closer to me, her hair forming a curtain of silky brown strands around her face. "So what now?"

"You tell me. Are you going to continue to hold out on me?"

I twist my lips to the side, holding back my smile. "Sort of."

"Sort of?" Exasperated, she lets out a long sigh. "Are you trying to torture me?"

"No, just looking for the right moment."

Eyeing me suspiciously, she asks, "Are you a closet romantic?"

"Possibly."

Slowly nodding her head in understanding, she says, "I can respect that." And as quick as she jumped on top of me, she hops off and holds out her hand to help me to my feet. "If you're waiting for the right moment to kiss me, I'll wait with you."

"You're going to wait?"

"I'm going to wait for you." *Who is this girl? How did I get so lucky?* For the second time today, she wraps her arms around my waist and hugs me tightly. And for the second time today, my heart stutters in my chest, my body melts into her, and I take one more step to becoming addicted to her sweet embrace. And this is also when I realize I'm so fucked.

CHAPTER EIGHT

ADALYN

"You're making it hard for me to think of other men," I say, putting my fork down and staring over our empty dishes at Hayden.

"Do you want to think about other men?" He leans forward, hands gripping the table.

"Not in the slightest." I play with my fork on my plate, and look at Hayden through my eyelashes. "Can I be honest with you?"

"Always." He relaxes into his chair, crossing his arms over his broad, expansive chest. There is a light patch of hair covering his thick pecs, trimmed short so you barely notice it's there. It's masculine, very appealing, incredibly sexy. His hair is ruffled from his peaceful slumber, and he's been sporting a lazy smile ever since I appeared in the kitchen.

There is an easygoing, fun-loving air about him I find intoxicating. By now, I would have thrown caution to the wind and kissed the man, but with Hayden, it feels different. It feels *okay to wait*.

"Can I ask you a question first?"

"Sure." He looks to the side and quickly says, "Maybe we can sit on the couch though?"

"I'd like that." Standing, he takes my hand and guides me to the couch where he sits and pulls me down across his lap so my legs drape over his, and my back is against the arm of the couch. Gripping my knee, he soothes his thumb over the bone, back and forth.

"What's your question?"

His touch is so gentle. It makes me feel cherished—worshipped—such a foreign feeling.

Fiddling with the end of my shirt, feeling a little weird without pants on, I ask, "Have you ever been in love?"

"In love?" He blows out a heavy sigh and rests his head on the back of the couch. "Nah, I don't think so, not the kind of love that builds a foundation for the rest of your life. I feel like I've had puppy love, you know back in high school when you think you love someone, it's new and exciting. But real love?" He shakes his head. "No. What about you?"

I press my lips together and shake my head as well. "No, I've never been in love, or a relationship for that matter."

"You haven't had a boyfriend before?"

"Nope." I twist my hands in my lap as my forehead creases with concern. "I know it's super early in whatever this is between us, but I thought I would let you know . . . I've never done this before, spent more time with a guy than one night."

Realization hits him and when I think he's about to grow angry, he surprises me and takes my hand in his, bringing it to his lips. "So you've never been on a date?"

"No, I've been on dates before, but second and third dates? Not so much, nor have I talked to a guy like I've talked to you."

"Does that scare you?"

I nod and lean my head against his shoulder as he wraps his arm around me, pulling me in close. "You're a professional hockey player, Hayden. You live in Philadelphia; you're only here for a short amount of time; it feels ridiculous to even think about starting a relationship with you, let alone my first one, and who knows if you really want a relationship with me, I'm just . . . ugh, I'm getting ahead of myself." I take a deep breath and say, "I guess I want to feel you out before I dive any deeper into this thing between us, because I'm already starting to feel things for you, and I'd like to nip it in the bud if you're not feeling the same thing." God, I sound like a rambling idiot. "No pressure or anything. It's not an ultimatum, sorry if it sounded like one. Ugh, can you tell I'm not good at—"

"Stop." Hayden pinches my chin with his thumb and index finger, bringing my eyes level with his. That smile, those eyes, his rumpled hair . . . it eases the tension building in my chest.

"Adalyn, I wouldn't have made dinner and breakfast for you, or tracked you down through multiple hospitals if I wasn't interested in you, if I didn't feel the same thing you're feeling. Believe me, I understand our lives are different, and when hockey season starts again, it's going to be hard, but I'm not worried about that right now. What I want to focus on is getting to know you."

"But what happens when you do have to go? Is it worth starting something?"

"To me it is." He twists his fingers through my messy hair. "I want more of you. I'm not ready to say goodbye, are you?"

I take a second, weighing my options. This is all new to me, getting to know someone on a deeper level, not jumping into the physical right away, feeling like I'm swept up into another world. The big question is, do I want to dip my toes into the unknown with someone who's bound to leave no matter what? Do I want to put myself out there with the huge possibility of getting hurt in the end?

"What's wrong?" he asks, cupping my cheek. "Why do you have that worried look on your face?"

Knowing he will appreciate my honesty, I say, "I don't want to get hurt, Hayden."

He lets out a long breath and pulls me in closer, resting my cheek on his chest. He kisses the top of my head and strokes my shoulder with his thumb. "I would like to promise I'm not going to hurt you, but I can't make that promise, because I don't know what the future holds, but what I can promise is to try. To put in the effort. To make you laugh. To make you happy. To continually make that beautiful smile appear on your lips. That's what I can do, and hopefully, everything else will fit into place if it's meant to be."

"So just like that, you're going to jump in, feet first?"

He nods against my head. "Yeah, I'm jumping in. Care to join me?"

Biting on my bottom lip, I squeeze my eyes shut, my nerves twisting and turning in my stomach. *Fuck, I don't want to get hurt.* Shit. Shit. Shit. I don't want to get hurt. Not by him. Not by one of the sweetest guys I've ever met. Because I know. I know he'd never intentionally hurt me, which gives him a lot of power, yet it doesn't make me powerless. He's such a good man. Kind. Giving. But I don't think I can survive being hurt by him.

Then again, I don't think I can survive saying goodbye right now, either.

Shyly, I look up at him and say, "If I jump in, will you catch me?"

Playfully, a grin spreads across his lips, lighting up his entire face. "Don't worry, I'll catch you, Adalyn."

~

Leaning against the door of my car, I play with the belt loops of Hayden's jeans. After cleaning up breakfast, we joked and teased each other for a bit before he changed and offered me a set of shorts to wear home.

"What are you doing for the rest of the day?"

Gripping my hips, his large hands pressing me gently against my car, he says, "I have some errands to run, and then I promised Racer I'd help him out with something tonight."

I can feel my disappointment take over me, my smile melting away. I was hoping I'd be able to hang out with Hayden tonight.

"Yeah? Sounds like fun," I say, faking my excitement for him.

Stupid Racer, what could he possibly want help with and why can't he ask Tucker or Aaron?

Chuckling and rubbing his thumbs over my hipbone, he says, "Tell me how you really feel."

Tilting my head to the side, I level with him. "You really want to know?"

"I really do."

I give his belt loops a few tugs before answering, loving how with each tug he leans in closer. "I was kind of hoping we could hang out tonight, since it's my night off."

"Is that right?" His smile is contagious but also cocky.

"You don't have to look so pleased with yourself."

"It's just nice to know where your head's at. I like a girl who is open and honest about her feelings, none of this having to read your mind bullshit."

"Oh, you're not a mind reader?" I tease him, poking his rock-hard stomach. And of course, he doesn't flinch. God, the man has fantastic muscles. It was so hard to hold back groans of pleasure earlier when my hands were *wandering*. I wanted to spend hours there, touching, memorizing. *Man, did I want to dip below his waistband.*

"No." He's silent for a breath before cupping my cheek and stroking his thumb over my skin. I let out a heavy breath as he squeezes in closer, his body flush against mine, towering over me, those dark eyes of his turning more sinister. "Want me to cancel with Racer?"

There is no humor in his question, no empty ask, and from the look in his eyes, his stone-like features, he's serious.

Sighing, I shake my head no. "Don't cancel on Racer. I'm sure he called because it was important."

"I don't like this sad face on you though. Maybe I can hurry things along with Racer, catch a late dessert with you tonight?"

"I can make chocolate cake."

A brilliant smile spreads across his lips. "You'd make me choco-late cake?"

"From a box, don't get too excited."

"It's still cute and thoughtful." Moving his other hand to my neck, he presses his thumb against my hammering pulse, his fingers tangling with my wild hair. Talking low, he asks, "Does that mean I'm coming to your place tonight?"

Wetting my lips, I try to keep my breathing even despite how erratic it feels, despite the close proximity of this man, despite how crazy in lust he makes me feel. "Yes, it does."

"Should I bring an overnight bag with me?"

"I'd be disappointed if you didn't."

He licks his lips, and his eyes search mine. His mouth so close, his body so warm, and I take a moment to savor this moment. The tension between us palpable, the lust seeping into a pool of need between us. Our touches, anything but innocent, the desire in our eyes about to explode.

I want him . . . bad.

"Then I'll see you tonight. Text me your address?"

"Of course." I swallow hard as he passes his thumb over my cheek once more.

I can see it in his eyes, the indecision. Is this the moment he wants, the perfect timing for a kiss? God, what is he waiting for?

"It doesn't have to be a big moment, you know. You can just kiss me." My lungs feel heavy, my legs tingling with need, my hands shaking as they grip him, clinging desperately to him, not wanting any distance between us.

Leaning down, I hold my breath, my stomach flipping with somersaults just as his lips press against my . . . forehead. He lingers for a second before pulling away and stuffing his hands in his back pockets, his chest pulling at the threadbare shirt stretched across his thick muscles.

"I'll see you tonight, Adalyn." He winks and takes off toward the cottage, making me more sexually frustrated than I've ever been in my life.

Deflated, turned on, and irritated, I get in my car, start the engine, and stare out the front window. Is this what it's like to be with a man who doesn't want me only for my body? If so, it's the most sexually frustrating . . . yet exhilarating thing I've ever experienced.

Now to get ready for tonight. I need to make it impossible for Hayden to NOT kiss me.

Damn it, I'm going to get that kiss tonight, and it all starts with a very thorough shower, shave, and then a much-needed shopping session.

~

"That dress is so hot on you," Emma, my best friend, says as she flips through a magazine on my bed.

I look at my reflection in the mirror. "But do I want to wear a dress? Should I do something more casual? We're just going to be here, would it be weird if I answer the door wearing a dress?"

Emma folds the magazine shut and leans forward, hands poised on her lap. "Let me ask you this. Are you doing your hair and makeup?"

"Of course, but I was going to go with a natural look with my makeup, not too much since it's going to be late."

Shrugging her shoulders and casually picking up the magazine again, she says, "If it were me, I would wear a dress and make it impossible for him not to stare at me. Works with Tucker every time, then again, he usually sees me in scrubs, so when I get dressed up, his eyes pop out of their sockets."

"I don't know." I pull on the hem of the dress that reaches mid-thigh. "Maybe something more subtle. This is a little slutty."

"Do the pink sundress. It's more casual but still pretty and looks great against your tan skin. It's going to pop, plus it gives you great cleavage." Tossing the pink dress at me from the pile that's formed on my bed, she says, "Put it on. Trust me, it's the winner."

Since there is no modesty between Emma and me, I take off the slutty-looking dress and put on the pink one. I adjust my bra in the cups of the dress and look in the mirror. Emma is right. It's casual but pretty and gives me great lines.

"And if you wear your hair down in loose waves, add a touch of makeup, he's going to be begging to kiss you."

Before we started trying on dresses, I filled Emma in on my little kissing problem with Hayden. To say she was giddy over our budding relationship is an understatement. It took her at least five minutes to stop squealing over everything I said, and now that she's calmed down, she's bound and determined to help me get that kiss.

"He's different than any guy I've ever been with. I could answer the door naked, and I'm pretty sure he still wouldn't kiss me. I can tell he's physically attracted to me, that doesn't go unnoticed, but I'm shocked by his restraint. For some reason, I thought athletes were horn dogs, you know, all that adrenaline and masculinity pumping through them."

"I think Hayden is exactly what you need." Emma peers at me, true honesty in her eyes, the kind of honesty only a best friend can give. "Ever since I met you, you've been one and done with men, never really continuing past a first date."

"Because none of them were worth it." I shrug casually.

"Or maybe because you didn't care enough to give the guys a second chance. But Hayden is different. I can tell you really do care about him."

I fiddle with the right strap of my dress, adjusting the length. Up and down, up and down. "Maybe it's because he's one of the first guys ever to treat me the way my brothers always said I should be treated."

Realization hits me as the words come out of my mouth.

It's true.

From as early as I can remember, my brothers have told me countless times how I need to be treated like a lady, how the guy I date needs to be open and honest. How he needs to respect me not only for my body but for my mind too.

Hayden is physically attracted to me, yes, but when I've given him the opportunity to push further, he hasn't taken it. And when he speaks of my job, of my education, he's in awe, like I have the hardest job he's ever heard of. It makes me feel . . . valued.

He makes me feel accomplished.

He makes me feel like I'm more than a pair of legs, like I'm a good human being.

And that's what my brothers want, for me to be appreciated for *who* I am. Not only what I look like.

"I think you're right." Emma gets up from my bed and stands behind me, both hands on my shoulders. She looks into the mirror, staring at my reflection. "He's a good guy, Addie. I'm really happy for you."

But . . .

"He's not here forever."

She squeezes my shoulder. "If it's meant to be, you'll work it out, but for now enjoy yourself, enjoy him."

"I don't want to get hurt."

"I don't want that either, so take one step at a time. If he's smart enough, he'll know that when it's time to go back to Philly, he'll make whatever is going on between you two work."

"You think so?" I bite on my lip, feeling so unsure.

Emma gives me a *get real* look. "Adalyn, he's one of the few high-profile hockey players out there we rarely hear about. He's not in the tabloids with women hanging off him at every event. And you've figured out by now that Racer, as much as he is a lunatic at times, he's good people. And by association, Hayden is too. I mean, he went around to hospitals in the area looking for you. That was so damn sweet. And, I'm pretty sure it means he's going to put in the effort where you're concerned." She presses her fingers into my brow, dissolving the tension in my forehead. "Now stop worrying. You have a cake to make."

Shit, I do. And it has to be perfect.

Like how Hayden seems to be. Perfect.

CHAPTER NINE

HAYDEN

"Can you stop dancing for the love of God and finish this damn thing?" I beg of Racer who won't stop dancing to the playlist he created "just for this occasion."

Huffing, he steps up next to me and starts hammering the two-by-fours into place. "You're telling me you can listen to *'Get your Freak On'* by Missy Elliot and not want to bust a move? Dude, she's a lyrical master."

"As much as I appreciate the beat, I have things to do tonight."

Racer cocks his head back. "Things to do? What could you possibly be doing at"—he checks his watch—"eight at night? Don't you go to bed early? Am I not your only friend here?"

Shit, I don't want to tell Racer about Adalyn, because I know he'll flip out. In *his* mind, he's my only friend here.

"Early morning stuff," I mumble.

"Early morning stuff, huh?" Racer pounds a few nails and then says, "Sounds to me like you have a late-night booty call you're not telling me about. Am I right?"

I can feel all color drain from my face so I quickly look away, hiding my panic. "Nah," I clear my throat, "just some training I have to do tomorrow morning. You know, basic training shit."

Racer is silent. I can feel his stare. His studying gaze waiting for me to falter, waiting for me to show my true colors.

"Who are you training with?"

"Huh?"

Racer lifts another board and hands it to me. I put it in place just as he leans forward, getting in my space. "Who are you training with tomorrow?" He enunciates every word.

"Uh, you know . . . Franklin."

There is no Franklin.

Where Franklin came from, I have no clue.

He doesn't even sound like a real person.

Who names their kid Franklin anymore?

I would have been better off with saying something like Blaze. Blaze is more believable, not . . . Franklin.

"Franklin?" Racer deadpans.

"Yup." I chuckle. "Good old Franklin. Killer on the ice, that guy. Has some of the best cuts I've ever seen."

"And what's Franklin's last name?"

"Dolittle." I nod, hating myself but trying to convince Racer that this Franklin Dolittle fella is real.

"Dolittle. You're going to go train with a guy tomorrow by the name of Franklin Dolittle."

"Yup, funny right?"

Suspiciously glaring at me, he pulls his phone from his back pocket and starts typing. Leaning forward to catch what he's doing, I ask, "What are you typing there?"

"Looking up this *expert on the ice*, Franklin Dolittle."

Without even thinking, I swat the phone out of his hand, sending it careening into a pile of wood on the floor.

"What the fuck, man?"

"Uh . . . sorry. Spasm." I shake out my arm and then give it a couple stretches across my body. "No need to look him up, 'cause he's aloof. Stays off the Internet, keeps to himself. He's only known in the underground hockey world. It's kind of like a black market of sorts but for hockey."

Jesus, I'm really digging myself a hole here.

Note to self: you're not good at lying.

At least you're not good at creating believable lies.

"Dude, you did not have a spasm."

"You don't know that." I whip my arm around in a windmill like motion. "This old thing spasms all the time."

Hands on his hips, looking me dead in the eyes, Racer says, "Stop fucking with me. What are you doing tonight?"

Shit.

Think . . . think . . . fuck, I got it.

Shrugging, trying to act embarrassed, I say, "Ugh, fine, you got me. I'm, uh, I'm taking a water aerobics class tonight. It's to help with my muscles. It's with a bunch of older ladies, and it's at eight forty-five. It's a, uh, black-light party class. We bring glow sticks and everything."

This is a real thing. My mom spent a good ten minutes on the phone with me the other day telling me about it. She was so damn excited it was hard not to get caught up in her enthusiasm.

Racer studies me and shakes his head. "You're not fucking going to some glow-stick swim party. I'm not buying it."

"You don't know. I actually really like black lights and glow sticks. There's nothing more exciting than a neon parade of sticks while dancing in the water. Don't make me feel bad about my extracurricular activities, dude."

"Okay." Racer sets down his hammer, goes to the woodpile and pockets his phone. "Come on, I don't want you to be late."

Ehhh . . .

I don't make a move.

I barely bat an eyelash.

I can see he's brewing something in his head, because he's acting *way* too cool right now.

"Are we finished?" I gesture toward the pile of wood we still have to frame out.

Racer picks up his car keys and jingles them in his hand. "Yeah, I'm good for the night, thanks for the help. Let's get out of here."

"Racer, man, you're freaking me out a bit."

"Why? You have a class to get to. I don't want to hold you back from your *glow stick* fun. Come on"—he nods toward the door —"let's get out of here."

Cautiously, I follow him out and wait for him to lock up the bridal shop he's been remodeling for some extra cash.

We walk to our vehicles, and I can't help but wonder what his game is. "Are you sure? I don't mind staying a little later. I can skip the class tonight."

"Hell no, there is no way I'm letting you skip your class, especially when I'm going with you."

Fuck, I knew it. I knew he was hiding something.

"You don't have a membership."

He shrugs, "I'll ask for a guest pass. I'm sure they'll be more than accommodating for Hayden Holmes."

"You don't have a bathing suit."

He shakes his finger at me. "Funny thing, I always have one in my truck in case I come across a lake I want to jump in."

"Dinner. You can't swim on an empty stomach." Can you see I'm grasping here?

"Isn't that reversed? You should never swim on a full stomach."

I drag my hand down my face, exhausted. "Fine, I'm not going to a fucking glow-stick water class."

Racer crosses his arms over his chest. "Then where are you going?"

There is no way of getting around this, not one I can think off the top of my head. Besides all my "lies" have been pitiful, so I might as well go with the truth so I can get out of here faster.

"I'm going to Adalyn's house, okay?"

Pretty sure Racer wasn't expecting that answer because his face falls in shock before turning brutally sharp with anger. His jaw ticks, his eyes narrow, and the veins in his neck start to twitch.

Okay, maybe the truth wasn't a good idea, after all.

"Did I not tell you to stay the fuck away from her? What the hell are you doing?" He takes a step forward, but I stand my ground. I'm a few inches taller than he is and have about twenty more pounds of muscles wrapped around my body.

"I'm sorry, but I like her." I run my hand through my hair. "I like her a lot."

"For how long?"

"Since I met her at your house. I went to each hospital in town and looked for her. Once I found her, I didn't let her out of my sight. I've taken her lunch, made her dinner, and treated her like a goddamn queen. And before you even ask, no, I haven't slept with her, and I have no plan of doing so anytime soon. I haven't even kissed her. I know she's fragile, I know this is new to her, and I know she's been hurt before. I have no intention of hurting her. When I say I like her, I mean it. I want to see where this goes."

Studying me, Racer's eyes bouncing back and forth, he grinds his teeth together, still not happy, but the crease in his brow lessens. "I don't like it."

"Didn't ask you to like it, didn't even ask for your approval, because either way, I'm still going to pursue her."

"She's my friend, Hayden, my good friend."

"I understand." I squeeze Racer's shoulder. "But I'm your good friend too. Trust me. You know me, you know the kind of person I am. I'm not the kind of guy who's going to purposely hurt someone, or get what I want and then leave. I'm honest and trustworthy. I will treat her well, I promise you that."

Moving his jaw back and forth, he sighs and lowers his head. "Fuck, you're right. If I had to choose someone for her, I guess it would be you . . . unfortunately."

"Don't be too excited about it," I joke.

"She's been hurt before."

"I know." I pat Racer on the back. "She told me. She told me everything."

"She did?" Racer looks surprised.

"Yeah, she did."

Nodding slowly, he understands the importance of Adalyn opening up to me. He gets it. "And you're going over there tonight to . . ."

"Eat cake." Racer suggestively raises his eyebrow at me. Rolling my eyes, I clarify. "Like, actual cake. Chocolate cake to be exact."

"Gah, chocolate cake. That sounds really good. Can I come too?"

"Are you mental? Of course you can't come." I make my way to my car. "Three's a crowd, man. Sorry."

Hopping in my car, I wave goodbye through the windshield and make a quick pit stop at the cottage for a one-minute shower, and to pack my overnight bag. Then I'm back in my car on route to Adalyn's place, which thankfully isn't too far away.

The conversation with Racer went a lot smoother than I expected. I can't tamp down the euphoric elation I'm feeling, or the giant smile I'm sporting. *That is* until I pull up to Adalyn's house and see Racer's rusty old pickup parked right outside.

What. The. Fuck.

~

Trying not to barge through the door with a serious chip on my shoulder, I take a calming breath and rap my knuckles on the wood. I run my hand through the short strands of my still-damp hair as the door opens. Adalyn's eyes are wide as she shakes her head and goes to shut the door on me, telepathically telling me now is not a good time.

Clearly Racer hasn't told her about our little conversation. The asshole. I bet he's sitting on her couch right now, eating my goddamn cake.

Before she can shut the door on me, I press my hand against the wood and push open.

Under her breath, she says, "What are you doing? Racer is here."

"I know." I push through the door and walk into her living

where Racer is perched on the armrest, a smug smile on his face and a plate of cake in hand.

That motherfucker.

"Hayden, what a pleasant surprise. What on earth could you be doing here at Adalyn's house?"

"What the hell did you not understand about the phrase three's a crowd?" I make my way toward him as he quickly shovels the cake in his mouth.

Talking with his mouth full, he says, "You must have known I'd show up. You say cake and I'm there, man. Sorry I'm not sorry."

I snatch the plate from him as he takes his last bite and point toward the door. "Say good night to Adalyn and leave."

"What is going on here?" Adalyn asks, stepping into the living room, looking so goddamn beautiful in a pink dress that the anger roaring through me starts to dissipate.

Racer lifts the hem of his shirt to wipe his mouth, showing off his six pack—how he has one, I have no idea—and says, "Romeo over here let the cat out of the bag before I got here. Not only did he tell me about that delicious cake, but he also let it be known that he has a huge crush on you."

God, why does he have to sound like a giant turd when he talks?

"You told Racer?" Adalyn asks, looking a little more angry than I expected.

"I did." I rub the back of my neck, casting my eyes toward Adalyn, giving her all my attention. "He cornered me, and I'm not a good liar. I'm sorry. I know you probably would have wanted to tell him, but I was honest."

"He was." Racer jabs me in the ribs, buckling me over as he walks past me. Pulling Adalyn into a hug, he whispers something in her ear and then pulls away. Winking in my direction, he says, "Hurt her and I'll rupture your nut sac with a hockey puck." He throws up the peace sign and walks out of Adalyn's house, leaving us alone.

What was the point of that other than Racer acting like a total dick?

Maybe he wanted to see if I was telling the truth.

Or maybe, he's a goddamn child and just wanted a piece of cake.

I'm going to guess it's the latter.

Silence falls in the room, making it extremely awkward. This is not how I wanted our night to start off, with this uncomfortable tension between us.

I break the silence. "I'm sorry, I didn't know what to tell him."

Adalyn shifts in place, her hands twined together. "It's okay. He said he was happy for me and that you were a good guy." Peering up through those impossibly long eyelashes, she adds, "He also told me to tell him if you're a dick to me at any point in time."

My eyes find the ceiling as I shake my head. "Of course he did." I take a few steps toward her until I'm able to grab her by the hand and pull her into my arms. I press a kiss against the top of her head and say, "I hate that he ruined the night for us . . ." She looks at me with a raised eyebrow. *How can chicks do that?*

"Okay. Okay. And I really hate that he ate my cake." Adalyn and my mom will get along well, given they both possess mind reading abilities. *But it's cake.*

Chuckling, Adalyn squeezes me tight. "He didn't ruin the night, just made it interesting. And I gave him one of my tester cakes. I made three today just to make sure your cake came out perfect."

I pull back to look her in the eyes. *He didn't eat my cake?* "You made three cakes?" Shyly, she confirms. "What was wrong with the first two?"

"Just testing out certain things. I added a pudding packet to the cake mix, making it extra moist. But I wanted to be sure the cake came out right, so the first was a test, the second was a forgetful moment for me—not spraying the cake tins—and number three came out beautifully. It's iced and ready to be consumed, untouched by Racer."

"Hell, that's fucking adorable." I give her another hug. "Thank you."

"It's the least I could do given everything you've done for me."

I take her hand in mine and let her lead me to the kitchen. "It's not a competition, babe."

Adalyn's apartment surprises me. I would have guessed her place would have been super colorful, but it's white. Almost everything is white, from her couch, to her walls, to her furniture. The only colors she has in the entire space are potted plants, throw pillows, and art on the wall. It's very clean and crisp, with mere splashes of her personality.

When we reach the kitchen, I'm struck by bright green dinnerware in the open shelves hanging over her counters. Not one upper cabinet is present, just shelves after shelves covered in all different shades of green dinnerware. It's . . . soothing.

"I like your dishes."

"Thank you." She takes down two plates and places them next to what looks like a three-layered cake covered in chocolate icing and chocolate sprinkles. Damn . . . I think I may have fallen in love.

"You made that?" I point at the cake that looks like a professional made it.

Her cheeks stain crimson as she cuts a big piece for me and a medium-sized piece for herself. There is what looks like some kind of cherry filling in the middle that has my mouth watering from the very sight of it. "I had a little help from my friend, Emma, but yeah, I made it for the most part. I hope you like it."

"Pretty sure I'm going to love it." I glance around her galley kitchen. "Where should we eat it?"

"Let's go out back. I have a partition on my deck. It will afford us some much-needed privacy."

She leads me to the back of her house and onto the deck, which is surrounded by three slatted partitions and white curtains. Setting the cake on the coffee table of her outside furniture set, she releases the white curtains, blocking us from her neighbors completely. Fuck, it's super romantic with the small lantern on the table offering the only light in the space.

We both sit and before she takes her plate in her hands again, I stop her. "Hey."

She looks at me with a question in her eyes, and all I can think is how fucking gorgeous she is.

"I didn't get to tell you how beautiful you look tonight."

That blush of hers takes over again. Will she blush the same way in bed, when I'm pulsing in and out of her? When she comes, does she blush, or does her face morph into something entirely more perfect, if possible?

"Thank you."

Passing my eyes over her body again, I take in her pink dress that's loose at her hips, but cinches in at her breasts, her cleavage killing me, and that pink makes her skin look unbearably smooth. It makes me want to run my hands up and down her entire body, slowly peeling away the fabric, revealing what's underneath.

Is she wearing anther thong? Is she commando? Is she even wearing a bra?

I take a quick peek, and it doesn't look like it. Fuck . . . it doesn't look like it at all, not with how her nipples are pebbling against the fabric.

"Are you going to eat your cake?"

"What?" I clear my throat and shake the images of her hardened nipples out of my head. Get it together, man.

"Your cake, are you going to eat it?" She thumbs at my solo plate on the coffee table.

"Oh yeah, sorry." I pick up the cake, and I'm quickly consumed by the chocolaty flavor. "This smells so fucking good."

She takes a forkful and I watch in fascination as her exquisite lips wrap around the metal tongs, pulling the chocolate, smooth and velvety. Her eyes shut, her head tilts back, her jaw moves erotically until she swallows, the long column of her neck, working the chocolate down, pulse after pulse.

Eating has never looked so sexy.

And never in my life have I ever paid such close attention to an everyday action.

"You like it?" I ask, my voice cracking, my focus traveling from the soft column of her neck, to her collarbone, to the swell of her breasts in that sweet dress.

The night I first met her, she wore simple shorts and a T-shirt. I've seen her in scrubs and I've seen her in jeans as well, but this dress? I know it's simple, but it's revealing and made for her body, accentuating her shapely legs, her full breasts, and her smooth skin.

"I think it's one of the best cakes I've ever had." She eyes my plate and asks, "What are you waiting for? Are you nervous I poisoned it? Pausing to see if I croak after taking a bite?"

Chuckling, I shake my head. "Sorry, I'm just a bit distracted tonight. You look so damn good, Adalyn."

"You mentioned that." Head tilted to the side, she licks some icing off her fork.

Dead. I'm slowly fucking dying inside. Was her mission to torture me, to get me to break tonight? Because she's doing one hell of a job. "Are you wishing you kissed me earlier now?"

I swallow hard.

I'm wishing I did a hell of a lot more than kiss.

"You're making it hard on a guy, that's all."

"Good." She lays her legs across mine and scoots closer, the hem of her dress kissing her upper thighs. "Because I'm going to tell you right now, if you don't at least kiss me tonight, I might go crazy."

She's as desperate as me at this point. Good. I've always been about delayed gratification when it comes to relationships. I like to feel the chemistry first; I like to know there's something real between us before I make the first move. Lust can cloud your outlook on a person and being a "celebrity"—someone in the lime-light—I like to make sure the woman I'm with is interested in *me* and not my profession.

"I'm making no promises." I take my first bite of the cake and quietly moan. Fuck, this is good. Probably not as good as biting into Adalyn, but I'll take this for now.

Poking my shoulder with her clean fork, she says, "And I'm making no promises of keeping my clothes on."

Fucking minx.

∼

Plates are cleared, light music plays in the background, and Adalyn is curled against me, my arm wrapped around her, my hand resting on her hip as she's tucked into my shoulder, her hand resting on my chest, her fingers lightly playing with the fabric of my shirt.

"Do you think your family will like me? Well, perhaps I'm asking more about your dad and brothers here."

A lonely cricket chirps in the background, adding to the summer-like ambiance surrounding us. Adalyn draped a blanket over us about half an hour ago once the temperature dropped. I feel goosebumps on her arms but every time I ask her if she wants to go inside or if she wants a sweater, she tells me she doesn't want to move.

"My dad? He's not a pushover, but he has age and life on his side to trust my judgment more than my brothers do. However, the boys are a tough crowd. Very protective. There aren't many men they would approve of."

"Hmm . . . do any of them like hockey?"

She chuckles and pushes against my chest. "You can't win them over with autographed paraphernalia."

Laughing and oddly loving the little jabs from her finger, I say, "A guy can try. Hell, to win them over, I'm not above whoring my teammates or myself out. I have access to all the Brawlers. I can get them to sign anything. Season tickets, done. What do they want?"

"None of them watch hockey."

"Whh-what?" I peel away and look down at her. "They don't

watch hockey? What kind of men are we talking about here? They live in the northeast for Christ's sake. Hockey is life up here."

Adalyn shakes her head. "Football is life."

Pressing my lips together in disgust, I shake my head. "Fucking football. Hockey is so much better."

"Yeah? How so?"

"Really? You want me to list off all the reasons why it's better?"

"I do. I'm kind of liking that you're going into a tizzy, so I want to hear all the reasons."

"Okay. First, I am not and do not get *in a tizzy*." I sit a little taller and disengage myself from her warm body. Ticking off the reasons on my fingers, I say, "Well, one, it's a longer season. Football is like two games long, and hockey is about seven months long."

"Sixteen games. Football is sixteen games."

As if I've been slapped, I scoot back on the couch. "Uh, excuse me . . . are you a football fan too?"

"Of course," she answers not even sugarcoating it for me. "I've never been to a professional hockey game before and forget about watching it on TV. You can never see where the puck goes."

What?

WHAT?

Shaking my head, blinking fervently, trying to comprehend what she's telling me, I say, "You've never been to a professional hockey game? You've got to be kidding me. But . . . but hockey is . . . God!" I stand from the couch and start pacing her small deck. "You're going to a game." I point at her, one hand on my hip. "You're fucking going, and you're going to enjoy it, damn it!" Now pointing to her house, I say, "Get up, we're going to review some game tape. That's your punishment. We are spending the rest of the night going over hockey highlights on YouTube."

Laughing, she shakes her head. "We are so not doing that."

"Uh, yeah we are. Come on, stand your pretty little ass up and march it over to your computer. We are reviewing every last hockey highlight tonight, and if we're lucky, I might let you watch a blooper reel here and there."

I pull on her hand to guide her up, but she stays put and pats the bench next to her. "Sit before you have a heart attack."

"Fine." I sit next to her while pulling my phone from my back pocket. Ignoring the multiple text messages and missed calls I've received since I've been here, I enter hockey highlights into the browser on my phone and start looking for some good material.

Palming my phone, she snags it from my grasp and puts it behind her back. "We are not watching hockey highlights."

"To hell we're not." I reach for my phone, but she has it tucked completely behind her, not exposing an inch.

She wants to do this the hard way? I have no problem getting handsy, especially when my sport is on the line.

Snagging her ankles, I yank her down the length of the couch, the hem of her dress rolling to just below her panty line. No time for distractions, I'm on a mission. Moving over her, one of my knees tucked between her legs, my hands straddling her slender shoulders, I try to dig around for my phone behind her.

Giggling and pressing hard into the couch, making it hard to find my phone, she blocks me. Her hair—fanned out on the cushion, her smile—beautiful and addicting, her laugh—a seductive sound igniting a heat of warmth to erupt over my skin. *God, she's so gorgeous.*

Even if she speaks blasphemy.

"Where is it?" I ask. "Give me my phone and no one gets hurt."

"Never." Like the vixen she is, she circles my waist with her legs, pulling my hips onto hers. At the same time, she links her hands behind my neck, trapping me.

Fucking fooled, that's what I am.

"What do you think you're doing? I'm mad at you."

She shakes her head. "No, you're not." Her fingers play with the short strands on the back of my head, a comforting touch. "Now tell me what the other reasons are why hockey is better than football."

Damn this woman. Just when I'm trying to pretend to be mad at her, she distracts me. Sighing, I lean back, taking her with me so I'm sitting upright and she's straddling my lap, her knees now pressed against the seat cushion. To keep her where I want her, I place my hands firmly on her hips, plastering her heated center to my lap.

She feels so fucking good.

Her thumbs rub a little patch of skin on my neck, soothing my tension to zero. Slouching, I enjoy the view in front of me, of this beautifully addicting woman, as I explain exactly why my sport is so much better.

"Besides the long season and numerous games, plus the badass trophy at the end, hockey takes more precision, more focus. Not only are we being tackled—using a football term for you—but we're doing it on skates while trying to control a small three-inch puck with a stick."

"What else?" She shifts on my lap causing a light groan to rumble from my chest.

"Uh, we have fights, all-out brawls, and they're not stopped right away like in football."

"Mm-hmm." Her hands fall to my pecs where her palms rest, her fingers playing with the patch of skin exposed from my button-down shirt. Unabashedly, she undoes two more buttons, and pulls my shirt open, exposing more of my chest.

Fuck.

Another shift on my lap, but this time, her hips continue to slowly move back and forth.

A low hiss escapes my lips.

Every part of me hardens, from my grip on her hips, encouraging her rocking, to the muscles in my chest where she's stroking my pecs, to my quickly growing cock.

"What else, Hayden?"

I'm blanking. What else is good about hockey?

"In hockey, there's . . ." *Shit, her hands feels so good.* "In hockey . . ."

What's good about Adalyn? The way her breasts sway with her movements, the way her nipples are so impossibly hard right now, and how she lightly bites on her bottom lip while she rocks above me.

"Uh . . . nachos," I mumble. "We have nachos."

"There are nachos in football."

"But these nachos . . ." She grinds on me. "Fuck . . . these nachos are . . . so good. Fuck, that's so good."

My head falls to the back of her couch, my eyes shut, Adalyn glides over me, her pace picking up now. Slipping her hands inside my shirt, she scrapes her fingers along my nipples and I swear to God, I nearly come apart.

"Adalyn."

"Hmm?"

"You feel . . . goddamn, you feel . . ."

"What?" Her head is bent forward now, her mouth near my ear. "How do I feel?"

"Fucking perfect," I hiss when she grinds down harder.

"Good." She nips my earlobe and then lifts off me in one swift movement, taking her warmth, her touch, her seductive ways with her.

"Wh-what are you doing?" I ask, watching her walk into the house.

"It's getting late. You should probably get going."

"Going?" My eyebrows shoot up. Pocketing my loose phone, I stand—painfully—my cock scraping along the crotch of my jeans. "What happened to staying over?"

Like a needy puppy dog, I follow her into her house and shut the screen door. She's in the kitchen fiddling with dishes when I come up behind her, pressing my front to her back, my hands to her hips, my mouth hovering near her ear.

"Are you playing hard to get now?"

"It's working, isn't it?"

"Maybe." I run my nose along the soft cartilage of her ear, down to her neck. Clamping her hands over mine, I feel her tense when I meander my perusal back up to her ear. "Do you really want me to go?"

"You know I don't." Spinning in my grasp, she places her hands on my chest as I lift her to sit on her counter, reminding me of a position we were in not so long ago. "Is this the moment you've been looking for?" Her voice is meek with a hint of desperation, like she's been waiting all her life for this one kiss, for my lips to be pressed against hers.

And for one of the first times in my life, I'm scared. I'm scared of what this kiss might do to me, of how it will change me as a man, because Adalyn isn't just any girl. She could be THE girl for any lucky son of a bitch.

No doubt in my mind she's someone you only come across once in a lifetime, and fuck if I'm not nervous to take that next step, to see if my gut reaction is right, that this girl is *my* game changer.

And I know kissing her will not just be our mouths connecting. It will be an unearthly experience. From how responsive she's been already with her soft mews and her apprehensive but also mostly confident touches. She's going to rock my fucking world and the question is . . . am I ready for it?

Because once I press my mouth against hers, once I conquer that first taste, it's going to be a steady downward spiral from there, of me losing any ability of staying away from her.

It's hard to stay away now.

It's hard to keep my hands off her now.

It's hard to not want to ask her every single question that comes to mind, because all I want is to know her better, to know everything about her.

And it's only been a few encounters.

Closing my eyes, I take a deep breath.

Standing in front of me, is a brand-new, unwritten page, a chapter waiting to begin, and I have to decide if I am ready to fill in the blank.

I am.

Stepping deeper between her legs, I slide my hands up her arms, reveling in the smooth feel of her skin, loving how goosebumps erupt from the rub of my worn hands. Cupping her neck, one hand gently twisting in her hair, I pull her head back an inch, parting her lips for mine. On an audible gasp, her eyes widen for a brief moment before softening when I bring my mouth a whisper from hers.

I pause.

Eyes locked, her hands gliding up my arms, anchoring her in place, our breaths mingling, her lashes beat, up and down, up and down.

Chests rise and fall in tandem.

The press of my thumb against her pulse.

Beat after rapid beat.

Holding my breath, my skin prickling with awareness, with the knowledge this is fucking it, I cut the distance between us and press my lips against hers. On a sigh, her body melts into mine, our mouths molding together.

Tentative at first, we explore, our lips light, our mouths not quite nipping, but not fusing together either.

We probe, we search, we delve into each other.

Her hands to my face.

My fingers tangling in her wavy brown curls.

Mouths open.

A gasp.

A moan.

A tightened grip.

The lightest touch of tongues.

Scooting closer, she wraps her legs around the back of mine, linking them together.

Tangling, molding, becoming one, the sweet taste of her mouth on mine . . . *I'm lost.*

Falling and falling fast, our kiss so deep, so intense with each thrust of our tongues, with each mingling of our lips, with every intake of desperate breath.

Tender, the way she moves her lips across mine.

Shaky, the way her hands tentatively explore the crevasses and divots of my broad and built chest.

Fearful . . . of the unknown, of what this means.

But so goddamn electrifying because the craving I've harbored for this woman is finally being sated.

Eyes closed, hands lingering, I slowly pull away and rest my forehead on Adalyn's trying to catch my breath, taking a second to steady the jittery, wobbly feeling in my legs.

"Wow," I mumble. "That was—"

"Unforgettable," she finishes for me, her nose rubbing against mine.

Exhaling, I say, "Yeah, it was."

My hands venture to her sides, memorizing every contour of her body in their path. "Where's your bedroom?"

Her eyes light up, and she hops down from the counter, taking my hand in hers in the process. "This way." She practically skips down the hallway, light and giddy.

The dark hallway leads to another white, clean, and crisp room. Smooth lines, monotone colors of whites and creams, with one light blue throw pillow on her plush white bed that looks like a cloud floating in the middle of heaven.

Angling in my direction, she reaches for the hem of her dress, but I stop her, gripping her shoulders and standing her upright. Confusion laces her eyes and I take no time in easing that confusion.

"I want to take this slow, Adalyn." I let out an unsteady breath. "That kiss back there, fuck . . ." I press a hand through my hair. "That rocked my goddamn world."

Shyly, she peeks up at me through her eyelashes. "It rocked my world too."

Unable to keep my hands off her for too long, I tip her chin up and press my lips against hers, my mouth smoothing along hers, lush and delicious, as expected. She sighs into me, holding on to my waist. I press my tongue against hers again, loving how she gives as much as I take.

Slowing down, my lips brush hers, the fiery passion we have for each other simmering like a pot ready to boil, but never getting hot enough.

I don't want it to get too hot. Not right now.

I need to know more about her. I want more time with her. I don't want to jump into this—into a physical relationship—when I know there is so much more I can share with this woman.

There is time for this connection to go beyond to the physical, but for now, I need to not get wrapped up in the sensation of her being so close to me and rather seduce her mind instead. I. Want. Her. I want what Calder and Rachel have. I want the depth of trust and friendship I've seen in my parents' marriage . . . *How is that possible so soon?* God, I want inside her, but I think I need inside her heart more than in her body.

Yes, I'm certifiable.

Completely.

"Can we agree on something?"

"Depends on what it is." Her fingers trace up and down my spine.

Tracing her pattern, matching it with my fingers, I say, "Can we both acknowledge this unimaginable pull between us? Can we admit to ourselves that the physical is there, that we both would have no problem taking this relationship to the bed?"

"Easily," she breathes out heavily, her fingers playing with the hem of my shirt.

"Can we also agree to wait?"

Sighing heavily, she rests her head against my chest, knocking it a few times with her forehead. "You're killing me, Hayden."

"I know but there have been too many times where the physical has taken the lead in developing a relationship and the communication has lacked. I don't want that with you."

"I can understand that." She bites her bottom lip, her thoughts running a mile a minute in that pretty head of hers. "But what about . . . you know . . . when you have to leave, go back to Philly?"

I nod. "This is for then. So when I do go back, we'll be okay. Because I can see a future with you, Adalyn, and that's why I want to build a solid foundation with you, something that can last. I want that chance. With you."

"So when you return to Philly, you want to stay in contact with me?"

"Fuck yes, I do. And I'm going to have you sitting front and center at as many games as you can get to, especially since I'm trying to make hockey your favorite sport."

"I don't know." She smiles. "That's going to be one hell of a task to accomplish. Think you can handle it?"

"I know I can." I press a quick kiss against her lips and then slap her ass, making her squeal. With a wink, I say, "Go get changed for bed, we have some making out to do."

"Making out?" she asks, adding in a lift of that well-defined eyebrow of hers.

Acting stern and pointing my finger at her, I say, "Just making out. If you start with your wandering hands, I'm going to jet out of here, taking my body warmth with me."

"That's just cruel."

"Then keep it in your pants, Adalyn." Smiling wickedly, I go to the living room to grab my overnight bag, reprimanding myself with the same warning.

Keep it in your pants, Holmes.

For the love of God, keep it in your pants.

CHAPTER TEN

ADALYN

Waiting impatiently, I tap my foot, check my phone for what seems like the thousandth time, and stare down the entrance of the movie theater.

Where the hell is he?

After dating Hayden for three weeks, I've become accustomed to his habits, and being late isn't one of them. He's always on time, annoyingly on time, to the point that I need to be ready ten minutes early so I'm not interrupted mid curl of my hair when he arrives.

Another habit? He likes to press his thumb against my pulse, and whether it's my neck or my wrist, it's like a sweet spot to him.

He also groans loudly when I happen to *accidentally* dry-hump him.

He's also really good at trapping me against a wall, the counter, a door, even poles, invading my space with his luscious scent and alpha-male stance, only to press the lightest of kisses against my lips and then keep walking.

God, the man is infuriating but also . . . sweet and sexy.

With one tiny kiss on my lips, he can make the earth shatter beneath me, cause my knees to quake, and leave me melting into a puddle on the floor.

It's scary what one touch can do to me, how a whisper in my ear can cause me to break into a cool sweat. Not to mention how alarming it is when I catch a glimpse of him, of that smile, of those dark eyes, the way I can feel and hear myself visibly sigh. It seems unhealthy to be so enigmatically affected by a man, but there is no way I can consider walking away, not when I wake up every morning to a text from him, or when he has lunch sent to me at the hospital, or when he's sitting on the steps in front of my place, with flowers in hand, waiting for me to get off work.

I know one thing for sure: he's ruining me for all other men, because he's the exception. He's the kind of guy that's one in a million.

The kind of guy you dream of.

The kind of guy you take home to your family.

The kind of guy you hope your brothers and sister like as much as you do . . .

The door swings open and a frantic Hayden searches the lobby, hair twisted and pulled from a worrying hand. When he spots me, his face softens. He makes his way through the crowd of moviegoers, carefully dodging their large buckets of popcorn and oversized cups of soda.

"Hey you," I say as he reaches me and pulls me into his side, planting a chaste kiss on my cheek. "Is everything okay?"

"Yeah," he answers breathlessly, walking us toward the usher. "I'm sorry I'm late." I hand the usher our tickets, and he directs us to movie theater seven.

Taking my hand in his, Hayden brings our connection to his lips and gently kisses my knuckles, eyes trained on me, his smile boyish with so much charm.

"Well, no need to worry"—I pat my oversized purse that is like a red flag to a movie theater attendant looking for smugglers—"because I brought the candy and drinks."

"Daredevil, I love it."

We choose seats in the very middle, a few rows from the top. They're great seats, and I'm surprised they're still available.

Situated, Hayden doesn't let go of my hand, not even when I bring out the candy and offer him a Junior Mint. And for some reason, he seems all shook up.

Leaning closer to him, the light of the pre-movie commercials casting a glow over us, I ask, "Are you okay? You seem kind of not yourself."

"All good," he whispers, squeezing my hand.

I don't buy it.

"What happened? There's something you're not telling me, and I don't like it."

Sighing, he leans in close and says, "I went to the wrong movie theater and when I realized it, I was so worried you might think I stood you up, that I sped here, was pulled over by a cop—of course—and then spoke to the guy for longer than I wanted because he recognized me. I had to take a selfie, he excused me from the ticket, told me to slow down, and now I'm here."

"Why does that frazzle you?"

"Because." He kisses the back of my hand again. "I didn't want you thinking I ditched you. This is your first real relationship, and I don't want to set a bad precedent of what to expect."

He's so sweet, how could he ever make me think sourly of him?

Lifting up the armrest that divides our seats, I scoot in and drape his arm over my shoulder, snuggling in close. Reaching up, I kiss his jaw. Two pecks on his scruff, my lips lingering. "You don't have to walk on eggshells around me. I grew up in a large household, so I can handle a lot."

"I know." He kisses my forehead and talks into my ear. "But it's my job to set the bar high so no other man has a chance . . . and so that *large* household doesn't want my neck."

His teasing tone makes me poke his rock-hard stomach, causing him to laugh into my ear.

Chills.

Crazy, wonderful chills spread over my body.

He makes me feel so . . . brand new. Like he's awakened a part of me I've never known before. He's introduced me to a personality I didn't know existed within me. Someone who can be content, thrilled, exhilarated all at the same time. A woman who doesn't necessarily depend on a man, but allows him to take care of her because he *treasures her.* Someone who doesn't need to shed her clothes to get a man to like her.

He's shown me my worth. But what about him? He makes it impossible to not feel *satisfied, adored.* But what does he need from me? Am I giving him everything he needs? I don't want him to feel as though I don't give. But how?

~

"I know, I know." Hayden is sitting on his couch, pulling on his hair, shirtless, shorts hanging low on his hips, with a boyish smile lighting up the room. "I miss you too, Mom, but I've been a little pre-occupied lately."

Our game of Boggle was put on hold when Hayden's parents called. Cringing, he apologetically said he had to answer since he hadn't spoken to his parents in a while. It was cute watching him dodge their questions, sidestep his mom.

"What has been consuming my time?" He looks directly at me and smiles openly, not even hiding his happiness. "A girl."

From his phone, there is a lot of chatter, like his mom is freaking out in excitement, but it's muffled, and I can't quite decipher what she's saying.

"Yes, a girl. Is it serious?" Scratching the back of his neck, he answers, "Yeah, it is." He pauses. "She lives in Binghamton, yeah, where I am right now." Another pause. "Racer introduced us." His smile grows; his eyes soften. "Incredibly beautiful, Mom. You will love her." Licking his lips, he motions with his finger for me to come closer. I shake my head no. "Great personality. Super smart.

She's a nurse and she's actually sitting right next to me. Want to talk to her?"

What?

Uh . . . no.

I shake my head fervently and stand to collect our dishes from a classic Kraft Mac and Cheese lunch with peas, but before I can move out of the way, Hayden snags me around the waist and brings me down on his lap. Turning the phone on speaker, he says, "Say hi to Adalyn, Mom."

"Oh Adalyn, it's so nice to speak with you."

Eyes wide, feeling so incredibly awkward, I say, "Mrs. Holmes, what a pleasure. You've done such a wonderful job raising Hayden. He's the perfect gentleman."

"He better be or else his father and I will have something to say about that."

"Don't worry, Mom," Hayden pipes in. "You taught me very well."

"That's right I did." You can hear the smile in her voice. "Now Adalyn, what do you like to do for fun?"

Relaxing into the couch, Hayden places his spare hand on my thigh and leans back, happy with himself, even though I still feel incredibly awkward.

Does she know we haven't had sex? Does she know her son has been walking around shirtless all day, driving me crazy with his taut abs, thick pecs, and forearms that seem to ripple with every word he writes on his answer pad? Does she know he struts around the cottage—swagger in every step—his shorts so low on his hips I'm practically panting for them to fall all the way down? Does she know he loves cooking meals for me and likes doing it shirtless, that he smells masculine and fresh, like he's been hanging out in mountain rain for three days straight?

Is Mrs. Holmes aware that when Hayden is around me, or when I talk to him on the phone, or when I shamefully use Google to search him, I turn into a lustful puddle of hormones, desperate and needy for one touch, one look, one kiss?

Probably not . . . and we should keep it that way.

"What do I do for fun?" I think about that. Well, before Hayden, nothing really, but now that he's around, my fun is whatever we decide to do together, or whatever he surprises me with. "Is it sad to say relax?"

Before his mom can answer, Hayden cuts in. "Like I said, Adalyn is a nurse and has a hectic work schedule. I covet every minute she can spend with me, because the work she does at the hospital is constant."

Gently, I run my fingers over his chest, loving the appreciation he has for my job. *For me.*

"Oh, I can't even imagine. You work at the hospital? That must be stressful and tiring."

"It is, but there are a lot of rewarding days when you see a patient walk out, healthy and ready to take on the world again. Those are the days I try to remember when I'm having a low moment."

Comforting me, Hayden pulls me closer into his chest and holds me tightly.

"So relaxing really is your fun, clearing your mind from everything you've seen during the week. I can't imagine. I really hope Hayden has helped you forget some of the real you see on a daily basis."

"He does." I rest my cheek against his chest and press my body into his, seeking his warmth, seeking his coziness. "There are days that take a toll on me and when I reach the nurses' station, there's lunch waiting for me, or flowers, or even a box of cookies from a local bakery . . . all from your son."

Mrs. Holmes gasps as if she is surprised someone recognizes she created the most beautiful human being ever and is validating it.

I have to be honest, I think she did. He might very well be the most beautiful human being.

"My, my, my, Hayden, you must really like this girl."

A scarlet heat warms my cheeks, my body igniting in an inferno when Hayden squeezes me and says, "I like her a lot, Mom." He likes me a lot. He just told his mom he likes me a lot. Simple words, yet coming from Hayden, they mean so much more. *Will I ever not be surprised by how I feel around this man?*

CHAPTER ELEVEN

ADALYN

"Thanks for coming with me, Adalyn." Hayden pulls his Porsche into a parking spot right in front of the arena marked off for him. There is a barricade around the entrance to the arena with security personal surrounding the area, blocking off the fans and media who have come to watch Hayden walk into a building.

Scanning the crowd, I read the homemade posters declaring their love for him, watch the grown men grip tightly onto the rails of the barricade to catch a glimpse, or unapologetically use their children as pawns to get closer to the professional hockey star.

This is very odd, such a strange sensation realizing for the first time that the guy you're seeing is . . . famous.

This is the first time I'm seeing Hayden worshipped for who he is, for the talent he possesses. It's eye-opening. I've known him as Hayden, the man who treats me like a queen, the man who makes me laugh, who makes me swoon. But I've yet to experience *this* Hayden. The superstar all the people outside have waited patiently to see.

Will I like that Hayden?

I'm so used to the relaxed, laid-back, chill Hayden.

But when he picked me up from my place today, dressed in an impeccably tailored navy-blue suit, the top two buttons of his crisp white dress shirt undone, and freshly buffed brown loafers, I was . . . taken back, enamored, spellbound. *Just like every person here.*

He looked like a different man, so professional, so grown up, but then I fixed my eyes on his and saw it, the sparkle he gets whenever he first sees me. His face lights up, the corner of his eyes crinkle, and he fills me with so much joy it almost feels impossible to breathe. All from one simple smile from him.

It's *the* ingrained look I'll keep forever in my memory.

"I promise we won't stay very long."

"Hayden"—I press my hand to his forearm—"I'm in no hurry to leave. I'm here for you."

"Thank you." Leaning over the console, he kisses me, his lips lingering for a second before groaning and pulling away. He starts to tug on the short strands of his hair but thinks better of it when he remembers the product he put through it this evening. "Maybe we can make out in the back for a few seconds before we go in?" He looks hopeful, like this actually might be a good idea.

It's not.

Because there are already camera lights flashing at his car, trying to catch a picture of him in his natural environment.

"Not a chance in hell, Romeo."

"Figured you were going to say that but might as well try." Pocketing his keys, he says, "Don't get out, let me open your door for you. The least I can do is look like a gentleman in front of all these people."

"You don't have to look like a gentleman when you already are one." I give him one last kiss before he pulls away.

Hopping out of the car, he shuts his door and waves to the waiting fans while rounding the hood, screams erupting, fans shaking the barrier, cheering for their homegrown hero.

He's so beloved, and it fills my heart with pride. Looks like I'm not the only one who's infatuated.

Opening my car door, he takes my hand in his and whispers, "Are you ready for this?"

"Ready as I'll ever be."

With a deep breath, I hop out and allow Hayden to guide me through the barricaded area and straight to the screaming fans hanging over the rails, holding out jerseys, T-shirts, hats, and hockey sticks for him to sign.

From his pocket, he takes out a black sharpie and starts making the rounds, keeping me close to him. He starts at the beginning, shaking hands, smiling into cameras, sighing autographs, graciously talking to the fans and asking them about their night.

He's smooth.

He's controlled.

He's in his element, doing his job, and making one hell of an impression.

If I weren't a fan already, I would be now.

The patience he has while talking to his fans is endearing.

And when he gets to a kid, not only does he bend down to give them a hug, he spends extra time talking to them, asking them questions about their favorite players, favorite games, favorite part of the sport.

Women are melting at his feet, moms oozing with joy for their children . . . and jealousy toward me as they eye me up and down.

But I don't take offense. I don't even flinch when I'm sneered at because I know it comes from a deep-rooted *and understandable* place of envy.

There is no questioning I know I'm lucky. I'm quite aware of the kind of man Hayden is, not just because of his athletic talent, but because of the real man he is, the one who will spend his time away from the gym and honing his skill to send me notes while I'm at work. The man who surprises me at work with candy bar bouquets to brighten my day. The man who will spend an entire night watching chick flicks because I'm in the mood. The man who effortlessly cooks me dinner after I've worked a long shift and then massages my feet after the dishes are done. He's an absolute dream. And I only hope I provide him the same. I hope I'm *his* dream.

"Who's the girl?" a reporter calls out, grabbing Hayden's attention.

Glancing up from the hat he just signed, he ropes an arm around me and brings me in close, despite my effort to give him some distance. "My girlfriend," Hayden answers before grabbing the next piece of merchandise.

And from those words, more lights start to flash, but this time, they're pointed directly at me, light after blinding light going off.

Leaning into me, Hayden whispers into my ear. "If you tilt your head down and let your gorgeous hair fall forward, it won't be so blinding."

I take his advice, my face still heating from his compliment, and follow behind him, my head tilted down, using my hair as a curtain from the onslaught of media. We spend a good twenty minutes outside, Hayden investing his time, making a lasting impression with every one of his fans.

I've been to football games. I've stood outside of the players' entrance, waiting to catch a glimpse of some of my favorite players. I've heard my brothers' voices go hoarse from screaming for their favorite quarterback to give them the time of day, and the best they could do was smile and wave in our direction.

Hayden is giving these fans a completely different experience than I ever thought imaginable.

It triples the beat of my heart for this man. Just thinking about him, of the impact he's having on these young minds, on their parents, it gives me sharp palpitations to my chest.

Genuine.

Delicious.

REAL.

Mine.

Taking my hand in his, he waves to everyone, thanks them for waiting, and heads through the door of the arena, thanking the security guards for their help as well.

"Mr. Holmes, we're so glad you joined us tonight. We're very grateful you could cut out some time from your busy schedule for us."

Busy schedule. *I want to snort.*

If only they knew what he did during his off time.

Work out.

Lift weights.

He does some light calisthenics and then texts me all day about the shows he's binging on Netflix. Or about the book he's reading. Or about the recipe he can't wait to try when I get to his place.

I know it won't be like that forever.

But his schedule is pretty wide open right now.

"Ah, anytime, Mr. Lewis." Hayden shakes the portly man's hand and then brings me forward into the conversation. "This is my girl-friend, Adalyn. Adalyn, this is Mr. Lewis. He's been heading up tonight's charity for the past five years, is that right?"

The sparkle in Mr. Lewis's eyes when Hayden speaks of him is endearing, like he just received one of the best compliments of his life.

"Mr. Lewis, it's a pleasure to meet you. From what Hayden has told me, this is one of his favorite charity events to attend."

"We are so lucky to have a homegrown professional hockey player in our midst. We're happy he can make the time for us."

Hayden pats the man on the back. "Any time." Looking around, Hayden asks, "Same as usual?"

"Yes, we have a little suite set up for the both of you with snacks and drinks. We just need you on the ice for the beginning of the game and then afterwards, the kids always enjoy it if you can sign some things."

"Of course, I wouldn't dream of skipping out early. I was actu-ally kind of hoping we might be able to stay a little later?" Hayden winks at Mr. Lewis who gives him a knowing smile. "Of course, not a problem. If you want to make your way to the ice, the game is going to start in a few, and the referees are expecting you to do a ceremonial puck drop."

"Sure." Hayden tugs me to the right and we walk behind Mr. Lewis who speeds up in front of us, talking into a headpiece, referring to Hayden as Mr. Holmes the entire time.

Mr. Holmes is in the building.

Mr. Holmes is heading to the ice.

Mr. Holmes would like some cake in his suite.

"Cake?" I give him a pointed look.

Wiggling his eyebrows, he says, "Just a little something, a little thank you for coming with me."

"You know you don't have to thank me, right? I love spending time with you, especially as your . . . girlfriend."

He winces and says, "I hope that was okay to say to someone we don't know."

I scoff. "Why would I be mad about that? Being able to lay claim to you is something I don't mind at all, especially with those envious women out there, baring their ravenous claws."

"They're fun, aren't they?"

"I didn't mind them too much to be honest. Just made me realize how lucky I am." Smiling, I wrap my hands around his arm and tuck myself into his side. Placing a kiss on my head, he keeps moving forward, drawing attention from everyone around us, true hockey fans having no qualms in staring while he walks by. Like the good guy he is, Hayden shakes hands, poses for quick selfies, and waves when he needs to while saying thank you for putting this together.

I've been watching football with my family for a very long time, ever since I can remember, waving pom-poms in the air. We watched pre-games and post-games. Interviews, montages, commentators, I've seen it all. But what you never get to see is this backstage stuff. You don't get to see how athletes act off camera, which I think is a true depiction of who they are as a person.

Hayden Holmes, in my opinion, is one of the most dignified and humble athletes I've ever seen, which makes him beyond attractive in my eyes. He has every reason to be the most cocky, self-centered man out there, but he's not. He's self-assured and most of all? Respects the hell out of me.

Set aside the muscles, the smirk, those devastatingly handsome features of his, or the multi-million-dollar talent he possesses, let's consider his character, how he treats others, how grateful he is to his fans, and his dedication to bringing the sport he loves to those who might not be able to afford all the gear and ice time.

It's impossible not to develop feelings for him.

It's impossible to stop my heart from exploding in my chest whenever he's around.

And it's obvious how impossible it will be to *not* fall for him and fall for him fast.

"This way, Mr. Holmes. Ma'am, can you please step to the side?"

Turning toward me, Hayden places a gentle kiss on my mouth, his breath minty, his lips soft and smooth with a hint of scruff prickling my chin. The combination is better than perfect weather on a beautifully brilliant summer day.

"Stay right here. I'll be back." Winking, he takes off, down a red carpet draped across the ice. From the Jumbotron above, his name and picture flashes in bold, the announcers call him out, and the arena erupts in cheers. The high school boys playing in the charity game pound on the sideboards with their sticks, their other hands in the air cheering him on. Their eyes are alight with awe.

It feels so unreal, to see someone you see as "normal and everyday" be worshipped.

There is a little fear in the feeling.

A little bit of unease.

I only met him a short time ago, and we've easily become hooked on one another, but we've been in a bubble. This is the first time our bubble is being poked. It's the first time I'm not in the comfort of Hayden's reassuring arms, because everyone else is pulling him in different directions.

"He's such a good guy," a lady with a low grey bun and maroon parka says, standing next to me.

Giving her my attention, I notice quickly how kind her eyes are, followed by the crooked smile that seems so natural to her. "Hi, I'm Ariel, I am second-in-command for this entire event. I heard you're Hayden's girlfriend."

"Yes, hi. I'm Adalyn." I shake Ariel's hand. "It's nice to meet you. I'm so glad I could be here. Hayden was telling me how much you guys raise for the community. Twenty thousand dollars is a huge deal."

Ariel offers me that crooked smile with a shake of her head. "That boy is very humble. *We* raised about ten thousand. *He* donated the rest but refuses to tell anyone. His goal is to provide as much equipment, ice time, and opportunity for those who are not as fortunate as he was. He desperately wants to keep the sport alive in his hometown."

Casting my gaze toward Hayden, I watch him . . . in awe.

Shakes hands.

Smiles.

Waves.

Laughs.

Jokes around with the captains of the teams and refs.

Poses for pictures, never once looking annoyed or put out.

Shit . . .

My stomach bottoms out, flipping like a gymnast as I can feel proverbial hearts forming in my eyes.

There is no stopping it. This isn't just lust . . . this is forming into something entirely different.

"He's a good guy," I whisper.

"The best. This is the first time he's ever brought someone and looked so smitten."

"You think he looks smitten?" I ask with a scrunch to my nose.

Ariel nods toward Hayden, who is staring me down, a giant smile on his face. "Oh yes, I most definitely think he's smitten. That smile, the one with the little crinkle in the corner of his eyes? That's reserved for you and only you."

For me and only me. Maybe, just maybe, I am the fulfillment of his dream too.

A girl can only hope.

~

"Do you want a drink?" Hayden asks when we enter the private suite the event organizers provided for us. There are stacks of pictures of Hayden to be signed, which will be handed out to the kids after the game, platters of food including mini corndogs, nachos, a pile of seasoned French fries, and a delicious-looking chocolate cake that has my mouth watering. To the right, there are two more platters. One of plain grilled chicken and the other of roasted veggies, and they're the platters Hayden goes straight to.

"I would love a water."

"Coming right up." He picks up a piece of broccoli and pops it in his mouth as he pulls a bottle of water from a small cooler under the counter. Like the gentleman he is, he opens the bottle and brings it to me, placing a kiss on my lips before handing me the bottle. "Want me to fix you a plate?"

"I can make one." I take in my surroundings, the kids skating around on the ice below us, warming up, the crowd dancing to the music that's booming through the speakers in the arena. "You're really loved, you know that?" I'm taking in the fans below with Hayden Holmes shirts on when he comes up behind me, wrapping his arms around my shoulders.

"Is it overwhelming? Seeing all this at once?"

"A little, but it doesn't bother me. I like watching you interact with your fans, making them smile, giving them an everlasting impression. It's sweet." I tip my head back to look him in the eyes. "You're sweet."

He kisses the tip of my nose. "My dad always told me it's about the game, not the fame. I've tried to live with that motto. Especially after this past season. Being a well-loved and successful rookie was something I never dreamt of, so I want to make sure I don't take that for granted. If we end up staying later tonight, I apologize in advance. I want to make sure to connect with every single one of those boys. I can always call a car service to take you home if necessary."

I shake my head. "No, I want to stay. I don't have work tomorrow, so I'm all yours."

"That's what I like to hear."

Moving his lips from my ear he nibbles on my earlobe, causing goosebumps to erupt over my skin. We have yet to have sex, but there have been some heavy make-out sessions, and when I say SOME, I mean a ton. If we're alone, it's what we do, and from the way Hayden is working his lips up and down my neck, I'm guessing that maybe he's planning for—

The door flies open, hitting the wall, scaring the crap out of me. I fling my water in the air, dousing Hayden in the process and screech, like we were just caught naked together.

"Ohhhhh, looks like we're interrupting something."

"And in front of the kids. Don't you have any class, man?"

Turning around, I attempt to focus on two men who look identical to Hayden. Tall, broad, the carved jawline, and the same panty-melting smirk.

Confused, I look between the three of them trying to understand if I'm seeing things . . . or if I'm drunk. I don't remember drinking, but who knows, maybe I started sleep drinking during my naps and didn't even realize it.

"What are you guys doing here?" Hayden asks, linking our hands together and taking me to the two domineering men, who like Hayden, are dressed in tailored suits.

"We were invited. You're not the only famous Holmes brother in town."

"Being famous for sleeping with every girl in your college dorm doesn't count." Hayden playfully punches one of the guys and then pulls them both into a hug. "Its good to see you guys. And look, you're starting to get some muscles in those noodle arms of yours. Your coach must be doing something right."

Noodle arms? Uh . . . pretty sure those aren't noodle arms under their suit jackets. They aren't as big as Hayden, but they surely aren't middle schoolers draped in rich fabric either.

"Yeah, we're coming for you, bro. Soon we'll be taking your ass down on the ice."

Hayden chuckles. "Keep dreaming, boys." Pulling me forward and protectively wrapping his arm around me, he says, "I want to introduce you guys to someone. This is—"

"Adalyn," one of them says, stepping forward with an identically charming smile that rivals Hayden's. "Mom told us all about you on FaceTime the other night. She was gushing about Hayden's new girl. She went on and on about how she's a nurse with a very pretty voice." Oh Jesus, that's embarrassing. Sticking out his hand, he says, "I'm Holden, and this is my twin brother, Halsey."

Hayden, Holden, and Halsey . . . their parents didn't give girls a chance.

"It's very nice to meet you." I shake both their hands. Halsey studies me, his eyes raking up and down my body while Holden flirts harmlessly by kissing the back of my hand.

But Hayden doesn't seem to find it funny as he swats Holden away. "Keep your distance." Turning to me, Hayden says, "Holden will pretty much try to seduce everyone and anyone. If you strapped a bra around a mailbox, he would try to take it out on a date." Holden nods his head in agreement, causing me to laugh. "And Halsey, he's the silent but deadly type, and I'm not talking about flatulence. He's a studier and when it's time, he strikes without warning."

Holden thumbs toward Halsey. "It's true. The dude doesn't say anything to girls, but then one look from him, THE look, and he's walking out the door, girl in hand. Freaky shit."

Not speaking much, Halsey shrugs his shoulders and grabs himself a drink from the cooler.

"Well, it's nice to meet you both." I bite my bottom lip and say, "Hayden has spoken nothing of the two of you, and I can see why." I wiggle my eyebrows.

Holden's mouth drops open and Halsey's eyebrow rises with humor. "Dude, your girl is totally hitting on us," Holden says.

"She's really not." Hayden pulls me toward the seats overlooking the arena, whispering in my ear, "My dick is bigger than theirs, keep that in mind."

Laughing, I pinch his side and take a seat next to him. "Seems like they put out though, so the smaller dick size is something I can overlook as long as I'm getting some."

"Ah, but they sure as hell wouldn't make you moan like I can."

I nonchalantly shrug my shoulders. "How can I believe that when you haven't once made me moan?"

Laughing in his throat and dropping his voice low enough that I can barely hear him, he says, "Two nights ago, when I was pulsing on top of you, my tongue wrapped around yours, my cock thrusting over your center . . ."

Oh God, I moaned so loud because dry-humping is a real thing, especially when the guy has a cock thicker than you've ever felt before.

My cheeks heat up, a crimson color most likely spreading over them. "That wasn't moaning." I press my lips against his ear. "That was begging."

"Christ," he mumbles, shifting in his seat and clearing his throat some more. "Adalyn, are you trying to get me hard?"

"Yes. For the love of God, yes."

"What's going on over here?" Holden steps up with a plate in hand, fries and corndogs toppling off the sides.

"Your brother won't have sex with me."

Corndog halfway to his mouth, Holden blinks his eyes rapidly and sits on the armrest of one of the chairs. "Excuse me?"

Hayden has his head in his hand, groaning as I smile to myself, pleased with my outburst. A little ribbing from his brothers might help. A girl can only wait for so long before she explodes.

I can only watch him walk around shirtless for so long.

I can only make out with him for so long before my need gets too overwhelming.

I can only dry-hump him so many times before I lose my ever-loving mind.

He's driving me crazy.

He's creating a monster with every day that goes by . . . sexless.

And let's face it, I'm so goddamn horny. He has driven me to the point of being so horny I can feel my skin crawling, trying to undress as quickly as possible whenever he's around. And when he smiles at me? Forget it, my bra pops open, my nipples wave, waiting to be tweaked.

"Adalyn," Hayden groans and then turns to me, mirth in his eyes. "Do you know what you just did?"

Uh-oh.

Holden starts laughing, putting his plate down on a little shelf in front of the seats and calls out to Halsey. "Dude, we have some twin tag-team duty to take care of. Hayden, the old fuck over here, is holding out on his girl." Pushing past Hayden, Holden squats before me and takes my hand. "Come with me, Adalyn. I'll show you a good time, a better time than this old man can show you. You need a young stallion."

Hayden pushes Holden in the shoulder, throwing his balance off and sending him against the chairs behind him. "Get out of here before I kick your ass."

Chuckling, Holden goes back to his plate of food where Halsey is sitting now, picking at the French fries. "There's something you have to know about our brother," Holden says, taking a seat. "He's one of the good guys, always has been. Works hard, is determined, and doesn't take his relationships lightly. You're going to be waiting a long time, so saddle up and enjoy the slow burn, because the man is the master at it."

Looking proud of himself, Hayden nods his appreciation and presses a kiss to the back of my hand. "It's true . . . the absolute master."

I just wish the absolute master *would get to the* saddle-up *stage . . . I'm* more *than ready to ride.*

"You have our numbers, so if you need anything, and we mean . . . anything"—Holden emphasizes the word with a wiggle in his brow—"you let us know. We're only a few hours away."

"Get out of here." Hayden steps in and pushes his brother away. "She doesn't need your numbers."

"Too late, we plugged them in her phone and made her text us so we had her number."

"You did?" Hayden turns to me, shocked.

"You were in the bathroom," I answer. "They pressured me. Don't worry, I'll give you a few more weeks before I search them out for my womanly needs." I wink, causing Holden and Halsey to laugh.

Shaking his head, he pulls his brothers in for a hug, one at a time, speaking quietly in their ears. Holden and Halsey both nod, a serious look on their face, listening intently to their older brother before pulling away and conducting a small secret handshake that makes me smile at the camaraderie between the brothers. They remind me of my siblings, how we playfully rib each other, but still love in our own way.

As I wait, I watch the three of them—all extremely handsome versions of each other—draw the attention from passersby, women making their intentions known with their eyes. There is no doubt in my mind the Holmes brothers were put on this earth to give the female race a run for their money. Their poor mother, what her life must have been like, raising three hockey players.

The smells.

The fighting.

The constant competition.

She has to be a saint.

Now it makes so much sense why she was so excited to talk to me. She's probably looking for a little estrogen to balance all the endless testosterone in the family.

Waving, I say, "Drive safe, you guys."

"Bye, Adalyn." Halsey holds up his hand while Holden mouths for me to *call him* like a fool.

When we start walking toward Hayden's car, I ask, "How on earth did you three not kill each other growing up?"

"There were some close calls." Hayden takes his hand in mine. "But we're pretty cool with each other now. There's some animosity between Holden and Halsey sometimes, twin-rivalry type shit, but we get along."

"I can see that. What did you say to them when you gave them a hug, if you don't mind me asking?"

"Never." He places a kiss on the back of my hand, holds the door to the arena open for me, and then unlocks his car. "I told them that even though it was summer break, they have responsibilities to continue training. They're going into their senior years, and it's important for them to keep focus if they want to go professional."

"They both want to play professionally?" He nods. "Do you think they're good enough?"

Hayden helps me into his car and stands in the doorway. "Yeah, no doubt in my mind they have the talent for it, but they just have to keep their heads in the game, that's all."

"Have they been known not to do that?"

Slowly Hayden nods, his lips pressed firmly together. "Competition is a funny thing. It's good to have a little competitiveness in you, because what else would be the driving force for you to grow as a human? But with my family, with my brothers, competition bleeds from our veins. It consumes us. It takes over every last inch of our bodies until we're helpless, unable to think of anything else. I've found ways to curb the feeling, to help ease the anxiety when I start to feel like it's overtaking me. But Halsey, and especially Holden, they run hot. They're still trying to learn how to control their fire. How to manage when they're feeling anxious."

Playing with the button on his suit jacket, I ask, "You've had issues with your competitiveness?"

"Big time. Last season, I went through ten mouth guards

because I was grinding down on them so hard. I don't like losing, Adalyn."

"That explains your Boggle fit." I pull him closer to the car. He ducks and grips the edge of the doorway.

"It wasn't a Boggle fit, it was . . . a small tantrum."

I turn toward him and unbutton his suit jacket. His tapered waist showcased by the tailored white shirt he has tucked into his waistline. Running my fingers along the buttons, I say, "That was a tantrum? I would hate to see what it's like when you have a fit."

"It isn't pretty."

"Do you always have to win?" I undo one of the buttons on his shirt and play with the opening, my fingernail grazing his bare skin.

"Yes."

Tipping my chin up, he searches my eyes right before placing a gentle, yet sultry kiss on my lips. A loud sigh pops out of my mouth when he pulls away. Smiling, pleased with himself, he says, "When is the next time you have off?"

"I have a four-day shift starting Thursday. And then Monday and Tuesday I have off. Why?"

"Come to New York City with me. I have a photo shoot with a sponsor Monday morning and want to take you with me. We can still do touristy stuff, get a hot dog from a street vendor, go on a tour bus ride, and silly crap like that. We can leave Sunday night after you get off work. The sponsor is flying me down. What do you say?"

"Can we go see a Broadway show?"

"Anything you want, baby." That grin, hell, I'll say yes to pretty much anything if it causes him to grin like that, with so much joy and excitement. It's *the grin* Ariel mentioned earlier. The one with the little crinkle in the corner of his eyes. He has a perpetual smile, really. It's just who he is. But I know and love *the grin*.

And to hear him call me baby so casually?

He has me wrapped around his finger. Without a doubt, he's starting to slowly capture my heart, one deep breath, and one gentle kiss at a time.

CHAPTER TWELVE

HAYDEN

"You're kidding me, right?" Adalyn asks, spinning around in the hotel suite. "This is huge and you can see all of Central Park." Growing serious, she finds me and says, "This is beautiful, Hayden."

I shrug. "I asked for a nice room, so I'm glad we were able to get one."

"Oh look at you, hands in your pockets, looking all cool as if this is nothing." She comes up to me and grabs my cheeks. "This is not nothing, Hayden. This is special for me, so if I forget to say it, thank you."

A burst of pride surges through me. I follow and believe in my dad's mantra, but *my fame* is paying off a little right now. Because that look on Adalyn's gorgeous face, a look that screams utter happiness, fuck what I wouldn't do to keep that look there. I would do anything to make her this happy.

"You're welcome." I pull her into a hug, kissing the top of her head. "And because you were able to get out of work earlier—"

"We can thank Logan for taking the last few hours of my shift."

I'm not thanking Logan for anything. Fuck that guy. "I got us tickets to see Hamilton."

Adalyn's eyes widen and she sucks in a deep breath.

"Before you go screaming, they aren't super great seats, and we have about an hour to get ready and get to the theater before it starts, so you better hurry."

"You got tickets to Hamilton? Oh my GOD!" Running in place, hands above her head, Adalyn celebrates.

Chuckling, I playfully smack her on the ass and say, "Go on, go get dressed."

Launching herself into my arms, she places a sloppy wet kiss on my lips and then skips into the bathroom, her bag trailing behind her while saying, "We're going to see Hamilton!"

I take out my phone and check my messages. Five missed calls from my publicist, James. I know he's freaking out about the shoot tomorrow since I've yet to confirm the details with him. Giving the guy a break, I call him back.

"Christ, Hayden," he answers on the first call.

"Yeah, sorry about not calling you back right away."

"You're giving me an ulcer, you realize that? I have to drink Pepto Bismal straight from the bottle because of you."

"Eh, just keeping you on your toes."

"No need, I'm doing fine on my toes myself. For the love of God, respond when I ask you to."

Chuckling, I look out the window, observing the clear blue skies, full green trees, and the skyline of the most enchanting city I've ever visited. "Well, I'm responding now. Got the details, I'll be ready for the car at seven tomorrow morning."

"And did you see they don't want you to shave? They want a good five o'clock shadow on your jaw."

"That won't be an issue."

"And have you been working out? I hope you haven't been eating any salt, because I can't have you bloated."

Jesus Christ, heaven forbid I look bloated.

"James, don't ask that question again."

"So I'm going to take that as *not* bloated."

"Move on." By now, he should know I take my workouts and eating seriously. And before you go harping on the cakes I've been eating lately, I ran extra the mornings after.

"I think that's it, except, you've asked for Adalyn to be seated on the set. You haven't mentioned Adalyn to me, but I heard she's your—"

"My girlfriend."

"Yeah."

Silence falls over the phone and I know I threw James for a loop, one I'm sure he's not loving at the moment. From the bathroom, the shower shuts off and the creak of a glass door opens. My mind goes straight to what Adalyn might look like wrapped in a white terrycloth towel with her wet hair hanging over her shoulders. My mind wanders, envisioning her lotioning her smooth, silky skin, brushing out her long brown hair, and letting the towel fall straight to the ground . . .

"Hayden, are you paying attention?"

"Huh?" I blow out a breath and turn my back to the bathroom.

"Your *girlfriend*. You know you have to run these things by me first."

That last sentence really grabs my attention.

"The hell I do. My personal life has nothing to do with my professional career, and I suggest you remember that going forward, or we're going to have a problem."

A long, irritated sigh.

He can sigh all the fuck he wants, but it's not going to change anything. I've never mixed my personal life with my professional life, and I don't plan on doing it now.

"Fine. I'll see you tomorrow morning."

"Yes, I'll see you tomorrow morning. Just a heads-up, James. If you at any point make Adalyn feel uncomfortable, you're done. Got it? None of this talking shit to her behind my back. I've seen enough movies to know where that leads. Stay the fuck away from her unless you are offering her a drink or are genuinely being a nice guy."

"It won't be an issue."

"That's what I like to hear. See you tomorrow." I hang up before he can say anything else. I plug my phone in its charger and rest it on the nightstand.

Walking to the closet, I open the doors to find a few black garment bags waiting for me. I don't take advantage of my "celebrity" status very often, but when I'm in need of a suit and all I have is jeans and regular shirts in Binghamton, I flash my celebrity card and have some suits sent to my room before we arrive.

I want to make sure I look nice for Adalyn and for some weird reason, I didn't want to wear the same suit she saw me in at the charity event.

Charcoal, light grey, textured black, and a steel blue. What to wear?

I guess it will depend on what Adalyn's wearing. I'll wait.

Still a little peeved about my conversation with James, I walk to the window where I look at Central Park. I like the guy, he works well with my agent and has scored me some great sponsorship deals, but he oversteps his boundaries often. I can take it when it's just me, but now that Adalyn is involved, I needed to lay down the rules.

The last thing I need is for James to start running his mouth about my hectic life, especially during the season, and spook Adalyn, because that would happen. She's already on edge about what will happen to us when the season starts up, me being in Phily while she's in Binghamton. I don't need any added pressure coming from James.

From the nightstand, my phone buzzes with a text message. Giving Adalyn her space and time to get ready, I answer the text message.

Calder: *Dude, haven't heard from you in a few weeks. The only* *reason I know you're alive is because your mom sent me an email with a picture of you, your brothers, and a girl . . .*

Leave it to my mom. Calder got attached to her weekly update emails she sends to family and friends. How did that happen? Easy, she took a picture of us after one of our games, asked for his email to send the picture, and now he gets the weekly emails. He thinks it's hilarious, loves keeping up with the Holmes. He's told me more than once that getting the Holmes email at the end of the week is one of his favorite things ever. Sometimes he knows more about my family than I do.

The fucker.

Hayden: *Yeah about that . . .*

Calder: *Yeah, about that. Who is she, man? She's hot.*

Hayden: *Uh, she's my girlfriend.*

Calder: *I'm sorry, I think I read that wrong. You just said she's your girlfriend.*

Hayden: *You read that right. We're in NYC right now, about to go to Hamilton.*

Calder: *What are the chances . . . we're in NYC too. Shea is with my brother, the saint, and I'm treating Rachel out. Let's meet up for drinks. I want to warn this girl.*

Hayden: *You're still tracking my iPhone, aren't you? You're stalking me.*

Calder: *Family and friends, dude. Don't give me the goods if you don't want me periodically stalking you.*

Hayden: *Your crush on me is getting out of control.*

Calder: *Feed my craving. Meet us after Hamilton. I'll get us a VIP spot and send you the details. Sound good?*

Hayden: *Fine, but keep your embarrassing stories about me to yourself.*

Calder: *That's cute . . . see you soon.*

The door to the bathroom opens, light shining from behind a curvy silhouette. My breath hitches when my eyes adjust to the light, and I can make out Adalyn's figure. Dressed in a long-sleeved black dress that comes to mid-thigh, hair loosely pinned up, she looks . . .

fuck, she looks so damn good. Light makeup, heavy mascara on her long, thick eyelashes, and a pop of red on her plump lips. Smoothing out her dress, she looks at me, her sweet seductive smile capturing me.

I rub the back of my neck, my body humming, my need for her becoming all-consuming.

"Would you mind zipping up the back of my dress?" She walks toward me, her flowery scent floating in my direction, spiking my yearning into overdrive.

"Uh, yeah . . . sure."

She turns around, and looks over her shoulder. The back of her dress is completely open, the zipper undone to just above the curve of her beautifully round ass.

Shit, all that smooth, tan skin, covered by nothing but the velvety fabric of the dress. Is she wearing underwear? She's not wearing a bra and I see no panty line.

Clearing my throat, I ask, "Are you wearing underwear, Adalyn?"

From over her shoulder, she smiles shyly. "Yes, it's small though."

Of course it is. Why wouldn't it be?

Not being able to stop myself, I take a second to float my fingertips up her spine. From the initial touch, her back arches and a small gasp releases from her lips, but before I can think about stopping, she melts into my touch. Stepping closer, I place my hand on the back of her hip, my thumb pressing into her ass while the other hand explores the bare expanse of her back. Her head falls to my shoulder. Her lips part, and when I snake to the front of her dress, her breath hitches.

Eyes closed, I take in ragged breaths, my fingers inching closer and closer to her front, my cock painfully hard.

It's been so goddamn long—and being with Adalyn has only spurred on my need—but I want to make sure we're in a good place before we commit to anything. I want to make sure she's ready emotionally because the minute I bury myself deep inside her, I know there will be no turning back. *She will be mine forever.*

But maybe for now, I can have a little touch . . .

My cock presses against her butt, she expertly grinds her backside into me, her hands moving to my neck, pulling my head down to hers. I kiss the side of her neck, using the hand that's gripping her hips to guide her with her grinding in just the right place.

Fuck, that feels good.

I grunt, the sound vibrating over her sleek neck. My hand on her stomach, she arches, wanting more of my touch, silently asking me to move north.

And I fucking comply. Inch by slow inch, I guide my hand to just below her breasts. When I halt my pursuit, a displeased groan escapes her.

"Hayden, please."

I squeeze my eyes shut, trying to find the willpower. Her fingernails dig into my scalp, spurring me on as she turns her head and finds my lips.

She kisses me.

Hot.

Wet.

Needy.

Her lips glide across mine, her tongue diving into my mouth; her moans are vocal and sexy. Her delicious ass, pressing, grinding, undulating against my rock-hard cock makes me want to do so much more, makes me want to taste so much more.

Moving my hand higher, my fingertips graze the bottom of her breast. Soft. Round. Smooth. I caress her right below her nipple, never touching, just teasing . . . tempting.

"Fuck, Hayden," she breathes heavily, her body rocking against mine, bringing on a wave of longing. "I need you."

I move my lips to her jaw, kiss her neck, squeeze her breasts with my thumb and index finger, slowly.

In and out.

In and out.

In and—

Adalyn spins in my arms, her eyes wild, her chest heaving, her hands pulling on the sleeves of her dress.

She's ready. Fuck, I'm ready.

"We're going to be late," I say, stunning myself, the words full of pain.

She halts in her pursuit to undress, her brow creased, her face falling flat with disappointment. Sadness consumes her with a hint of frustration I'm sure is starting to push her past her breaking point. Turning away, shoulders slumped, she adjusts her dress, fixing the mess I made of it. Her head tilts down. But . . . her silence speaks volumes.

Fuck.

I run my hand over my face, angry, turned on, and unsure why I'm still holding out. Maybe because in the past, most women have only wanted sex. Maybe I'm nervous once we finally do it, the spark will simmer out. Maybe I'm nervous she's going to leave me once she gets what she wants.

But then again, it's Adalyn, and the last thing I want to do is make her sad.

Cock throbbing, heart erratically thrumming, my body tingling with anticipation, I step forward and grab Adalyn by the waist, pulling her against me. Leaning forward, I nibble on her ear and lower my hand down her thigh to the hem of her dress. With little finesse, I drag the hem of her dress up to her hips and slip my hand into the waistline of her thong.

She stills in my arms, holding her breath, waiting for my next touch. Moving my lips to her neck, I suck on the juncture of her shoulder, marveling in the way she tastes, like vanilla and a hint of floral. So fucking good.

Her pelvis tilts forward, sending my fingers lower, across her smooth pubic bone. Fucking hell.

Kissing up her neck to her jaw, I glide my fingers farther down to her slit. With one finger, I move across the valley. She's fucking soaking.

"Jesus Christ, Adalyn." I pause, my breathing picking up, my cock so goddamn hard it's painful to stand, to have her rubbing against me. "You're drenched."

"Because of you. Because all I want is you," she whispers, lifting her chin, granting me more access.

Slipping my finger more, I press her clit, sliding along easily. Her moans are driving me crazy.

This isn't going to work. I can't do it like this. I need to taste her. Removing my hand, she protests. I don't listen. Instead, I lift her up and take her to the edge of the bed. Reaching up her thighs, I pull down her thong, exposing her glistening pussy, so pink, so fucking ready for me.

Spreading her legs, I move her dress up around her waist and slowly kiss my way up her thigh.

"Oh God," she moans, her head falling back, her hands pressed into the mattress behind her. It's a beautiful sight. Her nipples hard and erect against the fabric of her dress, her pouty lips partially open, her eyes shut, her silky hair dangling behind her like a chocolate waterfall.

I reach the center between her thighs, loving how aroused she is, how ready, and for the first time, I taste. Fuck I've wanted this for weeks, but I know what I'm like. One taste, and I'd have to be inside her body. Now? Now, I'm not waiting to taste. To take.

I press my lips against her, kiss her pussy gently, before spreading her lips and licking one long stroke up her slit. Her legs clamp around me, her body tensing from the touch. Loving her reaction, I repeat the long, languid stroke, tasting every inch of her.

Her body still tense, I lift my head and press my palm against her dress-covered stomach. "Relax, baby."

"It's just . . . I want this . . . so bad."

Softening, I say, "I'm not stopping now, so relax, Adalyn."

Letting out a long breath, she loosens up, releases the tension from her body and spreads her legs open for me. Thank. Fuck. I bring my mouth back to her pussy, kissing her gently before flicking her clit with my tongue in fast, short strokes.

Instinctively her hand goes to my hair. Her nails dig into my scalp with each stroke I make across her slick pussy.

I need relief right along with her.

Removing my hand from her stomach while keeping my mouth pressed against her center, I undo my pants and my cock springs free. I grip it at the base, and without even a second thought, I start stroking myself, using the pre-cum at the head to lube my hand.

I groan against Adalyn's pussy, the vibration making her back arch off the mattress, her hand grip my head tighter.

I do it again. I hum and suck her clit into my mouth, pulling on my cock at the same time.

Lick, suck, pull.

Lick, suck, pull.

Squeeze.

Fuck. Squeeze hard.

I groan louder, my mouth thrumming into Adalyn. She writhes on the bed above me, her body twisting, her hands desperately directing my head, her hips moving up and down, guiding my tongue.

I place my free hand at her entrance and slowly insert two fingers. Taking her in just at the right time, she flies forward, her eyes wide, her mouth agape. "Oh my God, Hayden."

Curving my fingers upward, I hit her G-spot and suck her clit into my mouth at the same time. Her walls clench around my fingers as she moans my name. Loud and feral.

"Oh God, yes. Oh fuck yes!" she screams, her head moving back and forth, her teeth biting down on her lip, her hips pumping up and down on my finger and my tongue.

My vision blackens, my sight tunnels in on her and her alone, and nothing else around us matters. Yanking on my cock, my hand moving at a rapid rate, my balls tighten, my stomach drops, and I come . . . fucking hard, my guttural groans mixing with the beautiful sounds coming from Adalyn.

Drop after drop, I squeeze everything out of me.

Her hips slow, her body slouches, and my mouth is pulled from her center. I leave my fingers where they are, lightly moving them in and out of her as she falls from her orgasm.

Slowly, I pass my hand over my cock, easing myself down as well, the high of euphoria eating me alive.

"Hayden?"

"Hmm?"

She sits up, her pussy clenching around my fingers again, and all I can think about is what it would feel like to be buried deep inside her. But I already know. Fucking heaven. Mind-blowing, out-of-this-world, heaven.

"Why on earth have you been holding out on me?"

I remove my fingers and sit up. "To hell if I can remember at this point."

Laughing, she hurtles her body at mine, tackling me to the ground where she slams her lips against mine, knocking the wind right out of my lungs.

~

"Are you sure you don't mind?"

"Not even a little." Adalyn cuddles into my side, holding on to the hand that's draped over her shoulder. She's still wearing that devil of a dress that made me lose my damn mind, but now she's paired it with exponentially dangerous black heels, bringing her lips that much closer to mine.

Easy access, just what I like.

After we, uh . . . got off, we raced to get ready and hailed a taxi, making it to Hamilton just as the curtain began to rise. It was a close call but so worth it.

And so was scoring the tickets, because Adalyn was enamored during the entire musical. Eyes bright and a huge smile on her face, her hand never left mine.

I can barely recall what the musical was about or any of the songs, because my attention wasn't center stage. It was to the right of me on the girl who is stealing my heart, one precious smile at a time.

The pub Calder picked to meet at is off Broadway, pretty close to the theater, but far enough away from the hustle and bustle . . . and picture-taking tourists, thankfully.

There are no windows to the front façade, just a giant neon-green four-leaf clover and a red awning covering the door. Opening the door for Adalyn, I press my hand to the small of the back and follow closely behind her. Inside, we're greeted by floor-to-ceiling mahogany wood, neon beer signs, red-leather booths, and a bar that stretches the length of the tavern. In the back, there are some closed-off booths with high backs, hidden from patrons. I direct Adalyn to the far-right booth. When we turn the corner, we find Calder and Rachel . . . making out.

Calder's hand is up Rachel's shirt and Rachel's hand is pressed against Calder's lap. Adalyn turns her head into my shoulder and giggles as I clear my throat, loudly.

Startled, Rachel is the first to pull away while Calder is still puckered up, leaning into Rachel and feeling for her lips. Palming his face, she pushes him away and nods up at us. "Company has arrived."

"What?" Confused for a second, Calder turns around, eyes lust-filled. "Oh shit, I forgot about you two."

Lips thinly pressed together, I nod my head. "Good first impression, dude."

"Shit." He runs a hand down his shirt and clears his throat while glancing at his lap. Shamelessly looking back up at us, he says, "Uh, in normal circumstances, I would stand to introduce myself but, uh . . . kind of have a situation here, so I'm just going to wave." He does that and says, "I'm Calder and this is my girl, Rachel."

"It's very nice to meet you." Adalyn motions to Rachel's shirt. "Um your bra is showing."

"What?" Rachel checks out her shirt. Gasping, she whacks Calder in the chest. "You could have told me, you fool."

Gesturing to his crotch, he says, "Kind of dealing with my own situation here. You're the one who got handsy, not me."

"Oh no, don't you blame this on me, you're the one who nibbled on my ear first and said how much you wish you could—"

"Hey-o, we have company." I gesture toward Adalyn, wishing my friends could pull it together.

Realizing the error of their ways, they sit taller, put some distance between themselves, and wave once again, looking like one giant hot mess.

"Hi, we're Rachel and Calder, and we're here to make you uncomfortable with boners and bras," Rachel says, gesturing to the other side of the booth.

Chuckling, Adalyn takes the seat closest to the wall and brings me down next to her, holding my hand. "Don't worry about it. Before we went to the theater, Hayden came all over the hotel carpet."

Rachel and Calder's eyes both widen as they lock gazes with me, mirth written all over their faces right before they tilt their heads back and laugh.

Meanwhile, my face is bright red, embarrassed as hell, but oddly equally turned on and proud.

"Babe, that's not the kind of things we talk about in public," I say, with a light lilt.

"Oh, must have missed that memo." Casually, she pulls a chip from Calder and Rachel's nachos and pops it in her mouth, smiling and chewing at me.

"Oh fuck, man. You have met your match." Calder claps his hands and laughs some more while Rachel leans over to shake Adalyn's hand with pride, a silent *thank you* passing between the two women.

Pretty sure Calder is right. I have most definitely met my match. I'm in awe.

"**O**h, I have one," I say as I take a sip of my beer and lick the top of my lip before saying, "Rachel, fuck, chuck, and marry." I clear my throat, "Daario Naharis, Khal Drogo, and Jon Snow."

I'm practically giddy over my question, knowing how much this is going to kill Rachel. She is a HUGE *Game of Thrones* fan, throwing viewing parties and dressing up in her GOT-themed clothing every time the show airs.

Slowly, Rachel lowers her pink Cosmo from her mouth, eyes locked on mine, a little vein in her forehead twitching. "You *bastard*."

Laughing, I reach over and pat her hand. "You have to answer. It's the oath we cheersed to before the game started. And as we have all known from the beginning of this friendship, a cheersed oath is one never to be broken." I might be a little drunk, but who's really counting beers tonight? At least I'm not Adalyn who's been giggling consistently since she downed her fourth drink.

"And you had layups. You just threw down the gauntlet with a fuck, chuck, and marry, Game of Thrones edition. Tell me how that's fair."

"It's not, but I never said I was fair."

Shaking her head, payback written all over her face, Rachel playfully points her finger at me. "Just you wait, Holmes, your turn is coming."

"Bring it on." I spread my arms. "You won't be able to stump me."

"Maybe not you . . ." She eyes Adalyn who's still giggling, playing with the stem of her margarita glass.

Eyeing Rachel suspiciously, I ask, "What are you up to?"

"Just you wait and see." Sighing heavily, she leans her head back against the bench and really puts some thought into her answer.

Next to her, Calder sways back and forth to the Irish music lightly playing in the background, occasionally biting down heavily on his bottom lip and drunkenly tapping on the table along with the beat. Drunk looks "good" on him.

"If I have to answer, which this isn't fair, because you know I love all of my men . . ." She presses her hand over her eyes, and swears under her breath. "Marry Jon, chuck Daario, and fuck that monster cock of a man Khal." Leaning forward, growing even more serious, she adds, "And for the record, I would teach that man how to not only please a woman, but how to make him come so hard, his eyes pop out of their sockets."

"She knows how to fuck, man." Calder falls into Rachel and places sloppy kisses all over her face, which she doesn't seem to mind, given how her mouth opens and her tongue starts prying Calder's mouth open.

Moving in close to me, Adalyn loudly whispers, "They sure know how to kiss and make noise when they do it, don't they? Top-notch noise level. Do you think we sound like that when we kiss?"

I shake my head. "Nah, we're classy, baby." I press a quick kiss across her nose and then throw a wadded-up napkin to break up the make-out session.

"Come on, I shouldn't have to tell you to keep your lips to yourself every goddamn second. We're playing a game."

Pushing Calder away, Rachel says, "He's right." She wipes her mouth with the sleeve of her shirt, all class flying out the window long ago. "I have an important question to ask." I don't like that look in her eye. Fixing on Adalyn, she taps the table in front of her to gather her attention and says, "Adalyn, fuck, chuck, and marry." Smiling devilishly at me, eyes locked, she says, "Hayden, Holden, and Halsey." She finishes her sentence with a giant smile and folded hands on the table.

Touché.

Tou-fucking-ché.

"You bitch."

Rachel throws her head back and laughs. She's so happy with herself, pleased as punch, and I have to hand it to her. She has all the right to be because that is a killer question.

Head tilted to the side, Adalyn asks, "You want me to compare Hayden with his brothers?"

Rachel nods her head.

"Well . . . that's easy." Turning toward me, Adalyn boops my nose with her little finger and says, "Fuck Holden, marry Halsey, and chuck Hayden. I like my men young."

From the other side of the table, Calder and Rachel erupt in laughter, holding on to their stomachs, wiping tears from their eyes kind of laughter. Adalyn giggles along with them, keeping her eyes on mine, a sparkle deep within her dark irises.

"You're in fucking trouble now," I whisper to her, leaning into her ear.

"Good, it's about time you punish me."

Shaking my head, my scruff brushing against her smooth skin, I say, "Nah, you won't be punished the way you're thinking. Looks like I just took another oath of celibacy."

Rolling her eyes, Adalyn groans and leans back against the booth, melting into the seat. "God, of course you did. You sadistic bastard."

"You're going to take care of my boy, right?" Calder asks, holding on to Rachel to steady his heavily swaying body.

Cuddled up to me, like she has been the entire night—well, almost the entire night—Adalyn nods her head and pats my chest. "Consider this guy in good hands."

"That's what I like to hear. He's a sensitive one, you know. Not a playboy. Takes his relationships seriously."

"One of his best qualities along with how sweet he is."

"And hot," I add. "Don't forget to mention how hot I am."

"And modest." Adalyn winks.

"You're good for him." Rachel presses her finger to Adalyn's forehead. "I approve."

"Me too." Calder steps up and copies Rachel, pressing his

finger to Adalyn's head, who then proceeds to bow to both of them afterward.

Talk about a bunch of drunk assholes.

After bowing, Adalyn presses her finger to Rachel and Calder's foreheads and says, "And I approve of you two as friends of Hayden's."

Clutching his chest like a dickhead, Calder let's out a long breath. "Thank fuck, I was nervous she wasn't going to like us."

"Not like you?" Adalyn tsks. "How could I not like you? First impressions are everything, and the fact that I was greeted by boners and bras . . . that is better than a butterscotch candy from the Queen herself."

"That old bird." Rachel looks up to the sky. "God, I like her. Do you think she wears a bra to bed?"

"Totally." Adalyn nods her head. "She's got those puppies on lockdown twenty-four/seven."

"Like the family jewels."

"And she doesn't let people take pictures of them just like the family jewels."

"Ugh, you're so right." Rachel shakes her head. "What a shame, the money she could make on selling those photos."

"Damn shame," Calder states and looks at his watch. "Shit, it's late. Hayden has a photo shoot tomorrow morning. Dude, you're going to be bloated from all the beer."

Yes. Yes, I am. James is going to be thrilled.

"Does it matter?" Adalyn asks.

Rachel cuts in, leaning toward Adalyn, gripping her forearm. "Adalyn, it matters big time. Have you not seen one of Hayden's underwear ads?"

"Underwear ads?" Adalyn pulls back, shocked. "Tomorrow you're going to shoot an underwear ad?"

"Uh, yeah, is that a problem?" I rub the back of my neck.

Studying me, giving me several once -overs, she crosses her arms over her chest and says, "Not a problem at all, as long as you know I will most likely be horny the entire time they're shooting you."

"Horny I can handle, jealous I can deal with . . . but mad?" I shake my head. "I don't want you mad."

"Why on earth would I be mad? Hell, I'll be popping the bubbly, celebrating the fact that everyone in that room is going to be wishing they were in my shoes." Standing on her toes, she presses a deep kiss across my lips, the flavor of tequila infused on her lips.

"Oh that was smooth." Rachel slow claps. "Well done, Adalyn, well done. She's a keeper, Hayden, so don't fuck it up."

"I don't plan on it."

No way will I fuck this up.

CHAPTER THIRTEEN

ADALYN

"Ughhhhh, I'm dying," I moan when I open the door to the bathroom.

The shower didn't help. Brushing my teeth didn't help, and the four Ibuprofens I took with a full glass of water when I woke up are not helping.

"I'm sorry, baby. You can seriously stay here. I'll order you some greasy room service, and you can sleep some more while I'm at my photo shoot."

Unlike me, Hayden is bouncing back from last night as if he had half a tablespoon of alcohol, got a full ten hours of sleep, and happened to have time to wear a homemade mud mask at the same time.

None of that is the truth.

In fact, we got back to the hotel at two in the morning, dragged our bodies into our room, and passed out. Hayden woke up at five, went for a run, did some kind of crazy workout routine, took a shower, and is now handsome as ever with his unfazed skin, eight-pack abs, and minty-fresh breath.

Meanwhile, I'm over here looking like I've been dragged

behind a subway car for five stops and then picked apart by sewer rats . . . and this is *after* a shower.

How can he possibly look at me and think, oh yes, this woman, this woman right here is who I want to take to my photo shoot?

He's insane.

He's crazy.

He's infatuated with me.

And it's the only reason I'm currently slipping on my white Keds and linking my fingers with his. "Take me to the photo shoot. I want to see you in underwear."

Chuckling, he says, "I can show you what I look like in underwear in private."

I wave him off. "It won't be the same. You'll be under all those lights, oiled up, and posey. I can't miss that. Plus, what if you need a fluffer? I'm not going to let any other lady touch your penis."

We're halfway to the door when he stops his pursuit. "Uh, what are you talking about? There are no penis shots."

"No? So this is like a David Beckham-type underwear ad?"

"Yeah." He chuckles. "What were you thinking it was? Because from the sounds of it, you were thinking this was X-rated."

I shrug my shoulders. "Hey, I don't know what you do to make a buck. I'm not judgey here, I just don't want other women touching your penis."

"Well, you have nothing to worry about. There will be no touching of my penis by anyone else but you."

We take the elevator to the main lobby where there is a car waiting for us by the curb.

"Funny you say I'm the only one who will be touching your penis, especially since I have yet to fully wrap my fingers around it."

"Maybe you should try harder." He holds the door to the car open for me, a giant small on his face.

"Try harder?" I raise an eyebrow at him. "Yeah, okay. Be careful what you wish for there, Holmes. I'm feisty, and you just tested me."

"You must be Adalyn." A suave-looking man in a tailored suit walks up to me. Slicked-back hair, freshly shaven face, and a powerful cologne advertising the man has made money.

My guess, he's made money off athletes like Hayden.

A Jerry McGuire-type, but a little more . . . sleazy-looking.

"And you must be James, the publicist." I lend out my hand and he takes it, placing a kiss across my knuckles.

Okay, not Jerry McGuire, more Philip Stuckey from Pretty Woman, but with a full head of hair.

"Hayden must have told you about me. I hope it was all kind."

Taking my hand back, trying not to wipe my knuckles on my shirt to rid of the feeling of his lips on my skin, I shrug. "Could have been kind, could have been irritated. Something about asking him if he's bloated?"

James grips his tie, shuffling it back and forth on his neck. "Got to make sure my boys are in top form. During the off-season, some of them let themselves go and forget about the photo shoots we have lined up."

"Well, nothing to worry here, as Hayden is in top form." I wink and scan the room, looking for the man of the hour. He's been in "hair and makeup" for what seems like an hour. What could they possibly be doing to primp him?

"They're spray-tanning him if that's what you're wondering."

Hmm, I don't like that this dude can read my mind. It ups the level of his skeeze factor.

"Spray tan, huh, I guess that makes sense. He is a bit on the paler side, still hot though." Looking James up and down, I ask, "Have you seen his eight-pack? Yummy, right?"

His brow pulls together. "Well, I wouldn't necessarily say yummy, but yes, the man has a nice stomach."

"Not just stomach, James. Abs, the man has abs." I pat his arm.

"Yes." He drags out the word, looking me up and down. He's

suspicious. I can see the assessment he's making of me, the first judgment.

And I'm not looking my best, that's for damn sure. I've seen better days. Pretty sure I still have a little bit of mascara residue under my eyes from last night. My wet hair is in the midst of air-drying, and I'm dressed in jeans and one of Hayden's T-shirts. The only thing holding me together right now is the Egg McMuffin we had on the way here and the venti coffee gripped in my hand.

"Can I ask you something?" James asks, sticking his hands in his suit pants pockets, his shoulder tilted in my direction, as if we're about to share a special conversation.

I take a sip of my coffee and look over the lid. "I would be surprised if you didn't."

Blunt. It's the only way to deal with this kind of men.

The kind of men who think they're doing the right thing by looking out for "their guys" when in fact, they're ready to blow everything up. I'm not stupid. I know what this man's end game is. He only makes money if his boys are performing well, if he's able to portray them as perfect specimens. So why would he want Hayden to have a "distraction" in his life. To publicists and agents, a girlfriend is a distraction.

And I have a feeling he's about to tell me that.

"How long have you known Hayden?"

"A little over a month. We met through a mutual friend."

He nods. "And it's going well between you two?"

"I'd say it is."

"And what is it that you do?"

"I'm a nurse at a hospital in Binghamton." Another sip of coffee. "Tell me, James, what exactly is your burning question? Are you trying to scope out information from me so you have dirt for the media? Are you thinking of every which way you can spin our situation so you can make me look bad and make Hayden look like a hero, in case things go sour?"

Silence falls between us as James chews on the side of his cheek, his eyes searching mine, calculating his next move.

Plastering on a fake smile, he says, "I would never dream of doing such a thing. I only want to get to know you."

"Well I have no desire to get to know you." I take down another gulp of hot liquid. "I know why you're really here, okay? I'm not a vapid airhead; Hayden has the whole package. He is not only extremely talented on the ice, but he's a kind human being, overtly attractive, and has a heart of gold. He's exactly what every publicist dreams of. So your number-one priority is to make sure no one messes with your perfect package. I get it." I lean forward, drawing him closer. "But I'm going to tell you right now, I'm not here to bring Hayden down. I'm here to lift him up, and I suggest you do the same instead of trying to dig for dirt from a girl who plans on sticking around for a very long time." I pat his check, putting an end to our conversation just as Hayden walks up, looking drop-dead sexy in a pair of white boxer briefs.

He places a kiss on the side of my head and looks to James. "Everything okay over here?"

"Oh yes," I answer. "James was asking if he could get me anything for my hangover. Sweet guy, this one." I thumb toward James who purses his lips.

Not buying it, Hayden eyes James, but before he says anything, he's called on set. "Got to go." Dipping his head down, he clasps my chin and gives me a slow, sweet kiss before taking off toward a well-lit set, draped in deep blue fabric. With his tan skin, white briefs, and popping muscles, he's looking so damn delicious.

I can't wait for the show.

James steps forward, close enough so only I can hear him. "I've seen it before, a woman takes down a man of Hayden's caliber. I've seen them lose everything, and I don't want that for Hayden. I only want what's best for him."

I nod and stand from my chair, wanting to move it closer. Before I excuse myself from the conversation, I look at James and give him a sweet smile. "Thank you, James. I really appreciate your concern for Hayden. But I'm going to tell you this once and only once . . ." I pause and pat his chest. "You can fuck off."

~

T est shots flash, people mill about adjusting lights and the backdrop, PAs stand around with headphones, waiting for their next request while Hayden does pushups on the floor, vigorously working up a sweat.

Me, I sit back in my chair, legs crossed, coffee halfway to my mouth while staring at my boyfriend.

When did shoulder blades become so sexy?

Because Lord Jesus, Hayden has a set of shoulder blades that will tickle any women's fancy. With every drop to the ground, they form into peaks, surrounded by bulge after bulge of muscle. From his traps, to his shoulders, to his biceps, sinew flows effortlessly, ripples with precision.

Up and down.

Up and down.

I'm transfixed, unable to move, unable to pull my eyes away.

"You about ready?" the photographer, Hildi, asks.

"Yeah, ten more," Hayden calls out, his voice strained.

Pumping up and down, he shows no struggle in his last ten pushups. His large hands spread over the ground, his forearms working overtime, his head tilted down, giving me the perfect view of his tight, round ass in his white briefs.

Oh heavens.

That ass.

What was he thinking bringing me to this photo shoot? Was this another way for him to torture me?

Because it's working.

Hopping to his feet, Hayden rubs his hands together, dusting them off, his chest popping, his abs flexing, his body looking better than ever with a light splattering of hair across his thick, barrel-like chest.

A low thrum starts to form between my legs.

My veins are tingling with awareness.

I'm turned on.

From pushups.

And I want more. I've become a harlot for pushups. *Why am I not filming this?* Because then I can watch pushups on replay for hours on end.

I make a mental note to ask Hayden to perform more pushups for me later.

Hayden is put into place, music booms over speakers, and like a seasoned professional, he starts posing for the camera, making little adjustments with his arms and hands.

Grabbing on the back of his neck, head tilted up.

One hand behind his back, abs flexed, pecs full, nipples hard.

Smiling, hand over face as if he's the shyest, yet hottest man on earth.

Both hands pulling on the edge of his underwear, biting on his lip . . .

Oh fuck, that one right there, that's the shot.

The set around me stills, women motionless as Hayden moves effortlessly, listening to Hildi's direction, occasionally peeking over to me, that boyish smile made only for me appearing.

I prop my chin on my hand and lean forward, eyes traveling from his powerful shoulders to the well-defined divots in his stomach, to the V that leads straight to his bulge.

Ugh, and that bulge. It looks so . . . heavy, so full, so fucking hot, all I want to do is run up to him, pull his underwear down and start sucking him off.

Yeah, did you cringe? I said it, I said suck him off, and I'm not ashamed of it. If you were in my position, you would be thinking the same thing.

Hayden's attractive, but it wasn't his looks that made me fall for him. It's the kindness, the warm heart he carries in his chest, the thoughtful man he's proven to be. It's things like holding off on the physical side until we got to know each other better. It's the loving texts in the morning, the flowers at work or lunches delivered, or the way he calls me baby without even giving it a second thought.

I've fallen for him for all the right reasons, and in many respects, that was Hayden's intention and desire. He's clearly and rightly beloved, because the man the public sees is not that dissimilar to one I've grown to adore. But it's not what James thinks. I haven't fallen for the larger-than-life pinup-worthy hockey star.

That being said, I'm happily taking a selfish moment. I'm looking past his beautiful qualities and focusing on the pure physical here.

I'm letting my eyes eat him up for the first time because I'm finally getting the chance.

Nothing but a pair of underwear, he stands before me, those dark, mysterious eyes smiling, his strong, square jaw posed and sharp, the scruff on his face adding to the sex-appeal. His body, tall and thick with muscle. His forearms and biceps like cannons. His bulge so freaking enticing I feel myself inching forward on my chair.

I lick my lips as if trying to savor the sweetness of our last kiss, wishing we were tucked away in our hotel room, lying in bed, slowly tracing each other's bodies with our fingertips instead of me watching him from a few feet away.

Tilting his head back, he shows off the long column of his neck, his Adam's apple poking out. All male. Masculinity drips from him. The hum between my legs forms a solid throb as my breath turns shallow, my body aching for him.

Please touch me.

Please take me somewhere private.

Please bury yourself deep inside me.

"That's a wrap!" Hildi shouts, startling me out of my stupor.

Eyes blinking rapidly, I stand from my chair and clap along with everyone else, unsure of what to do.

Hayden eyes me while he speaks with the photographer, his gaze never leaving mine even when he speaks with her.

I take a step forward and his eyes darken, smolder, giving me a once-over.

Another step and he takes a deep breath.

One more.

Thanking the photographer, he closes the space between us, snags me by the arm, and bypasses everyone on set, taking me down a long hallway and into a room to the right. Slamming the door shut, he locks it, and spins on his heels, looking almost . . . angry.

"What the hell was that?"

Caught off guard, I step back. "What was what?"

He approaches me, his body vibrating. "You know what I'm talking about." Pressing me against the wall, his height towering over me, he adds, "The licking of your lips, the searing *I'm going to eat you alive* look you were giving me through that entire photo shoot." His hands trap my hips against the wall. "Do you realize how hard it was to not only look away from you, but to not get fucking hard with the way that perfect pink tongue of yours would peek out and touch the tip of your lips?"

"Oh."

"Yeah, oh."

"Well . . . you know, it wasn't easy on me either." I puff my chest forward, my nipples hard and rubbing against his chest. "Watching you practically pull your underwear down in front of everyone, the way you would bite your bottom lip, or flex your muscles in just the right way. It was hot." I whisper, "So hot."

Not able to take it anymore, needing to show him how serious I am, I place my hands on the waistband of his briefs and inch my fingers inside.

"Adalyn, what are you doing?"

"This." In one swift movement, I bring his briefs down past his growing erection, letting them fall to the ground.

He sucks in a deep breath and hisses when my hand squeezes around him. "Adalyn," he chokes out, "there are people outside."

"Good for them." I glide my hand up and down his erection, feeling it grow quickly in my grasp, followed by a pained look on Hayden's face. "I want you, Hayden. I need you. I can't wait any longer. This thing between us, this sexual chemistry, it's eating me alive. Your tongue and fingers are not going to hold me over." I squeeze is erection hard. "I need this."

"Fuck," he breathes out. "Adalyn, we can't do this here. I had plans for this moment."

"Well, you took too long." I strip my shirt over my head, reach behind me and unclasp my bra, letting it fall to the floor with his briefs.

Darkening eyes meet mine. A tick of his jaw. A flex in his neck.

"Goddamn it," he says between his teeth before he reaches for my jeans and unbuckles them. I help him and push them down to the ground along with my underwear. "This is not how it's supposed to be." He strokes my cheek.

"Not everything can be planned, Hayden. Sometimes you have to throw caution to the wind and be in the moment."

"Is that what you want? This?" His voice goes deeper when he says, "You want me to fuck you against this wall?"

My breath hitches as I swallow hard and nod. "I do."

"You're going to have to be quiet."

"I'm not making any promises."

Searching my eyes, indecision clear in the pull in his brow, I can see he's concerned. He pictured this moment differently, but there is no more waiting where I'm concerned. There is no more waiting. There is no more teasing. We're done with that.

Taking charge, wanting to ease his worry, I bring his hand between us and press it between my legs, letting him feel how much I want this, how turned on I am.

His finger slips past my slit and he groans, his forehead connecting with mine. "Fuck, Adalyn."

"Do you feel that, Hayden?" I move his hand up and down, sliding along with ease. "This is how hot I am for you, how needy I am. This is from watching you and nothing else." I press his finger inside me, loving how he adds another finger, stretching me. "I've waited, Hayden. I've waited so damn long to find out what it feels like to have you pulsing inside of me, to have you groaning out my name while you hover over me, complete ecstasy written all over your face." I squeeze the base of his cock. He coughs and swallows hard. "A little piece of me has died inside every time we've gotten so close, every time I've itched to feel your rock-hard cock in my hand and you've pulled away." I shake my head. "Not this time. I'm not waiting. I'm taking what I want. And I want you, Hayden. I want your heart, I want your thoughtful mind, and I want your sexy body. Right here. Right now."

The air stills, my words hanging heavily between us, the sexual tension thick.

Is he going to make a move, or am I going to have to help him take the next step?

Before I can decide, his lips crash down on mine, needy and demanding, stealing my breath, draining every last ounce of air from my lungs.

Cupping my cheeks, he licks my lips, parting them with his tongue, diving deep into my mouth. Relief washes over me when he pushes me farther into the wall, his hips pinning mine, his cock, hot and stiff, grazing between my legs.

Shifting with our movements, his length creates a heady friction, awakening a part of me I haven't felt in a while, a tingling sensation that reaches from the tips of my toes to the root of my hair.

Taking his shoulders in my hands, I steady myself and pull him closer so my pebbled nipples are rubbing against the fine hair on his chest, the sensation adding to the sultry experience.

With each passing kiss, each press of his cock against my wet center, I get lost.

Lost in the feel of his mouth on mine.

Lost in his gentle, yet demanding touch.

Lost in the explicit groans rumbling from his brawny chest.

In this moment, I'm not Adalyn, and he's not Hayden. We're becoming one. It's scary, terrifying actually, because from this moment on, I know I'll never be the same. *From this point on, I'll be his, and he will be mine.*

CHAPTER FOURTEEN

HAYDEN

This wasn't what I had planned. This wasn't how I envisioned making Adalyn mine for the first time, but her speech, the way her eyes pleaded with me, and the way she consistently eye-fucked me while on set has left me no choice.

I need her . . . now.

My mouth works over hers, licking, sucking, fusing together. We've made out before, but there is a sense of urgency in our kisses this time that's different.

Moving my hands down her neck, past her shoulders to her sides, my fingers graze her soft skin, spreading goosebumps along every inch of her body. The little pebbles encouraging my touch.

Her stomach, her ribs, my thumbs caress every crevice, every bone to her breasts. I caught a quick look at her full, round tits when she took her bra off and I'm amazed with myself that I've been able to keep myself away from them for this long.

But no more.

Cupping them into my palms, they fit perfectly, barely over-flowing. Her nipples are hard as my thumbs pass over them, stiff and turned on. And when I squeeze, her mouth drops open wider, a gasp passing her lips straight into mine.

I repeat the action, increasing my cupping with each squeeze until she's writhing beneath me, her pussy rubbing desperately against my aching cock.

But I don't give in.

Instead, I squeeze her breast and then pinch her nipple, rolling it between my fingers. Plucking, pulling, pinching. I alternate between the two, until she's moaning desperately into my mouth, our kisses becoming sloppy, our mouths all over each other, her lips pressing across my mouth, my jaw, my cheeks.

My lips fuse to her chin, her neck, her collarbone. Lifting her arms against the wall, I pin her and bring her breast into my mouth, nibbling on her nipple.

"Oh God, Hayden." Her hips slam into mine, seeking relief.

I move to the other breast, nibbling harder and sucking her nipple into my mouth, yanking on it, which only seems to spur her on more. Gripping both of her wrists against the wall with one hand, I reach between her legs and easily slide in as she spreads for me, giving me more access.

Pressing my fingers inside her, I let her rock on my hand for a few strokes before I can't take her soft moans anymore. *I need to be inside her now.*

Releasing her wrists, I grip her waist and lift her up. Getting the idea, she wraps her legs around my waist and links her ankles, locking herself in. My cock slides up and down her wet center, gliding along her clit.

"Get inside of me, now," she moans into my ear.

"Hold on to my shoulders." Reaching between us, I guide my length along her slit until the head of my cock is at her entrance.

Squeezing my eyes shut, so painfully hard, I slide myself in, inch by slow inch.

So wet.

So warm.

So goddamn tight.

MEGHAN QUINN

"Yes," she hisses into my ear before her mouth lands on my shoulder.

With each inch she slides down on me, her teeth bite down on my shoulder. Feels so good. So right.

After a few seconds, I bottom out. We both let out a feral groan when I hit that special spot of hers, her teeth sinking deeper.

I welcome the pain.

I'm turned on by the pain.

I want so much more. I want her to bite down on more than my shoulder. Fuck, I want her to play with my nipples again, to grip my balls and roll them between her fingers.

Right now, I need to fuck her against this wall.

Pulsing my hips, I slam into her, thrust after thrust, never letting up. I keep a constant pace, a pace that throws Adalyn into a spiral of passionate ecstasy. Hands on my shoulders, she moves up and down on my length as well, pushing down when I'm rising up, meeting in the middle for an explosive feeling, so rich, so overwhelming that the sounds coming out of her mouth are inaudible. I can hear my name, I can detect some curse words, but that's it.

And it's sexy seeing how much I cause Adalyn to feel.

It's sexy to see how she so easily falls apart and loses control.

And yet, despite her sedated body, she's still present, she's still moving with me, clenching around me.

"Feels so goddamn good," I whisper into her ear. "So good, Adalyn."

She bites down on my earlobe and says, "Harder. Fuck me harder, Hayden."

Christ.

This woman. A biter, a dirty talker, a fucking queen in my arms.

I give her what she wants, slamming into her, her back hitting the wall, our attempt at being quiet washed away with unbridled passion.

Moaning into my mouth now, she clamps around my cock, her body stilling, her hands trembling. She gasps and then murmurs a slew of curse words as her pussy contracts around my cock, the sensation so powerful, so overwhelming that within seconds, my balls are tightening and I'm coming pulse after pulse.

I come so hard and so long I almost forget where I am when I moan her name, the sound echoing in the small dressing room.

If people *were* wondering what we were doing in here, they sure as hell know now.

Fuck, but was it worth it.

Slowing my hips, I take a deep breath and open my eyes to find Adalyn staring back at me. A lazy smile passes over her lips as she gives me a quick peck to my nose.

"That was so fucking hot," she whispers, not that she needs to, not after what we just did. "Well worth the wait."

"Yeah?"

She nods. "Yes, you were easily worth the wait."

"God, Adalyn. Phenomenal. You are phenomenal." Actually, there are no words to describe that. Being inside her . . . touching her . . . fucking *her*. She's everything . . . *She's quickly becoming my everything.*

She's everything.

I thank God I met this girl. *My girl.*

With another gentle kiss, to my lips this time, I become lost in the feel of her once again. I'm so fucking glad I took the time away from my normal crazy and went to Binghamton when my season ended. Without *that* decision, I never would have met Adalyn, the woman who didn't steal my heart, but to whom I gladly gave it. *She's becoming* my *everything.*

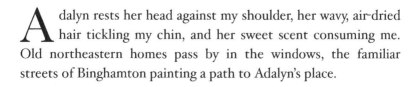

Adalyn rests her head against my shoulder, her wavy, air-dried hair tickling my chin, and her sweet scent consuming me. Old northeastern homes pass by in the windows, the familiar streets of Binghamton painting a path to Adalyn's place.

The past two days have been . . . Fuck, I don't even know how to describe it.

Life-changing.

I can remember getting the call to play professional hockey. I remember where I was sitting, what I was watching, what I was eating.

My parents' house, on their big brown sectional, watching the movie Ratatouille with my mom because it was about a cooking mouse, which my mom thought was adorable. We were eating homemade beef Wellington. Fancy feast for two movie watchers. But that's how we rolled. My phone rang, and it was my agent.

The room stilled, the air around us heavy, my mind whirling with *holy fucks* and *I can't believe I did it*. It was singularly the proudest, more exciting moment of my life.

Little did I know, it was going to be rivaled.

The past two days . . .

They've rivaled the feeling I had when I first found out about being signed with the Brawlers.

I'm happy. I feel at peace with Adalyn in my arms. It almost is like my life is coming full circle, everything falling into place.

Now . . . to have the talk with her.

Living in Philadelphia while she lives in Binghamton is going to be inconvenient, especially with her nurse schedule, but I really think we can work it out and hopefully—if I'm a lucky son of a bitch—she'll consider moving to Philly, even if it's not immediately, given she's new to her job.

The town car pulls in front of Adalyn's house and idles. "We're here." I kiss the top of her head. It's late and if she didn't have such an early shift tomorrow morning, I'd suggest I follow her into her house. But she needs a good night's sleep, especially considering what little sleep we've had over the past two days.

"Mmm . . . but I'm so warm, and if I leave this car, I'm going to have to face the real world, and I'm not sure if I'm ready for that. Ten more minutes."

I chuckle as she tries to snuggle in closer. "Ten more minutes, babe, will lead you to falling asleep in this car."

"Nothing wrong with that. Don't you want to just take a little nap, have a little snuggle time?"

Groaning, I wrap my arm around her and squeeze her tightly. "I want nothing more than to stay in the tiny bubble we created, but you have work tomorrow, and I have to get back to my training."

She waves me off. "You're fit enough, you'll be fine. I mean, how many more muscles do you really need?"

"All of them, babe. All of them." I chuckle and kiss her forehead. "Come on, I'll walk you to your door."

Grunting with disapproval, she lifts off me. "You know, if I didn't know any better, I'd think you were trying to get rid of me." Stiffly turning on the seat, she asks, "You're not getting rid of me, are you?"

"Yup, that's been my plan the entire time."

"I knew it." She shakes her fist to the sky. "Played, by Hayden Holmes. It will be my *InTouch Weekly* article I sell out of desperation and payback."

"When they're interviewing you, can you at least mention my sizable cock?"

Eyes narrowing. "I'll mention its size for sure, but I'm going to tell you right now"—she hops out of the car and leans in through the door—"it's not going to be in your favor."

"You're the devil."

The driver takes her suitcase to the sidewalk and she takes it from him with a thank you. Walking up the pathway to her house, she says over her shoulder, "You have no idea, Holmes. Get ready for the wrath of Adalyn. Ohhhhh boy." She laughs manically, as I follow closely behind her. "When my brothers get ahold of this information, you can bet your tiny macaroni that there will be a bounty put on your head. First person to rupture your nuts with a hockey puck wins."

I squeeze my legs together when we reach her front door. Fuck, that would hurt. "Damn, if I would've known the psychotic nightmare you'd turn into, I never would've asked you out." I pull her in by her hips, smiles on both of our faces.

"You should always do your research, Hayden, especially a man in your position. You never know who the psychos are going to be. We might seem normal at first, but that's how we get you. *Then*, we flip a switch and tear your world apart."

"Noted." Sighing, I press my forehead against hers. "Did you have fun?"

All joking aside, she grips my shirt and nods. "I had an amazing time. Thank you for taking me and giving me some memorable moments to lock away forever."

"Memorable moments, huh?"

She nods and plays with the collar of my shirt. "Being fucked in a dressing room. Blow jobs in town cars. Sex in the shower." She moans. "That was my favorite."

Town car blow job was a close second for me.

"Are all your memories sexual?"

"Mostly, since you held out on me for so long, but spending time with Calder and Rachel was amazing. Seeing Hamilton was so much fun. Going to the top of the Statue of Liberty and geeking out like tourists is right up there. Oh, and don't forget about the pizza. Ugh, the pizza was so good."

"The pizza, let's fly back for the pizza."

"Okay." She attempts to pull me back to the car but I stop her. "Ugh, you're no fun. Where's your adventure?"

"I have no idea why I'm the responsible one here. I'm not the one who has to get up early tomorrow and be present enough to perform medical tasks on real-live human beings."

"Well . . . when you put it like that." She twists her lips to the side. "Damn it, Hayden. Ugh, you're right. Putting in an IV with zero sleep isn't very responsible or fun."

"I prefer my nurses to be well rested." I lean closer to her ear and add, "And fucked."

Shivering in my arms, she looks at me through her eyelashes. "Well, you took care of the second half of the sentence."

"And I'm trying to take care of the first half." Hooking my finger under her chin, I bring my lips to hers, sweetly kissing her, not diving too deep, and not pressing too hard. "Go on, go get some sleep. I'll text you in the morning, okay?"

She nods and pulls me into a hug. I wrap my arms around her slight shoulders and breathe her in one more time. "Thank you again for the past two days. It was exactly what I needed."

"You're welcome, baby." I want to talk about our future. I want to tell her we need to have a serious conversation. The words are on the tip of my tongue but I push them down. If I tell her we need to talk, she's going to worry. She'll want the conversation now instead of getting the sleep she desperately needs. So I keep my mouth shut. We have time, and it doesn't have to be discussed right now.

"Dinner tomorrow?"

"I'll cook. Come to my place after work?"

"I'll be there." Reaching up she presses a gentle kiss on my chin and steps away. "Have a good night." Winking, she takes her suitcase and unlocks her door. Hands in my pockets, I watch her every move until she waves and shuts the door on me.

Hopping off her front porch, I jog to the waiting car the whole time wishing I was snuggling next to Adalyn rather than going back to an empty cottage.

One night, that's all. One night isn't going to change anything.

CHAPTER FIFTEEN

ADALYN

Oh that feels so good.

I love it when the water is so hot in a shower that it feels like it's blistering my back. I once saw a piece on *The Today Show* that talked about taking cold showers in the morning to wake you up, get you started for the day.

What a load of crap.

I tried it once and I was miserable. Such a bear. All my coworkers steered clear of me that day, because who in their right mind wants to take a cold shower in the morning?

Sadists, that's who.

I go for the opposite, and you know what, a blistering hot shower is better.

There I said it, I put it out in the universe.

Hot showers wake you up if you do them right. Turn them scorching, singe your skin, and then you are good to go. Trust me on this.

Turning the shower off, I wring out my hair and reach for my towel just as my phone starts to ring on the bathroom counter. I always bring my phone into the bathroom with me so I know how much more time I have to fuck around before I actually have to get ready for work.

Stepping on the yellow bathroom mat, I glance at the screen and see Emma's face pop up. Smiling, I answer it.

"Hey girl."

"Ugh, I miss you," Emma groans. "We haven't had our morning chats in so long." It's been a ritual of ours when getting ready for our early shifts, we call each other at least twice a week to catch up. It's been a while.

"That's because you were on a little mini vacay with Tucker. Not my fault."

"It was worth it, but I don't want to talk about that, I want to talk about your New York City getaway with the famous Hayden Holmes."

Needing to dry off, I put the phone on speaker and set it on the counter. "It was amazing. I got to hang out with his friend, Calder, who is also his teammate along with Calder's girlfriend, Rachel. They were so much fun—"

"Not as much fun as me."

"Never." I chuckle. "No one is as much fun as you."

"Good answer. You may continue."

Just a little friend reassurance break. Like anyone could take her place. Emma is my girl. We've been through far too much together, especially during our first year of nursing school.

"We also did some silly touristy things like the Statue of Liberty and touring Ellis Island. And his photo shoot. Oh my God, Emma. I know you're madly in love with Tucker, but I am one hundred percent positive if you were there, you might have considered leaving him."

"That good?"

"Ugh, so good." I sit on the lid of the toilet, towel wrapped around me, and start applying lotion to my body, prepping my face for what little makeup I put on. "He was in underwear and that was it. The lights made every indent and crevice of muscle stand out, and then he starts pulling down the waistband of his briefs."

"Oh damn."

"Oh damn is right." Opening my drawer, I shuffle around for my brush, not paying attention to what I'm doing. "It was so hot. Every woman in the area stopped what they were doing and watched." My hand connects with something plastic and I move it to the side still searching for my brush.

"Please tell me you guys had sex. For the love of God, tell me you finally did it."

Laughing, I stand to look in the drawer. "Oh yeah, we had—" I pause, my words falling from my lips when I focus on the plastic thing my hand was hitting. Oh fuck.

Oh fuck, oh fuck, oh fuck.

"Adalyn, are you there?"

"I . . . am."

Picking up my birth control pills with shaky hands, I slowly open the top.

"Is everything okay?"

Swallowing hard, eyeing the pills in the pack that should have been taken, I shake my head. "No, it's not."

"What's going on? Do I need to drive over there?"

Deflated, I lean against my bathroom wall and fall to the floor. "Emma . . ."

"Yes? What's going on?"

Taking a deep breath, I count the amount of pills I've forgotten to take.

Six.

Six freaking pills!

How on earth could I forget six freaking birth control pills?

"Umm, let's say someone forget to take their birth control pills and then had . . . um, unprotected sex against a wall in a dressing room. What are the chances they could get pregnant?"

"Please tell me you're asking for a friend."

"I wish I was."

"Oh Adalyn, what the hell were you thinking?"

Pressing my hand against my forehead, I groan. "I wasn't thinking. The man had me so horny from his photo shoot and holding out on me, that I kind of just jumped his bones the minute the opportunity presented itself."

"Which was in a dressing room against a wall?"

"Yes, but for what it's worth, it was the best sex I've ever had . . . until he took me back to the hotel and fucked me in the shower."

"Let me guess, no condom?"

Oh Jesus Christ.

What the hell was I thinking? Did I really lose all common sense the minute Hayden's penis made an appearance?

Thinking back . . . I cringe. Yup. All common sense when out the door once pants were shucked. I'm one of those girls. One of those girls you look at and think in this day of age, how can you possibly forget about birth control or condoms? *And I'm a freaking nurse.* I should know better. *Ugh,* I do know better.

Two words: Hayden's cock.

Oh God, it is such a nice cock. Long and thick with the perfect head. Slightly curved up so every time he pulsed inside me, it was reaching for that one spot, that one spot he hit every time.

"Oh Adalyn." I don't have to answer; my silence is enough. She knows. "How is that possible?"

Burying my head in my knees, I say, "It was the dick. The dick did it to me."

Sighing on the other end of the phone, Emma says, "Damn the dick. Damn all the dicks."

My sentiment exactly.

∽

I'm not pregnant.

Nope.

After my revelation this morning, my minor slip-up on the no-baby train, I have convinced myself I am in fact not pregnant. There is no way Hayden's athletic sperm, which I'm sure is super healthy and ready to impregnate, broke through my superior eggs. Nope, my eggs are on total lockdown.

Not only do my eggs laugh at little sperm who try to break through, but they are reinforced with steel metal and surrounded by sperm-eating acid.

You read that correctly: sperm-eating acid.

There are only a few of us who possess such defenses in our uteruses, and I am one of them. A medical marvel I must say.

And to hammer it home, I've spent the entire morning talking to my uterus, telling her that she's still a single lady and she's not eating for two.

It has helped. I've completely forgotten about forgetting to take my pills, or letting Hayden pound into me thrust after thrust with nothing separating my superior eggs from his athletic man-sperm.

Yup, not thinking about it at all.

Not one bit.

Leaning against the wall of a hospital, I squeeze my eyes shut.

I'm so pregnant.

My nipples have been tingling all morning, isn't that a sign? That has to be a sign. And my scrubs are tighter. It's not my imagination, they are tighter and yeah, I might have been eating more cake than normal, but it's because I'm pregnant.

There is life inside of me.

Shit . . .

I can't think like that. You are not pregnant, Adalyn.

Repeat after me: you are not pregnant. You are not pregnant.

"Hey there." Logan bumps my shoulder, leaning against the stark hospital wall with me, glancing at the clipboard clutched to my chest. "Holding back some secret information?"

"What?" I take in the clipboard I have a death grip on. "Uh, no, just . . . God, I don't know what I'm doing."

"Ah." Logan knowingly nods his head. "So you've heard."

So I've heard? Heard what? Oh God, can he tell I'm pregnant already?

I know, I'm in the medical field, I know how babies are conceived, it doesn't show that quickly but I'm borderline hysterical right now so my mind is not quite making any sense.

"When I saw it trending on Twitter, I immediately thought of you."

Okay, my possible pregnancy is definitely not trending on Twitter, because not enough people would care to make an idiot nurse who forgot to take birth control pills a trending topic. Although, as a society, we should continue to educate the youth about pregnancy. And I would be a prime example of what *not* to do.

Wanting to play it cool, as if I'm in the know, I say, "Oh yeah, why did you think of me immediately?"

His brow pinches together and he lifts off the wall. "Uh, because you're dating him."

For a brief second—very brief—I think that maybe my pregnancy is trending on Twitter, but I shake that thought straight from my head.

Don't be a moron, Adalyn. For Christ's sake, you're not pregnant.

"Dating Hayden." I nod, lips pressed together, still unsure what Logan could be talking about.

"From the blank look in your eyes, I'm going to assume you don't know."

Guilty.

"Yeah, I didn't check the old Twitter yet today." I've had embryos on the mind. "What's going on? Did his underwear ad go viral?"

"No . . . Adalyn, he was traded."

My eyes blink rapidly because my ears must be deceiving me. With my finger to my chin, disbelief consuming me, I say, "I don't think I heard you correctly. Did you say he was traded?"

"Shit, he didn't tell you?"

"Does this look like someone who is in the know of their boyfriend being traded?" I stare at Logan, at his deep green eyes, trying to make sense of this. Traded. Like . . . to another team?

Massaging my forehead with two fingers, I ask, "When you say traded, what exactly do you mean?"

Logan breathes out a heavy sigh and takes me to the nurses station where he sits me down in a chair. This is good, because in case I decide to pass out, the fall is shorter to the ground. No need to be a battered possibly pregnant woman with a boyfriend who has been traded. Battered makes me look pathetic.

Taking my hands in his after removing the clipboard, Logan forces me to look at him. "Addie, he's been traded to the Quakes."

"Mm-hmm, I hear ya. The Quakes. Sounds like a fun team." Swallowing hard, I ask, "By chance, do you happen to know where the Quakes are located?"

Logan pauses, his eyes softening with regret as he says, "Los Angeles."

I've seen hysterical women before, when their eyes bug out of their sockets, their hair looks wild, like they played around with the electrical socket for far too long. They bare their fangs and start hissing at everyone within a three-foot radius. I see hysterical women at least once a week, and I always wonder what it must be like to be in their shoes, to want to chuck a tongue depressor across the room and demand non-latex gloves. But I've never been in their position. I've never felt so passionate about something that I've felt the need to karate chop every throat that crosses my path.

And I'm not saying I'm hysterical, because I'm more in shock than anything, but I can feel the hysterics. I can feel the need to strap on a black belt and take innocent victims under my steely slice of a hand. If a tongue depressor were in reach right now, I would consider stabbing Logan in the ribs with it.

But I'm not there. I'm not at *that* level. I'm just itching to get there.

"Question." I prop my chin on my hand, trying to act as casual as possible. "Is this trade final?"

"It's final, Addie."

I hold up my finger. "One more question. What is the distance between Binghamton and Los Angeles?"

Pity is written all over Logan's face when he says, "It's not drivable."

Yup.

I start nodding my head, bobbing it up and down, trying to comprehend what Logan is telling me. Hayden, Captain Sexy Cock, is moving to Los Angeles, where palm trees flank the streets and snow is a mythical ice crystal that falls from the sky in far-off lands.

I, Adalyn, General Forgets Her Pills, will be staying in Binghamton, New York, which is located two miles down from Jack Frost's tundra of an armpit, with a possible demon baby that can bypass sperm-eating acid.

I'm not a mathematician, but I'm pretty sure the two don't add up.

"I'm sorry, Addie, but maybe it's for the best. Because what were you two—"

"Adalyn."

That voice. It vibrates down my spine, sending chills across my skin. Turning in my chair, I find Hayden standing at the desk, his eyes searing Logan in half from under the bill of his baseball cap.

"Can we talk . . . alone?"

"Oh, hey there . . . Hayden, is it?" I don't know why I said that. His jaw ticks, his eyes focused on Logan's hands that are holding on to mine. "I mean, of course I know it's you." I laugh awkwardly. "Didn't recognize you for a second. Hats can be deceiving. It's why so many celebrities wear them. What better way to hide yourself than under the brim of a hat. Oh, is that why you're wearing one now?" I zip my lips. "Don't worry, I won't tell anyone it's you." Clearing my throat, I say to Logan, "This is my friend, Franklin. He's from Switzerland and knows nothing about hockey."

"Adalyn," Hayden says with more force in his voice. "I need to talk to you."

I pull on my ear. "I hear ya, but I have some nurse duties to attend to." I stand and look around, looking for anything to show I'm doing my job. Logan hands me the first thing he sees, a pee cup. I hold it up to Hayden. "Urine isn't going to collect itself."

Walking toward a room on the corner, Mr. Glasco's room, Hayden jogs up to me and pulls on my arm, halting me in place.

"Adalyn, we need to talk."

"Is there a problem here?" Logan asks, eyeing Hayden's grip on my arm.

Furious, Hayden, talks from between his teeth. "This is none of your concern."

"It is because Adalyn is my friend."

"And she's my fucking girlfriend," Hayden spits back.

Shaking his head, Logan mutters under his breath, "Not for long," and walks away.

"Hey, what the fuck is your problem?" Hayden asks, pushing Logan to the side.

Oh God. Okay, pushing in hospitals should not be happening. Before Logan can retaliate, I step between the two men, putting hands on both of their chests. "Logan, go check on room sixteen's vitals." When he doesn't move, I look him in the eyes, pleading. "Go, please."

Not happy, Logan adjusts his shirt and turns toward room sixteen. One guy down, one more to go. Bringing my attention to Hayden, I muster up all the strength I can find. "You need to leave. Now."

"Just give me a few seconds."

I hold my hand up in front of his face so he sees I need him to stop. "We can talk later. I have to do my job and you're making a spectacle. I wouldn't come on the ice, interrupting one of your games, saying I need to talk to you. So I expect the same kind of respect."

His jaw moves from side to side, the veins in his neck popping with anger. He looks like he's about to explode. Seems like he hasn't had the best of days. I'm right there with him.

Letting out a heavy breath, he asks, "You're still coming over after work?"

"Yes, I'll be there." Even though I want to avoid this conversation like the plague.

"Okay." Leaning down, he places a chaste kiss on my cheek and takes off, his retreating back acting like a prelude of what's to come.

We need to talk.

I can only imagine how that conversation is going to go. *He hasn't made any true commitments to me. He hasn't spoken about what our future looks like.* He's said this is the real thing, but when it came to working out something for when he went back to Philly, that was never discussed. Why would it be? Before Monday night, we hadn't even had sex. *He hadn't been inside my body, so why discuss a future that may not have been in the cards. And now that he's moving across the country? Why bother talking at all?*

Los Angeles. New York.

How could we possibly make that work?

⌒

So this is what walking the plank feels like?

But instead of a gaggle of bloodthirsty sharks at the bottom of the plank, it's the end of a relationship I never thought I wanted. And I don't want it to end. I want all of this to go away. I want my boyfriend to stay in Binghamton. I want our bubble to remain intact. I want to walk into this house, throw my arms around Hayden and love him. *I want him to be mine.*

I don't want to have this talk.

I don't want to break his heart.

Sighing, I knock on the door of the cottage I've come to love, a sanctuary I used to hide away in after a long day of being on my feet.

It's no longer a hideaway. It will be the place where I put on a brave face, and try to make it through this conversation without breaking down at his feet.

Hayden opens the door in what seems like a panic. His hair is standing on end, his clothes disheveled, a pinch to his brow. "Fuck, I thought you weren't coming."

"There was an accident on the way over here that delayed me." There was no accident. I might have stopped off at a gas station and ate two Twix bars before coming here. I blame it on the non-existent baby in my uterus.

Not saying a word, he pulls me into his chest and wraps his arms around my shoulders. For a brief moment, I allow myself to feel this man's warmth, taking in his masculine scent, committing it to memory, allowing myself to get lost in his touch.

But only for a second.

Because my heart is already raw.

He's been traded.

Traded.

No matter how many times I say it in my head, I still can't fathom what this is going to do to us, what kind of relationship we're going to be able to maintain. I was nervous about him going back to Philly, trying to work that all out, but now that he's going to Los Angeles, that changes everything, it puts a giant chasm between what we have, what we share.

I don't want to lose him, but how can we make this work? My mind is completely blanking.

Placing my hand on his chest, I put some distance between us, stepping away, trying to gather my thoughts.

"What are you doing?" He studies me, and I'm sure he wonders why I stepped out of his embrace. Maybe because it's too much, having him that close, knowing I'm grasping for any kind of link to keep us together. Maybe because I don't want to lose the one person who's ever made me feel like I deserve more than a one-night stand. Bending at his knees to look me in the eyes, he says, "He told you, didn't he? Logan told you."

The anger in his eyes, the worry, it slays me as I take a step back. "I would have found out somehow," I answer, looking up in time to see Hayden blow out a frustrated breath and rake his hand through his hair while turning to the side. His arms flex, his fists opening and closing. "He took any opportunity to get between us. I should have fucking known." I've never seen this kind of anger in Hayden. The way he clenches his fist, like he's about to blow his hand through the wall, the strong tick in his irritated jaw, the rise and fall of his proud chest; it's startling.

"What are you talking about? Logan was being a friend. He thought I already knew and wanted to make sure I was okay."

Spinning on his heels, Hayden boils with fury, nostrils flared, and jaw clenched. "Don't be so fucking naïve, Adalyn." As if he slapped me in the face, I take another step back. I really don't like this side of Hayden. I get that he's upset and frustrated, but he doesn't need to take it out on me or Logan. "I drove as fast as I could the minute I found out I was traded. I wanted you to hear it from me, but you didn't give me the chance to fucking tell you. You sent me home."

"Because I was working." And I didn't want to have that conversation in the middle of the nurses station. Surely he can understand that.

"You've taken time away from your job for me before, and this was no different."

"This was entirely different. I wouldn't want to have this conversation at work." I swallow hard.

Raking a hand through his head, a sardonic expression clouding his eyes, he says, "What did he say to you? What did he tell you? Might as well see what the gossip is."

Taking another step back, my back hitting the wood of the front door, I say "He said what happened. I don't understand why you're being so mean to me right now."

"I'm fucking frustrated that I couldn't tell you, and I can see doubt in your eyes. You're not giving me a chance."

"Excuse me if I'm having a hard time trying to wrap my head around the news. I need a second to comprehend everything,

Hayden." Trying to come up with anything to make this situation better, I ask, "Do you have a choice in the matter?" There is a little drop of hope that maybe he can turn down the trade, even though, I know that's generally not how it works in football, but a girl can hope hockey is different.

"What do you mean?"

"Like . . . can you say no to the trade?"

Chuckling with distaste, he shakes his head. "That's not how it works. I don't get to decide things like that."

"So you're moving to Los Angeles." I say it more as a statement rather than a question, letting the words sink in, coming to terms with the giant bump in our road.

"I don't have a fucking choice," he shouts, his arms tossed in the air.

And just like that, I can see my future being laid out in front of me, bricks of despair leading the pathway.

We won't get our forever.

This man has shown me what being with a good man can truly feel like, this man has doted on me, spoiled me, made me laugh, made me . . . come. God, he's not real, he's not forever, he's temporary, and that right there is what's breaking me.

"But you have a choice," he whispers, stepping forward. "You can come with me." His voice is so soft, shaky with his request as if he's nervous to ask.

"Go with you?" We've been dating a few weeks and he wants me to fly across the country to be with him? Is he insane? I shake my head. "I don't have a choice either, Hayden. My life is here. My job is here. My friends are here. My family. I can't just pick everything up, move across the country."

"If you wanted to, you could."

"What does that mean?"

He shakes his head. "Never mind." His hands go to his waist, and he stares at the floor.

"No, what did you mean by that?"

He grips the back of his neck. "I don't know, Adalyn. Maybe

I'm a little fucking sensitive right now, but . . ." He pauses and I can see the wheels in his mind spinning. "Fuck, what about Logan?"

"What? What about him?"

"I don't know, just seemed like you two were fucking comfy at the hospital."

Is he serious?

Is he really questioning my friendship with Logan, questioning it against the way I feel when I'm with him? Is there really any kind of competition? Does he not remember our conversations about Logan? How he hurt me, how he's just a friend, and will *always* be a friend? Is he really so blinded right now he can't see how much I wish I could stay in his arms forever?

"You can't be serious right now, Hayden. I know you're upset, I get that, I'm broken over this too. But I can't pick up everything in my life and move across the country. Who's to say I would be able to find a job?"

"You wouldn't have to work. I would take care of you."

"Hayden, I went through four years of schooling hell to become a nurse, so I'm not about to give that up."

"Then that's it?" He nods, even angrier, a sarcastic laugh escaping him. "You're giving up? Just like that. Treating me like every other man you've ever fucked. Taking what you want and not bothering to give it a chance."

I suck in a harsh breath. My heart splinters in half, his words so destructive to my already fragile being. Never in a million years would I have expected Hayden to use my past against me, to throw it in my face so easily as if it's a thought he's held in his head since we've been together.

And yet, he did.

Tears well up in my eyes, my hand finds the handle to the door and I open it, needing to escape, needing to find fresh air.

And I see it, the minute he regrets the words that fell out of his mouth. Anguish hits him hard, but it's too late. His words are hanging in the air, adding to the pain already resting heavily on my chest.

"Adalyn . . ."

"No." I shake my head. "I can't." I look to the open the door, casting my head down, not able to make eye contact. "Let's call it like it is." Using his words against him, the ones he so clearly regrets now, I say, "Let's say I took what I wanted with no intention to give us a chance. Let's call it a fling and move on."

"A fling?" The word rolls off his tongue with utter disgust. Isn't that what *he* meant? Isn't that a nicer way of rearranging what he said? "Is that what this has been to you? A fling?"

No.

Not even a little.

This has been so much more than a fling. This relationship has changed me. Hayden has opened my eyes to my worth. He has shown me I deserve so much more than a one-night stand; I deserve someone who will respect me, challenge me, and make me feel beautiful inside and out.

But my truth doesn't matter right now. Because setting aside how he broke my heart with his meanness—even though I know he didn't mean what he said—what would happen if I told him this was so much more to me than a fling? What would be the point? He'd want to try to make it work. He'd move to Los Angeles, I'd stay in Binghamton, and we'd FaceTime every night. He'd never be able to visit me with all the training he'll have to start soon with the new team. I won't be able to visit, because my schedule is far too demanding. We'll get in fights because we never see each other and then the inevitable will happen: We'll break up.

So why go through the pain? Why hang on to something that is broken already? There's no point. It's better to end things now than to give each other hope.

Summing up all the courage I have, I tell one of the biggest lies of my life.

"It was just fun for me."

It hurts.

All of this hurts.

I'm broken.

Cut.

Bruised and battered, his assumption of me still swarms around in my mind.

I can't make eye contact with him. I can't possibly see the hurt I've caused him, and I can't let him see the hurt he's caused me. This is hard enough as it is. Living with that image in my mind will be too much.

Letting go of my hand, he takes a step back, his voice so full of anger I'm startled when he speaks. "Fucking look me in the eyes when you say that."

Breathe, Adalyn. One breath at a time. Push back the tears, push down your feelings.

Taking a deep breath, I lift my head. Hayden is vibrating with stormy eyes, glowering. There is an infinitesimal twitch in his jaw, and from the look of it, his fingernails are digging painfully into his palms.

"Say it," he repeats, emphasizing each word with barked precision.

Tongue-tied and on the verge of breaking down, I twist my fingers together, keeping my eyes locked on his. "This was just fun for me."

"Fuck," he bellows, turning away from me and pulling on the back of his head, his biceps pulsing under his shirt.

Oh God, this is so terrible. The world seems to move in slow motion as Hayden angrily paces the living room, and I can't breathe. With each pass of his distraught body, my heart stutters in my chest, spinning, colliding, then falling to the ground.

I can't take much more of this. It's too much. "I'm going to go."

Whipping around, Hayden heaves, looking like he's about to explode any second. "So that's it. You're just going to leave?"

"Well, you didn't expect me to stay for dinner, did you?" The words are so bitter falling from my lips.

I hate myself.

I truly and utterly hate myself.

"Fuck, I actually thought you gave a shit about me, Adalyn. But I guess I was wrong. You got what you wanted, didn't you? And now you'll leave."

"It wasn't like that," I croak out, needing to defend myself. I'm trying to leave with dignity, but I won't be dragged through the mud in the process.

"Oh, it wasn't? It seems like it. We fucked and now you're on your way. Isn't that what you did with every other man you've ever been with?"

Low blow.

Again.

But it's justified. That's the message I'm giving him.

Twisting my lips to the side, I attempt to steady the shake in my jaw, the weariness in my voice, the tears willing to fall, but I can only hold back so much. A lonely tear falls down my cheek, and I quickly wipe it away but not before Hayden sees it.

The crease in his brow lessens, the anger in his features softens. He can see it, can't he? He can see the lies in my eyes.

"Adalyn." His voice shakes, his body moving toward mine, but I step away and shake my head.

"I have to go." Stepping back towards the open door, I make an attempt to leave, but Hayden presses his hand against the door, his overbearing body eating up the space between us.

"You don't really want to go, do you?"

Another tear.

"Don't do this. Just let me go."

"I . . ." His voice deceives him. "I fucking can't." Lifting my chin, he searches my eyes, his eyes darting back and forth, looking for something, for any kind of tell. "Can we talk? Please?"

Lowering my head, I shake it. "There is no use, Hayden. There is no point in dragging on the inevitable. You're moving to Los Angeles. I'm staying here. Let's call it like it is."

"And what's that?" he grinds out.

Lifting my gaze, I hold my breath. "A summer fling I will forever remember."

Twisting his lips, his jaw shifting back and forth, he punches the door behind me before lifting away and shouting, "Fuck."

Not able to take any more, my heart crumbling into an unfixable pile, I turn my back and slip out the door. I jog to my car, and the minute the door shuts, I let out a wail of a cry and rest my head against the steering wheel. Catching my breath, I start my car and look out the window where I find Hayden standing in the frame of his front door, both hands pulling on the back of his neck, the lift of his shirt showing off a patch of tan skin on his narrow waist.

Pulling myself together, I wipe the tears from my face and put the car in reverse. All the while, Hayden keeps his eyes trained on me, never detaching, never letting go.

That was without a doubt the hardest thing I'll ever have to do.

To walk away from the man who stole my heart.

To say goodbye when all I want to do is stay.

When all I want to do is love.

CHAPTER SIXTEEN

HAYDEN

T his is the last fucking place I want to be right now.

In Philadelphia.

At a child's birthday party, holding some fucking princess tea set under my arm.

I've been home for a fucking day. One day and I'm already itching to drive right back to Binghamton, to the hospital and shake some sense into Adalyn.

How the fuck could she just leave like that?

I know I meant more to her. I could see it in her eyes. I could tell from the way she broke down in her car, so why is she turning away from me?

Why is she ignoring my calls and texts?

Because of distance? We can work that out. It's a minor detail. But the connection we had, that doesn't come along very often. Hell, I've never felt the way I feel about Adalyn for any other woman.

It might have happened fast, I might have attached quickly, but fuck, how could I not? She was so kindhearted, strong, feisty, and so incredibly genuine. She was nothing like the women I've met throughout the last year. I love her brain, her crazy wit, her vulnerable looks she'd give me when she was unsure. She seemed interested in me as a person. She could trash talk my brothers. She talked to my mom on the phone, for fuck's sake. *And seemed to enjoy it once she was off the call.* And her body? Her fire? She's a goddess. She was the whole package. She made me feel like myself with no pretense. She showed me I'm more to her than a famous hockey player. At least she did leading up to our last conversation. I still can't understand how someone can switch from mellow and content, wanting more of me, to agitated and indifferent, desperate to leave. To leave me.

Christ. I rub the outer parts of my eyes with my hand when the door opens. Someone I don't know greets me with a smile, letting me know the party is in the back. I could have guessed that from the noise spreading to the street when I pulled up.

Handing over the gift, I make my way to the back of the house where I find Calder standing at the grill, looking like a master in command.

A flash of pink catches my eye, shooting across the pavement of the pool area. Shea, Calder's daughter, is bouncing on her feet asking her dad when Uncle Hayden is going to arrive. I should be touched, warmed to the core, but I feel nothing.

But because I have to, I put on a happy face and grab Shea by the waist.

"Right now." Shea squeals loudly. "Were you worried I wasn't going to come?" I spin her around for a few turns.

"You're late."

"I know, please forgive me."

Shea ridiculously sighs. "Fine, only this time, though."

"Thank God." I smile devilishly at the little girl, one thing on my mind. I start walking toward the pool, and Shea understands her fate in seconds.

"No, no, no." She laughs, squirming in my arms.

"Oh, it's going to happen, little girl. Get ready, you're about to get wet." Like the "uncle" I am, I count to three then toss a bathing-suit-wearing Shea into the pool, who luckily, knows how to swim.

Dusting my hands off, I come face to face with Calder's grilling spatula. "You realize you started a war, right? And Rachel is ALWAYS on Shea's side. It's hell, man."

I grab a beer from the cooler next to the grill and say, "Oh please, you fucking love it."

"I do."

Speaking of Rachel, she walks up to Calder, a plate of patties in her hand, a glittering ring on her finger. I wasn't surprised when Calder told me he proposed in New York City. I'm seriously happy for them.

"Hayden, I'm so glad you could make it. Where's Adalyn? Did she have to work?"

Taking a giant gulp of my beer, I nod. "Yeah. Work."

"Ugh, that stinks. I really wanted her to meet Shea. I think they would get along so well."

There's one vital thing you need to know about Calder. When it's off-season, Calder shuts himself off from the world and he spends every waking moment with his family. He turns off his phone, leaving his landline open for emergencies, and steps away from social media and everything that has to do with hockey. The only routine he keeps is his workouts, because that's a requirement as a professional athlete.

So I'm not surprised when Calder doesn't mention my trade, or that Rachel is talking about Adalyn as if our world wasn't flipped upside down with the news of my relocation.

This is going to be hard. I thought telling Adalyn I got traded was going to be difficult, but having to let my best friend know I won't be sharing the same logo on my jersey as him . . . Fuck, I'm going to hate every second of this.

And then there was my family. My parents immediately called me, understandably upset about the news and me having to move so far away. My mom cried for far too long on the phone.

Will Calder cry? Nah, he'll be upset though.

No one expected it, a rookie with a stellar first year to be traded. It's almost unheard of, but it fucking happened. And all I can do is bend over and take it up the ass.

"Uh, hey I have to tell you two something."

"What?" Rachel brings her arms around Calder's waist, holding on to him tightly. Her face falls flat when she takes in my demeanor. "Oh no, did something happen with Adalyn? Did you two break up?"

Why are women so goddamn intuitive? There is no way I would be able to pick up on something that well. I swear, there are women out there that are mind readers, Rachel being one of them.

"Yeah, we did."

"Nooo," Rachel drags on, disappointment in her voice. "Why? You two were perfect together. I really liked her." Calder gives Rachel a squeeze, silently telling her to cool it. It doesn't work. "Did you talk to her about possibly moving to Philly? Was that it?"

I guzzle the second half of my beer and shake my head. "No, I asked her to move to Los Angeles."

"Los Angeles? Why the hell would you ask her to move there?"

Glancing at Calder, I catch the understanding in his eyes before he closes them tightly and mutters under his breath. "Shit."

"What? What's happening?" Rachel looks between the two of us.

"I've been traded, Rach." I reach into the cooler and pop open another beer.

"Traded? What the hell for?"

Running my tongue over my teeth, I say, "My agent thinks it's from the last game, my temper, and the press conference after. The owner didn't like it and traded me."

"Because of one game? That's . . . that's . . . preposterous. Oh my God, they are such morons. You were the best rookie last season, and you led the league in goals." Rachel begins to slow clap obnoxiously. "Good job, Brawlers, way to get rid of a future Hall of Famer because he was mad about losing."

If I wasn't so fucking black inside right now, I might have laughed from how outrageous Rachel is acting.

"That is so . . ." She pauses, her eyes traveling to the sky, thinking for a brief moment. "Uh . . . Calder, does this mean you can be traded?"

He shakes his head, bringing his beer to his lips. "I have a no-trade clause in my contract, so we're good, babe."

"Ugh, why didn't you have that in your contract?" Rachel asks.

"He was a rookie, Rach. It wasn't an option."

"This is such bullshit." Tell me about it. "So you're going to the Quakes? In Los Angeles? That's so far away?" A light bulb must go off in her head. "And that's why Adalyn and you broke up?"

Gulping down some more beer, I say, "That's why she broke it off with me." I swallow hard. "It's why she said what we had was just a fling."

"She said that?" Calder asks, looking genuinely surprised. Join the club, man. "Didn't seem like a fling when we were in the city."

"It wasn't." I shake my head, the beer bottle posed at my lips. "It wasn't to me."

"And it wasn't to her," Rachel adds. "There was more to it than a fling for her, so don't you believe her for one second about that."

"I don't know." I take a seat in a bar stool. "She was pretty quick to leave." Sighing, my shoulders slouched, the beer hanging between my legs now. "It doesn't matter anymore. She said she didn't want to move. I have no choice. It's over." In less than twelve hours, two important and life-changing choices were denied me. You'd think being a professional athlete some things should stay in my control. Clearly I have that all wrong, because nothing is in my control. And that *fucking sucks*.

Calder and Rachel exchange glances, pained and sullen. They don't have to say anything else. I know how much this sucks, how much I wish my life were playing out differently right now but unfortunately when your profession is at the mercy of others, there is nothing that can be done. And as much I wish Adalyn were by my side, I'm not about to give up hockey to try to make things work with a girl who seems to have given up on what we had. *Without hesitation.*

We had an epic few days together, but within twenty-four hours of being back, she was done. *Done.* Yes, there were tears, but at the first mention of the trade she made up her mind. *Was she right?* Was it inevitable? Even if I stayed in Philly? Would she have given us up even if I stayed? Had I read her completely wrong during the time we were together?

If she's not going to answer any of my messages, why bother? *Move on.* As much as I hate that term and the pain it's going to cause me, I have to do it. She doesn't want me. *Maybe she never did.*

I have to turn the page, mentally say goodbye to the girl I cherished, and start a new chapter.

～

S mog.
It's everywhere.

It's suffocating.

It's dirty and fucking depressing. It's a representation of my life. A dark cloud hanging over a bright spot.

This should be exciting for me, or so I was told by my agent. A new city, a new team, a new chance to dominate.

But I have no desire to look on the bright side, not when my finger hovers over Adalyn's number every day. Not when my mom continuously calls me to cry into the phone, not when I have absolutely zero friends here.

I've been in Los Angeles for three weeks and there is nothing I like about it.

I've met some of the guys on the Quakes, and they're cool and all, but I came from a team that was one game away from playing for the championship to a team with the worst record in the league.

Worst fucking record.

It's not like this trade was an upgrade for me. It was a kick to the goddamn balls.

Sitting in my high-rise apartment, my legs kicked up on my coffee table, I survey the smog-soaked air, going over an interview I had this morning at a local TV station. Good Morning, Malibu. The hosts, Noely and Dylan, were nice, both huge hockey fans, super excited about me being here. Hell, every Quakes fan is ecstatic, and it's nice to be welcomed so warmly. We talked about random things; Dylan seemed to want to get me to talk more to Noely but luckily, before things could get super awkward, I had to leave for another radio interview.

Could have been worse. Could have been like the interview yesterday where the girl tried to grab my crotch when I went in for a handshake.

Sighing, I unlock my phone and bring up Adalyn's contact information.

What is she doing right now? Working? Hanging out with Logan?

That fucking shithead. He couldn't have given me the chance to tell Adalyn myself? No, he had to be the turd that he is and open his mouth. Just goes to show you the kind of guy he is. *And the look on his face at the hospital.* He was gloating. Especially when he walked away prophesying Adalyn wouldn't be my girlfriend for much longer. He knew what he was doing. Clearly he knows Adalyn better than I do too, because he was spot on. Not even twelve hours later and she was gone.

And do you know what's driving me insane? How different my outcome would have been if I had been the one who told Adalyn. I don't think she would have had the chance to doubt what we have, to convince herself this was a fling.

Would we still be together? Fuck, at this point I'm going to say no. She won't answer my calls. She won't acknowledge any of my texts, not even when I told her I made it to LA safely. It's like she's completely forgotten about me.

Maybe I read her wrong. Maybe I really was a fling to her.

Fuck.

Leaning my head against the back of my sofa, I sit in silence. Alone.

So fucking alone.

Bringing my phone to my eyes, I press on Calder's name, calling it for the third time this week.

"Hey man, how's the sunshine?"

"Shitty."

"Still not feeling it?"

"I don't know, man." I drag my hand over my face. "I'm in such a fucking funk right now. Training starts next week, and if I don't show up on the ice ready to prove myself, none of the guys are going to think I'm worth the paycheck the Quakes forked out."

Yeah, the trade came with a nice pay rise, but that's meaningless to me. *How could I enjoy more money when I have no one to share it with?* I couldn't care less about the money.

"Is it Adalyn?"

"Fuck . . . it is."

"Hayden, dude, you have to let go. It's been weeks and she's said nothing to you."

"I know. I know."

"Go on a date. That morning show you were on earlier. Rachel was telling me the girl is part of this dating app called Going in Blind. Sounded like something pretty legit. Maybe you should try it."

This makes me laugh. Straight up throw my head back and laugh.

"I'm serious. You might meet someone."

"On a fucking dating app? Dude, I am so not a dating app kind of guy."

"Really? Because I could totally see you doing it. The excitement you get when you're matched, treating the girl out to a nice meal, acting like the goddamn gentleman that you are."

He has a point. But a dating app? In a city where I know no one? Not a good idea.

"Calder, I could easily get shanked. Is that what you want? For me to get shanked now that I'm your competition?"

"Why do you immediately think someone is going to try to kill you?"

"Hmm, I don't know," I say in a condescending voice. "Maybe because I'm a professional athlete, maybe because yesterday some random girl tried to grab my balls, maybe because the dating circuit is crazy and you never know who you're truly meeting. For all we know, the person could have a clean record, look absolutely normal, but in real life, she collects the heads of cats and pets them every night before she goes to bed."

There is silence on the other end of the phone before Calder says, "Wow, way to exaggerate. You took it straight to headless cats. Dude, you need to get out more. Hence the dating app."

"I'm not doing a dating app. That is one of the worst ideas you've ever had."

"Suit yourself. But I'm going to tell you right now, it would help me out."

Stretching my neck side to side, I ask, "How would it help you out?"

"Because, instead of having to sit here and have hour-long conversations with you on the phone, you could be out on a date, sweating over if she's going to shank you or not."

Chuckling, I ask, "Getting sick of these phone calls?"

"Not me. Rachel." Lowering his voice, he adds, "She now refers to you as my secret lover."

"Sounds about right. No offense, but it's either you or my mom at this point, and my mom ends up crying every time I talk to her."

"And your brothers?"

"They have their heads so far up their asses, I'm not sure they know what the hell is going on around them."

"So that leaves me."

"Yup."

Calder pauses. "I'm signing you up for that dating app."

"Fuck you, man." We both laugh. The sound is nice and sheds a little brightness on my gloomy fucking day.

CHAPTER SEVENTEEN

ADALYN

I t's not like this is life alternating or anything. *Just look.*

This will change nothing.

This won't rock my world at all.

Staring at the brown napkin covering a pregnancy test, I consider throwing it away without looking.

I've gotten this far using the denial tactic, and it's worked great for me. It seems like yesterday I was having a mighty good time in Hayden's dressing room, being absolutely irresponsible, riding the dick train against a wall. What a memorable and slutty moment for me.

Groaning, I press my hand to my forehead, stressed.

I really don't have to look at the results. I know what it's going to say. There is no doubt in my mind what that little stick is going to say and yet, here I am, still holding out hope.

There is a knock on my door. "It's been five minutes. You have to come out at some point."

Emma is standing on the other side of the door of the janitor's closet. I locked myself in, wanting some privacy while I did this at work because Emma couldn't wait any longer.

"I'm not ready to look."

"Well, I am. Let me in and I'll tell you what it says."

"Yeah, I'm not ready for that either."

Emma sighs. "Sweetie, no matter what, you're going to have to look, and you know whatever the outcome might be, I will be here for you."

"Will you be the father?"

Chuckling, she taps the door. "I'll be whatever you want me to be."

Leaning my head against the door, I reach behind me and open the door. Emma slips in and gives me a big hug.

"You know, don't you?" she asks me.

"I would be pretty ignorant to think it's negative."

"You never know. Your body might be playing tricks on you. Sometimes you feel pregnancy symptoms when you're not pregnant."

I pat her hand. "Thank you for making up crap for me to make me feel better, I appreciate it."

"Anything for you." She eyes the napkin. "Shall we?"

"Might as well."

Like the good friend she is, she slips her hand in mind, squeezes it tight, and rips the napkin away, revealing a pink and white stick. Bending at the waist, we both get close to read the results.

It's clear as day, written in black.

Pregnant.

Yup, pretty much what I thought it would say. Not because I had unprotected sex during ovulation, but because I've puked every morning this week, leaving me green for the rest of the day and running on fumes by the end of my shift.

Standing tall, Emma wraps me in a hug, her arms comforting me for a brief moment. "Don't you worry. You're not going to have to go through this alone. We will be here for you. I talked to Tucker about it last night, and if you need to stay with us, you are more than welcome. We're here for you."

"Thank you." A tear slips down my cheek. "I appreciate it, but you guys are in that lovey-dovey stage of your relationship, so the last thing you need is some pukey, pregnant woman staying with you. I'll be fine."

"Do you want me to at least go to your first appointment with you?"

I am so glad Emma is my friend. "I love you, you know I do, but you have a man and a wedding to plan. I don't want to take away from that." Taking a deep breath, I say, "Let's pretend this doesn't exist right now. You focus on the wedding. I'll focus on taking prenatal vitamins and drinking lots of water. How does that sound?"

"You can't ignore this."

"I know." I pick up the pregnancy test with the napkin and grip it tightly.

"When are you going to tell Hayden?" And there it is, the name I've been trying to avoid. After he stopped calling and texting, I thought maybe forgetting him would be easier, but it's been the opposite. It's been impossible because now, I have a growing reminder of the time I shared with him.

"I'm not," I say, opening the door and trying to casually hide the pregnancy test along my wrist, tucking it in close.

"What?" Emma comes up behind me. "You have to tell him." She pulls on my arm, forcing me to stop. "He deserves to know."

"I understand that. That's why when the baby turns eighteen, I'll pin a note on their shirt and send them to Hayden to tell him. It's much easier that way."

"Adalyn. You have to tell him."

"Tell him what?" Logan joins us, chomping down on an apple, studying the both of us.

I can feel the color drain from my face as Logan looks between Emma and me and then down at my hand.

"What's going on?"

Logan is the last person I want to know about the pregnancy. He's protective of me, maybe a little too protective *and* territorial.

If he finds out, those basic instincts are going to kick in. He's going to want to be a part of this. He's going to want to be there for me every step of the way. And that shouldn't be a bad thing, right? But Hayden hates him.

"Just talking about popsicles," Emma says, rocking on her heels, trying to play it casually.

Logan doesn't buy it.

"What's in your hand?" He nods to the pregnancy test, his eyes narrowing.

"Highlighter, a pink one. I like to highlight things."

Once again, smarter than I'm making him out to be, he grips my arm and brings it to his eyes. His face morphs into shock and then turns hard. "Are you pregnant?"

"Umm . . ."

"Adalyn, are you fucking pregnant?"

"Maybe." I try to smile but I'm sure I look more like I'm in pain than trying to pass this whole thing off as no big deal.

Dropping my hand, his gaze bounces back from Emma to me, trying to comprehend what's going on. "It's Hayden's, isn't it?"

"We don't have to go into details." I wave him off. "This is no big deal. Just have a human growing inside of me. I really think we should treat this as any other normal day. Don't you have some rounds to make? Emma, I know you have to get back to your floor."

Logan has other plans. Discarding his apple in a trash can behind him, he grabs both our hands, leads us back into the janitor's closet and turns on the light above us, turning the small space into an interrogation room.

"How the hell did you get pregnant? Aren't you on birth control?"

"About that." I twist my foot on the ground, trying to avoid all eye contact. "I might have been a little forgetful."

"Jesus Christ." Logan runs his hands through his hair. Why the hell is he so distraught over this? It's not like he's the one who impregnated me.

"You don't have to be so upset." I awkwardly pat him on the shoulder.

"Not be upset?" His brows shoot up to his hairline. "Adalyn, you're one of my best friends and you're pregnant with a man's baby who now lives across the country. Believe it or not, you're going to be doing this on your own, as much as you like to pretend that's not the case."

And reality hits me square in the chest thanks to Logan.

"You have to tell him," Emma chimes in.

"Why?" Logan asks, looking peeved.

"Because it's his child. He deserves to know."

"But he took off. What's he going to do, send her texts, asking how she's feeling?" Pausing, Logan asks, "How are you feeling?"

Needing some support, I lean against the door of the closet. "Not well. I've been so sick."

"This is exactly what I'm talking about." Logan's fist clenches at his side. Man, his anger goes from zero to sixty quickly. I don't think I've ever seen him so upset, so . . . mad. "He's not here, and you're doing this all on your own."

"She still needs to tell him." Emma, the morally correct between all of us. She's always been like that. Do the right thing; it's her motto. It's why she's so sweet and hard to be mad at, especially when she harps on things like this.

"He doesn't need to know," I finally say.

"Good," Logan says while Emma says, "What?" at the same time.

"This is just going to mess up his life. He already went through a big change, and he doesn't need this."

"This is messing up your life too," Emma points out. "Why are you not putting this on him as well?"

Feeling my chest start to constrict, my eyes prickling with tears, I put my head in my hands. "I can't see him again." Tears start to fall, and my throat grows tight. "And Logan is right. What can he really do? His schedule is beyond crazy, and he won't be here for me like I need him. And I hate to admit it, but his publicist was right. Hayden needs to focus on him, on his new team, on making the best of his career. This is going to throw off his game." *This is going to change my whole life.*

"You're being absurd," Emma says, growing angry. Emma is normally slow to anger, so the fact that she's so upset about this shows how much she cares. She's the ultimate caregiver but can't see how keeping Hayden out of the equation for me is the only way I'll cope at the moment. She's possibly right, but I'm still too raw. I had Hayden for what feels like five minutes, and then he was gone. It hurts. I hurt.

"This is not on you. You should not have to take responsibility for all of this. He was the one who didn't wear a condom, so he was just as reckless. It's equal responsibility. You know I love you, Adalyn, but you're really making me mad."

"I'm making you mad?"

"Yes." She steps in front of me. "There are so many women who take the blame for getting pregnant when that's not the case. You were both there when it happened, both irresponsible. He deserves to know so he can be as supportive as possible. Even if it's from a distance." Giving me a cold hug, she opens the door and adds, "You know I'm here for you, but you need to not be stupid about this. You're single, you live alone, and you have a grueling work schedule. You can't do this on your own, as much as you think you can. He deserves to know his responsibilities need to include you and his child. And he's the sort of man, from what I know, who would not run from that. Not only that, going at it alone will make it that much tougher on you." With a sad smile, she leaves me alone in the closet with Logan.

"She's right." Logan crosses his arms over his chest, his scrubs pulling tight around his arms and chest. "You can't do this alone."

"I don't know how I can tell him, Logan. Emma is right, he'll want to drop everything to help me, and I can't do that to him."

Lips thin, pressed tightly together, Logan shakes his head. "You don't have to tell him, but you are going to need help. How often have you been sick this week?"

Sighing, I close my eyes, my head resting against the door. "Every morning, sometimes at lunch, and the occasional nighttime nausea."

"Christ. Okay." He pulls on my hand, bringing me into his chest where he wraps me up in a tight embrace. It's comforting being supported by a strong body, and it's times like these that I wish I was attracted to Logan. *Because he is here.* "We need to make you an appointment to see a doctor and then we will go from there."

"We?"

He nods against my head. "Yes, we. You will not be doing this alone. I'm going to be there every step of the way."

"Logan, that isn't—"

"Try to stop me, Adalyn. Try to fucking stop me."

~

Thank God Logan is here, because with every second that passes with my legs in these stirrups, my anxiety heightens and the need to cry consumes me.

He sits at my head and calmly strokes my forehead with one hand while the other holds my hand. "It's going to be okay. We've been through this during college. They're just going to do an internal ultrasound, make sure everything is okay, and then let us know about the blood work."

"I know." I take a deep breath, despite my breaths feeling shallow. "I'm just nervous. I haven't told anyone but you and Emma and lying here, it makes it so much more real. What will my family say? The boys will want to kill Hayden."

"We will deal with them together. As for now, let's focus on the appointment and keeping hydrated." He hands me my water bottle but I don't take a sip. "Come on, Addie, please have a little."

I shake my head. "I'll throw it up. I'm feeling way too anxious right now, and my stomach is rolling."

There is a knock on the other end of the door and Dr. Rose

Dallas comes through the door, holding my chart. "Adalyn, how are you?"

"Pregnant," I sigh.

She chuckles. "I can see that." She looks over at Logan and asks, "I always thought you two had chemistry."

"Oh, he's not the father," I quickly say, not wanting any gossip to spread around the hospital. "Logan is being a really good friend."

"My apologies. Was the father not available?"

"You could say that." I swallow hard, my mind going to what Hayden must be doing right now. Hanging out by the ocean, getting a great tan, watching bikini-clad women prance around in front of him. And here I am, about to be probed by a lubed-up stick.

Men have it so easy.

"Okay, well I'm glad Logan is with us today. It says you've had severe morning sickness over the last week and a half."

"Yes, it's been at least twice a day, sometimes three," Logan answers for me, taking charge. "She hasn't been able to keep food down, and hydrating has been a chore." Smiling, Dr. Dallas gives Logan a once-over and then turns back to me.

"You have to make sure you're drinking fluids, Adalyn. You know better than that."

"I know." I shut my eyes, calming my racing heart. "I'm going through a lot, and I think my anxiety is making me more nauseated than I need to be."

"That can be a big factor in having hyperemesis gravidarum, extreme morning sickness. It's also more common in first pregnancies."

"How long do you think it's going to last?"

"Unfortunately, there is no timeline for hyperemesis gravidarum. Women see a drop in nausea around week twenty, but there are the lucky women who continue to deal with morning sickness their entire pregnancy."

"Bet I'll be one of those lucky women," I say sarcastically.

"It's a possibility, especially if you can continue to stress your body with worry."

"And what about her nursing schedule. Should she cut hours?"

"What?" I snap my head toward Logan. "I can't cut down on hours. Are you insane? I have student loans to pay off and a child on the way."

"But you're working twelve-hour shifts, Adalyn. You're not taking care of your body like you should and you're extremely lethargic."

"I'm going through a lot, okay? It will get better."

Cutting in, Dr. Dallas asks, "Are you working seven to seven?" I nod. "It's the best shift at the hospital. Just make sure you're taking breaks, drinking as much electrolyte-replacement fluids as you can, peeing clear, and eating protein. Saltines when you're feeling sick, but replenish with lots of protein."

She goes over a few more things while getting the ultrasound ready. Suggesting I start taking more B6 vitamins and offering some holistic oils to help calm my anxiety, warning me if I don't start taking care of my body, I could end up in the hospital as a patient rather than a nurse.

That's the last thing I need.

Dr. Dallas inserts the wand, and my eyes shut as she shifts it around. Here I am pregnant, legs spread, an ultrasound tool lodged up my vagina, and the father is across the country without a care. I never expected a moment like this in my twenties, but here I am.

"Ah, look, there is it."

Turning to the side, the screen lights up with white waves surrounded by black. Right in the middle is a tiny circle that looks more like a lima bean than anything.

"From the looks of it, you're almost six weeks along."

Sounds about right.

Logan squeezes my hand as I stare at the screen. Dr. Dallas is taking measurements and printing pictures, but the entire time, my mind is whirling with what I created. What Hayden and I created.

That tiny blip, that little baby is going to be born into a crazy, chaotic world. A mother completely freaked out, not knowing what the future will hold, and an oblivious father losing nothing. Life will simply go on for him, and *I* will eventually become a tiny blip on *his* radar. And I know that's on me, but right now, I feel resentful and sad.

A tear slips down my cheek.

This baby deserves so much more.

CHAPTER EIGHTEEN

HAYDEN

I can't believe I'm doing this.

I stand outside the restaurant, looking up at the neon sign. Going in Blind.

Christ. This was a stupid idea, but when Calder told me he made me a profile a few weeks ago on the dating app, I didn't really have an option.

I was matched with a few profiles but didn't jump on them. I wasn't interested. But after a few more weeks of feeling so damn alone, I decided to give it a try, if anything to at least not spend another night alone in my apartment watching Jane the Virgin on Netflix, which if I have to be honest is a good fucking show.

But I'm regretting it now. As much as I like to think I'm over Adalyn, I'm not.

I'm so not fucking over her. *I don't want to be over Adalyn. I want her to be mine.* I think of her every goddamn day. I wonder what she's doing. I wonder if I should send her flowers or lunch at work. I consider punching a wall every time I think about Logan being around her. Fucking happy as ever. When I'm clearheaded, I know that Adalyn didn't dump me because she has feelings for Logan.

But fuck if it doesn't sting that he gets to see her every day, and right now, I'd settle for that. So, instead, I'll focus on hating the bastard.

Taking a deep breath, I close my eyes and tilt them to the sky. You can do this, Hayden. The profile suggests the girl was nice, she declared her love for Tom Hanks, which tells me she's a classy lady. She could have said Zac Efron or Ryan Reynolds or some other Hollywood heartthrob, but she went classic with Tom Hanks. Leads me to believe she's not going to be someone chasing after hockey players for one thing . . . the celebrity chaser.

Making my way through the doors, a beautiful African American woman at the hostess desk greets me. Her hair is pulled back, black eyelashes flutter, and a warm smile tugs on her lips.

"Welcome to Going in Blind. How can I help you?"

"Uh, yeah." Hands stuffed in my pockets, I take in the ambiance of the restaurant. Fun and intimate with its modern aesthetics and exposed white brick walls, but the mood lighting creates a romantic feel. "I have a date with ShopGirl."

"Ah yes, she's waiting for you at the bar. She's the blonde in the black turtleneck. Shall I show you to her?"

"Nah, that's okay. I got it. Thank you, though." I tap the desk and head over to the bar after the hostess tells me where we'll be sitting for the evening. My date seems to be looking a little . . . loose. Her hand grips tightly onto a small tumbler, which she then tilts back, her head craning to accommodate the dump of liquid down her throat.

This should be fun . . .

"ShopGirl?"

The blonde spins around in her chair, her movements erratic and very . . . wobbly.

"IceBiscuit?"

When making a profile you had to choose a username. Can you tell Calder made mine?

Hmm, taking her in, I can't help but think . . . I know this girl. We've met before. Where have we met—

It hits me.

Noely Clark, the morning show host whose friend tried to hook us up. What are the odds?

"Pecs," she mutters under her breath, her eyes glossy, taking in my chest, trying to peer through my shirt as if she has X-ray vision.

Before I can ask her if she's okay, her hand falls to my chest where she starts playing with the fabric of my shirt. Her face bright red, most likely a side effect of the alcohol she's already consumed, she takes me in, observing my jeans, the black button-up shirt she's playing with, to my face where she tilts her head to the side.

Realization hits her slower than let's say someone who wasn't chugging back what smells like a bottle of whiskey.

Shaking her hand away, as if my chest was on fire, she stands from her chair and with all the grace of a bottle of vodka, she stumbles forward falling to her knees right in front of me.

Popping up quickly, like a gymnast, she throws her arms in the air and bows to her left and right while saying, "Nine point five, not a perfect ten, but I'll get there." Laughing nervously, she rights her shirt, and lowers her arms. "They don't score like that anymore, but who's really going to say fourteen-point-two-six-seven? I mean, especially when the viewers don't know the degree of difficulty. You know? Gymnastics, am I right?"

Fuck, I feel awkward for her, but I have to appreciate her ability to try to recover. "Uh, are you okay?"

"Yep, fit as a fiddle." She motions with a low fist pump across her body.

"Good." Scanning the restaurant, I say, "Never thought I'd run into you here. Are you ShopGirl?"

"I am but you can call me, Noely. Noely Clark." Awkwardly she grabs my hand from my hip and shakes it. "Nice to meet you."

Puzzled, I laugh. "I remember who you are, Noely."

"Oh yeah, of course." Her face seems an even brighter shade of red now. A part of me thinks she would be humiliated if she saw how embarrassed she looks, and that's why I don't mention it.

"This is weird. I, uh, I didn't think I'd be matched with you, so I'm feeling nervous and intimidated. Because, you know, you're all hot and whatnot with your hockey body and strong thighs and nice hair. And I'm sure if you turned around right now, I would see your high, tight ass." Her hands cup together as she pretends to squeeze an imaginary butt. Oh hell.

"Thanks." I eye the bar behind her. "Started early on the drinks?"

"Maybe. Third blind date and rough day equals more drinks for me."

That explains it. Should I suggest we do this another night? Or maybe never? It's not that I don't like Noely or find her attractive. She's beautiful, but I kind of feel like I'm cheating on Adalyn, which is ridiculous. It just feels weird.

Although, Noely confessed to this being her third date and having a bad day, I can only imagine how much she would drink if I told her we should go home. From the thin thread of sanity she's hanging on to, I'm going to assume that isn't a good idea.

"Got ya. Should we get some food in you so you don't pass out onto your dinner?" Food will help . . . hopefully.

"Good idea." Oddly, she bops my nose in agreement. Don't know what to do with that. I'm going to blame it on the booze.

"Veronica said we have the table in the back." I guide her wobbly legs past the other patrons in the restaurant, her eyes fixed on a man in a suit having dinner with a woman who's chest is practically resting on the table exposed for everyone in the restaurant.

Talk about obnoxious tits. Damn, not my cup of tea.

When we reach our table, I help Noely into her seat and then take mine across from her. We're off to the side, which provides some privacy, and I'm sure it's going to be necessary with the amount of alcohol Noely has already consumed. If she ends up passing out on her plate, at least we won't be in the middle of the restaurant, making a spectacle.

"What are the odds we were set up with each other?" I ask, folding my napkin over my lap.

"Great ones." In an attempt to look like a seductress, she licks the outer rim of her lips and fingers the rim of her water glass.

Yikes.

Trying not to embarrass her, I hide the laugh that pops out of me with a cough, covering my mouth with my arm. Oh Christ.

Is that her sexy face?

Is this her way of showing men she's interested?

I'm going to guess no. She was entirely more put together than this during our first conversation.

"Eh, these words look all jumbled to me." Probably because the menu is an inch away from her face. "I've had the lobster and the steak on my other dates. What's left?"

Not having a chance to really look at the menu, I stumble for a few seconds but then say, "Uh, the butternut squash gnocchi with brown butter sauce."

"Sign me up." She taps the table and leans back in her chair, hands behind her head, her chair wobbling a little too far back for a second before she catches herself and awkwardly smiles with her eyes wide.

The girl is completely twisted. "How many drinks did you have, Noely?"

Leaning forward in her chair, she shout whispers, "Is my booze showing?"

"Just a little." I hold up my fingers, showing her just "how little."

With her hand blocking her mouth from the rest of the dining room, she says, "At least it isn't my nipple that's showing."

Okay, well that's a positive way of looking at things. Yes, I guess it could be worse if in fact her nipple was showing. Finding humor in her drunk antics, I take a deep breath and allow myself to laugh. Maybe this is just what I need, a little laughter in my life.

"Hey, you've definitely got that going for you."

She lifts her drink and says, "To not showing nipples."

I can toast to that. "To not showing nipples."

I've been on my fair share of dates. Not that I'm a manwhore, but I like to think I've shared a meal with a variety of women. The girls who don't eat anything, the ones who like to pick at salads, the ones who spend so much time talking they forget to eat entirely, and then there are the women who like to pick off your plate, thinking it's okay to share food on the first date. It's not. At least not with me. Let's get to know each other a little before we're cutting into each other's steak.

But with Noely, I'm adding a whole new kind of woman to my dating portfolio.

Sitting across from me, napkin stuffed in her turtleneck, is my very . . . aggressive eating date. It almost looks likes she was recently rescued from a desert island and the minute the waiter put her pasta dish in front of her, she went to town, straight up using her fork as a shovel. I wouldn't be surprised if she tips back her plate into her mouth like she did with her drink earlier at the bar.

"God, I'm ravenous. This is so good, don't you think?" She's hovering over her plate, forking bite after bite in her mouth, talking with a full mouth.

I've never seen such a thing.

"Uh, haven't had a chance to take a bite."

I have a forkful halfway to my mouth when she reaches across the table and lifts the fork to my mouth while saying, "Eat, eat. Enjoy."

Wanting to see if the gnocchi is really good or if the alcohol has taken over her taste buds as well, I take a bite, letting the brown butter sauce set on my tongue. Fuck, this is a ton of calories, but hell, call it eating my sorrows. I'll work it off tomorrow.

"That is good."

"Best dinner option I've had since I've been here. I mean, the steak was melt-in-your-mouth steak. The lobster with mashed potatoes? Boy, were those smooth on the tongue. But this gnocchi, talk about a myriad of flavors."

"It's pretty damn good." I chuckle. Eyeing her from over the table, I say, "So you keep saying this is your third time here. Am I really your third blind date?"

She points her fork at me and nods, eyes squinting. "You are. You're the third guy I needed for my tripod of dating. Do you feel special?"

Not really. I feel like I'm on a date that's trying to tell me something. Like maybe I shouldn't be dating yet. Then again, I've had more fun tonight than I have in a while, so maybe I should feel special.

Plopping more gnocchi in my mouth, I answer, "I do feel lucky. From the looks of it, I get to experience the looser side of you."

"Eh, eh, eh." She boldly waves her finger at me. "You're not getting in my pants, so don't even think about it. I didn't shave my legs, so not going to happen, fella."

Oh fuck.

I snort cough and take a sip of my water, trying to hold back the bout of laughter eager for release. "Didn't mean loose as in, sexually loose. Just, you know, personality loose."

"Oh." Eyes to the ceiling, she ponders my answer. "Misread that one, didn't I?"

"Just a little."

"Are you going to tell your hockey buddies you went on a date with Noely Clark from Good Morning, Malibu, and she told you she didn't shave her legs?"

"First thing tomorrow morning." I smile. Even though my hockey buddies consist of Calder and Calder alone right now. "So what happened with the first two dates?"

"Are you asking me to provide a postpartum on my first two blind dates?" Anything to help me forget at this point.

"I mean . . . not really. Was wondering what went wrong. Did you not shave your legs for those dates as well?" I tease her, liking how she can easily take it.

"I shaved and wore a dress. Both times." As if to throw it in my face, she crosses her arms over her chest.

"You wore a dress?" My eyes grow wide. "And you wore a turtleneck for me? That's some messed-up shit, Noely."

Laughing, a little too loudly—thank you, whiskey—she says, "With a statement necklace. I didn't wear a statement necklace on my other dates, so frankly, you're the real winner." She showcases her necklace with her fingers, touching the gems carefully, like she's on QVC trying to make a sale.

"Am I?" I cock my head to the side. "I get turtleneck with unshaved legs and the other guys get dresses with no sight of hairy Mary anywhere?"

"Hey." She leans forward and whisper-shouts. "Don't make me pull my pant leg up right now. It's a light stubble. A stubble!"

"Keep the pant legs down there, lady. No need to disgust people in the middle of their dinners."

Lips pursed, she says, "You're a freaking smartass, you know that?"

"Well aware." And for a second, I'm starting to feel like myself again. "So tell me about the dates. You shaved your legs and wore dresses, so that wasn't the problem. What happened? Fart by accident?"

Her mouth drops open in shock, her eyes wide. "I will have you know, all flatulence was held in, thank you very much. It wasn't anything like that. The first dates actually went really well, like, super well. It was the dates after that kind of fell apart."

"Give me examples. I want to make sure I don't screw anything up this go around."

Not that I'm looking to start anything with Noely, but you never know. She might be fun to hang around with, a good friend I can possibly rely on. My first friend out here.

"Well, the first guy, man, was he . . ." She pauses and glances toward the table she was looking at earlier, her face softening, her eyes yearning. Hmm . . . does she still have feelings for Mr. Suit over there? Pointing behind her hand, she motions to the suit and boobs. "Right over there, the guy with the girl whose boobs are swallowing her neck whole, that was my first date."

Conspiratorially leaning forward, I follow her finger even though I know exactly who she's talking about. It's hard to miss the boobs. The girl has nothing on Noely. She looks far too fake, whereas Noely has that all-American girl feel: gorgeous, funny, and personable.

Then again, Noely has nothing on Adalyn.

"He seems like a nice guy. I mean, his eyes are trained on that girl's face rather than the blatant display of cleavage. There's something to be said about that." Which is true. Any pervert would be spending his night eyes deep in her cleavage, but this guy has the respect to keep his eyes trained forward, listening intently to the woman. Date number one can't be that bad.

"Maybe he's scared of her boobs; maybe he's afraid they're going to pop out any minute and eat him alive."

"Possibly, but from his stand-offish body language, I think he's prepared to defend himself from an attack from man-eating tits." I smile, drawing the attention of Noely's eyes, her tongue wetting her lips while she concentrates on my mouth.

Oh boy.

Straightening, she says, "Well, he has issues with privacy. I accidentally said his name on TV, his first name, mind you, and he broke a gasket. Lost his damn mind. Paraded around kicking trash-cans and plucking weeds from the side of the street only to toss them in my general direction." Doubtful, but I like her drunken and exaggerated stories. "The rage on that one. He was sweet at first. Boy ooo-ee, talk about LOSING.YOUR.SHIT." She rolls her eyes. "Such a shame, you know?" She motions to her body, really emphasizing her turtleneck. "He could have had all of this."

"Statement necklace and all."

She wiggles her eyebrows. "It's growing on you now, isn't it? Aren't you glad I wore the turtleneck?"

"Couldn't be more pleased. What's cleavage when you can stare at a statement necklace all night?"

Affirmed, she slaps the table. "That's what I'm talking about."

Drawing attention from the other diners from her loud proclamation, she catches the suit staring at her and twiddles her fingers at him . . . obnoxiously. "Ahoy, Jackie Boy."

I watch the exchange. The suit doesn't look pleased with Noely's antics but not in an annoyed way. He's . . . angry, like he can't believe she's on a date with someone else.

Jealousy.

That's what it is. It's evident in the way his jaw clenches tightly together and how his brow is knitted together, or from the death glare he's giving me.

Despite Noely's attempt to say hi, he doesn't say anything, but instead turns away, back to his date.

"Well," she huffs.

"That was rude," I finish for her.

"You're telling me." She leans her chin into her propped-up palm. "God, technology has really desensitized us. If I sent him a text message with a waving emoji, I bet he would reply with a smiley face."

"He doesn't seem like a smiley face guy." Not even in the slightest. The dude has some serious alpha-male tendencies going on.

"Yeah, he doesn't, does he?"

"More like"—I rub a hand across my chin—"a dress shoe. That's what he would send. Two dress shoes because three is preposterous and one is inexcusable." I think Noely's crazy is rubbing off on me.

"God, you're so right. He would send me a freaking dress shoe as a hello. And here I am, sending him the cha-cha girl in her red dress freaking ole-ing around his ass and he sends me a dress shoe."

Fuck, she's funny.

"Men." I roll my eyes and take a sip of my water. "Not me though, I wouldn't send you a dress shoe."

"No? What would you send me? Wait." She holds up her hand. "Let me guess." She taps her chin with her finger, probably mentally scrolling through the many emoji options. "Hmm . . .

well, not knowing you all too well, I'm thinking you'd send me the dragon and cucumber."

"What?" Where the hell did she come up with that? A question follows my laughter. "Dragon and cucumber? Where did you even come up with those?"

She flits her hand in the air. "They just came to me. I'm right, aren't I? You would totally send me the dragon and cucumber emojis."

"What does that even mean if I sent those to you?" Cucumber could be something sexual, but dragon? Is it supposed to mean fire-spitting penis? Fuck, I sure as hell hope not.

She shrugs. "Some hockey code I would figure out two months from now and then laugh my ass off."

Maybe it is fire-spitting penis. Maybe some kind of code for a venereal infection. Yeah, I would so not send her the cucumber and dragon emojis.

Wanting to make it clear, in case she knows some kind of hidden meaning, I say, "There is no dragon and cucumber hockey code, I can promise you that."

"Okay, then what would you send me?"

"I feel a little inferior after the dragon and cucumber mention, but I would send you the wilting rose." Just off the top of my head.

"Wow." She sits back in her chair, arms crossed over her chest. "Well, that's freaking depressing. Uh, thanks for my wilting flower."

"And then I would follow it up with a candle, a clock, and a baguette." See if she can get this. I will be impressed if she did, also slightly disappointed if she doesn't. To any fan, it would be a slam dunk.

"Eh?" I can see her little drunken mind trying to figure what those emojis mean. It's cute.

"Guess you're not one to communicate in emojis, because any pro would know I'm trying to say Beauty and the Beast, meaning, *hey come on over and snuggle with me while we watch the movie*." I shake my head. "I thought you were better than that, Noely."

Shocked and disappointed, she hangs her head in shame. "Well, I hate myself now. Of course, baguette." Shaking her fist to the air, she shouts, "Baguette!"

A snort pops out of me. This is the most interesting date I've ever been on, and even though I didn't want to come—and I'm still hung up on someone else—in the end, this might have been the best decision I've made since I've moved here. Because for once in quite some time, I have a smile on my face. I've laughed even. Despite the smog, maybe I'm beginning to lift my eyes to see through it.

CHAPTER NINETEEN

ADALYN

"Adalyn, are you in here?"

I rest my head against the cold porcelain of the third stall toilet in the employees' bathroom. There has to be millions of germs permeating my skin at the very moment, but I don't care. It feels good.

The toilet feels good.

Never thought I would ever say such a thing, but this toilet, the one I'm bear-hugging right now, it's my best friend. It's cooling my clammy skin, making me believe there really are miracles out there, because this toilet is a miracle to me. Plucked from the porcelain factory, brought to this hospital, and installed just for me.

"Adalyn?"

"Errrrrrr," I groan, my eye partially open, pressed against the white surface, my face smeared across what I'm hoping is NOT a pee-coated surface.

Soft steps sound along the grey-tiled floor, stopping in front of my stall that I left unlocked because when you're about to throw up, you don't have time for pleasantries such as locking your bathroom stall door.

"Oh Addie." Emma pushes the door open. "What was it this time?"

Swallowing hard, my stomach rolling again, I say, "Mr. Martinez. He had me lotion his ankles. The scaly skin was just . . ." My stomach constricts and before I know it, my head is buried in the toilet again, the last of my saltines from lunch exiting my body.

Whoever said pregnancy is rewarding and a beautiful experience is a freaking con artist and should take the fast pass lane to go fuck yourself.

Hovering over me, Emma soothingly rubs my back, not needing to hold my hair, because I've learned by now that a tight bun at work while pregnant is my savior.

"I shouldn't have asked, I'm sorry."

Breathing in lovely toilet water, I spit and say, "No, I knew there was another one coming. I'm glad I got it out." Rolling to my side so my back is against my new best friend, I lean my head against the toilet seat. "I hate life right now."

Emma squats down next to me, taking a seat. "I know. I wish there was more we could do. You still don't want to take those anti-nausea pills Dr. Dallas suggested?"

I shake my head. "No. I really don't want to take any medication. I'm going to get over this, just have to get to that twenty-week mark."

"That's eleven more weeks to go."

"Eleven weeks is nothing. These last nine have seemed like a blur, they went by so quickly." Seeing as though for the first two weeks after my last missed period, I was blissfully ignorant that I would get pregnant.

Lies, all of it lies. Time stood still the minute Hayden left for California. Honestly, I don't know what day of the week it is anymore. But I don't want to take drugs.

"Don't be stubborn." Emma pushes a stray hair out of my face.

"You can't keep running to the bathroom every time you have to lotion someone's ankles."

"It's not just applying lotion to ankles."

"You know what I mean."

"I know." I sigh. "It will get better. We just have to make it through these next couple of weeks." Lifting my head, I ask, "Can you help me up?"

"You have toilet all over you."

"And that's an issue because . . ." I pause and get real with Emma. "You wipe asses at least once a week for total strangers. Pretty sure a little toilet face isn't going to harm you."

Rolling her eyes, she straightens and helps me to my feet. "Let's get you washed up."

We spend the next few minutes trying to disinfect my face and arms and brushing my teeth. I was smart. After the first day of throwing up at work, I brought in a toothbrush and toothpaste with me and keep it in my locker.

I splash one more round of water on may face and dry off. I've looked better, but at least I'm not as ghostly white as I was this morning. There is a small amount of color in my cheeks, making me look a little more human.

"Here. It's not water, but it should help." Emma hands me a ginger ale. "Drink up. Want me to get you some Powerade?"

I scrunch my nose up then take a big swig. "That stuff is way too sugary for me. Last night I was throwing up neon orange."

"Okay, I can score you some Pedialyte if you would want."

"Yes, that would be amazing. The clear kind. I'll suck it down quickly."

"Not a problem. I can grab some. Why don't you sit on the couch for now and take a second to gather yourself."

We both make our way to the common sitting area in the employees' lounge. There are a few doctors watching ESPN, drinking sodas and dabbling in some free pizza that was brought to the lounge. I consider eating a piece, but think better of it. Pretty sure the demon inside me will reject the pizza just like everything else I try to eat.

The only things that don't make me throw up right now are saltines, bland chicken, and applesauce. God, I love applesauce, the unsweetened kind. I have so many jars of it in my house right now, that you would think I had stock in the company.

"I'll be right—"

"Hayden Holmes is looking smooth as ever on the ice this pre-season, showing no signs of a bump in the road during his transition." One of the doctors turns the volume up on the TV as everything else around me fades away.

"I can't believe the Brawlers traded him," one of the doctors says, leaning forward in his seat.

"Rumor is because he lost his cool at the press conference after their loss at the end of the season."

"If that's true, the Brawlers are the most idiotic organization in the hockey."

On the TV ESPN plays a short montage of highlight clips. I've never seen Hayden play hockey, because I've never paid attention to the sport, but seeing him now, floating effortlessly along the ice, the determination in his eyes, the way he handles his stick with such precision, taking shot after shot at the goalie, it's impressive and incredibly sexy.

Emma tugs on my hand but my attention is glued to the TV, and when Hayden comes onto the screen, I freeze. Hair wet from his helmet, his shoulders looking impossibly large from his shoulder pads, he smiles boyishly at the interviewer and laughs from a question I didn't quite catch, my attention entirely focused on the man who stole my heart.

Looking toward the ground, his straight white teeth showing, hand gripping on the back of his head, his deep voice comes to life in the small staff lounge. "They've been amazing. The Quakes organization has really opened their arms to me and made me feel welcome." When Hayden looks at the camera, there is a smile on his face, but his eyes . . . they aren't happy.

Empty, soulless. Not the same eyes that greeted me when I first met him, or the eyes that stared at me while pulsing inside me.

"And how is Los Angeles treating you?"

"Love it." Hayden grips the collar of his shoulder pads as he speaks. "It's a huge change from Philly, but I've enjoyed soaking in the atmosphere of California. I very well might be in love."

In love.

The words vibrate through my body. *He's in love.*

Because I'm selfish and wish I were still very much involved in Hayden's life, I shamelessly hoped he was miserable in California, that despite not having a choice, he still wished he was in Binghamton with me. And for a small glimpse of hope, I thought maybe that was the case with his empty smile, but now . . .

He's laughing, joking, LOVING the state, the team that took him away from me. It's a hard pill to swallow. Incredibly hard.

"Hey, are you okay?"

My stomach rolls, my inability to swallow my saliva fast enough startles me. I'm going to lose it. Running to the bathroom, I throw open the first stall and dry-heave into the toilet, nothing left inside of me to rid.

Silently, tears fall from my eyes as my stomach convulses over and over again.

Why can't he be miserable? How is it fair that his life simply moves on and he's *in love*? I saw what I wanted to see—unhappy eyes. I was wrong. Oblivious Father: 1. Freaked-out Mother: 0

How I wish he were as miserable as I am.

Wrapped up in my robe, tucked under fluffy blankets, with a water next to me and a saltine in my hand, I open my computer. From a few feet away, a mint and eucalyptus candle burns, filling the air with a soothing smell that has eased the tension in my stomach. When I was at Bath & Body Works today, I bought six of the same candles, because it's the one thing that's been able to soothe me. Now if only I can find a way to burn one while I'm at work. If they came as those tree air fresheners, I would wear ten around my neck.

Netflix is calling me. My brother Sean was telling me about a show his wife is "making" him watch, *Grace and Frankie*. He said it's really funny and I should give it a try. Needing a laugh, I decide to take his suggestion.

At least that's what I told myself.

Lips pursed to the side, fingers hovering over my keyboard, I pause in my attempt to watch something funny, my mind deceiving me.

Type it in; go ahead. Netflix. N-E-T . . .

But my fingers don't listen, instead, they type out something entirely different.

I focus on the screen in front of me and squeeze my eyes shut.

Hayden Holmes press conference.

Don't press enter. Don't you dare do it. You don't need to watch his press conference that supposedly got him traded. This will do nothing to help your situation. There is no good in watching it.

Enter.

Oh my finger, what a defiant bitch.

Okay, no need to actually watch the video, despite the multiple links that pop up.

Oh look, there he is, headlines claiming Hayden as angry, a poor sport, and loses his temper. That's not who he is.

Why am I defending him?

Maybe he is an angry tyrant, and I have no clue. I mean, we were only together for a little over a month. That's not enough time to show your true colors . . .

Although, he did just lose the game that would have put them in the championships. If I were one step away from the biggest trophy in my sport, I'm pretty sure I wouldn't be a smooth-talking fella either.

But what did he say?

My finger hovers over the first link. This is stupid, and you're just going to regret it in the end. This is a toxic tendency, watching videos of people who are no longer in your life just for the hell of it.

All this is going to do is upset you. Now go on, go watch Netflix.

My finger clicks on the top link.

Son of a bitch.

Angry with myself but also strangely pleased, I sit up and turn up the volume of my computer.

The first thing I notice in the video is Hayden's posture. He's hunched over, arms folded on the table in front of him, baseball cap pulled low over his forehead. His eyes are barely visible, his jaw pulsing, his shoulders tense.

Focusing on the interview, I listen intently, watching Hayden's body language with each question asked and each answer he speaks into the microphone.

"Do you have any regrets about that fight with Marcus Miller?"

Leans into the microphone. Unapologetically. "No."

Flashes of light instantly bounce off him. He doesn't flinch.

Sips his water.

Looks around the room.

Tense and vacant.

"So you don't think the fight cost you advancement in the playoffs?"

Flinch, flexes his forearms, bites his bottom lip.

Pulls on the brim of his hat. "The shots O'Reilly deflected cost us our advancement. He played a hell of a game and shut down our offense."

"You were tied heading into the last five minutes of the game, right before you were sent to the penalty box, leaving your team short a man. You don't think that has anything to do with the loss?" Shoulders tense even more and a different man appears.

The man I became accustomed to is no longer in sight. He's morphed into an annoyed and bitter-looking man. Clenching his

223

jaw, he works it back and forth, his knuckles white as ever, his fingers digging into his palms.

He clears his throat, pinches the microphone and then . . . right there, you can see the minute he loses his cool, the second his professional media training is thrown out the window. Lifting his eyes for the first time, he makes eye contact with the reporter asking the question, fury slicing through his pupils.

"Tell me, Bob, if someone came up to you and slapped a hockey stick across the back of your legs, would you bend over and ask for another? Or would you have retaliated? From the look of it"—Hayden gives the man a once-over—"you would have bent over, but that's not how I handle things. Miller deserved to be brought down to the ice and I won't apologize for my actions." Hands digging into the table, he stands, his chair falling over. "Unless you have any other questions about the actual game, I'm done for the night."

More lights flash at him. Reporters call after him.

But he retreats, looking ready to kill.

The video ends and I let out a long pent-up breath, my heart stuttering. *Oh, Hayden.*

Melting into my couch, I lean my head against the cushion and have a very bad thought. The kind of thought anyone watching me would shake their head at, scream, and say don't do it!

But I'm feeling wild.

I'm feeling crazy.

I'm pregnant and have no sense of reason.

I'm doing it. I'm going to Google Hayden.

I know, I know, nothing good will come of this, but I never said I was smart.

Typing his name into the search bar, I have a small moment of pause, but before I can consider not doing this, my finger presses the enter button, once again being incredibly defiant.

Squinting, hand partially covering my eyes like blinds, I peek at my computer screen to be met with a small picture of Hayden holding a blonde woman's hand.

Outraged, I bring the computer inches to my face, a gasp popping out of me. "Who is that?"

I click on the picture and start searching for names, trying to tell myself it could be old, it could be someone he used to date, it could be—

Noely Clark, Good Morning, Malibu host.

What?

Leaning back on the couch, I stare at the picture of them, the way they look so good together. Her California-blonde hair, perfect figure, and insanely cute high heels next to Hayden, who towers over her, his hand two times bigger than hers, his stride long but also protective . . . of her.

Oh hell.

This was a bad idea.

How could he? How could he date someone so soon?

I mean, I know, I was the one who called it off, I get that, but he looks so cozy with her, so comfortable. Where did he meet her? Did she interview him? Did a mutual friend set them up?

I need to know more or my mind will start making up stories, and that is not a good situation to be in. Taking a deep breath, I start to type Noely Clark into the search engine when there is a loud knock at my door. Startled, I close my computer quickly and stuff it under my couch, as if I was caught watching porn. Jesus Christ.

Taking a deep breath, calming my nerves, I open the door.

Outside, looking handsome as ever is Racer . . . who is giving me a death glare.

Uh-oh. Looks like I have other things to worry about other than Hayden moving on with . . . well, just moving on. Period.

Wanting to seem as casual as possible, I say, "Uh, hey there, buddy."

"Don't you *hey buddy* me."

Stepping past me, he shuts the door and takes me to the couch, forcing me to sit. "Do you have something to tell me?"

Ignoring him, I ask, "How's Georgiana?" Racer started dating a girl he met through a project he's been working on. She's lovely actually, and is helping Emma with her wedding plans. She is stubborn and driven, the perfect match for Racer.

"She's great, testing my—" He pauses and gives me *the raised-eyebrow-I-won't-allow-you-to-sidetrack-me* look. Yeah, it's a thing. "Oh no, you don't. Don't distract me with my girl." Eyeing my stomach, he says, "Tell me."

Sighing, I flop against the cushion of my couch. "It seems like you already know."

"I want to hear it from you."

I drape my arm over my eyes. "I'm pregnant, Racer."

Cursing under his breath, Racer asks, "Is it Hayden's?"

"Yes." It's a one-worded answer, one that hangs heavily in the air. He warned me, he warned Hayden; he was against our pairing from the very beginning. Maybe in some weird cosmic way, Racer knew this would happen; we were going to be entirely too irresponsible and get pregnant.

"Jesus, Adalyn. Does he know?"

I look to the side, wincing. "No, and don't tell him, or I swear to God I will chop off your cock. I'm not kidding, Racer." I lift up and look him dead in the eyes. "I will slice you up."

He winces and adjusts his pants, scooting away from me. "Why aren't you telling him?"

"More importantly, who told you?" Getting angrier by the second, I pin Racer with a glare, and *he* now looks more nervous than anything.

"Uh, no one told me. I could sense it, smell it."

I whack him right in the stomach. "Gross, don't say you can smell pregnancy. What the hell is wrong with you?"

He chuckles softly.

"Emma told you, didn't she?" Shakes his head, lips sealed. "Racer!" I jab his side.

"Ouch, fuck." He rubs his ribs. "Are your fingers made of metal?"

"Who. Told. You?"

"You know, you're really scary pregnant."

"Which should tell you I'm not afraid to cash in on my threat." I glance down at his crotch, which he covers quickly.

"Fine, it was Tucker. He let it slip and told me not to say anything, but the guy is fucking dense. Of course I would say something to you." Becoming fatherly, Racer says, "How on earth in this day in age can you *accidentally* get pregnant? Do I need to have a conversation with you about safe sex?"

"Clearly not anymore." I sigh and lean against Racer's shoulder. He shifts so his arm is around me. "It was heat-of-the-moment stupidity."

He kisses the top of my head. "And why aren't you telling him?"

"What good is it going to do now?"

"That's a weird way of putting it." Racer is rarely serious; he goofs around most of the time. But when his voice turns stern, I know a rare moment is about to happen. He's about to be very honest and levelheaded with me. "It's not about what good it's going to do; it's about a man knowing that he created a child with another human being. It's about doing the right thing. You can't keep this from him as much as you wish you could. This isn't your secret to keep. This isn't your burden, because this baby isn't only yours. It's a product of both of you, and no matter how much you think this new journey is only yours, you're wrong, *and* you're being selfish. He deserves to know, he deserves to have a chance to do the right thing, so don't take that away from him."

For the record, I don't like it when Racer gets serious and level-headed, because every time he does, he's always right.

Slowly, a tear rolls down my cheek. I don't say anything, and I don't need to as his words sink in. There is no response other than *you're right*, so I stay silent, allowing myself to hide within his comfort. Because right now, I need my friend, and I need him badly.

CHAPTER TWENTY

HAYDEN

C *amaraderie.*
> *I want someone to lean on other than just my teammates.*
> *The physical is not what I'm interested in right now.*
> *I want to build a foundation with you.*
> *Being traded out here, it's been one of my worries, not having someone in my seats, cheering me on. To be in the stands for me.*
> *It doesn't matter anymore if I like her. It's over, and I'm starting a new chapter in my life.*

All things I've said to Noely over the last two weeks.

She's sweet, funny as hell, caring, her family is obsessed with me—literally obsessed—and fucking hysterical. They are the support system I've been trying to find since I moved to California. It's the first time since I moved that I feel part of a family again. Listened to. Acknowledged.

And yet . . . I can't stop thinking about Adalyn.

How fucked up is that?

I have this perfect woman who's interested in me, who's taking it slow because I asked, who's cheering me on in the goddamn stands at an exhibition game, and I can't seem to get one girl out of my mind.

I should be excited. I should be over the moon right now.

We just had our first pre-season game. I slayed it on the ice, and I had Noely and her family cheering for me in the stands. I'm having celebratory drinks with a beautiful woman and yet . . . I'm unhappy.

Trying to give Noely the attention she deserves, I ask, "Did you have fun tonight?" I got her and her hockey-fan family tickets to the game tonight. I also scored them jerseys. I'm making the effort but my heart isn't in it.

"I did, thank you so much for inviting us. And before you even ask, I had the nachos, extra jalapenos."

"My kind of girl." I tilt my beer in her direction and take a pull, my lips pressed against the bottle. Come on, Hayden, make an effort.

I must not do a good job because after she takes a sip of her drink, she flatly asks, "Do you like me?"

Fuck.

"What?" I chuckle, trying to play it off. "Do I like you? That's an odd question to ask. Of course I like you, or else I wouldn't be here with you. Why do you ask?" Smooth, good job.

"I don't know. I know you wanted to take things slow, but it almost feels like we're more like friends than a new couple. You've been to my place twice now, at night, and not even a little kiss."

It's because I can't get myself to kiss another woman.

I run a hand over my face. I might as well call a spade a spade. I can't keep dragging her along, because it's not fair to her. "It's not you—"

"Oh God, the classic it's not you, it's me line." Her face falls flat and I instantly regret what I'm about to say.

"I don't mean for it to sound cliché."

"I know you don't, but man, it still stings." She takes a large gulp of her martini and sticks the olives in her mouth, chomping down, looking anywhere but at me.

I fucking hate this so much. "Let me explain, Noely, before you get upset, or get drunk. I mean, I do like drunk Noely, but I'd rather you be present for this conversation."

Even though I asked her to be present, I can tell she's already checked out, and that's on me.

Sitting back, olive spear still in hand, she says, "What's going on, Hayden?"

It's now or never. I suck in a deep breath and lay it all out on the table. "During the off-season, I spent the last couple months on the East Coast in my hometown. I spent a lot of time with my good friend who introduced me to this girl."

"You don't need to say anything else. I get it."

Leaning across the table, I place my hand on Noely's. "Please let me talk."

Her features soften as she gently nods her head. So goddamn understanding. "I'm sorry, go ahead."

"I met this girl, and she was different. A little outlandish, spoke what was on her mind, and she kind of captured me. She was different than anyone I've ever met."

"She sounds lovely," she grits out. Ehh, maybe I shouldn't talk about how great of a girl Adalyn is in front of Noely. She doesn't seem to care too much for it. I don't blame her.

"She was. We spent almost every waking hour with each other when she wasn't working or I wasn't training. And then I was traded." I shake my head. "She walked away easily, a reaction I wasn't prepared for. I was kind of hoping, after our time together, maybe she'd consider moving to LA."

"But she didn't . . ." Noely finishes for me, a sense of sadness falling between us.

"She didn't. I told myself it was okay, what we had was just a fling, as she so delicately said. But I know deep down, the feelings I had for her were going to take a long time to shed."

"Is that why you joined the Going in Blind program? To get over her?"

"That and to meet new people, to maybe find someone to take

my mind off her." I sigh. "And then I met you. It's going to sound lame, but I didn't think going out with someone else was going to be so much fun. I really enjoy your company, Noely."

She winces and I realize my mistake. No girl wants to hear their company is enjoyed, not when they want to be romantically involved with you. But fuck, I can't lie to her, and I don't want her doubting herself. It's so fucking true when I say it's me, not her. Maybe if I was in a different place, a healthier mental state, I would be more apt to asking her out again and giving this a real shot.

But I'm not there.

"I really enjoy your company too, Hayden." The words sound like she's trying to speak them past razor blades in her throat. It's strained. "But . . ."

A heavy breath escapes me. "Fuck, I don't know, Noely. I want to move on, I want to start something up with you, because you make me happy. You make me laugh, and we have so much in common, plus you're fucking hot. I couldn't have asked for a better match when it comes to the Going in Blind program. But I don't know, there is something stopping me. Rather, someone, I should say."

Her face falls flat. "I get it, Hayden. I really do. I like you a lot, but I'm not going to come in second to someone who's still on your mind, you know? It's not fair to me."

"I know. It isn't at all. Shit, I feel like a total dick." I run my fingers through my hair, hating myself, hating Adalyn . . . No, I can't fucking hate her, no matter how hard I try. "This isn't how I wanted this to go. I thought I could push through, but I think I need some closure." Fuck, I so need closure.

"Closure is helpful." Noely twists the stem of her martini glass with her delicate fingers.

"Yeah, I guess. I need to make a phone call."

"Sounds like it. For what it's worth, I really appreciate you being honest, because being strung along when your heart and mind are somewhere else is not something I like to participate in."

"I thought I owed you that much." Taking a second, I lock eyes with her and say, "Can I ask you something?"

"Of course."

"If I can . . . you know, find closure, do you think it's possible you'd be open to trying this again?"

"You mean try dating again?"

Try this again . . .

It's something I say out of pure desperation to not make her feel so fucking awful, but do I really mean it? If I'm honest, not really, and what kind of a dick does that make me?

A massive one.

But fuck, I was her third date in this program. *Third* date. I know this is going to be a blow to her self-confidence, and I don't want that to happen. She's such an amazing woman, and I don't want *my* inability to get over Adalyn to be a setback for her. She's looking for love, and she deserves it.

"I'm not sure, Hayden . . ."

At least she's smart enough to read the hollowness in my question. It's why she's going to succeed, why she's going to find someone to love. While I lose again.

Once again, I open the door to an empty apartment, toss my keys on the side table in the entryway, and click the door locked behind me. What a long fucking night.

I spend ten minutes getting ready for bed running through my routine, stretching my achy muscles and putting some Deep Blue on the sore spots.

Flopping onto my mattress, I pull the sheets over my lower naked half and scroll through my phone, checking out highlights from the game, listening to commentators, studying some of the videos, and responding to some texts. One from my dad congratulating me on the game, wishing he was there. *Tell me about it.* A few from my brothers complimenting my "wicked" slap shot, one from my mom telling me she loves me, and one from Calder telling me I looked fat on the ice tonight.

I chuckle from his text, missing his friendship.

There are a few guys I've started to get to know on the team, but I still feel new, like I'm imposing on their territory. It doesn't help that the media is blowing up my trade, making it seem like a godsend to the Quakes, that I'm going to "save" the organization.

Think about it.

If you were on a team and this newbie comes around surrounded by hype, putting down your previous seasons, wouldn't you be a little resentful? Fuck, I would be. Because these guys work hard, they work incredibly hard, and it almost seems like the media is forgetting that.

Opening my email, I take a few seconds to scroll through the messages, not bothering to open any from my publicist or agent. I'm about to close out when one of the subject lines catches my attention.

Hayden, this is Adalyn's friend, Emma.

Emma? What the hell is she doing emailing me?

Wait . . . is Adalyn okay?

My body fires up, heating with concern. I open the email immediately.

If this isn't Hayden Holmes, I'm sorry. If this goes straight to Hayden's publicist, I beg for you to send it to him. Don't be a dick like you were to Adalyn in NYC.

My jaw clenches. Fucking James. *Why didn't Adalyn say anything about that?*

Hayden, I'm sorry to bother you, but I felt the need to email you. First of all, everything is okay, no need to freak out. I wanted to let you know that I looked up your schedule, and you're going to be in NYC for a game against the Stallions in a couple of weeks. I know it's a bit of a drive and I have no idea what your free time is like, but if you could spare some time, you really should visit Adalyn.

I'm not going to go into detail, but I HIGHLY suggest you come visit. If anything, just to say hey.

I hope you get this. I hope it's okay that I emailed you. And just to reiterate, everything is okay, just a short visit would be totally cool. Okay, I'm going to go.

Good luck with the season and I hope you're doing well.

Emma

Could she be any more evasive? I read the email a few more times, trying to read past the lack of information, looking for any clue as to what she might be talking about.

Why would she want *me* to visit Adalyn? Especially if nothing is wrong?

There has to be something wrong or else Emma never would have emailed me. Maybe there is something wrong, but it's nothing urgent.

Does Adalyn need help? Did she have another run-in with Logan? I swear to God if this has to deal with Logan, I'm going to lose my fucking shit.

I'm tempted to write back to Emma, to ask her what's going on, but I stop myself. She said to pay Adalyn a visit, but can I even make that happen?

I pull up my schedule for when I'm in New York City. It would be almost a four-hour drive to Binghamton from the city, but a quick flight. I can probably get a private jet to take me there. I have time after an afternoon game, and then I can take a different flight than the team to Chicago after that.

Mulling over my decision, I try to consider if it's worth it? At this point, I don't think I have a choice because I need closure. *She doesn't want me, and I need to let her go.* If I don't visit Adalyn, I don't think I'll ever get the balance back in my life.

And fuck do I need my balance, because I feel like my sanity is hanging on by a thread.

Looks like I'll be making another trip to Binghamton.

～

W hat a fucking shitty loss.

It's been two hours since I left the ice, took a shower, and jetted to Binghamton. Coach wasn't too thrilled about me taking a separate flight, but I lied and said it was a family matter. At this point, I feel pretty comfortable with the fact that the Quakes aren't about to ship me to another team.

Although after the game today, they might have a good case.

My head was not in the game. It's been hard to focus while on the ice, ever since Emma emailed me, but I've pushed through. Today was a different story though, because knowing I was hours away from seeing Adalyn, I was distracted. I couldn't remember plays, I was missing shot after shot, and my focus wasn't sharp like it normally is. What a fucking disaster.

The Uber driver turns onto Adalyn's street, the quaint neighborhood barely lit by the yellow street lamps lined along the sidewalk. Five houses to go.

Four.

Three.

Two . . .

"This it?" the driver asks.

Glancing out the window at the small, white one-story home, I say, "Yup, this is it. Thanks, man."

"Not a problem. Have a good evening."

I step out of the car, my duffle bag in hand and survey her house. The living room light is on, blinds shut, but no sign of movement. Her car is in the driveway indicating she's home, sending me into a fit of nerves.

Fuck. I shouldn't be shaking over walking up to her house, but I am. I'm apprehensive about Emma's reasoning for asking me to visit.

I guess there is only one way to find out.

With my heart pounding in my chest, my veins shaking, and my mind going a mile a minute, I walk up and knock on the front door. I plant the hand that's not holding my duffel bag in my pocket and rock back on my heels, my breathing non-existent as my chest tightens.

The telltale sound of locks being unlocked echo through the silent night air right before the door opens. It takes my eyes a second to adjust, but when they do, I'm greeted with a very shocked Adalyn at the door. Her hair is piled on top of her head, knotted in a messy bun, her face devoid of all makeup. Eyes wide, mouth parted in shock, she steps forward, partially closing the door behind her.

"Hayden, wh-what are you doing here?"

What am I doing here? Hell if I know at this point.

"Uh . . ."

"Who is it?" comes a male voice from inside the house, sending my head snapping to see past the door. I catch a quick cringe from Adalyn before the door is opened all the way up and reveals Logan standing protectively behind Adalyn.

You have got to be fucking kidding me. Is this what Emma wanted me to see? Was she trying to make me jealous? Did Adalyn set up this whole thing with Emma to throw her new relationship in my face? *Why the fuck would Emma do that to me?*

"Hayden, what are you doing here?" Logan asks, wrapping his arm around Adalyn, his hand resting on her hip.

Blood boiling in my veins, my eyes narrow in on the formfitting shirt Adalyn is wearing, the one Logan is stroking with his thumb, the one that . . .

Wh . . . what?

Is the light really that bad here or am I seeing things?

Peering at Adalyn, I watch her squeeze her eyes shut tightly and turn into Logan who pulls her into his chest.

My eyes go back to Adalyn's stomach, wondering why she is holding it so . . . protectively.

Brow creased, head tilted, a light sheen of sweat glazing my skin, I keep my eyes fixed on her torso. When I speak, my voice cracks. "Adalyn, are you okay?"

Adalyn shakes in Logan's arms. He soothingly rubs her back

and whispers into her ear, but thanks to the quiet night, I can hear everything he says.

"Just breathe or you're going to make yourself sick again. Take deep breaths, Addie."

Sick? Again?

"Excuse me." Adalyn takes off running into her house, leaving me alone with Captain Shithead.

We stand there, silently staring at each other, Logan with his hands on his hips, me clenching my fist at my side ready to plow it through his cocky-as-fuck grin.

"You should probably leave. You being here isn't good for her."

"You can fuck off." I push toward the door, but Logan blocks me.

Grunting while he speaks, he says, "You can't just show up when it's convenient. This is going to destroy her."

"I'm going to destroy your pathetic ass if you don't let me through this fucking door. As a reminder, I take men down for a goddamn job, so I suggest you don't fuck with me." Pushing him to the side, I make my way into Adalyn's house and go to her bathroom. The door is partially cracked, the light on, the sound of her throwing up on the other side.

Without a second thought, I drop my bag, push through the door, and fall to my knees next to her. Head in the toilet, hands on the seat, she heaves while I rub her back, my heart aching.

Letting out a long breath, her body slumps as she rests her forehead on the toilet seat. "What are you doing here, Hayden?"

I don't answer her, instead I ask, "How long have you been sick like this?"

Taking her in, I notice how pale her skin is and how much thinner she is besides what looks like a baby bump. And now that I think about it, her eyes looked sunken when I opened the door, tired and weary.

"Since I've been four weeks pregnant."

My teeth grind together, the tension in my body starting to

grow stronger with each passing breath. "How far along are you now?"

"Twelve weeks."

I hold her gaze for a moment before looking away without saying a word. I stand from the position on the bathroom floor and walk out to the living room where Logan is sitting on the couch. When he sees me round the corner, he stands and puffs his chest out. What a fucking douche.

Growing serious, I say, "You need to leave. Now."

"I'm not going anywhere."

Stepping in closer, I try to hold back the anger pouring out of me, but I fail miserably. Taking him by the shirt, I speak inches from his face. "I need time alone with her to work this out, and I don't need you hovering over us. You can either gather your things and leave with your dignity still intact or I can escort you myself, but I will guarantee you won't like it."

Not flinching, not even disturbed by my threats, he says, "I've been the one who's taken her to her doctor's appointments, the one who's been making her dinner, making sure she's getting some sort of food in her body. I've been the one shuttling her around when she's been too sick or too tired to drive herself, and I've been the one who's been there to scoop her up off the bathroom floor when she's far too exhausted to make it to her room." Pushing against my chest, dislodging my hand from his shirt, he straightens up. "I suggest you respect the fact that I've been taking care of your problem." Bending down, he picks up his keys from the coffee table and leaves, slamming the door behind him.

Fuck.

My problem? Is she pregnant with . . . No. Surely she would have told me *that*.

Logan's words ring through my head, breaking me down, killing my soul with the thought of Adalyn by herself, going through this all alone when I should have been here.

"Oh." Adalyn's stunned voice has me spinning around. "I . . . I thought you left."

I shake my head, pulling on the back of my neck, feeling absolutely deflated. When Emma emailed me, I never expected this scenario. Adalyn was on birth control. I remember seeing it in her bathroom, and I watched her take it a few times. I thought we were safe.

Hating that I'm going to ask, but wanting to make sure, I look her in the eyes and say, "Is the baby mine?"

Lips pressed into a thin line, she nods her head. "It happened in New York City."

"But you're on birth control."

Twisting her shirt, a patch of her skin making an appearance, she focuses on the ground. My eyes focus on the little bump pushing past the waistband of her pajama bottoms. "I might have missed some days accidentally." Her head snaps up. "I swear I didn't do it on purpose, I wasn't trying to trap you or anything. I just—"

"Adalyn, being careful isn't your sole responsibility. I didn't wear a condom, so that's on me. This is on both of us."

We stand there in silence, the awkward realization we're going to be parents hitting me hard. "Were you going to tell me?"

When I tear my gaze from her stomach, I catch a glimpse of a lonely tear caressing down her cheek right before she wipes it away.

"Were you, Adalyn?"

Remorse fills her face when she shakes her head no.

"Why the fuck not?"

"Why would I?" she asks meekly.

Stepping forward, anger taking over my body, I answer, "Because it's my goddamn child, Adalyn. I have a right to know about it, and I have a right to be a part of its life."

"You lead a different life than I do. Do you really think you can be there for this baby . . . for me?"

Is she serious?

"Plenty of hockey players have kids. Fuck, Calder has been a single dad from the beginning. He makes it work. You can't blame this on my profession. How could you not tell me? What the fuck, Adalyn?"

"You live across the damn country, Hayden," she shouts. More tears fall from her eyes. "You're here now for what, a few hours and then you have to take off to your next stretch of games. As much as you like to think this can work, it can't. You want to be a part of this, I get that, but let's face it, when it comes to logistics, I'm going to be a single mom with a flyby baby daddy. So excuse me if I didn't believe you needed to know yet. Whether you knew or not, it wouldn't make a shitload of difference to me right now. Or when the baby is born. *I* will be raising a child all by myself. And I'm fucking terrified."

Turning away, she walks to the back of the house where her bedroom is located. The soft click of her door sounds through the silent house.

Instead of going after her right away, I take a seat on her couch, trying to gather myself. What a fucking disaster.

I'm going to be a dad. A fucking dad.

Christ.

I attempt to let that sink in as my head drops past my shoulders, my hands clasped in front of me. But she wasn't going to tell me . . .

What kind of man does she *really* think I am to believe I wouldn't want to know? If there was one thing she should have understood it's that I'm not a man to ditch those I care about. And a baby? Our baby? *What the hell, Adalyn? How could you be so callous? What did I do to deserve that?*

And then there's the fucker who most definitely moved in once I left. *Is Adalyn not the girl I thought she was?*

I'm going to be a dad, sooner than I would have liked, but fuck if I'm not going to be in this child's life. My parents gave me a beautiful childhood and opportunities to better myself; they gave me the world, and that's exactly what I want to give my kid.

And doing it with Adalyn? Hell, I don't think I could have

chosen a better person to partner up with. The only problem is our distance.

From the back of my pocket, I pull out my phone and send a text to Chris Thompkins, the goalie on our team who's been working with me lately after practice. I have an idea, but I just need to know if he can help me.

CHAPTER TWENTY-ONE

ADALYN

I am going to kill her.

Emma is dead to me. Absolutely dead to me.

Technically I don't know if it's Emma who told him, but I'm ninety-nine percent sure it is. Racer is too scared to be castrated, and Logan would probably prefer Hayden to never know at this point. So that leaves Emma.

Ugh.

I bury my head in my pillow. Breathe, Adalyn, breathe. This isn't good for the baby, none of this stress or anxiety is good for the baby and yet, I can't seem to find a happy place.

Hayden deserves to know about his baby, I understand that, but I never wanted him to find out like this. He was blindsided, although he would have been blindsided no matter what. But with Logan here, protecting me . . . God, no wonder Hayden is so angry.

I have no idea if he's still in my house. I didn't hear the front door open and close, but then again, I've been crying into my pillow for the last half hour; I might have blocked out any other sounds in the house.

Rolling to my other side, facing the door, I wish I had X-ray vision so I could see if he was still here or not. *Do I want him to be here still?* Not really. It was easier when he wasn't here, because I could go on thinking there really was no daddy to my baby. But now, it's real. This whole clusterfuck is real.

Sighing, I snuggle in closer to my pillow, trying to get my rest when the door to my bedroom cracks open, startling me.

"Hey," Hayden says, stepping in and shutting the door behind him. The only light in the room is from the moon outside, casting just enough brightness in the room to make out each other's features.

Sniffling, I answer, "Hey, I thought maybe you might have left."

Shaking his head, he comes to my bed and sits next to me, his hand going to my back where he lightly strokes it.

Briefly, I shut my eyes, indulging in his touch again, in his large hand soothing me.

"I needed a second to understand everything." His voice is more calm, more Hayden. "This is life-changing, Adalyn, and I'm still trying to wrap my head around it all."

"I can understand that."

Moving his hand up and down my back, he asks, "Who knows?"

"Logan, obviously." Hayden's face hardens, but I continue before we can dive deep into the Logan conversation. "Emma and Tucker . . . Racer."

"Shit," Hayden mutters. "What did *he* say?"

"That he was going to kill you, but then I told him if he came after you, I would castrate him."

Chuckling, Hayden says, "I appreciate that."

"It was more for Racer's protection, because even though he's a strong guy, I don't think he could take you."

"Damn right." Hayden winks and the weight that's been pressing against my chest ever since I found out I was pregnant eases. "What about your family?"

I shake my head. "Haven't told them yet. Haven't had the courage to do so."

"Your brothers are going to kill me, aren't they?"

I sugarcoat my answer. "Stay in California and I think you'll be okay." I chuckle and let out a little sigh. "I'm sorry, Hayden, I didn't mean for this to happen."

"Adalyn"—he presses his palm against my cheek—"neither of us planned for this to happen, but it did and now *we* need to figure it out."

"I'll share custody, if that's what you want. I'm just not sure how. I guess during the summer, the baby can be with you and during your hockey season I can—"

He presses his fingers against my lips, halting the thoughts coming off the top of my head I seem to be speaking out loud. The last thing I want to do is figure out custody so early on in the pregnancy, but I feel insane, like I need some sort of way to figure this all out.

Softly, looking me square in the eyes, he says, "Move to California."

Did I hear him correctly?

Move?

I'm not one to guffaw, but this is the perfect time for it. I let it rip, a loud, obnoxious guffaw.

"I'm serious, Adalyn."

Sitting up, using my pillow as a barrier against my headboard and putting a little space between us, I say, "Come on, you're joking."

"I'm dead fucking serious."

Okay, maybe he was hit in the head with a puck tonight. I didn't watch his game, but I'm now tempted to go back and search the highlights. Surely a puck to the head would be on there.

Patting his forearm, I say, "You've had a big night, finding out you're going to be a dad and all, not to mention the exhaustion you must feel from your game and traveling. Don't worry, I won't hold your crazy against you."

"Adalyn," his voice now stern, "I'm perfectly fine. I thought about this, and it would be perfect."

"Perfect?" I raise my brow at him. "Perfect for who?" I point at him. "For you? Because it seems like that's the only person it would benefit. I, on the other hand, would be moving to a foreign state with no job, no place to live, no friends, just to be close to the man who impregnated me? Yeah, I don't foresee that happening."

"You can stay with me."

Guffaw number two.

"Hayden, don't you think that would be awkward?"

"Why?" He looks genuinely confused.

"Uh, maybe because we're not seeing each other anymore?"

"You broke it off. I never said I didn't want to be in a relationship."

Now I point at myself. "I broke it off? You're the one who was traded. What the hell was I supposed to do? Wait around and have a long-distance relationship with a guy who's on the road for half of fall and all of winter and spring? It would never work, Hayden. I didn't have a choice, so I moved on."

His hand retreats to his lap, my words apparently stinging him more than I expected. *Does he think I mean Logan? That we're together? Do I clarify that?* "I would have tried to make it work."

"I have no doubt." Looking at my lap, my fingers locked together, I add, "But I wouldn't have been able to make it work, and sometimes you just know. When I found out you were traded, I knew. We weren't meant to be." *When I saw you'd moved on with another woman, I knew we were done.* It still stings, but what can I do? Now he wants me to move, for what? To be the *other woman he once fucked and knocked up*? Why the hell would I want that?

Silent, there is tightness in his jaw with the way his cheeks pulse and his hands clench together. He's not happy with my honesty, but I'm not about to string him on.

"That's beside the point. You wouldn't be alone in California. You would have me. And a job, I have a really good lead for you. Chris, the goalie on the team, his wife works in a doctor's office, a family practitioner, and they're looking for another nurse. It would be a better job, not on your feet all the time, pays well, and you would be in California, where I could help." He sighs. "I wish we were in a different situation where I work your typical desk job and could be there for you whenever you need me, but unfortunately this is the best I can do. And I will do anything you need. Don't want to live with me? Fine, I'll get you an apartment across from mine. Need a doula or a mid-wife? Done. Need friends? I will fucking find some. I just . . ." He pauses his throat growing tight, my heart sputtering in my chest. "I want to be a part of this, Adalyn. I know I'm asking more than anyone should ask of another person, but please, please consider it. I don't know how else to fix this, to not lose out one of the best things to ever happen to me."

Shit . . .

~

"I can't believe you're moving." Emma turns off the freeway toward the airport. "What am I going to do without you?"

I pat her arm. "You'll be perfectly fine. You have Tucker."

"But he's a boy . . ."

"A hot one."

Sighing as if she's seen him for the first time, she nods. "So hot and so good in bed but still, you're moving for your baby daddy. Who does that?"

"I have no clue." I look out the window, reconsidering my decision. This is stupid, this is really stupid. But then again, when I talked to Chris's wife, and they offered me the job after an hour-long conversation on the phone that included great benefits, maternity leave, good pay, and the ability to go home at four, how could I say no? Hayden found me a great place to live, because I refused to stay with him, and it's decently priced too. A two-bedroom apartment on the second level overlooking a courtyard.

But my family, oh boy . . . they did not take it well. I told them about the pregnancy. My mom fainted, my dad grunted past his newspaper, my sister didn't have much to say given the hard time she's going through, and my brothers well, they stole my phone and tried to find out who the guy was. Thank God I have the thing password protected. When they asked why I was moving across the country to be closer to a guy I didn't plan on dating, I told them it wasn't about me, it was about the baby, and there was no option for him to move to me.

The only brother that was okay with the move was Sean, and I think that's because he secretly wants to be an actor and could stay at my place while trying to pursue his dream.

Not going to happen.

I've seen his acting, and it's pure crap. I love him, but it's crap.

"Are you having second thoughts?" Emma asks, soft and concerned.

I nod, keeping my eyes fixed on the changing leaves outside my window. "Of course I'm having second thoughts. I would be concerned if I wasn't. But I don't know, Emma, I feel like I have to, like I need to give Hayden a chance to be the dad he deserves to be."

Stopping at a light, Emma turns toward me and levels her glare. "Is there more to this you're not telling me about? Do you . . . love him?"

"No." I answer quickly, shaking my head. "I don't plan on getting romantically involved with Hayden."

"You don't?" Emma quirks a brow in my direction. "This coming from the girl who was obsessed with him this past summer. You're just . . . over him like that?"

"I have to be." I suck in a deep breath. "I have to be over him, Emma."

"Why?"

"Because"—I turn my gaze toward the window when Emma starts driving again—"when he was traded, when he left, it nearly destroyed me. He has his new life now, and well, I'm not part of that. I won't allow myself to fall for him and then be destroyed by him again. I won't let that happen."

"And what happens when he's at an away game and something happens with the baby or you go into labor? At least if you're here you have me, Tucker, Logan, and Racer to count on."

"Don't worry." I add, "I won't be alone."

CHAPTER TWENTY-TWO

HAYDEN

E xhausted, sore as fuck, and barely able to walk up the stairs in front of me, I take a second to collect myself.

Adalyn chose a time to move out here when I was out of town. I begged her to reconsider another time when I had a home stretch, but she insisted upon getting started at her job as soon as her two weeks' notice was up at the hospital. She didn't want to skip a beat in paychecks. She made that quite known. And when I offered to help cover some of her costs, she nearly bit my head off. I blamed it on the hormones not because she wanted nothing to do with me.

This is the first night I will actually get to visit her, check up on her, and make sure she's doing okay, that she's fitting in at her job. Which honestly, I already know she is because I've been checking up on her through Chris. Would it have been better if I went straight to the source? Of course, but she barely texts me back when I text her and forget about phone calls, those go unanswered. I'm desperate, and Chris was my only source of information, and according to him, the staff adores her and she's quickly become friends with everyone. That doesn't surprise me. She's passionate and dedicated in everything she does. It's hard not to like Adalyn. I'm just wondering why she's so adamant about keeping me at an arm's length.

Gripping the bouquet of flowers tightly in my hand, I hold the handrail that leads up to her second floor apartment and take one step at a time, my muscles screaming at me with every step. Goddamn, I don't think I've been this sore in a long time, but when I'm not on the ice or in the training room, I'm practicing with the boys, putting in extra time, learning the plays, and driving puck after puck into Chris.

At first, the extra time put a target on my back, like I was trying to show up everyone, but they get it now. They're observing what level of commitment it takes to be on a team like the Brawlers.

If only my muscles would get the idea.

When I reach the top of the stairs, I take a left and head to the end of the outside hallway and the corner apartment. Adalyn thinks she got a steal when it came to this apartment when in reality, I pay half her rent without her knowledge, making it an irresistible place to live. It's two blocks from my apartment, in a good area, and has two bedrooms, one for the baby, one for her. Hopefully though, she won't have to use the second bedroom because I'm bound and determined to win her back. Despite the circumstances of when and how I saw her in Binghamton again, and how she barely spoke to me while I was there and since, I knew why I'd struggled so much in California. She had become my best friend. She'd become someone I thought of first to talk about my day. And when I was so suddenly cut off from that, my heart ached. It was why nothing could have happened with Noely. My heart has an Adalyn-sized hole, and only she can heal that.

There is no denying she still has feelings for me. I saw it in her bedroom when we talked about the baby. She's holding back though, and I need to work out why and correct it. We're having a child together. There is no other option.

I have time. I have plenty of time because I'll be damned if Adalyn isn't mine.

I fucking love her. I loved her before I knew about the baby, and I love her more now that she's carrying my child.

I knew the minute she caught me snooping in Racer's house she would change my life, and she did. There is no turning back because life without Adalyn is a life I don't want to live.

Standing outside her apartment, I take a deep breath and give the door a knock. I quickly adjust the baseball cap on my head and make sure my shirt is righted just in time for the door to open.

With a big smile, I look up to a very familiar set of eyes.

Just as quickly as I plastered the smile on my face, it is quickly washed away.

"What the fuck are you doing here?"

Gripping the edge of the door, a shit-eating grin on his face, Logan chuckles to himself. "Good to see you too, Hayden. Glad to see you have your anger under control."

Stepping in closer, I ask again, "What are you doing here?"

"Oh, did Adalyn not tell you?" He shakes his head. "Must have slipped her mind. Pregnancy brain and all." Thumbing to the apartment behind him, he says, "I live here with Adalyn. I moved here as well, wanting to make sure she had someone to rely on, someone to take care of her."

Never have I felt such boiling rage take over every vein, muscle, and bone in my body. Searing white-hot anger rips through me and the urge to swiftly punch Logan in the face is so goddamn real I have to take a step back in fear of what I might do.

"Who is it?" Adalyn asks, coming up behind Logan. When she sees me, her eyes widen and her mouth parts open. "Oh, Hayden. You're back from your road trip."

Grinding my teeth together, I speak through my anger. "Adalyn, a moment. Alone."

Stepping past Logan, she nods and directs me toward the courtyard. Staring Logan down for longer than I should, I follow Adalyn down the back steps and into the courtyard. Behind my tumultuous rage, I can appreciate the bags under Adalyn's eyes have become softer and she's looking like she has some color in her face.

Sitting on a bench, she curls her legs close to her body and wraps her long cardigan around her knees, bringing them close to her chest.

Not even bothering with the flowers anymore, I set them in front of her and take a seat, one of my arms spanning across the length of the bench, the other dragging my hand over my face. "What the fuck, Adalyn? You didn't tell me douche nugget was moving out here."

"I didn't know how to tell you."

"Easy." I give her my attention. "You pick up the damn phone when I call you and you tell me."

"You already hate him, I didn't—"

"You're damn right I hate him. I mean . . . fuck," I press my fingers into my brow, squeezing my eyes shut, "Are you seeing him?"

"Like as in dating?"

"Yeah, are you two dating?"

Fiddling with her cardigan, she doesn't answer me right away, making my heart stammer in my chest and my skin prickle with pure hatred.

"No," she finally answers.

"Why did it take you so long to answer?"

Turning her head toward the fountain in the middle of the courtyard, she says, "This is none of your business, Hayden. I moved out here for you. If I bring someone with me, that's my choice, not yours."

"This is my business when that douche is sharing an apartment with my girl." The word slips past my lips before I stop it. Adalyn tilts her head in my direction, a slight shake to it.

"I'm not your girl."

Well I'm fucking aware of that now.

"But you're his?" She doesn't answer, sending me into a heated frenzy. "So basically you're going to give that shithead a second chance when he treated you with nothing but disrespect after he slept with you, but you're not looking at me twice when I had *no choice* in our breaking up, when I wanted nothing more than to try to continue seeing you." I stand now, pacing back and forth, my mind whirling. "Fuck, Adalyn, do you realize what this is doing to me? That kind of pain you're putting me through? Why him? Why not me?"

"Because . . ." Her lips quiver, her inability to look me in the eye driving me insane. "You make me hurt too much."

Halting my pacing, I drop my hand from the back of my neck. "What?"

"He's easy, Hayden. He's mindless. He doesn't make me ache like you do. I've had a bad enough pregnancy, I don't want to make it any harder on myself."

"So you're going to fuck a guy I hate with every bone in my body and play house with him, with my baby, because he's easy? Are you hearing what you're saying?"

"We're not fucking as you so eloquently stated."

"Does he kiss you?" I hold my breath, waiting for her answer. I want those lips for me and me alone. Luscious and plump, so addicting I could spend hours pressing my mouth against hers. I don't think I can stand knowing Logan gets that privilege, gets to taste her, touch her . . .

"We're friends, Hayden."

"But he wants more." It's not a question; it's a statement. I'm not an idiot, I know when a guy is infatuated, when he's fucking lost over a girl because that dumb-as-shit look Logan gives Adalyn is the same damn look I have on my face.

"I have a feeling he does." She presses her chin on her knees, staring down at the bench.

Scratching the heavy scruff on my jaw, I decide to try to calm myself, tamping down my anger because that's not going to get me anywhere. Instead, I go for a more gentle approach. Sitting down next to her, I rub my thumb over her cheek, drawing her attention.

"Adalyn, do you hear what you're saying? You are aware he has feelings for you. Why would you do this to him? Aren't you playing him? Using him?"

"No, I'm not. He's only a—"

"Not in *his* eyes. And I don't believe that you, someone so kindhearted, so giving and selfless normally, would do that."

She looks away, and I can see she's trying to deny what I'm saying is true. If she wasn't confused, weakened by the weeks of being sick, I'd run now, because I don't want someone so thoughtless handling my heart either. I know it's not the real her, though. *Unless I have read her very badly, but I no longer think so.* But I don't want her focusing on him. I want her heart as it is completely interwoven with mine.

"What can I do to make this work between us?"

She searches my eyes, her brown to my brown. "Hayden," she sighs, "It was a fling, let's keep it—"

"Don't you fucking lie to me about what we had. Respect me enough to never use that word again. It's an insult, one I don't deserve."

Giving in, she says, "I'm sorry, but it still doesn't change anything. I don't think I'm cut out for the world you live in, Hayden."

"How do you know? You haven't been a part of my world for long enough, you haven't given me a full chance to show how you and the baby can fit perfectly into it."

She shakes her head. "You're caught up in the pregnancy. If it weren't for the baby, we would still be three thousand miles apart."

"Not in my fucking heart." Taking her hand, I press it against my chest, letting her feel how wildly it beats for her. "You have been buried inside here since the day I first met you. Why do you think I traveled around Binghamton going from hospital to hospital looking for you? Because I knew leaving Racer's house without your number was one of the biggest mistakes of my life, second to letting you walk out of the cottage the day I was traded. This isn't a fling for me, this isn't because of us having a baby together, and this isn't because you live out here now. This feeling I have for you, this powerful, all-consuming feeling, it's fucking real and I'll be damned if I don't try to earn your heart every day for the rest of my life."

"Hayden . . ." A tear falls from her eye that I quickly wipe away with my thumb.

"Don't say anything, I don't need an answer. I need a chance. Let me prove to you the hurt you harbor for me was a one-time thing. This between us is real, Adalyn, and if I have to spend every day of my damn life proving that to you, then I will. Let me prove it to you, will you do that? Will you give me a chance?"

Taking a deep breath, she looks up, her eyes watery and blood-shot. Peering into the distance, she says, "That day, the day you were traded, I remember waking up feeling different, thinking about our little getaway in New York City. I knew I was pregnant. I had a feeling I was, and when realization crashed all around me I'd never felt more alone before in my life. And then"—she buries her head in her hands—"I saw you were dating that morning show host—"

"Listen to me, Adalyn. She was nothing. I was so goddamn lonely out here, you weren't talking to me, the guys on the team had their own lives, and I needed someone to talk to, someone to keep me from feeling so alone. I never even kissed her, because she was a friend. And when *I* realized her feelings were different than mine, that I didn't think of her as anything other than a friend, we went our separate ways."

Looking at me now, she says, "So then you know what it feels like to feel like you're facing a new situation all by yourself." She takes pause. "I know I have no right to be upset about Noely, but it still stung. It still bit me straight to the core, it still does. I never want to feel like that again. Logan might not be who I want, but at least I won't be alone." Standing from her crouched position she picks the bouquet up from the bench and tucks them against her arm. "Thank you for these, but I should get back inside, it's getting late."

Walking away, her long cardigan blowing in the light breeze, my soul cracks in half as once again she tries to put more distance between us.

Not this time.

Catching up, I stand in front of her, halting her retreat. Tipping her chin up, I step in close, feeling the strong pull between us. "You said Logan is not the man you want, but the man who is there. Who's the man you want?"

She tries to look away, but I force her to keep her gaze set on mine.

"Tell me, Adalyn, who do you want?"

She bites her bottom lip, wet droplets rolling down her cheeks. "You, Hayden. You're the man I want but can't have. The man I need to stay as far away from as possible, because there is no doubt in my mind, you're the man who can break me, and with a baby on the way, I can't be broken. I need to be strong."

Despite her confession at the end, hope blossoms in the pit of my stomach. She wants me. That's all I needed to hear. There is a chance, and it's up to me to show her, even though I have a busy schedule, I will always be there for her; I can make our relationship work. I won't break her. If anything, I will make her stronger.

"No one said you can't have me, Adalyn." Stepping in closer, my grip still holding her chin in place, I lean forward, inches from her mouth. "I'm all yours for the keeping, and I don't mind showing you exactly how much I fit into your world, how you fit into mine."

"Hayden, I can't—"

Pressing a chaste kiss across her lips, not lingering, I pull back, silencing her. "Promise me two things. Please, this is all I ask, just two things, after not telling me for so long, give me this chance." Her heavy lids part open, revealing those whiskey-brown eyes, giving me an opening. So goddamn beautiful. "Answer my phone calls and texts." Cautiously, she nods her head, swallowing hard. I press another chaste kiss against her lips and lift barely off her mouth when I say, "And don't let that fuckhead touch you. You're mine, and I'm going to prove it. Be patient with me, baby. I promise what we have will be night and day compared to any connection you've ever had with Logan."

Placing another light kiss across her lips, I allow myself to linger for a moment longer than anticipated but pull away when she parts her lips.

She's going to have to wait if she wants more, because we are nowhere near the end of the road for our relationship. No, we just started a brand new trip, and this one is headed for forever.

Game on. Adalyn will be mine.

CHAPTER TWENTY-THREE

HAYDEN

I put my car in park and stare at the office building in front of me. I would have preferred to woo Adalyn in private but now that fucking Logan lives with her—which don't even get me started on—I have no choice but to visit her at her office building because I'll be damned if I have to stand there, talking to Adalyn with Logan's shit-eating grin staring back at me.

I pick up the bakery box next to me and head into the building, pulling my hat down on my forehead, hoping I'm not recognized. I don't want to draw any attention to myself, because all I want to do is say good morning to my girl, tell her to have a good day, and then head off to the rink for some training.

Heading to the second floor for suite 210—thank you, Chris—I turn the corner to a span of glass windows only to see Logan talking to Adalyn in the office entryway.

Spinning against a wall to hide myself, I mutter, "Son of a bitch!" Clutching the pink pastry box close to my stomach, I lean past the corner of the wall, one eye peeking past.

What is he doing here? I swear to God, if he's working with Adalyn as well, I'm going to straight up chuck these pastries at the glass windows, stomp my feet, and throw a goddamn tantrum. It is not beneath me to do so.

Intently, I watch their every move, their body language and the way the fucker leans in toward her, laughing as if Adalyn said the funniest thing. She's funny, but come on, throwing your head back and laughing so early in the morning. Can we say desperate?

Leaning in closer, Logan wraps his arms around Adalyn's shoulders, hugging her.

My nostrils flare as my hands accidentally crush the corners of the pastry box. If he goes in for a kiss, I will see red.

Holding my breath, my eyes trained on the man who's making my life difficult, I wait. Adalyn rubs his back, he returns the touch, and I'm two seconds from making a Hayden-shaped hole through the glass of the office.

He says something to her, squeezes her again and then pulls away. I wait on bated breath for their next move. "Get out of there, you motherfucker," I whisper. "Stop lingering and move the fuck on." Leaning in a little farther Logan holds Adalyn's attention, and I'm itching to make my move to break them up when Adalyn steps away and waves.

Jesus Christ.

I scurry back behind the wall and let out a long breath. The glass door to the office opens and Logan takes off down the stairs, reaching into his back pocket to pull out his phone.

"Trip, you motherfucker, trip." To my disappointment, there isn't any thumping down the stairs . . . unfortunately. I wait a few seconds before rounding the corner, puffing my chest, and walking toward the office while attempting to un-crinkle the corners of the pastry box.

When I enter the office there are no patients, thankfully, and the receptionists seems to be out of sight as well as Adalyn. Walking up to the counter, I lean over and say, "Hello?"

"We're closed right now," Adalyn calls out.

"Hey, Adalyn." Her head pops around a partition. Mouth parts in surprise.

"Hayden, what are you doing here?" Her eyes scan the area behind me probably wondering if I ran into Logan. Thankfully I was spared conversing with him.

I nod with my head. "Come here and find out."

Stepping out to the front, her baby-blue scrubs bring out the pink in her cheeks and are starting to fit snug to her little pregnant belly. I can't help it. My eyes go straight to the bump.

Pulling on her shirt, she says, "I have to get some new scrubs, these are getting a little tight."

"You look beautiful." Standing awkwardly, I pull her into a hug, wanting to erase the last one she just received. "How are you this morning? Did you get sick?"

Shaking her head against my chest, she says, "No, thankfully. Lo-uh, I made eggs this morning and some toast and ate it first thing, which seemed to settle my stomach."

I'm not stupid, she was going to say Logan made her eggs. Trying to seem as casual as possible, she doesn't need more stress, so I give her a squeeze.

"That's great to hear. And you have your water?" Dumb question but I don't know what else to say, I want to show her I care, but I really have no idea how to go about doing that, so water talk it is. This used to be so much easier.

"Yes, got my water." She steps back and fiddles with her hands in front of her, avoiding eye contact. Christ, from where I stood, she had a much better conversation with Logan, and it's about killing me to know that.

"Got the office some pastries. There is a place around the corner that sells really good apple fritters. Thought you and the ladies might like to pick at them throughout the day."

Adalyn tilts her head to the side when she speaks to me. "That was very thoughtful of you, but don't you have a game today?"

"Yeah, but I don't have to report in until later. When I have a home stretch, I'm around quite a bit." Hint, hint. I'm not gone all the time. "Which reminds me"—I reach into my back pocket—"I have some tickets for you and the staff here for the game on

Sunday. Don't feel like you need to go, but if you are interested, here are a few tickets. And I put your name on the list for the family and friends suite for after the game. They usually have drinks and snacks afterwards. It's fun, and you get to greet the players when they come off the ice."

"Oh, thank you." She takes the tickets. "I'm sure the girls will love to go."

"Chris's wife should be there." I put my hands in my pockets. "Shannon, right?"

Adalyn nods. "Yes, Shannon. She told me she goes to every game." Looking at the tickets, she jokes, "Couldn't get tickets for tonight?"

Chuckling, I shake my head. "Thought it would be polite to give you a week's notice."

"How polite."

I want to tell her the tickets are for the staff here only and no one else. Basically, no Logan.

"Wednesday night we have off, I have some press stuff going on tomorrow, I was thinking maybe I could take you to dinner."

"I don't know if that's a good idea, Hayden."

"As friends," I say quickly, grasping at anything at this point. "I would like to hear about your birth plans and"—I take pause, swallowing hard—"have you found out the sex of the baby yet?"

She shakes her head. "I want to wait right now. I'm still trying to make it through one day without throwing up, I don't think I could put a sex label on this baby because right now, all it is to me, is demon child."

Laughing, I nod. "Yeah, I don't blame you there." Taking a step forward, I lace my fingers with hers and rub the pad of my thumb over her knuckles. "Please have dinner with me, Adalyn?"

"I go to bed early."

"How early?"

"Ten." She chuckles.

"That's not early, but don't worry, I'll get you home before bedtime." I pull on her hand. "Please."

She concedes, and heaves a heavy sigh. "Okay, what time?"

"Don't sound so pained about it," I joke, squeezing her hand. "What time works best for you?"

"How about five?"

"Dining with the early birds, I like it. I'll pick you up."

"I can actually meet you—"

Not going to fucking happen. I shake my head. "I'll pick you up." Gesturing toward the pink box, I say, "Enjoy the fritters, hand out the tickets, and make sure to keep one for yourself. Have a good day." I bring her knuckles to my lips and kiss them softly. Wiggling my eyebrows, I say, "Don't forget to text me back, because I have some great conversations planned out."

Laughing, she takes her hand back and folds her arms across her chest, a glint in her eye. "Is that right? Real riveting text conversations?"

"Get ready to be blown away."

She rolls her eyes and shakes her head. Taking the box with her, she walks behind the reception desk. "Don't hype it up if you can't deliver, Holmes." That right there—that look, the teasing lilt in her voice—that's the Adalyn who stole my heart. That's the girl I've been craving, and seeing that little glimpse of her gives me hope.

"I always deliver, babe. Always."

～

Hayden: *Did you know alligators swim out of the way of a manatee's path?*

Adalyn*: Is this the mind-blowing text conversation you were talking about?*

Hayden: *Just a soft opener. What did you think?*

Adalyn: *I think it's kind of strange.*

Hayden: *Fun facts are always strange but useless information you can utilize to impress others.*

Adalyn: *Is that what you're doing? Trying to impress you?*

Hayden: *If I am is it working?*

Adalyn: *I want to say yes to save your pride . . .*

Hayden: *Please, no pity yeses, I don't think my heart can take them.*

Adalyn: *I think you could have opened up with a more useful fact.*

Hayden: *Manatees and alligators aren't useful? Odd . . . give me a good example of a useful fact.*

Adalyn: *Because of water weight, a women's shoe size can grow one full size bigger during pregnancy.*

Hayden: *So what you're trying to tell me is that you would like to borrow my shoes. Anytime babe, you don't even have to ask.*

Adalyn: *Don't you wear a seven in men? That won't work.*

Hayden: *Feeling spicy today, are we?*

Adalyn: *I think it's the sugar high from the fritters.*

Hayden: *How many have you eaten?*

Adalyn: *I don't want to say.*

Hayden: *I've seen you take down an entire sheet cake, so your fritter consumption won't faze me.*

Adalyn: *I didn't take down an entire sheet cake. Don't you dare text lie.*

Hayden: *It's called embellishing for comedic effect.*

Adalyn: *Well since I'm feeling larger than normal, you can cut down on the embellishing, funny boy.*

Hayden: *Honest comment coming - - > You look gorgeous.*

Adalyn: *You just want to know how many fritters I've eaten today.*

Hayden: *Yes but I do think you're gorgeous, so you can't change my mind about that.*

Adalyn: *Took an extra dose of charming today, I see.*

Hayden: *To match your spice. Now tell me, how many?*

Adalyn: *This is so embarrassing . . . four.*

Hayden: **eyes pop out of sockets* FOUR??*

Adalyn: *I hate you.*

Hayden: *Nah, impossible.*

"Are you ready, Holmes?" Chris asks, sitting next to me, wrapping his goalie stick.

"Yeah, feeling good. What about you?" I nudge his shoulder with mine.

"A little beat up from this weekend, but other than that, ready to go." Eyeing my phone in my hands, Chris says, "Shannon told me you took fritters to the office this morning."

I lean back against the locker. "Just trying to win over my girl."

"Yeah, well, don't drown the rest of us in the process. Shannon was telling me how we've lost our spark, because I don't take her bakery treats at the office."

"Oh shit." I laugh. "Did she say that?"

"Called me once you left, asked me to bring her a latte to go with the fritter that the handsome new guy brought into the office."

"And did you?"

"Of course I did. I can't have you showing me up. I brought lattes for everyone, damn it."

Laughing and shaking my head, I say, "That is one happy doctor's office."

"They're Quakes fans, that's for damn sure."

"Bribing nurses and doctors with lattes and fritters, we might be onto something."

Chris nods his head as my phone buzzes in my hand. "We should bring it up to PR. I'm sure they would have a field day with it."

"Yeah, I'm sure." Zoning out, I open my text from Adalyn.

Adalyn: *Pizza should be on the list of things pregnant women should eat. Dairy, protein, veggies, and grains. What more can you ask for?*

Smiling to myself, I respond back.

Hayden: *It's on my list of pregnancy-approved foods along with four apple fritters a day.*

Adalyn: *Funny. Aren't you supposed to be getting ready for a game?*

Taking a picture of my socked-up legs, I send it along with a comment.

Hayden: *It's the calm before the storm in the locker room right now. Waiting for coach to come in and do his spiel.*

Adalyn: *Oh, huh, for some reason I thought you couldn't have phones in the locker room.*

Chuckling, I type her back as fast as my fingers will work. This is a moment, a moment I can show her that in fact I might have a game, but even during that time right before it, we can still be connected.

Hayden: *This isn't one of those hipster parties where you're required to put your phone in a bowl before you enter the house. A good amount of the guys have families, and they're usually FaceTiming with their kids leading up to the game.*

Adalyn: *I see that you're trying to prove a point.*

Hayden: *Is it working?*

Adalyn: *I don't really want to talk about that right now.*

Hayden: *Fair enough. Are you going to watch the game tonight?*

Adalyn: *I can't, sorry. We don't have cable.*

We.

One single word can turn my fucking stellar day into pure crap.

We, meaning Adalyn and Logan. From the mere thought of them curling up on her couch together, snuggling to watch me play, causes my stomach to roll and my skin to break out into a sweat. Fucking Logan. I still don't understand why he's an outside factor I need to work around.

Needing a second, I take a sip of my water and squeeze my eyes shut, trying to rid of the image of Logan wrapped around Adalyn out of my mind.

"Dude, are you okay?" Chris asks, "You look pale."

"Fine." I scratch my beard.

"You don't look fine. Does this have to do with the person who's texting you?"

Melting into the locker behind me, the hardwood cutting into my back a bitter welcome. "It's Adalyn. When she moved out here, her friend moved with her."

"Logan, right?"

My eyes snap to Chris. "You know about Logan?"

"I know of him." Chris bites the roll of tape, finishing off a section of his stick. "Shannon was telling me about him the other day, how he's always at the office, picking up and dropping off Adalyn. He hovers, but when Shannon asks Adalyn about him, all she says is he's a friend."

"Yeah, that's the term I keep hearing too. Friend."

Reaching over, Chris squeezes my shoulder. "Coming from a guy who married way out of his league, I'm going to tell you this. Don't sweat the stuff that doesn't matter. If you want Adalyn, focus on her, not him."

Focus on her, not him. Fuck that's good advice. Advice I wish I had early on. And it seems easier said than done, not to focus on him, but I'll try, especially if it stops the sharp, pulsing pain I get every time I hear his name. With that new mantra running through my head, I type Adalyn back.

Hayden: *Such a shame, you'll be missing a good show. Don't worry. I'll give you a play-by-play on Wednesday.*

She's quick in texting back making me believe she's giving me her full attention right now. I like that.

Adalyn: *Will this play-by-play be at the dinner table with straws and sugar packets replacing hockey sticks and pucks?*

Hayden: *If you're lucky.*

Adalyn: *Do you know where we're going to dinner? The baby likes to plan these things out.*

I smile to myself. This is the first time she's referred to the baby as a real thing, and fuck if it doesn't wash away the sour feelings I was having about Logan. Forget all of that, she just mentioned the baby. *Our baby.*

Hayden: *You tell me, what is the baby craving?*
Adalyn: *Pizza.*
Hayden: *Then pizza it is.*

~

H **ayden:** *Good morning, beautiful.*
       Adalyn: *Good morning. Congratulations on your win last night.*

Hayden*: Did you get cable just to watch me play? Wow, that's going above and beyond for your baby daddy.*

Adalyn: *Don't flatter yourself. I looked it up this morning while sipping some tea.*

Hayden: *First of all, it's cute that you checked. Thank you. Second, only tea this morning. Captain Cock Blocker didn't make you eggs this morning?*

Adalyn: *LOL, he's not a cock blocker, and I wasn't feeling too great this morning, so I drank some tea to settle my nausea.*

Hayden: *I'm sorry you weren't feeling well. Are you doing better now?*

Adalyn: *Yes. I brought a protein bar with me to work in case I felt hungry this morning, so I'll be good.*

Hayden: *Pregnancy seems like a real joy ride.*

Adalyn: *You're lucky all you had to do was stick your penis in me. Carrying this child is a whole different world.*

Hayden: *I can't even imagine. That's why I'm trying to be the best partner in all of this. If you go to the oven in the break room, I believe you'll find something staying warm for you in there.*

Adalyn: *Did you bring me more fritters?*

Hayden: *Better. Go look.*

Adalyn: *OMG is that breakfast pizza?*

Hayden: *Yup, fresh from the oven, full of all your daily nutrients: dairy, veggies, and grains plus an additional protein with the eggs.*

Adalyn: *I'm so happy right now.*

Reading that at seven thirty in the morning made my entire day. A picture buzzes on my phone and I quickly open it up to find Adalyn munching down on a slice of the breakfast pizza, a huge—albeit full—smile on her face. I save the picture to my phone and text her back.

Hayden: *Even with a breakfast pizza shoved halfway down your throat, you're still gorgeous.*

Adalyn: *I'm positively glowing. I can feel the pizza aura lighting up the space around me.*

Hayden: *Then my job here is done. Have a good day, Adalyn.*

CHAPTER TWENTY-FOUR

ADALYN

Hayden: *You don't want to know what I'm doing right now.*
    Adalyn: *You did that on purpose, open up a text like that so now I have to know what you're doing. Well you know what, I don't want to know. Nice try.*

Hayden: *It involves baby powder.*

Adalyn: *Damn you! What are you doing?*

Hayden: *I knew that would get your attention. I'm currently wearing a gladiator costume that's less than comfortable in the thigh region.*

Adalyn: *Time out. Why are you wearing a gladiator costume?*

Hayden: *It's the reason I couldn't take you out tonight and I had to revert to tomorrow night.*

Adalyn: *A gladiator costume is not a valid reason.*

Hayden: *It is when I have to do a commercial in it.*

Adalyn: *LOL, okay, now I'm really interested. Are you sponsored by Trojan now? A little ironic, don't you think, given our situation.*

Hayden: *Ha. Not sponsored by Trojan. It's for the league. They like to do skits with all the teams for bumpers in between commercials. I'm assuming since I'm the new guy, the Quakes nominated me for this shit.*

Adalyn: *That's fantastic. Do I get a picture?*

Hayden: *No.*

Adalyn: *Ahh, you're all cranky because you're chafing, aren't you?*

Hayden: *This baby powder is pure shit. We will not be using it on our kid.*

I pause, reading his text a few times. OUR kid. That's kind of weird and scary and . . . comforting. Despite Logan being here for me, I've felt so alone during this pregnancy, maybe because whenever I envisioned myself being pregnant, I envisioned being married, owning a home, and cuddling up next to my husband every night. Unfortunately, I don't have that luxury with this pregnancy.

Adalyn: *I don't think baby powder is used that much anymore with babies.*

Hayden: *Shit, really? Well good thing because it doesn't work. How have you been feeling today?*

Adalyn: *Good, the breakfast pizza was exactly what I needed. The lunch pizza you sent to the office was even better. Do I need to prepare myself for dinner?*

Hayden: *I would tell me now if you would like to pass on a dinner surprise.*

Adalyn: *Depends, what's on the pizza menu?*

Hayden: *Hawaiian pizza, extra pineapple.*

Adalyn: *Bless you, Hayden Holmes. Bless you.*

∼

Adalyn: *Are we going anywhere fancy for dinner?*
Hayden: *It's not Subway if that's what you're asking.*
Adalyn: *I'm trying to decide what I need to wear, smart ass.*
Hayden: *Bikini.*
Adalyn: *Over my dead body.*
Hayden: *Okay, okay, lingerie works too.*
Adalyn: *I thought this was supposed to be a "just friends" dinner.*
Hayden: *Do you not wear lingerie for your friends?*
Adalyn: *Want to ask Logan?*

Hayden: *Ohhhhhh low blow, babe. Low fucking blow . . . do you wear lingerie for him?*

Adalyn: *No.*

Hayden: *Cool. Cool. Not like I cared or anything.*

Adalyn: *You're so full of shit.*

Hayden: *Can't show all my cards right away, got to play it cool.*

Adalyn: *Oh is that what you're doing? Could have fooled me.*

Hayden: *It's the new way of acting cool, something these youngins came up with.*

Adalyn: *When you say youngins you make us seem so old.*

Hayden: *Well we are having a baby together. That is a very adult thing to do.*

Adalyn: *We're having it out of wedlock.*

Hayden: *Fishing for a proposal?*

Adalyn: *Just tell me what to wear.*

Hayden: *Anything you feel comfortable in.*

Adalyn: *Comfortable right now is sweatpants.*

Hayden: *Then I look forward to seeing you in your comfy threads.*

Adalyn: *I'm not wearing sweatpants, jeeze.*

~

A**dalyn:** *Heads-up. I just ate a sleeve of Oreos.*

Hayden: *I can see you're starting to feel better. I hope you still have an appetite for dinner.*

Adalyn: *Pretty sure right now, with the way I'm feeling, I'll be eating my dinner, your dinner, and the patrons' next to us.*

Hayden: *I'll ask for a secluded table then, this place isn't a family style restaurant.*

Adalyn: *Rookie mistake with a pregnant woman. Always go family style.*

Hayden: *Making notes now. Should I highlight family restaurant for emphasis.*

Adalyn: *I recommend it.*

Hayden: *Done.*

Hayden: *Leaving my place in a few to pick you up.*
     Adalyn: *I'll wait outside in the front of the complex.*
Hayden: *No way, I'll come get you.*
Adalyn: *Logan is here.*
Hayden: *I'll be sure to slow down enough by the curb for you to get in.*

<hr />

Hayden's black Porsche Cayenne pulls up to the curb, the sleek car polished and glittering under the streetlights. Popping out of the car, Hayden rounds the hood and opens the door for me as I reach for the handle.

"Can't let me be a gentleman?"

Smiling, I pat his chest. "Not a date, remember?"

"Doesn't mean I still can't open the door for you. Let me be old-fashioned; there are few of us left in the world."

I settle into my seat, the soft leather sucking me in like quicksand. Forget the restaurant, I can eat here and be the happiest person on earth.

"I wouldn't be too sure about that. We millennials think old-fashioned is cool."

"We also think we can find our next love on Tinder."

I point my finger at him right before he shuts my door. "Hey, there are Tinder love stories out there, and they're beautiful."

Chuckling, he shuts the door on me and walks toward his side of the car. I take that moment to peruse his choice of clothing. Dark wash jeans, a light blue button-up shirt, sleeves rolled to his elbows, and his hair styled messily to the side with a mild amount of scruff on his jaw, highlighting his dark features. There is also an air of confidence about him I haven't seen in a while. It's sexy.

When he gets in the car, he turns to me and asks, "Are you all buckled up?"

"Yup." I snap my seatbelt and notice something on Hayden's face. "Hey, look at me for a second."

He clicks his seatbelt in place and puts the car in drive. "It's a faded black eye, nothing to worry about."

"A black eye? Where did you get a black eye? Did you get in a fight on the ice?"

"Nah, just being stupid and messing around the other day at practice. Didn't wear a helmet and got an elbow to the face."

"Why weren't you wearing a helmet?"

He pulls out onto the street, one hand steering, the other resting on the gearshift, the thick sinew in his forearm flexing with every shift he makes.

"Call it being an idiot."

"Well, don't be an idiot," I say, irritated. "Skating without a helmet is really stupid, Hayden. You could give yourself a really bad head injury."

"I was being careful . . . enough."

"Doesn't seem like it." I fold my arms over my chest, causing my growing cleavage to make an appearance.

At a stoplight, Hayden eyes me from the side, his eyes traveling down my body, quickly taking in my breasts and then turning away. He clears his throat and says, "You act like you care about me, Adalyn."

"I do. You're the father of my baby, so it would be great if you wore a helmet while skating. I don't think that's too much to ask. You didn't wear protection while conceiving this child but from here on out you'll be wearing protection on your head, your shoulders, your shins, and even your balls."

That causes him to throw back his head and laugh. "You're concerned about my balls?"

"Only because I'm sure if you didn't take care of them properly you would whine more than the baby when they get hurt and there is only so much whining I can take, especially from a grown man who should know better."

"Brutal."

We spend the rest of the drive making small talk, talking about things like the weather, the ever-present sun in California, and the lack of rain. Really boring, but it fills the silence. I've had easier conversations with Hayden before, but for some reason, with the elephant in the room—ahem, the baby—we seem to be awkward as hell.

Will it always be like this?

I sure as hell hope not because if we're going to remain friends, I'd like some sort of camaraderie between us. It will probably take time and more nights like this.

Pulling in front of a brick building, Hayden puts the car in park and hands his keys to the valet right before opening my door. Taking my hand in his, he helps me out of the car but doesn't let go as he guides me into the restaurant. I allow it because I've held hands with friends before . . .

When I'm drunk.

On the side of the dark brick, painted in white is a very modern logo with the name Waffle Me in the middle of a circle, established in 2016. That makes me giggle. Usually when a restaurant claims establishment, it's at least twenty years, but I guess you have to start somewhere, and a waffle joint is exactly where I would want to start.

After my pizza-day extravaganza, I texted Hayden earlier and asked him if we could maybe not have pizza tonight. Waffles seem right up my alley.

When we step into the restaurant the sweet aroma of home-made waffles hits me along with a myriad of smells ranging from sweet maple syrup, to fried chicken, to chili. The seating is modern and sleek, wood-slatted benches, black leather cushions, and clear partitions hanging from the ceiling, giving parties privacy. I like it here. Casual and comfortable, just what I need, especially in my leggings and tunic.

"Hello, I have a reservation for Sergio Valentino."

The hostess checks her computer and nods, grabbing two menus, she motions to follow her. "Right this way, Mr. Valentino."

With his hand on my lower back, we follow the waitress to a curved booth in the back. She places the menus on the table and says, "Your waitress will be right with you. Her name is Sandy."

"Thank you." Hayden helps me into the booth.

When I get settled, I hold my menu but give my attention to Hayden. "Mr. Valentino?"

He shrugs, a smirk tilting the ends of his mouth up. "You've never used a fake name before?"

"Never had to."

"Ah, come on, there's always a time to use a fake name. Next time you order a coffee, give them a fake name, if anything, it will give you a little giggle when they call it out, and you know it's not really your name."

I stare at him for a few beats. Did he just say giggle? "Are you nervous?"

Rubbing his palms on his pants, he nods. "Yeah, a little and I have no fucking clue why?" Turning toward me, he takes my hand in his and laces our fingers together. Staring at our connection he speaks, his voice soft and gruff. "It's not like I haven't spent time with you before. It's not like we haven't been alone together. Hell, I've been inside of you before. I know what you taste like on my tongue, but for some reason, tonight seems monumental."

"We're just here to hang out, Hayden, nothing more."

Slowly moving his head up and down, he squeezes my hand and looks at me past his dark eyelashes. "You might think we are just going to be friends, but as much as I wish I could settle for that, I can't, but out of respect of your request for tonight, I will remain friendly. But if I say out-of-character things like . . . giggle . . . please know it's because even if I might seem like I have it altogether on the outside, being by your side unable to claim you like I want to is twisting me up in knots on the inside."

Unsure what to say to that, I turn to my menu while the words swim around together, making it incredibly hard for me to understand.

This is going to be a long, hard night and not in a good way. I'm pretty sure I'm going to leave tonight with a heavy heart and a confused mind.

～

"**D**id you take a pregnancy test or did you see a doctor?" Hayden asks, wanting to know more about the pregnancy, about all the moments he's missed.

"Pregnancy test with Emma in a janitor's closet."

He takes a bite of his banana and caramel waffle and quirks an eyebrow at me. "A janitor's closet?"

"I didn't want to do it in the staff lounge because frankly, there was already so much gossip among the staff in the hospital, I didn't want to add fuel to the flames."

"Why not wait until you got home?"

"Emma. She begged me to take the test. She swore my boobs looked bigger and needed me to confirm the pregnancy."

Hayden turns away from me and pushes some waffle around on his plate. "Yeah, I'd say Emma is right on that front."

Chuckling, I playfully swat Hayden. "Hey, don't be looking."

"It's hard not to, Adalyn." Looking at my breasts, he says, "They're kind of in your face."

Glancing down, I attempt to shift my shirt but there is no point in trying to cover them up, as none of my clothes fit anymore so if the ladies are out, they're out.

"Nothing fits like it used to."

He holds up his hands. "I'm not complaining, just agreeing with Emma, that's all." Nodding toward my plate, he asks, "Can I try your salsa waffles?"

"How long have you been waiting to ask that?"

"Ever since you ordered them." His fork hovers over my plate.

Rolling my eyes, I give him the go ahead, but not without collecting my own bite. Together, we try each other's waffles and both marvel in their flavors. Sweet, caramelly, with a hint of buttermilk and banana. So good.

"Damn, I got the wrong waffles."

"I was thinking the same thing." I reach in for another bite, which causes Hayden to chuckle.

Resting his fork on his napkin, he lifts both our plates and swaps them. "There. Better?"

Grabbing another bite, I shove it in my mouth and close my eyes, dying over the caramel taste. "So much better. I thought I wanted savory, but boy was I wrong, it's all about the sweet for me tonight."

"What has been your weirdest craving so far?"

"Weirdest? Hmm." The prongs of my fork tap my lips while I think. "I would have to say when I asked Emma to bring me a brownie from the cafeteria and a small condiment cup of honey mustard."

Fork halfway to his mouth, salsa dripping off the waffle, Hayden's eyes go wide. "I like you, Adalyn, but if you tell me you dipped a brownie in honey mustard, we might have to part ways."

"What if I told you I ate the brownie and dipped my finger in the honey mustard? Does that make a difference?"

"I mean, it's better, but I'm still judging you a little."

"Don't judge me, judge the baby."

"You're insane." Hayden eyes the table, disgust written all over his face.

I cut the brownie on the table in half and dab a little honey mustard onto his plate. "This is your fault, you know that, right? You're the one who got me thinking about brownies and honey mustard and here we are, ready to divulge in our baby's guilty pleasure."

Sniffing the brownie and honey mustard together, he winces. "I think you're right, the baby is a demon."

"Come on." I nudge his shoulder with mine. "Give it a try. You never know, your new favorite dessert might be sitting in front of you right now."

"Pretty sure it isn't."

"Hayden, don't make the pregnant woman ask you again. Pick up a piece of that brownie, dip your pinky finger in the honey mustard for your brownie chaser, and follow my lead."

Shaking his head, he does what I say and holds the brownie bite to his mouth. Watching me first, I eat the brownie, chew, swallow, and then clean my pinky finger off, getting every last drop of honey mustard. "Mmm . . . so good. You're turn."

Apprehensive and possibly a little scared, he eats the brownie, eyes his fingers and then pops it in his mouth, sucking off the yellow-colored condiment.

Wincing, his throat muscles working up and down, he finishes swallowing and takes a big gulp of his water. Sticking his tongue out, he pats it with his cloth napkin and then politely sets it on his lap.

"Yup, the baby is a demon."

"As long as we're in agreement, I'm good with that."

"Thank you for dinner, I had a good time." Hayden pulls up to the curb of the apartment building and puts the car in park.

"So did I, almost felt like old times, huh?"

"After the awkward faded, yeah, it did."

Rubbing his hands together, he turns in his seat and says, "Now to finish our dates like we used to."

He obnoxiously puckers up and leans forward. Palming his forehead, I push him back. "As I can remember, you didn't kiss me for a very long time. And don't forget, this wasn't a date."

He laughs. "Yes, you keep reminding me of that." Moving back to his side of the car, he says, "I forgot to ask, are you liking your new job?"

"Love it actually. When I was at the hospital, I truly wondered if I was in the right profession, but at the new office, I feel at home. The doctors and staff are amazing, Shannon has been so sweet, and I'm not draining my body like I did at the hospital. I think it's one of the reasons I haven't been as sick as I was at the beginning of the pregnancy."

Growing silent, Hayden stares at his hands that rest on his lap. "You know, I never really told you how sorry I am that I wasn't there for you, at the beginning. It kills me thinking about you being so sick and me not there to help you."

"You didn't know."

"I should have checked in."

"You did." I touch his shoulder, wanting him to look me in the eyes. "You checked in, but I didn't respond." Not only that, I deleted every one of his texts, unable to face the reality that I was pregnant with a man who lived across the country.

"Why didn't you?"

The light and breezy atmosphere between us immediately turns heavy and emotional like there is a weight above us, pulling the air from the car.

"Because I didn't think we could honestly reach a point like this, where we could be friends, live near each other, and both be involved in the pregnancy."

"Friends." He breathes out the word with a heavy dose of disappointment lacing it.

Not wanting to get into that conversation right now, I reach into my purse and pull out a few pictures. "I almost forgot; I brought these for you to have." I hand over the pictures and turn on the light that rests above the dashboard of the car.

It takes Hayden a second to realize what he's looking at, but the moment he does, his face softens and his eyes well up with tears.

"Uh, I thought maybe you could hang one in your locker or something. I don't know if you guys do that or not—"

Clearing his throat, Hayden says, "This is perfect." He wipes at his cheek before I can catch a tear falling from his eye. "Tell me what I'm looking at."

I didn't expect this, his reaction to be so sweet, so heartfelt. It's cutting me deep, an arrow straight to my soul with Hayden's name attached to it.

Feeling overly emotional, I take a second to catch my breath before leaning over and describing everything in the picture. We spend the next five minutes looking through the photos, marveling at the little human inside of me.

Passing a thumb over the picture, Hayden says, "This means the world to me, Adalyn, that you would give me these pictures. Thank you."

"Of course, it's your baby too."

Moving his focus to me, he tilts my chin up, our eyes connecting, fusing together. "Our baby, Adalyn. This is our baby."

Under the dim light of the car, parked in front of my apartment building, Hayden moves in closer, his thumb and forefinger gripping the tip of my chin. I have room to move away, I have plenty of time to stop him, to tell him no, but the emotional side of me, the side that just watched a grown man cry over ultrasound pictures of his child? That side allows the softest press of Hayden's lips against mine.

He doesn't linger, he doesn't part my lips with his tongue, and he doesn't search for more. It's a light brushing of our mouths, but it speaks a thousand unsaid words. He still has feelings for me. I know this. But there is something else . . . appreciation.

Like he's thanking me for being the mother of our child.

Feeling weak and a bit wobbly, I pull away and tightly grip the strap to my purse, holding on to it like a lifeline.

I want to be with this man. I want to give him my heart. I want to be the one he spends the rest of his days with, but there is this dark, scary unknown that keeps creeping in on me full of what ifs.

What if he's traded again?

What if he meets someone better on the road?

What if I'm too much for him to handle?

What if what we had in Binghamton was truly a summer fling, and we both don't realize it until it's too late?

What if I truly end up being alone?

Putting some distance between us, I reach for the handle of the door and put one foot on the pavement.

"Adalyn . . ."

"Thank you for dinner, Hayden. Good luck on your road trip."

Now outside of the car, I give him a quick wave and shut the door before he can say anything else. Tonight was enough, seeing him fawn over the baby was enough, actually it was too much for my heart, my stupid, stupid heart.

When I open the door to my apartment, Logan is sitting on the couch, shirtless and in a pair of Nike shorts. He looks up from his laptop and takes off his black-rimmed glasses. "Hey." His brow creases. "Are you okay?"

Maintain a neutral face. Do not cry. Logan will only want to talk about it, and that's the last thing I want to do right now.

"Good," I say with a cheery smile that feels so incredibly forced.

"Okay, you'd tell me if he said something to you, right?"

"Of course."

I hang my purse on the coatrack in the entryway and take out my phone, Logan watching every one of my jagged movements. Does he notice how robotic I feel? Can he tell I'm on the verge of breaking down? Does he see my need to bury my head in my pillow?

"Where did he take you?"

Guess not.

"This really good waffle place. I'm stuffed though, so I think I'm going to call it a night. I'll see you in the morning."

Eyeing me suspiciously, Logan says, "Okay, let me know if you need anything."

"I will. Night." I give him a quick wave, skipping out on the hug he usually asks for every night and fast-walk to my bedroom where I shut my door and fling myself on the mattress, burying my head into my pillow.

I lie there for I don't know how long, my tears silent, soaking into the pink Egyptian cotton sheet set. Why can't I just say yes to Hayden? What's holding me back?

Is it what James said to me in New York City?

I've seen it before, a woman takes down a man of Hayden's caliber. I've seen them lose everything, and I don't want that for Hayden. I only want what's best for him.

Am I letting him get into my head?

Is it how quickly he went out with someone after we broke up?

Is it the high-profile woman he went out with? Does he deserve —*need*—someone like that?

Or is it the fear of becoming one of those women who wait around for their man, who wait around for a man to take care of them, to shield them, support him?

Am I so scared to be alone that I'm pushing away someone who wants to never let me be alone again?

Confused more now than ever, I turn to wipe my nose when my phone vibrates with a text. I don't even have to look at it to know who it's from.

Hayden: *I want you to know one thing, Adalyn. The pictures you gave me, the pictures of our baby, it reminded me of something. If I never get to win back your heart again, at least I'll have a piece of it in the child we share. Thank you for going out with me tonight. Sleep well, baby.*

Shallow breaths take over, my heart pounding in my chest, as more tears fall past my cheeks while I read his text over and over again.

I don't think I could be more confused.

At least that's what I thought . . .

CHAPTER TWENTY-FIVE

ADALYN

Hayden: *Good morning. Did you sleep well? Get some eggs? Drink some tea? Think about me at least three times?*

Chuckling, I put down my mascara brush and pick up my phone.

Adalyn: *Slept okay. I had some eggs and toast with some water this morning, happy?*

His response is immediate.

Hayden: *You failed to mention the thinking about me part.*

Adalyn: *I did on purpose.*

Hayden: *Ouch. That's okay, another knock from you to my ego isn't going to kill me. Although, it wouldn't hurt you to say how handsome I looked last night.*

Adalyn: *You're absurd.*

Hayden: *Just admit it. Dapper, that was me. Mr. Dapper Dan.*

Adalyn: *I don't think men who qualify as dapper beg people to call them dapper.*

Hayden: *There was no begging involved, just trying to nudge you in the right way of thinking. Come on, admit it.*

Adalyn: *Your hair looked nice.*

Hayden: Bingo! I'll take it.

He's so ridiculous, smiling I respond back.

Adalyn: And you smelled good too.

Hayden: Okay . . . that's not fair. Now I'm hard and on an airplane to San Jose.

Adalyn: Men are disgusting.

Hayden: Hey, I don't say women are disgusting when you get wet.

Adalyn: It's because we don't announce it like our coffee order in the morning.

Hayden: You should . . . it's sexy foreplay. Are you wet from this conversation?

Adalyn: No.

Hayden: Eh, it was worth a try.

~

H *ayden: Just got back to the hotel, have a second to chat?*
      Adalyn: Yeah, is everything okay?

The phone buzzes in my hand. Pausing Netflix, I shift my computer to the other side of my bed and answer my phone.

"Hello."

"Hey." Soft, deep, comforting, Hayden's voice brings chills to my skin. "How are you?"

"Good," I answer on a swallow. "Is everything okay?"

"Yeah, why wouldn't it be?"

"Well"—I pause and read his text again, pulling the phone away from my ear—"you asked if I had a second to chat? Made me think that maybe you had something specific to say."

"Nah, just wanted to hear your voice. That's all."

Sighing and relaxing into my mattress, the tension rolling off my shoulders, I say, "You know, it's not nice to scare pregnant women."

"Did I scare you?"

"Sort of," I answer honestly.

"Ahh, I'm sorry, baby. I didn't mean to. I wanted to chat, that's all. I know you go to bed soon, so thought I'd catch you before you drifted off."

Baby. He's been throwing that term of endearment around so casually, like this past summer. Does he realize the kind of effect it has on me? The kind of wave of heat that rushes through my body every time he says it?

He probably does. That's why he keeps saying it, to weaken me.

It's just another piece of Hayden that's been so different than every other man who has ever attempted to be with me.

I made a mental list in my head, trying to figure out why I've been so apprehensive, and at one in the morning, after my mind had been racing, it hit me. Hayden was my first when it came to an emotional relationship. Beside my dad and brothers, he was the first man to treat me like a lady, to respect me, to emotionally grab me and pull me into his universe while wanting to be in mine.

He chose to get to know my mind, my soul, rather than only my body.

He was the first to challenge me.

He was the first to shut me down when I tried to make things physical, telling me there was time for that.

And he was the first to truly break my heart.

Logan hurt me, but he didn't break my heart.

And being that I've never fully given my heart to another man, I wasn't expecting Hayden's departure from my life to hurt so bad, for it to affect me so much, for it to positively consume me.

I can't do that again. I can't risk that feeling again. I only had him in my life for such a short time, but he took over everything in my heart. Reorganized my priorities, my time, my focus. And I can't risk going back to such a dark place where I missed him terribly, where I cried more than I'd ever cried in my life. Losing Hayden's presence stole something essential, and I'm terrified of giving that away in case I lose it again. I need to be whole, strong, to be able to work and raise a baby on my own. I need to feel strong . . . *but that's what he's offering. His strength so I'm not alone.* No. I've told him I need to be strong. *On my own.*

And yet, here I am, talking to him, worrying that maybe something was wrong with him. Will I ever be able to separate myself, have a clean break?

Thinking about it for a second, I don't think I will. He's the father of my child, he will forever be in my life, whether I like it or not.

"Are you there, Adalyn?"

Pulling myself back in the conversation, not letting my negative thoughts take over, I say, "Yes, sorry. Just thought of something. So, uh, your trip was good?"

"Yeah," he says hesitantly. "But I don't want to talk about that. I've been all hockey all day, I like to decompress at the end of the day. I showed my mom the photos you gave me today."

Oh wow. I wonder how she took that? God, she probably hates me now. "Um . . . what did she say?"

"She didn't say much actually." *Oh. That's worse than I thought.* "She was so quiet I thought I'd lost the connection. Turns out she was having one of her silent-cry moments. Does your mom do that?"

"The silent cry? Hmm, not so much, but I know what you mean. Was she angry? With me?"

"God, no. Adalyn, she thinks you're amazing. I didn't tell her about when I found out. I just said we didn't want to say anything until you were past the first trimester." This man. *How can he protect me from his mom's wrath when I held back from telling him about his own baby?* "She told me to give you her number. If you want it. To talk about pregnancy . . ." He's silent, and I wonder what he's thinking. "Anyway, she's happy, Adalyn. She's so looking forward to having a grandchild to cuddle and fuss over. And she's really looking forward to meeting you."

"Ah . . . that's nice. She's nice." *She's nice? That's all I've got?* My mom wasn't exactly thrilled about the pregnancy, she mostly worried about me and going it alone. *My baby will have two grandmothers.* And I felt even worse thinking that in not telling Hayden,

I would have denied his mother knowing her own grandchild. *God.
I'm awful.*

"So, tell me, have you thought of names?"

"Names?"

"Baby names. Do you have any that you like?"

Oh . . . do I have names? I think about the little note section I
have in my phone for names I've heard and liked. Should I tell
him? Why the hell not? We're going through this process together.

"Maybe."

Chuckling, I can hear him shift, probably getting more
comfortable wherever he is. "Hit me with them."

"I want to hear yours first, just in case mine are stupid, I can
adjust based on what you say."

"What?" He laughs. "No way, that's not fair. I asked you first."

"And I'm the one who has to push a watermelon out of a quar-
ter-sized hole, so guess who's going to win this battle?"

"God, I like you pregnant. So damn feisty. It's sexy as hell."

"I was feisty before." Truth, being one of nine meant I had no
choice but to learn how to stick up for myself.

"True, but it's like you have an extra pinch of cayenne in you."

"Stop avoiding the question. Tell me your names."

"Fine, but no laughing, okay?"

"I can't make any promises." Turning to my side, I get comfortable, interested to hear his choices.

"Brutal, baby, totally brutal." Clearing his throat, he continues,
"Okay, if it's a boy, I was thinking something like Melvin."

I take pause, letting the silence stretch on the phone. "No, you
were not."

"Yes, I was. Melvin Holmes. It has a good ring to it, and it's my
great, great grandfather's name. He was a good man."

"A man you never met."

"Doesn't mean I shouldn't name my firstborn after him."

"Not happening. Sorry. Granddaddy Melvin is not happening."

"Okay, give me one of your boy names then." His voice is challenging, yet playful.

Thinking back to my list, I don't go with my number one, instead I toss up number two, wanting to gauge his reaction. "How about Reign."

He takes no time in answering. "Are you kidding?"

"What's wrong with Reign? You're just disagreeing because I didn't like Melvin."

"Melvin was a joke." I knew it, the bastard. "And I can't possibly have a son with the name Reign. Should his middle name be sunflower?"

I roll my eyes. "Reign, spelled r-e-i-g-n."

He pauses. "Oh . . . still no."

Even though I'm a little upset, I didn't think he'd go for that name, which is why I threw it out there first. I couldn't possibly have him hate my number-one pick.

"Fine, give me a real boy's name that you like."

"Hayden Junior." He chuckles on the phone.

"You're impossible. I'm hanging up now."

"Wait." The mirth in his voice continues. "I don't have a boy's name really, but I have a girl's name."

"If you say Adalyn Junior, I'm going to hang up."

"No, this is real. I promise."

I switch the phone in my hand. "Okay, go for it."

"If we have a girl, I really like the name Madeline."

The name rolls of his tongue with such love that it makes me actually have to pause, my mind envisioning Hayden with a little girl, running toward him, her eyes big and brown like his, her little knees all pudgy, calling out Daddy while he says her name. *Madeline*.

It's beautiful. The whole picture in my head, it's beautiful.

My eyes begin to sting. For fuck's sake, it's just a name, but for some reason the name hits me hard, harder than I thought because it truly isn't just a name.

It's an image.

It's a conceivable future.

"You hate it, don't you?"

Holding back my tears, my throat growing tight, I shake my head even though he can't see me.

"It's . . . beautiful, Hayden."

"Really?" Joy exudes him.

"Yes, really beautiful. I could see it."

"So does that mean it's on the table?"

"It does."

There is a knock on my door when I hear Hayden say, "Fuck, yes!"

"Uh, hold on one second."

Pulling the phone away from my ear, I put it on mute and call out to Logan. "Yes?"

He pops his head through a crack in the door and takes me in, his eyes slowly giving me a once-over, heat filling them when his eyes land on my bra-less breasts, my nipples hard, poking past the flimsy T-shirt.

"Am I interrupting you?" he finally asks when his eyes reach mine.

"Just on the phone. What's up?"

"Tomorrow night. I'm working a late shift tomorrow so I'm starting at eight. Want to go out and grab dinner together beforehand?"

Logan's job alternates between early, mid, and late shifts. He leaves the apartment at six thirty on his early shifts, which means we don't always cross paths until the night on those days. Because I've been so tired, we've mostly eaten at home each day, but going out sounds like fun for a change.

"Yeah, that sounds fine," I answer casually.

He winks at me. "Perfect, it's a date. I'll make reservations for six. Wear something sexy." Tapping the molding, he shuts the door, leaving me slightly confused. *Wear something sexy?* That was a joke, right? Because sexy right now for me is a pair of leggings and fuzzy socks.

"Adalyn, you there?"

Ridding all thoughts of Logan out of my head, I turn my attention back to Hayden, taking the phone off mute. "Sorry about that. I had to answer a text." The lie feels dirty coming off my tongue, like I'm trying to hide something and I'm really not. Logan just asked me to have dinner with him as a friend, and I accepted as a friend. That's that.

"Not a problem. Everything okay?"

"Yeah, everything is fine. Thank you. Although, I should probably get to bed soon. The baby has been wiping me out."

"I bet. I can't imagine what it would be like to be having a demon sucking the life from you every day."

That makes me snort laugh. I wipe at my nose when I say, "Men will never know the tribulations we go through to bring life into the world."

"Well, for what it's worth, I think you're superwoman and I mean that." He grows serious. "You've battled severe morning sickness, weight loss, and all the hormones that go along with your body changing with the baby. You've moved across country after spending week after week working long hours in the hospital to be closer to me as a favor. You've learned a whole new job, in a foreign city far away from your family, and you still have that beautiful smile on your face. I'm in awe, Adalyn, and I'm not just saying that. You truly are awe-inspiring."

Biting on my bottom lip, heart sputtering in my chest, I weakly say, "Thank you."

"Of course . . . now this is when you tell me how amazing I am at hockey and being a supportive baby daddy."

Chuckling, I wipe away a stray tear. "I've yet to see you play hockey, so I can't speak true to that, but the supportive thing, you've been incredibly supportive. The pizza alone has been a savior, not to mention the cute texts checking up on me."

"Just want to make sure my girl is okay, that's all, even from afar. Which reminds me, there should be cinnamon buns at the office tomorrow morning for you and the girls. Don't eat too much. Baby demon sent me Morse Code using its umbilical cord that it wanted cinnamon buns."

"You realize how disturbing an image that is?"

"I can't picture the baby without horns and a two-pronged fork, so is there something wrong with me?"

Now that he says it, the image is firmly planted in my head now. "Yes, something is seriously wrong with you."

"And yet, you had unprotected sex with me, so that tells me there is something alluring about me."

"It's because you made me wait so damn long. I was desperate to see what all the fuss was about."

Chuckling, he says, "Your words, baby. *That was so fucking hot. Well worth the wait.* And I couldn't have agreed more."

He's right. I did say that. Because it was. But I can't reinforce that right now. "Don't gloat too much, you were just average."

"Oh bullshit." Too much for holding back, a laugh pops out of me. "FaceTime me right now. I'll make you come in two minutes." Tempting, since I've been feeling more and more turned on with every day the nausea fades.

I must take too long to answer because Hayden says, "Thinking about it? Are those pregnancy hormones kicking in?"

"What? No!" I answer entirely too quickly. I might have painted a giant sign over my head that says I'm horny.

When I think Hayden is about to laugh, he doesn't, instead he grows even more serious than before, more intense. "Are you horny, Adalyn?"

"This is not something we should be talking about. I should go."

"Answer the question, Adalyn." Firm and so male, his voice is like a lightning bolt straight to my core.

"No." I don't even believe myself, my answer so weak, so unconvincing.

"Do your nipples ache? Is your pussy throbbing? Are you wet?" Back to the wet conversation.

As much as I'd like to deny it, I'm so incredibly wet right now, just from hearing his voice drop lower on the phone, the deep rumble shaking me from the tips of my toes to the apex between my legs.

"Adalyn, I'm waiting on an answer."

"Hayden . . ." I draw out, hating how quickly he's heated my body, how quickly a few questions have brought back vivid memories of him hovering over me, pulsing in and out, his long, thick cock rubbing me in such a sensual way I can practically feel the thrusting right now.

"Answer me."

Biting on my bottom lip, my hips slowly starting to rotate, looking for some sort of relief. I should not be talking about this with him. I should hang up right now. I shouldn't be leading him on when I have no clue what I want, but the strong need I have for him holds me back.

"Yes." It's one word, one simple word, but it shifts our conversation from casual to hot in seconds.

Hayden's breathing picks up, his groan loud, echoing through the phone.

"Fuck, do you have a vibrator?"

"We're not doing this on the phone, Hayden." There, some sense has been knocked into me.

"Saturday," he groans. "I get home around noon, have dinner with me."

"I'm not having sex with you." And I'm standing firm with that statement.

"Say yes to dinner."

Reaching between my legs, under my underwear, I press lightly on my clit and try to hold back my moan.

"Fuck, Adalyn, what are you doing?"

I don't answer him, instead, I say, "See you Saturday night."

Hanging up, I toss the phone to the side and start moving my fingers through my slit, pressing down on my clit, letting the built-up tension in my body slowly ease. Spreading my legs wider, I sink into the pillow just as my phone buzzes next to me.

Knowing exactly who it is, I take a moment to read his text.

Hayden: *I swear to God, if you're pleasuring yourself right now, I might not be able to control myself on Saturday.*

Smiling, I talk to text.

Adalyn: *Good thing I'm not telling you what I'm doing right now.*

He responds immediately.

Hayden: *Send me a picture.*

Adalyn: *Never. Night, Hayden.*

Hayden: *You're mine, Adalyn. And I'll be sure to show you that Saturday.*

With those last words read, I lean on the memory of his chiseled body above mine, his sexy voice rattling through my ear, and bring myself to orgasm for the first time since I've been without Hayden.

And oh my God, was that much needed.

CHAPTER TWENTY-SIX

LOGAN

M y brother's words play on repeat in my head as I help
Adalyn into her chair, her soft, brown hair brushing the
back of my hand when she sits down.

Do something, or you're going to regret it forever.

Moving out to California was the first step. Although moving
away from Binghamton has been a wish of mine for a while. This
was the perfect excuse to getaway, start a new chapter in my life,
hopefully with Adalyn.

Being there for Adalyn was the second step.

Taking her to dinner is the third step.

Making my move is the fourth.

The fourth is what terrifies me. What if she turns me down?
What if she still has feelings for Hayden? From the conversations
we've shared, there is nothing going on between them, but after
her date on Wednesday, she's been weird, a little standoff-ish
with me.

That's why I had to act quickly.

But acting quickly means I didn't have enough time to pump
myself up, and fuck do I need time.

This is Adalyn, the girl I've lusted after for years. The girl I foolishly screwed things up with.

Because of nerves!

Fucking nerves.

I had the best fucking night of my life with her wrapped in my arms, and the next morning I blew it. I didn't know what to say, I didn't know how to react, and because of that I ended up saying the completely wrong thing.

That was a mistake.

Those words will haunt me until the day I die, I'm sure of it, especially if I've lost Adalyn forever.

Why did I say those words? Besides being an idiot, because when I woke up with her by my side, I went to reach for her, and in that split second when my arm began to wrap around her . . . she flinched.

Fucking flinched.

I was spooked and instead of spending that morning worshipping Adalyn all over again, I balked and said the last thing that should ever have come out of my mouth.

Now I'm in the midst of trying to win her back, playing the friend role with the hopes that when Jackass fucks up once again, I can swoop in and take the spot I never should have lost.

Although, after the other night, it seems like my time is running out. So with Hayden out of town, I have to make my move.

"That dress is gorgeous on you, Addie."

Blushing, she folds her napkin on her lap. "Thank you. It was the only nice thing that fits." Scanning the dining area, she leans forward and whispers, "This place is really nice, Logan. You didn't have to bring me here."

"I wanted to. Thought you deserved a nice night out, especially since the morning sickness has died down and you're eating more. Thought a little celebration was in order. A feast-a-bration."

A big smile spreads across her face. "A feast-a-bration, I like that. Does that mean we can get two sides to share?"

"You can get all the sides you want, Addie."

After Emma, Addie, and I graduated from college, one of the first things we did was go to a fancy steakhouse for dinner to celebrate. We always wanted to go to one of those places where the only thing served to you is a piece of steak on the plate, and if you wanted potatoes, it was an additional charge.

Fancy and ridiculous.

But we loved it. We ended up ordering way too much, spending a good chunk of our graduation money, and had the best time, drinking our champagne with our pinkies lifted high in the air.

I wanted a repeat of that night. I wanted to remind Adalyn how great we are together.

Staring at her menu, she says, "These prices are high, Logan."

I reach across the table and take her hand in mine, rubbing the back of her knuckles. "Don't worry about it. It's on me."

"Oh no, I don't want you to—"

"I asked you out, Addie, so it's on me. Just enjoy the night. The last few weeks have been hell; let's celebrate what's to come."

"Are you sure?"

"Positive." I give her a wink and turn to my menu. "The filet sounds amazing with the truffle butter."

"And the roasted cauliflower with cheese and the salt-boiled potatoes with rosemary."

"And the house onion rings."

Peering up from her menu, she smirks. "Looks like we might need a to-go bag like last time."

Smiling as well, I say, "Leftovers at midnight are already calling our name."

"Yeah but this time, I won't be drunk eating them."

"Which means you have no excuse to not follow proper leftover etiquette."

She shakes her head in mirth. "There is no leftover etiquette. If you eye it, you eat it. Simple as that."

"Which means some people don't even get a chance to eat them."

She shrugs and takes a sip from her water glass. "The benefit of growing up in a big family. I learned to be quick on the trigger where food is concerned. I have no shame in it."

"Clearly."

We put our orders in with the waitress, I order a Coke and Adalyn sticks with her water, claiming she hasn't gotten in her daily ounces yet today, but a part of me wonders if she's sticking with water because it's free.

"How have you been liking your new job?"

"It's been good. The hours are much nicer; the doctors are awesome and have encouraged me to go for my degree to become a physician's assistant. They have a program in the office that would pay for it after I've been there for six months."

"Really? That's amazing. Are you going to do it?"

I nod and take a sip of my Coke. "Yeah, being a nurse never was the long-term plan, but I wanted to see if the medical field was something I could do for life before going all the way, and honestly, I don't think I could see myself doing anything else at this point. I love helping people."

"You were born to be in the medical field. You're so kind and gentle with your patients," she says.

"So would you say I have excellent bedside manner?"

She rolls her eyes. "You still have rough hands, they could use a little more lotion."

I hold up my hands for both of us to inspect them. "These are man hands. There is nothing wrong with that."

"They're like sandpaper."

"They are not." I laugh. "You're so full of it. If we're talking sandpaper, let's talk about your elbows."

She points her finger at me, humor in her shocked expression. "That was one summer. How dare you bring that up again?"

"Hey, you cut a hole in leather with those crusty elbows of yours."

"Oh my God, you're the worst, I did not."

I shrug. "I have photo evidence to prove it."

"Fine . . . prove it." She folds her hands on the table and waits.

Fuck, she's totally calling my bluff. I wouldn't expect anything less from her.

"Oh my God." Adalyn leans back in her chair, pats her face with her napkin, and in the most ladylike manner, rubs her belly. "Now I know what they mean when they say you're eating for two."

"Two?" I raise my eyebrows in question. "Adalyn, you ate for an entire platoon. What happened to leftovers?"

"There are still leftovers, so don't make it seem like I ate all the food. You had a part in this massacre as well." She motions to the almost-clean plates.

Playing with a potato on my plate, I say, "It was really good, wasn't it?"

"So good I might cry myself to sleep thinking about that truffle butter."

"And you know, oddly, I was okay eating it even though in the Urban Dictionary it's known as something else."

She scoffs. "Ugh, those Urban Dictionary people. They have taken a delicacy and ruined it with their perverted minds. They have taken away my ability to shout in the middle of crowded area that I love truffle butter. Jerks."

Chuckling, I say, "Because you're often shouting into crowds about fine foods."

"I would more often if Urban Dictionary didn't ruin it for me."

"Want me to write them a letter?"

She plucks a piece of lint off her dress. "Yes, I think that might help. I get them wanting to be creative but if we could keep fine foods off the table, that would be appreciated."

"It's a fair ask. I'll craft my email tomorrow."

Nodding and closing her eyes, she says, "You're a good man, Logan, a very good man."

Paying the check and grabbing our small amount of leftovers we head to the car. "There is an overlook over there, want to go check it out?"

Adalyn looks over my shoulder and smiles. "Would love to. I don't think I've ever seen the city at night." We put the leftovers in the car and head to the lookout. There are a few people milling about but not enough to make it crowded.

Walking to the rock wall, we take in the cityscape.

"It's so pretty at night. No smog distracting your view, glittering lights sparkling among the dark palm trees. Makes me think of La La Land."

I chuckle. "That movie. Don't even get me started."

"Besides the end"—she touches my shoulder—"it was a good movie, admit it."

"I can't admit to a movie being good if the end sucks. Sorry, but I will never be a fan."

"But . . . Ryan Gosling," she defends.

I shake my head. "That's not going to work on me."

"Fine, Emma Stone."

I shrug my one shoulder. "Eh, she's beautiful, but she didn't give me the feelings like Rachel McAdams did when she was teamed up with Ryan in The Notebook."

"You're absurd. Emma and Ryan by far have more chemistry."

Turning toward her, I point to my chest. "I'm absurd? You're the one saying Emma and Ryan had more chemistry in La La Land, than Ryan and Rachel in The Notebook. Take a poll right now. Twenty bucks says Rachel and Ryan win. Go ahead ask the people around us."

Taking in the couples around us, she turtles in on herself and shakes her head.

"Aha, because you know I'm right."

"No." She swats at me. "It's because I don't want to disrupt their evenings with your childish ways."

"Ahh, I'm childish now, huh?" I wrap my arms around her and bring her back to my chest, my hands linking in front of her belly.

For a brief moment, I pause, trying to memorize this moment. The way she smells, sweet and fresh. The way her hair brushes against my clean-shaven face, soft and airy. The way her body fits against mine, petite and curvy. The way my heart is so goddamn full at this very moment.

"Are you cold?" I whisper into her ear.

She shakes her head and sighs, looking toward the cityscape. "How many movie stars do you think are driving around the streets right now?"

My lips curve up. "At least fifty."

"Got to be at least fifty. There are so many movie stars, and they're always going places."

"Yup, always going places." I chuckle. "Can't stop those movie stars."

"Real busy bees. Do you think we'll ever run into one living here?"

Bending my head, I pull her in a little closer so her cheek is almost caressing mine, just a few inches shy. "I sure as hell hope so because then what was this move all about? The whole point of us relocating here was to run into a movie star. What a letdown that would be if we never once bump into Jake Gyllenhaal at Taco Bell."

"Blasphemy, that's what that would be." She takes a second to think and then says, "Is that who you want to bump into? Jake? Because I don't recall you being a super fan."

"For some weird reason, it was the first name that came to mind. But now that you asked, who do I want to bump into? Hmm." I take a moment to really think about my choices. So many celebrities, so many opportunities. "I guess if I had to choose one, I would say Mark Hamill."

"Mark Hamill as in . . . Luke Skywalker?"

"The one and only." I kiss the top of her head and squeeze her tighter. "What a freaking dream that would be."

"Huh, I kind of thought you would pick a girl."

"Why, when I have all the girl I need in my arms right now?"

The minute she stiffens in my embrace, I know my words are

unexpected, maybe a little too soon. Fuck though, I feel like I can't hold back any longer.

"Are you ready to go?" I ask, not wanting to have this conversation with random people milling about us.

"Uh, yeah. It's getting late."

The door clicks shut behind me as I lock up, while Adalyn walks into the living room, her hand playing in her hair.

The car ride wasn't silent like I thought it would be. Instead, we talked about the celebrity she would want to run into—Scott Eastwood, because The Longest Ride "did her in"—and what she would do if she ever did run into him. Her response was cute, which was most likely cry like a banshee while trying to talk to him at the same time. She's confident that Scott, or Scotty as she likes to call him, would be very understanding and cool about her "fangirl" moment.

We felt normal. We felt like the old us, but now that we're home, I know I'm about to throw a wrench into our normal.

Taking a deep breath, hands on my hips, I ask, "Can we talk for a second before you go to bed?"

She's in the midst of taking her shoes off when she nods, not knowing what's coming her way. "Of course, what's up? Are you moving out already?" She playfully pouts, and I can't help but think, possibly, if this doesn't go my way. There is no way I can continue to live with her if there is no future with her. That would be like dangling a glass of bourbon in front of an alcoholic. I know this because that's what it has felt like for the last few weeks. Being friends with Addie is easy because I love her so fucking much. But it's also brutal because I want more. *Surely it's our time.*

Nerves ratcheting up my spine, my voice feeling tight and shaky, I try to ease my body, telling myself this is Adalyn. I've known her for a long time, we've shared an amazing night together, there is no reason to be nervous, even if she moved out to California to be closer to the man she has a baby with.

That's nothing to worry about . . .

"Not moving out." I take a seat on the couch and pat the cushion next to me. "Take a seat."

Trepidation in her every move, she slowly lowers herself. "Okay, you're starting to make me nervous. Is everything okay?"

"Yes," I say quickly, taking her hands in mine. "Everything is fine, I'm just . . . fuck, I'm nervous, Addie."

"Nervous? Why? Are you sick?"

"No." I shake my head. "I'm . . . I'm in love."

"Oh." She sits back, keeping her hands in mine, then she does the one thing I never would have expected her to do. She laughs.

Brows pinched together, feeling slightly offended, I ask, "What's so funny?"

Removing one of her hands to mine, she presses it against her chest and says, "Oh, I'm sorry, Logan, I just thought . . . I don't know . . . that you were sick or something, not that you were in love. I was preparing myself for this big cancer scare. You're in love." She squeezes my hand. "That's amazing. Who's the lucky girl?"

Oh fuck, this is awful.

This is so fucking awful.

What's worse than a girl laughing when you say you're in love?

I have the answer. When she's completely clueless as to who you're in love with. Even worse when it's her.

Has she not noticed the way I look at her, the way I care for her, the way I fucking lust after her every night when we're snuggled up close, watching Netflix? Have I not been obvious enough?

"Who is it? Do I know her?" Adalyn continues.

Wanting to punch myself in the face to end my misery, I nod my head, lips tightly pressed together.

"Oh. Hmm . . . oh does she work at my office?"

Oh, for fuck's sake.

"It's you, Adalyn."

Eyes rounded, mouth parted, realization hitting her, she stays seated next to me, and I watch as my words soak in.

I don't say anything else. I don't know what else to say, because it's almost as if the confession has made me tongue-tied. Like the look in her eyes, the *deer in the headlights* look has clammed me up. Hell, I don't know what I was expecting.

Best-case scenario: she fans herself and melts into my arms, telling me she loves me too.

Worst-case scenario: she slowly backs away, moonwalk style, and locks herself in her bedroom where she pretends she doesn't speak English.

From the looks of it, I might see her cute self moonwalk out of this living room.

"Ho-how long?" She breaks the silence but doesn't look at me. I try to tell myself it's nothing to worry about.

"I don't know, a few years now."

That gets her attention, snapping her head up, she parrots, "A few years? And you're telling me now? I don't . . . I . . . but you said we were a mistake." Standing now, she begins to pace the living room. "You broke my heart that morning, Logan. Do you realize that? You made me feel so worthless, so . . . used."

Fuck.

"That morning, that day, those words. I wish I could take them all back." I stand, feeling awkward being the only one sitting. "You have no idea how much I've regretted saying that. From the moment the words left my lips, I knew it was a huge mistake."

"Then why say them?"

"Because I was terrified, Adalyn. I'd slept with the girl I'd been pining after, and when I went to reach over for you, you flinched."

She scoffs. "I didn't flinch."

"You did, Addie. You flinched, and like a dick, I thought I would try to save face and not make it hard on you. I said what I thought you were going to say."

Staring at me, confusion in her brow, her eyes narrowed, mouth still parted, she shakes her head. "I don't understand. Why not just say your true feelings?"

"Because." I grab the back of my neck. "Because you were a girl who went from man to man. At the time, I thought maybe I was different, but when you flinched, fuck, I thought I was just another number, another one of those guys."

"Are you kidding me?" She throws her arms up in the air. "Logan, you are my friend, one of my best friends. Do you really think I would have slept with you and then left?"

"I don't know. I was so goddamn shocked you actually gave me a shot."

"I can't believe this. And what now, you decide to tell me you love me when I'm knee-deep pregnant with another man's baby? Can you say poor timing, Logan?"

"I know, I know." I run my hands through my hair, frustrated with myself. "Believe me, this isn't how I wanted this to go down, but I thought I could get over you. I told myself I could, but the minute I saw you with him, I lost all ability to think straight. I was hoping it was only a fling, but when things started to get serious, I started to go crazy. But then he left. I knew it was my time to make my move, but I wanted to give you time to grieve the loss of your relationship—"

"And then I found out I was pregnant," she finishes for me, realizing my struggle with my timing.

"Talk about a blow to the fucking gut. But he was gone, and I was there. I told myself I didn't care that it was his baby; I wouldn't be the paternal father. I still wanted to be there, I wanted to be with you."

"And you were." Her eyes well up with tears, her face growing somber and the tension easing out of her shoulders, the anger dissipating. "And you moved out here."

"Because I love you, and I can't seem to let go." I take a step forward. "No matter how much I try to convince myself I'm not in love with you, I can't. You're ingrained in my heart, Adalyn." I point to my chest. "Right here, you have permanent residence."

"Logan . . ." She breathes out, her eyes widening when I take another step forward and wrap my arm around her waist, pulling her close to my body. Her hand falls to my chest, grasping for balance, her little baby bump poking my stomach. So fucking sweet.

I cup her face, tucking a loose strand of hair behind her ear, and search her eyes. "This right here, this is where I want to be. I don't care if you're having another man's baby. I don't care if we're living in this tiny apartment forever with a screaming baby in the next room, because as long as I'm with you, that's all that matters."

Her eyes search mine, her voice lost, so instead of waiting for her to speak, I bend my head forward, breathing in her scent. Mint and vanilla. Her fingers curl into my shirt, my hand grips her hip, holding her in place while I caress the softness of her cheek with my thumb, my intent worn on my sleeve.

Inches from her mouth, I say, "I love you so much, Adalyn, and all I want is to be with you." Closing the distance between us, I press my lips across hers, taking a moment to soak in the feel of her soft mouth against mine.

I don't push her. I don't part her mouth with my tongue despite wanting to, and I don't spend more than a few seconds exploring her lips. Pushing away, shock in her eyes, hand to her lips, she steps out of my grasp and backs up, tripping over the coffee table and falling backward. Luckily I catch her arms before she can tumble to the floor.

"Jesus, Adalyn. Be careful." I right her but she keeps walking backward to her room.

Shaking her head, she says, "I . . . I can't do this right now, Logan."

Trying not to get upset, I nod my head. "I'm not going anywhere, Adalyn. I'm here."

With that, she shuts her bedroom door, leaving me alone in the living room, my actions hanging heavily in the air.

So there was partial moonwalking. But it's not like she slapped me across the face when I kissed her. Maybe she didn't kiss me back, but I also caught her completely off guard tonight. She was expecting to go to dinner with her friend, which she did, but then I hit her hard with my feelings. That's a lot for a someone to take in, let alone a pregnant woman who's highly emotional.

I need to be patient. I need Hayden to screw up again and when he does, I'll swoop in. Adalyn knows how I feel. I put it out there, now I need to wait.

Patience. This is a marathon, not a sprint.

CHAPTER TWENTY-SEVEN

ADALYN

R emember when I said I've never been more confused?
I was wrong.

This is confused.

And to add to the level of confusion, Hayden is on the way to my apartment to pick me up. He said he would come to the door but there is no way in hell I'm going to let that happen.

He fought me about it, saying he's cool with Logan, and I'm going to guess after last night, he's not going to be cool with him at all.

Can we just take a moment to consider what happened last night?

Logan, my dear friend, who I've been through everything with from bad one-night stands to learning how to insert a catheter . . . we've gone through it together. The good, the bad, and the incredibly ugly.

And out of the blue, he goes and tells me he loves me and then kisses me.

What the hell?

And for the record, before you go judging me, HE kissed ME.

There was no reciprocating of the kiss. No, I was pretty much a dead fish hanging off his lips last night. He must not have kissed a lot of women lately because when he pulled away, he looked fully satisfied.

He must have been kissing carps for a while if that was pleasing to him.

But he's in love with me.

In love.

The big L word. Where the hell did that come from?

In all honestly, I'm not being naïve here. After our night together, I really thought there was no chance in hell Logan and I would ever be a couple. Anyone in my position would think the same thing.

This was a mistake.

It's clear-cut. There is no going forward from there.

Oh and don't get me started on the "flinch," because that's so ridiculous. For all I know, I could have had an ill-timed muscle spasm. I'm pretty sure I wouldn't have flinched if he went to snuggle with me.

Ugh, men.

A flinch.

That's what this all comes to. A freaking flinch. How about you ask me, did you just flinch or did you have a morning chill? I was naked after all. I could have been cold. A little shiver is what scared him off.

Absurd.

It's times like these I miss Emma. It hasn't been easy being so far away, but we have managed to connect most days either in the mornings before a shift like old times, or in the early evenings when we were both finished work. This morning, I tried calling Emma to talk about Logan's declaration, but we couldn't catch each other. She'd worked a morning shift then was helping Racer at the bridal store he's working at. I was taking a nap when she called back. And her phone was off when I tried her back. I knew what that meant. When she hasn't spent much time with Tucker, she turns off her phone and it doesn't come on until . . . well, until *she* has come . . . well, multiple times. And he's good for it. For. Hours. But I needed my friend. I still couldn't get my head around Logan saying he'd been pining for me. I'd thought he'd been into Emma before she got together with Tucker. But he said he'd been pining after me for years. Did Emma know? Had she seen that? God, I was so confused. Part of me felt angry that he'd waited until we were here because it was *his turn to make his move*. It was so . . . contrived. Yes, he is amazing in how he packed everything up and left the East Coast to support me in LA. I'll never forget that. But knowing he was doing it with the intention of making his move because things with Hayden didn't work out. *Gah.* The whole thing was absurd.

Rolling my eyes, I snag my purse, check myself in the mirror one last time, and make my way to the front door. Logan is on the couch, his computer propped on his lap watching something on Netflix.

Trying to be sneaky, I tiptoe to the door but not having an invisibility cloak at my disposal in such a small apartment makes it impossibly hard to sneak out without going undetected.

"Where you off to?"

Okay, I practiced this in my room. I wore jeans and a regular white shirt with leopard-print flats. Casual but still nice, not looking all gussied up for a night out.

"Shannon is picking me up. We're going to the movies and then dinner." My voice sounds a little robotic, but I plaster on a huge smile, showing off every last one of my teeth.

"What movie?"

Ha, got it covered and looked up times to make sure what I said matched up.

"The new Marvel movie."

"Really? I didn't know you were into Marvel movies." I'm not. He shuts his computer. "I'll tag along, let me grab my wallet and shoes."

What? Who just invites themselves like that? Think, Adalyn.

Pretty sure Hayden won't be happy to take me to a Marvel movie with Logan.

"You can't," I shout. Laughing nervously, I play with the strap of my purse and say, "Shannon wanted a girl's night."

Raising an eyebrow at me, he asks, "Why are you looking all fidgety?"

"I drank a can of real Coke a few second ago, pounded it hard. The sugar makes me feel high as a kite." I wipe my forehead. "Man, look out, high pregnant woman coming through."

Now his brow is creased when he steps closer to me. To say I'm a good liar under pressure is not necessarily correct. I feel like he can see right through me.

"You drank one of my Cokes without asking?" He tsks at me. "That's a roommate no-no, Adalyn. You should know that. Just poor etiquette." When he reaches me, he pulls me into a hug and kisses the top of my head. "Have fun with Shannon, and tell her I said hi, okay?"

"Yup." I swallow hard. "We'll be out late, so don't wait up."

"Okay. Be careful. Call me if you need anything."

With another kiss to the head, he sends me on my sweaty way, waving at me from the door. Thankfully he shuts it, not watching me the entire time.

It's not like I'm already having a difficult time here, Logan has to come into the mix and throw me for an entire loop.

Outside, waiting for Hayden, I try to process everything. Logan is my friend, a boy I once briefly saw myself with long ago, a boy who broke my heart, who kept me guarded. But he's also been there for me when I've needed someone the most. He's protected me, guided me, and has been my rock.

And then there is Hayden.

He pulls up to the curb in his sleek car, a pinch in his brow when I open the door. "I told you I would come to the door. I don't want you to have to wait outside for me."

"It's fine," I say, getting immediately in and buckling up. Taking a second, fidgeting with my purse, I tell myself to forget the bomb

Logan dropped on me last night. Hayden deserves my full atten-tion, especially when he's making such an effort. He drove straight from the airport to here, and I'm sure he's exhausted.

"How was your flight?" I ask casually. He eyes me for a second before he starts driving.

"Fine, got in an hour of sleep. You know, it's dark out, Adalyn, something could have happened to you."

"Hayden, I'm fine." I touch his arm that's gripping tightly onto the gearshift. "It's really okay."

Exhaling heavily, he looks unhappy but moves on when he asks, "Do you like Chinese food?"

"Love it. Did you get us some?"

"Yup, should arrive shortly after we do."

We're not in the car for more than five minutes when Hayden is pulling into an underground garage and parking in a spot reserved for him.

Out of the car, he guides me to the elevator where he has to flash a key card to get started and presses the tenth floor. When we were pulling in, I didn't realize that one, he lived so close, and two, the building was more than ten floors. It didn't seem that tall when we drove into it.

"You're pretty close, aren't you?"

"Planned it that way." Reaching out, he links my hand with his and leads the way when we step off the elevator. The hallway is a light shade of green with grey flooring, and modern, sleek-looking lights illuminate the dark but clean hallway.

It doesn't take long to reach his unit, 10A. Not releasing my hand, Hayden opens the door and lets me in first. The room opens up to a span of windows overlooking the city below. To the right is an open-concept kitchen with dark cabinets, chrome hardware, and subway-tile backsplash. It's beautiful and a great size for entertaining. To the left is a spacious great room connected to a dining room. All the furniture is dark, just like the cabinets, with accents of white and green. There isn't much personalization to the space, just a few picture frames on a credenza, but it's the view that's breathtaking. It's what draws me.

Walking toward the windows, I take in the busy streets below, wondering once again if there are any celebrities below us. Hell, are there celebrities in this building? Hayden is technically considered a celebrity, but in my eyes, he's just sweet and handsome Hayden, not this mega-star everyone deems him to be.

Although, the people closest to Scott Eastwood must think the same thing.

"Would you like anything to drink?"

"Water is great," I call over my shoulder, spotting my apartment. "I didn't realize how close you were to me. You can see my place from here. You know, I could have walked here."

That statement makes Hayden laugh, deep and throaty . . . and oh so sexy. "Adalyn, I didn't even want you waiting outside after I realized what an idiot I was being. Do you really think I would want you to walk here, in the dark? Yeah, not happening and don't attempt it, or I'm going to be really mad at you."

"It's a nice area, Hayden."

Coming up behind me, he hands me my water and places his hand on my hip. Possessive, marking his territory, even though it's just us in his apartment. It's as though no time has passed, and it's simply how we stand when close to each other. *Easy.*

"I don't care." His thumb rubs across my side, silently letting me know he's looking out for me.

"This place is beautiful," I say, taking in the room. "So open and airy. And the ceilings, they're so high. Who knew apartments could feel so big?"

"I wanted to get you a better place, Adalyn, but your budget—"

I silence him with my hand to his lips. "I love my apartment, and it's perfect. I was just admiring yours."

Eyes softening, he lightly kisses my fingers and then links them with his. He brings me to the couch where we both take a seat, facing each other. Hayden's large arm, defined and full of rippling sinew, spans across the back, his hand toying with a strand of my hair. Our propped-up knees knock against each other, our bodies are close, but still a reasonable distance for a conversation.

"Out of your brothers, who's your favorite?"

"What?" I laugh, surprised by his question.

"You have to have a favorite. Hell, I have a favorite brother and mine are twins."

"I understand the question, I'm just confused where it came from. I figured you would ask how I am, how the baby is or something like that."

Becoming serious, Hayden says, "I love that baby growing inside of you with everything in me, Adalyn, but you are more than a vessel carrying my baby around. I want to know more about *you*."

A little surprised, it takes me a second to gather myself. This is why I haven't been able to erase Hayden from my life . . . from my heart. Because just when I think I can do it, that I'm strong enough to put distance between us, he says things like that, pulling me right back in, firmly planting himself in my life. *Because he cares for you, Adalyn. He never stopped.*

Clearing my throat, I say, "Favorite brother, huh? Hmm, that's hard since I have so many, but if I had to choose one of them, I would probably go with Patrick. He's closest in age to me, and growing up, he's who I played with the most. He's the one I stay in contact with the most. Plus it helps that I like his wife the most. She's fun, and when we first met, she made it known she was here and sticking around so no need to try to weed her out. She's a tough cookie and takes a lot from the family. She tells us to fuck off when she wants to but is so incredibly loving."

"Sounds a lot like someone I know." Hayden tugs on the strand of hair he's playing with.

"I guess we are a lot alike. What about you? Who's your favorite brother?"

Before he answers, he eyes me up and down. "Does this stay in the vault?"

"The vault?"

"Yeah"—he nods—"the vault. Does this stay between us and

only us? Once the words are uttered out of my mouth, you have to keep them to yourself, locked up in the vault."

"Ah, I see. You don't want me telling your brothers you have a favorite."

"Exactly. Because, believe it or not, they'd never let me live it down, and that is something I really don't want to live through. They know me as loving them equally, just like all parents apparently love their children equally."

"Load of crock." I tap his knee and lean forward as if telling a secret. "My dad says I'm by far his favorite, which makes complete sense because my sister has always been quiet and at times aloof, independent, and of course, all my brothers are numbskulls. But when it comes to my mom"—I shake my head in disappointment —"Shane is her favorite."

"Shane?"

"Middle kid. He's her project."

"What do you mean by that?" A small chuckle pops out of that enticing mouth of his.

"Starting as a teenager, he's always been 'lost' and my mom has made it her mission to help him find his way."

"As every good parent should."

I grip his arm for emphasis. "I think so too, don't get me wrong, but when your mom goes to your college classes with you, there's an issue."

"Oh fuck, did she really?" The curve of his smile brings out the joy inside me. It relaxes me, helps me forget about everything else and enables me to focus on one thing: the man in front of me. *The man who looks at me as if I'm his world. As if every word from my mouth is vital to him somehow. The man I wished could be mine.*

"I wouldn't lie to you. She wouldn't have done that with any of her other kids. She's a total Shane fan."

"Well, seems like your dad is the smarter parent." Winking, Hayden flashes me that straight white smile, melting me with one look at a time. This is what I've missed the most. Yes, our chemistry was out of this world, but despite only knowing Hayden a short time, our friendship had been so effortless. I've missed him. Missed this. I like learning things about him, because I truly like the man.

"Okay, so tell me your favorite brother. This is all in the vault."

"Promise?"

"Promise."

Giving me one last once-over, he deems me worthy of such private information and divulges one of his deepest, darkest secrets. At least that's what I tell myself; it is for more of a dramatic effect.

"Favorite brother would have to be Halsey."

I lean back, a little surprised by his confession. "Huh, I would have guessed you were going to say Holden."

"Yeah, why's that?"

"I don't know. He's more outgoing and fun. It seems like you would have had more good times with him growing up. Halsey is so reserved and quiet. Barely entertained unless on the rare occasion you can grab a little smirk from him."

"That's why I like him more. He doesn't like someone to be nice. You have to earn his approval and when you do, he's a good time, more so than Holden, because he comes without the asshole attitude. I love both brothers, but Holden can be a dick a lot, and that gets on my nerves after a while."

I can see what Hayden is talking about. Holden can be obnoxious at times, at least from what I experienced, and for some reason, earning someone's approval sounds more appealing to me as well.

"Do you think I earned Halsey's approval?"

"Do you really want to know?"

Uh-oh, am I not going to like the sound of this?

"Umm . . . maybe?"

Chuckling, Hayden playfully tugs on my hair again and says, "He said you were cool."

"Oooo, cool. Is that good?"

"It's the first step to earning his approval."

"Then I'll take it."

"Are you judging me for eating straight out of the carton?" I ask, a mouthful of lo mein about to be shoved in my mouth.

"Not even in the slightest. I think it's cute." Eyeing the other cartons, he says, "I wish I'd asked what you wanted beforehand, because I'm going to have a lot of leftovers, when I shouldn't be eating all these leftovers."

Playfully, I flip up the hem of his shirt, showing off his corded stomach and say, "Pretty sure your abs can handle it."

He pushes his shirt down and takes mock offense. "It's not polite to lift a man's shirt when he's eating."

"Please," I scoff, giving him a giant eye-roll. "With the kind of abs rubbing against that tight shirt of yours, you're lucky I'm not making you eat with your shirt off."

"Making me, huh?"

"Yeah." I wave my chopstick at his body. "When a pregnant woman tells you to take off your shirt, you do it."

Laughing, he reaches behind him, his hands posed below his neck, gripping onto his shirt. "Say the word, babe, and I'll put on one hell of a show for you."

"Don't." I shake my head and pat my protruding belly. "You'll give me a complex."

"Are you being serious right now?" Hayden's features harden when he looks me up and down. "Adalyn, you're gorgeous—"

"I don't feel anywhere close to gorgeous." I sigh. "And believe me, I'm not saying that to fish for compliments. Nothing fits anymore. I feel like I'm not pregnant enough to be cute, I just look super bloated."

"You don't look super bloated. You look sexy."

That makes me laugh out loud, because the last thing I feel is sexy right now. I'm two forkfuls of lo mein from rolling down the elastic waistband of my jeans and calling it a night.

Setting down his carton of Chinese food, he dusts off his hands and scoots closer to me, taking my carton from me as well. Looking more serious than ever, Hayden says, "Touch me."

"What?" I nervously giggle as he comes even closer, the crisp white of his shirt stretched across the expanse of his chest, his biceps framed under the fabric, enticing me.

"I want you to touch me, anywhere you want, just touch me."

"Why?"

Scooting closer so now there is no room to retreat, he says, "I want to show you how unbelievably sexy you are to me. Despite what you might think, you're drop-dead gorgeous, Adalyn, and the fact that you're carrying my baby just heightens the need I have for you. So touch me. Let me show you."

Trepidation steels my nerves, my hand shakes, and I'm unsure if I should touch him. This was not in the plans—or at least not in my plans—to be this close, to be sucked into the sensation of having him near me again.

Touch him. It seems like such a simple request, but behind the simplicity is a myriad of emotions waiting to consume me.

One touch. I know that's all it will take to open up the flood-gate of memories I shared with this man. Am I willing to risk the onslaught of emotion to follow?

"Touch me," he repeats, his voice rumbling over me like a cloak of comfort, reverberating up my spine, sending my hand forward to his forearm.

Tentatively, with the pads of my fingers, I run them over the well-defined sinew of his thick forearm. The muscles beneath me flick and flutter to my touch, dancing beneath my hand.

Peering into Hayden's heavy-lidded eyes, I'm taken back to a moment in the hotel room in New York City, my head buried between his thighs. My mouth on his cock, my tongue lapping at the head, his eyes fluttering shut, his teeth pulling on his bottom lip, his corded neck straining with every single lap.

Heat consumes me. A wave of lava erupting over my skin, the sound of his grumbly moans echoing through my memory.

"Do you feel that, Adalyn? Goosebumps spread over my skin, the heat of your touch warming me immediately? A light touch does that to me, having you near me sends my body into a frenzy, so the next time you try to put yourself down again, think of this moment. Because you might not feel like yourself, but to me, you're more beautiful than ever."

Clearing his throat as my fingers continue to travel along his arm, he scoots back on the couch and pulls on the chocolate strands of his hair. "Uh, I'm going to pack some of these boxes up. I'll meet you in the kitchen. I have something planned for us."

Standing from the couch, he starts gathering boxes, and I finally open my mouth. "How many women have you been with?" I don't know why I ask the question, and frankly I don't think I want to know, but for some self-loathing reason, I'm curious.

Not looking at me, he says, "Doesn't matter. There's only been one woman I've ever truly cared about." Eyeing me with a look I can only describe as loving, he adds, "And she's sitting on my couch, driving me fucking nuts with the way she keeps wetting her lips."

My tongue on route to wet my bottom lip, I suck it back into my mouth, causing Hayden to chuckle to himself and retreat to the kitchen, his backside flexing with every step.

I might be in trouble.

CHAPTER TWENTY-EIGHT

ADALYN

"That's not how you whisk eggs. You're just stirring them."

I look down at the three still intact eggs, their yolks barely breaking. "No, look they're starting to break apart." I point into the bowl.

"At that pace, we're going to be eating cake at midnight. I'll show you how it's done." From behind, Hayden traps my body against the counter, his arms circling around me. Taking my hand in his along with the fork, he whisks the eggs sharply in the bowl, beating the poor things to death. Lips next to my ear, he says, "See, like this. Like you're whipping them."

Whipping.

Why does that word make me want to do naughty things? Hell, watching his forearm whisk the eggs makes me want to do naughty things. Look at how his wrist rotates incredibly fast, never letting up. And his fingers, long and strong, telling the fork exactly what to do, beating the eggs into submission.

Submission.

Whipping.

Forearms.

Wrists.

Oh Christ, I need some water.

Pregnancy hormones are in overdrive tonight. It doesn't help that Hayden is wandering around his apartment without socks on. Yes, he's barefoot in jeans and a white T-shirt, looking casually handsome, his large feet padding across the floor.

They're feet, uncovered man feet, and from the mere sight of them I can feel a dull throb start in the base of my stomach.

We are talking overactive hormones here. Never in my life have I lusted over feet, but by golly do I want to play with his.

Don't worry. I'm quite aware something is wrong with me.

"Adalyn, the milk."

"Huh?" I look up, my hand whisking in the air, carrying the motion on after Hayden has already stepped away and started mixing all the ingredients together.

"The milk, hand me the milk."

"Oh yeah, the milk. Gotcha." I give his side a playful punch that makes him chuckle, his brow drawn close together, confusion of my actions written all over his face. *Don't worry, buddy, I'm just as confused as you are.*

Milk already measured out, I give him the glass Pyrex cup and lean against the counter, my hip hitting the hard edge. Hayden's talking, but his words aren't registering. Instead, my mind is focused on the way his biceps swell with each pass of the mixing spoon in the bowl. Up and down, up and down, testing the elasticity of the cotton shirt he's wearing. Is it going to snap? It looks like it.

Come on.

Snap.

Snap, you little cotton—

"Hey, where are you right now?" Hayden tilts my chin up, forcing my eyes away from his cannon of an arm.

"Sorry, just thinking about things." Not things I plan on sharing. Nodding toward the mix, I say, "What does it taste like?" When Hayden said he wanted to bake a cake with me, I inwardly softened, the wall around my heart being broken down one brick at a time.

"Want to taste it?"

I nod vigorously. I reach for the bowl, but he swats my hand away only to stick his finger in the bowl and offer me a taste.

Holding his finger in front of me, he waits for me to taste the chocolate flavor about to drip off the end. Not feeling shy about licking his finger, I lean forward and stick my tongue out, flicking up the dripping of batter about to fall. Keeping my gaze trained on his, I notice how his pupils grow, his eyes narrow, and then I open my mouth and slip his finger inside. Looking up at him, I allow my lips to encircle his finger while my tongue works its way around his finger, lapping up the chocolate.

His sharp stare stays on me when I ever so slowly bring my teeth down on his finger, lightly dragging them to the tip along with my lips. When my mouth pops off, I lick around my lips and smile at him.

For a moment, we stand there, staring at each other, our eyes locked, our bodies breathing together in time, heavy and deep, our chests rising and falling.

"Tell me no." He lets go of the bowl and takes a step toward me.

Eyes wide, delicious chocolate on my tongue, my body humming for one touch, one taste, my lips stay sealed.

Taking another step forward, closing me in against the counter, he repeats himself, gripping my cheek. "Tell me no."

I know I should. I set ground rules. I told him we were over. I said we were just going to be friends, *but for the life of me*, I can't get myself to tell him no.

I can't utter the words. Instead, my hand grips one of the belt loops of his pants and pulls him in the last inch. Growling like a caveman, he bends at the waist and effortlessly scoops me into his arms only to usher me past the kitchen, living room, and down a hallway. With a push of his foot, he opens the door to his bedroom. The ten-foot ceilings give the room a heavenly feel along with the all-white bedding and giant California king.

Just when I think he's about to toss me in the bed, he gives it a second thought and gently sets me down, going down to his knees in front of me. Reaching behind him, he grips the back of his shirt and pulls it forward over his head revealing his expertly chiseled body.

God, how could I forget what he looks like without a shirt? This image should be burned in my mind, on constant replay, like a screensaver on my phone, always there.

Lifting my shirt, he reveals the spandex of my jeans, completely horrifying me. I scoot away, pushing my shirt down. God, it's like he just revealed my Spanx without any warning.

"Don't scoot away from me." He pulls on my legs, bringing me closer to him.

"Don't look at my pregnancy wear. Close your eyes. You should never see elastic where there should be zippers and buttons."

Chuckling, he doesn't listen to me. No, he lifts my shirt and pulls down on the elastic of my very stretchy jeans, revealing my little baby bump. Sitting back on his heels, his hand washes over his face, the look of sincere wonder reflected in his beautiful eyes.

Sitting up, he leans on his elbows, his arms straddling either side of me, and he brings his lips gently to my stomach where he kisses my bump. Peering at me, tears filling his eyes, he conveys with his awe-inspired look how happy he is.

Unable to control my emotions, my eyes dampen as well, watching him kiss me from the top of my belly to the bottom, his fingers lightly caressing the sides.

Even though it's an intimate moment, the farther south he kisses, the more my body heats, the more I wiggle beneath him, looking for more, needing more.

Continuing his journey south, he brings the rest of my jeans down with him until they're pulled off and tossed to the floor. Hands trailing back up my thighs, they stop when they reach my panties.

Eyes dark and lustful, he gives me a dangerous look. "Lace thong. Fuck, Adalyn."

Instead of ripping it off right away, he fingers the delicate lace, testing the waistband and the edges that encase the apex between my thighs. Fingers dancing dangerously close to where I so desperately want him, my head falls to the mattress and my back arches off the bed.

I moan loud and hard when his fingers trace over my slit. I'm so wet, more wet than I ever imagine being.

"Take my thong off, please," I beg. He does and the minute the fabric is off me, I spread my legs and place my calves over his shoulders, pulling him in close.

When I think he's going to laugh, he doesn't. His stare turns more dark, more serious, more intense.

Turning his head to the side, his lips graze my thigh, nipping and licking, his hands sliding under my ass, cupping each cheek in earnest, bringing my center closer to his mouth. Hovering above me, he flicks his tongue, barely passing over my wet center, a whisper of a touch.

Writhing under him, I push myself forward, hunkering my legs down so he has no place to go.

"Please," I beg. God, I'm so turned on, so in need of release. *Of him.*

Hands still cupping my ass, he presses his mouth against my pussy and with one smooth stroke, moves his tongue up the valley between my legs, hitting my clit in the process.

"Yes," I moan, my legs hooking Hayden in even closer.

Long languid strokes, his tongue plays with my arousal, keeping the same pace, the same pressure. It's mind-blowing, intoxicating.

"More," I demand, feeling how easily his tongue slides against me, how incredibly aroused I am.

Muttering against me, the vibrations of his voice making my stomach drop, he says, "Tastes so good. So fucking good."

A spark of my undoing shoots up my spine, his tongue working up and down my clit, licking, kissing, sucking. Pulling it between his lips, humming—

"Oh God," I scream, unable to hold back. I'm right there, my heart hammering in my chest, my clit pounding against his tongue, my legs starting to go numb as my stomach bottoms out on me, a ripple of pleasure tearing through me. Flicking his tongue over my clit, I convulse on him, my body jerking every which way, his grip holding me down, keeping his face firmly planted between my legs until I don't think I can take any more.

"Please, oh God, I can't . . ."

Releasing his mouth, he flips me over on the bed, pulls me up on my knees and brings my back to his chest, his rock hard erection pressing against me, his jeans an unwanted barrier.

"Shirt and bra off. Now."

Doing as I'm told, I race to get naked as I hear him disrobe himself from behind.

I toss my clothes to the side and kneel on his bed, waiting for his next move. I don't have to wait for long when his hands reach around me, his warm, strong body flush against mine. Bending his head forward, his cheek against mine, he looks down my front, groaning in my ear.

"These fucking tits. Shit Adalyn, they're so goddamn big."

That's the honest truth. I'm all tits and belly in my pregnancy. It's been very difficult to find things to wear.

As he cups them, the weight heavy in his hands, I lean my head back and moan softly, loving his touch.

"Goddamn, you feel good." His thumbs pass over my nipples and I cry out in pleasure. "You like that, baby?"

"Yes." The words fall out of my mouth in a long, drawn-out syllable.

Taking my cue, he passes his thumbs over my nipples again, his hands still cupping my breasts, squeezing and teasing.

My breasts have always been sensitive, but now with all these hormones running rampant in my body, sensitive isn't the right word to describe how they feel.

So heavy, so delicate, so taken over by the aching need to be played with.

Using his index finger and thumb, he rolls both of my nipples at the same time between his fingers.

"Oh my God!" I shout, bucking my ass into his cock, falling forward, my hands propping my upper half on the mattress. Head falling forward, my hair a privacy curtain from the intense expression I'm wearing on my face. I grind my ass into his cock, my pussy clenching with every grind, with every pinch of his fingers he continues to play on my breasts.

"I'm going to come," I announce, surprising myself as another orgasm rips through me.

Hayden stills behind me as I moan in front of him, my head dropping to the mattress.

"Baby," he whispers, his hand now soothing up and down my spine.

And just like that, that little touch, my body hums and need once again overtakes me. Cheek pressed against the cool white comforter, I rock my hips against him, begging him to take me one more time.

"Make me come again," I whisper.

"Jesus fucking Christ," Hayden mutters before gripping his length and placing it at my entrance. Stroking my hips, his hand covering my ass, squeezing, he thrusts inside me, filling me whole with one stroke. Stilling above me, I can feel the tension rolling off him. "Fuck. So tight, baby."

"So full," I say, moving my hips backward, savoring the way he feels inside me. "I need you to move, Hayden. Please fuck me."

Not saying a word, he grips my hips tightly and pulls out only to forcefully thrust back inside me, his balls slapping against my skin, the sound so erotic. Pulling out again, he repeats the process, refusing to speed up, keeping consistent with each thrust. His grip growing tighter and tighter until he thrusts so deep, he stills, hitting me where I need it the most.

Deep inside me, I spasm around him and grind my hips, swiveling, my impending orgasm starting to blacken the world around me.

"Fuck, fuck," he groans, picking up his pace now, his strokes fast and hard, burying my face in the mattress, muffling the sounds of his orgasm, but I feel when it happens, when he comes inside me, his white-hot arousal filling me, sending me over the precipice.

Like a feral cat, I scream out his name, my hands ripping the comforter, my pussy contracting relentlessly around his arousal, pulling everything from him, every last drop until we both collapse to the bed, our bodies sweaty and spent.

After a few minutes, once our breathing evens out, Hayden scoots me to the top of the bed and pulls me under the covers with his body wrapped around mine, his hand protectively covering my belly, and his face buried against my neck.

He doesn't have to say anything. I know how happy he is, because in this moment, this quiet moment, I feel that mile-long smile of his against my skin. And because of that, I can't help but smile myself.

~

"Are you okay?"

"Hmm . . ."

A nose nuzzles my neck, a strong body wrapped around me.

"How are you feeling? I can't believe I lost control and fucked you so hard. I hope the baby is okay."

"The baby is fine," I sigh, kissing the arm encompassing my shoulder.

"I'm sorry. I've wanted that so badly. Ever since that morning, ever since I said those words, I've wanted a repeat, and I lost my mind. But, God, Addie, I can't tell you how much this means to me. How much it means that you chose me over him."

"Hmm?" In my sleepy haze, I swear Hayden just called me, Addie. He never calls me Addie.

"And this baby, I'm going to love it with everything in me, just like I love you."

Strong arms turn me over in bed and I come face to face with Logan, a curve in his lip and sexy, ruffled hair.

"What the hell," I scream, scooting out of his grasp as I'm torn from a dream.

Eyes adjusting to the dark room and the worried man next to me, Hayden, tries to hold on to me as I back away.

"Adalyn, is everything okay?"

Scooting far away, I nearly tumble out of bed before Hayden catches me, moving quickly on the bed.

"What's going on?" He's not angry, just incredibly concerned.

Hayden, yes that's Hayden. I had sex with Hayden, not Logan. I had sex . . .

Oh God. I had sex with Hayden, when Logan kissed me yesterday and told me he loved me. And that dream, what was that about?

It felt so real, being in Logan's arm, his lips grazing my skin, his voice rumbling over my body, igniting a fire deep within me. But it wasn't Logan. It was Hayden, right?

"Baby, you're scaring me, is everything okay?"

I shake my head, unable to look Hayden in the eyes. Scrambling out of his grasp, I search for my clothes. This was a mistake, a huge mistake. I should have never had sex with Hayden, especially when I'm so unsure of anything.

Logan loves me.

Hayden wants me. Hayden needs me.

I'm having Hayden's baby.

I don't want to lose Logan.

I don't know what to do.

Bra is the first thing I find, so I strap that on followed by my pants and shirt, forgetting my lace thong entirely. Not even looking back, I go to the entryway where I slip on my shoes and snag my purse from the console table. Before I can open the door, a strong hand halts the door in place. From the corner of my eye,

Hayden's body appears, covered in athletic shorts and that's it. His chest is heaving. I can only imagine the death glare he must be giving me.

"What the hell is going on?"

"I need to go home," I say, keeping my eyes fixed on the door in front of me, willing it to open on its own.

"Why the fuck do you need to go home?" Angry Hayden, just like the day at the cottage when I broke things off. It's the same tone in his voice, the same furious vibe pulsing off him.

"Logan will wonder where I am." The words pop out of my mouth before I can stop them. I go to correct myself, but nothing comes to mind. So instead the mention of Logan's name hangs in the air between us, like an impossibly large pink elephant.

"Do you care if he knows you're here, with me?"

I play with the strap of my purse, unable to answer Hayden's question.

"Look at me, Adalyn." When I don't turn around, he carefully moves me so I'm against the door, forced to look him in the eyes—his distraught and sad eyes. "Do you have feelings for Logan?"

Do I have *feelings* for Logan? Good question. He's my friend, a man I once saw myself having a future with. I could see us fitting perfectly into each other's lives. And then . . .

That was a mistake.

Those four words knocked me on my ass, tainted my view of him.

But after last night, I don't even know anymore. *But I just thought the same words about Hayden, and I'd wanted him with every fiber of my being.*

"I see," Hayden says, taking my silence as an answer.

Pushing off the door, he runs both his hands through his hair, his muscles straining, his features a picture of pain.

"Fuck, I don't want to have to fight for you, Adalyn. I thought . . ." He pauses and shakes his head. "I thought we had something." Going to his couch, he sits down and bows his head forward, both hands gripping the back of his neck, a man completely and utterly hurting. *Suffering.*

Go to him, I tell myself. Hold him, reassure him. Tell him it's going to be okay. But every time I get the courage to take a step forward, Logan's pleading and loving eyes flash in front of me.

I'm stone, unable to move. And with each passing second I don't move, I'm slicing the man before me right in half.

"Fuck," he mutters and stands from the couch. Shaking his head, he grabs the keys from the console table and opens the door. Somberly, he says, "I'll drive you home."

The drive is deathly silent and what should be a five-minute drive feels like an hour of pure torture, my mind racing a mile a minute trying to think of something to say, some kind of reassurance to end the pain Hayden is so visibly going through.

When we reach my apartment, Hayden parks the car and looks out the window, his hand gripping his chin, contemplating something. Unsure of what to say, I reach for the door handle when Hayden grips my arm.

Still staring out the window, he sighs and takes a second before he brings his focus to me.

Deflated and dejected, he removes his hand from me and says, "Before you go up to your apartment, I need you to know something." His throat tight, he clears it and continues, his voice strained. "The day I met you at Racer's, I knew the universe I was living in was altered by your presence. I knew at that moment I would never be the same. My instinct never fails me. I was right. Over a little Northeast summer, I grew to know this incredibly funny, authentic, and beautiful woman. I learned about your family, your younger years, your fears, and your loves. With each story you told, each passing glance you gave me, every part of your body you let me own, I fell deeper and deeper in love with you." My breath catches in my throat. "And then you told me you were pregnant. Yeah, I was shocked at first, but after the shock wore off, it was solidified. The woman I met over a stack of unpaid bills was the woman I would never be able to let go." Shaking his head, his shoulders slump as he looks past me, up at the apartment. "And yet, here I am, having no choice but to let you go."

Passing his hand over his mouth, he brings my hand to his lips and presses a gentles kiss across my knuckles.

"I love you, Adalyn. You are my dream girl, the mother of my child, and the woman I want to spend the rest of my life with, but I can't compete with another man if you love him. I won't. I don't want to ask you to choose. But I need to know if . . . I need to know if you'll love me. If not, I'll back off. Still be there for you and the baby, but I won't . . . I won't fight."

His words rip through me, tears falling from my eyes.

"Tomorrow is my home game you have tickets for. After the game, the families of players greet us when we come off the ice after the game in the players' hallway. I've put your name on the list. If you come tomorrow, if I see you waiting in that hallway, I'll know you're mine forever. But don't show up if you have any question about wanting to be with me, because the next time we're together, I want you wholeheartedly. I want all of you. Do you understand?"

I nod, tears streaking down my cheeks.

"This is it, baby." He wipes a tear from my eye. "No more fucking around. You're either with me or you're not. And if you're not, I will be civil when it comes to our baby, but don't expect me to be nice to him."

Pulling away, he stares out the window, ending our conversation.

Such all-consuming sadness blankets me as I squeak out his name, "Hayden."

He shakes his head. "You either show up tomorrow, or you don't. That's it, Adalyn."

With that, he unlocks the door, the click of the locks echoing in the car, sending a clear-cut sign to me there is no negotiating. I either want him or I don't.

And what's scary is I'm *almost* positive I want him, but the words fail to leave my lips.

CHAPTER TWENTY-NINE

ADALYN

S leep has eluded me.

How could I possibly sleep when Hayden's sorrowful eyes are burned in my memory?

What have I done?

This is such a mess, and I'm the one to blame.

Logan came into my room this morning with a muffin and some tea, but I asked him to leave it on my nightstand. When he asked if everything was okay, I told him I was really tired from getting in so late.

And when he came in at lunchtime to see if I was okay, I told him.

I told him I didn't love him the way he loves me. The words fell out of my mouth before I could even think about how they might hurt him.

But the decision almost seemed too simple after Hayden dropped me off. Logan, although sweet and caring, and a beautiful human I always want in my life, he's not the man I'm grieving. I've had my time to grieve Logan, and he's a chapter in my life that's closed.

But leaving Hayden's car last night, due to my feelings of total despair, I could barely walk up the stairs to my apartment without breaking down.

And right there was evidence enough that the man I needed by my side was the man I destroyed with my silence.

I hate myself.

After Logan left my room, I cried. Not for the loss of Logan, but for the loss of Hayden, the dent I put in our relationship. No, not dent, but the chasm created by a dagger straight to his heart. And what's worse is I've now done that twice. I've. Done. That. Twice. And he's not a man who deserves to be treated like that once, let alone twice.

Many times I thought about calling him last night but once again, I was apprehensive. Deep down, I know he's the one, but when it comes to pulling the trigger, I'm gun-shy.

Now it's an hour before his game; I stand in front of my mirror, questioning my decision to go to the game. If I don't go, Hayden will assume it's over forever, but if I do go, I'm giving myself over to him—my heart, my broken and battered heart.

But not going isn't an option.

Adjusting the elastic band of my jeans, I take a look at myself one more time. I look like a moose. The Quakes shirt Emma gave me with Hayden's name and number on the back is entirely too tight around my stomach but I keep it on, wanting to show my support.

I forgot to hand out the tickets to the other girls in my office so I'll be sitting in a row all by myself. It might be better actually, because I'll be a nervous wreck the entire game, and I'd prefer not to be asked what's wrong every two seconds. Going to the game by myself will be much better.

I make my way to the front of the apartment complex where I told my Uber driver to meet me. Driving into Los Angeles doesn't sound appealing to me right now, especially when I haven't done it yet. I've only driven to work and around my little area. To be honest, Logan has done most of the driving if we've gone somewhere.

Oh Logan.

God, he was so upset. It kills me to think of his reaction. But then again, we're better off as friends. I hope after this blows over he still wants to be my friend.

What a mess.

My Uber driver pulls up just as my phone rings in my purse. I hop in the car, buckle up, and give the Uber driver a quick hello before pulling my phone out of my purse.

Racer.

Leaning back into the seat, getting comfortable. I answer. "Hey Racer."

"How's my girl doing?"

He sounds chipper. Recently he's fallen in love, the big teddy bear that he is. But I wonder, did Hayden call him? Do he and Hayden talk about us, about the baby? It seems like Hayden is more of a private man, one to keep his personal business to himself. Which honestly, I am too for the most part. I can't remember the last time I divulged all my secrets to Emma. Can you blame me? Last time I involved her in my big news, she interfered big time.

I know, I know, she was in the right, but still!

"Doing all right," I answer, sounding less than convincing.

Racer doesn't miss a beat. "What's going on?"

Sighing, I watch the palm trees pass by the window while I gather the courage to talk to Racer. "Logan told me he loved me."

There's a pause and then, "Oh, for fuck's sake. I told you taking him out there was going to be a bad idea."

"I didn't bring him out here. He wanted to come. He wanted a change, he wanted out of Binghamton. I thought he was coming out here as a friend."

"Addie, I love you, you know that, but I think anyone could have foreseen what was going to happen. He moved across the country with you, shares an apartment, takes care of you, so it's obvious he's a man in love. If I was single, I don't think I would have done the same for you, and you're one of my best friends, but that's a huge life change for someone to do who's not in love."

When he puts it that way.

Ugh, I'm so stupid.

"It was nice to have someone here."

"Hayden is there."

"Part-time, Racer. He's here part-time, and I was flying across the country, pregnant, uprooting my life—"

"And is that it?" Racer's voice grows more serious. The easy-going and fun-loving Racer has been switched out for the more serious one.

"What do you mean?"

"Why did you move out there, Adalyn?"

"Well," I stumble over my words. "Because Hayden asked me to."

"If I asked you to move for me, would you?"

Probably not.

"What's your point, Racer?"

The driver swerves to the side, drawing my attention to the front where he's playing around on his phone. Uh, can he please concentrate on the road? Someone is not getting a five-star rating, that's for damn sure.

"My point is, you need to figure out why you're out there."

"Did Hayden call you?"

"No."

I drawl out his name, "Racer, did he call you?"

"He didn't. Why, what happened?"

I cross my leg and rest my hand on my belly, a new habit I'm becoming accustomed to. "Logan told me he loved me then the next day, Hayden and I, umm . . . you know."

"Had sex. It's okay to say the words."

Not when I'm in an Uber car two feet away from the driver.

"Yes, that. And I must have fallen asleep after, because the next thing I remember is waking up next to Logan, him holding me and caressing me. It was so real that when I woke up, I freaked out and couldn't get away from Hayden quick enough." God, I really hate myself. "I then proceeded to tell him about Logan."

"Oh, Adalyn."

"I know," I groan. "Ugh it was a mess. Racer, he was so distraught." Taking a second to gather myself, I say, "He told me he loves me."

"Of course he does, Adalyn. Christ, you're just realizing that? I could tell he loved you when he was still here in Binghamton."

A tear trickles down my cheek and I quickly wipe it away, not wanting the Uber driver to catch me crying, making me the odd story he tells his friends and family at the end of his day.

"I don't know what my problem is. Why can't I just let him love me? Why am I having such an issue with this?"

"Because he's the first guy you've ever loved, and it's terrifying. He's the first guy who's ever treated you like you deserve to be treated. The first guy to stick around. The first guy to capture your heart."

"And he left."

"No, Adalyn, you left." The way he emphasizes "you" sends a fearful chill up my spine. "You were the one who left. You gave up before he even have a chance to break your heart."

"I didn't want to hold him back."

"You're holding him back now," Racer says, fighting with me. "You're holding him back from being the man he wants to be. Damn it, Adalyn. He wants you, he wants the baby, he wants a family . . . with you."

Another swerve of the car. Sitting up, I say, "Sir, could you please not look at your phone while you drive?"

"Is everything okay?" Racer asks, extremely concerned.

Whispering into the phone, I say, "Yes, the Uber driver is just texting and driving. I'm actually on my way to Hayden's game now to—"

My words are cut off when the driver misses a stop sign and sails through the four-way stop without even looking. It all happens in slow motion: the screech of wheels, me shouting "look out," the Uber driver swerving, and the impact of another car to the driver's side, careening the little Toyota Corolla into a small ditch to the right, hitting a fire hydrant.

Disoriented, confused, and upside down, water starts to flow into the car from the broken hydrant, and fills up quickly.

CHAPTER THIRTY

HAYDEN

N ever in my life have I played this hard. Not during the playoffs, not when being recruited, not even in college.

Each land of my skate on the ice, I push forward, skating faster, quicker, more precise. My footwork on fire, my stick handling incredible, my focus homed in on one thing and one thing alone: the puck and pushing it past the goalie.

I can't think of last night and the way Adalyn felt in my arms again, so soft and made just for me. I can't think about the way she called out my name when I was buried deep inside her, claiming her. I can't think of the way she felt pressed against my body, sleeping soundly, her breaths in rhythm with mine. And I sure as fuck can't think about the dead silence when I asked if she had feelings for Logan.

And the biggest thing of all, I can't focus on whether or not she's here, sitting in the stands, cheering me on.

I need to keep my head in the game, skate hard, and win this game.

Skating toward the puck, I snag it with my stick, spin off a defender and break through toward the goal, the puck juggled back and forth with my stick.

Focus, Hayden.

Haines is weak on the upper left. You've already scored two goals on him tonight in the upper left. Should I go for a third? Will he expect it?

No. He won't expect me to go for another upper left.

Pushing to the right, I fake, cross the puck to the left and slip it up into the corner again. The siren above the goal sounds off, the crowd cheers, and I wave my stick above my head as I skate toward my celebrating teammates.

Gloved hands pat my helmeted head, my eyes traveling around the arena, fans erupting, the score four to two with a minute to go.

This is one hell of a game. I just hope Adalyn is here to see it.

She's never seen me play, and that fucking stings. My entire career I've been surrounded by friends and family who've seen me play, who've supported me, been there for me, and the one person I want here, I can't be sure is actually cheering for me.

The rest of the game finishes in a blur, leaving the score at a four-to-two victory for the Quakes.

Helmets off, we shake hands with each other, congratulating one another on one more win to add to our record. It's a long season so we need to keep focused on one win at a time.

Gathering my gear, helmet tucked under my arm, I take a deep breath and follow the team in a solid line through the players' entrance.

Staying in the back, my nerves a mess, I consider what I might do if I don't see Adalyn waiting for me in the hallway. Hell, what can I do if she's not there? I can't keep throwing my heart down in front of her when she has no urge to pick it up off the ground. You can't force someone to love you. It's a tough pill to swallow, and I hate that it's one I might have to.

Stepping onto the carpeted area, I lift my head to take a look around. It strikes me as strange not to see Shannon there congratulating Chris but I continue looking for my girl. Mendez and O'Brien are giving high fives to their children, while Halstrom and

Bidwell are kissing their girls off to the side, giving themselves some privacy.

Scanning the area, I search for the brunette with whiskey-colored eyes and a smile that knocks me on my ass. My heart splutters in my chest, the weight of my gear feels heavier, making it harder to breathe.

But I don't see her.

Not giving up yet, I casually stand in place, off to the side, scanning the entire area, making sure she's not hiding behind any pillars or trapped behind security.

But the farther and farther I get into the hallway, I feel the crack of my heart as it starts to ripple through my chest. Realization starts to set in.

She's not here.

She's not fucking here.

Biting down on the side of my cheek, holding back the angry scream I want to expel, I make my way to the locker room. The team publicist asks me to do an interview but with one look in his direction, he sees the anguish in my eyes and, without asking what's wrong, he gives me space and turns to another player.

Players, media, staff members all congratulate me on a good game, their praise barely touching the deep wounds busy forging a hole in my soul.

Ignoring the banter in the locker room, the media grabbing interviews with players, and the playful ribbing regularly conducted after games, I shuck my gear as quickly as possible and head to the showers where I single out a shower head in the far corner, and let the scalding water burn onto my back. My palms pressed against the tiled wall, my head dipped down, water slicing over my body, I allow myself to have a fucking moment.

I can't believe it. I can't believe she didn't fucking show up. There was a small part of me, a part of me that was holding on to the summer, holding on to what we shared last night that maybe, just maybe she'd be waiting for me when I got off the ice. *That maybe she loved me too.*

This is what true disappointment feels like, like utter despair. When the woman you love rejects you for another man, for a man you completely despise. Beaten down and battered, feeling more empty than ever, I let the guys pass by me, their conversations hushed when they spot me. But I don't move. I stay in that position, letting the water attempt to comfort me. But it's no use. I'm going to have to find a way to co-parent a child with the woman I'm in love with, who doesn't love me back. *I'm going to have to find a way to accept that a man I loathe will spend every day with my child* and *the woman I love.* Fucking hell, this hurts.

"Fuck," I mutter, tears stinging the backs of my eyes.

Taking some soap, I lather my body and hair and rinse it under the lukewarm water now, the only guy left in the showers. When I towel off and head to my locker, the room has cleared out. Perfect, I don't have to deal with anyone.

Approaching my locker, my phone buzzes against the wood of my cubby, but I ignore it and instead, sit down, resting my arms on my legs, hands clasped together, trying to figure out what I'm going to do next.

Why did I think this was going to be a good idea? Why did I think I could pressure her into choosing? Should I have done more? Should I have told her I loved her sooner? Should I not have given her any time or space when she moved out here? And Logan, fuck, I never should have let him live with her. That's the perfect combination to fall in love with someone. Friends to lovers, it's written in all the books.

Shit.

I rub the palm of my hand into my eye as the door to the locker room slams open and a frenzied Chris comes barreling into the locker room, spotting me immediately.

"What the fuck are you doing?" he asks.

"What does it look like?" I answer, not in the mood for whatever Chris has to say. "I told Darryl I'm not doing any media today."

"Have you checked your phone?"

"No." I stand and reach to undo my towel when Chris levels with me, his eyes full of worry. "What's going on?"

"Everyone has been trying to get in touch with you. Adalyn was in a car accident."

The blood drains from my body, leaving me feeling lightheaded and pale as a ghost. Chris's words hit me hard.

Adalyn was in a car accident.

"Wh-what?" I choke out, my throat growing tighter and tighter.

"Logan called Shannon, said Adalyn was in a bad car accident and is in intensive care right now at California Hospital. They've all tried to call and text you."

Ice freezes over my veins, frozen as a fucking iceberg, unable to move, unable to fully comprehend what he's telling me. "Is . . ." I swallow hard, my voice coming out in a squeak. "Is she okay?"

"I don't know, man. They have no idea what's happening. No one will tell them anything."

Stunned, I stand there, unable to move, unable to speak. Adalyn was in an accident.

What about the baby?

Fuck . . . *the baby.*

"Dude, are you going to get dressed? I can drive you over there but you can't go in a towel."

Sitting on the bench of my locker, I put my hands in my hair, pulling on the strands, still in shock. The world slowing around me, my last words to Adalyn trying to reach my brain. What were they? They weren't I love you. Instead of loving her, I gave her a goddamn ultimatum.

Choose me.

Choose me.

It was all I wanted to yell and scream at her.

It's not like I said something like I need you. Come back to me. Be with me. You are the reason why I want to be the best dad I can be, because you inspire me to be a better man.

I didn't say anything like that.

"Hayden, man. Are you going to be okay?"

I shake my head, the room spinning on me. I grip the bench behind me, my nails digging into the wood, wanting to rip the entire thing off the wall and throw it across the room. I'm so fucking angry, I'm fucking scared, I'm fucking torn in two.

"She has to make it," I choke out, tears hitting me fast and hard. Breaking down, I bend forward, head in my hands. "She has to fucking make it."

From my side, Chris pats my back and hands me my clothes. "Come on, man. Get dressed and we can get to the hospital."

Empty and split in half, I walk through the motions of getting dressed and grabbing my things before Chris guides me to his car. I barely register him driving when my phone buzzes in my hand. Adding to the top of the plethora of texts on my phone, Racer's name pops up, right next to his multiple missed calls.

Does he know something?

I read his text.

Racer: *CALL ME!*

Fumbling with my phone, I hit the call button and he answers immediately.

"Fuck, man. Fuck. Do you know?" His voice is strained, barely audible.

My throat so goddamn tight, I answer, "On the way to the hospital now. Do you know how she is?"

"I know nothing. I was hoping you did. Fuck, Hayden. I was on the phone with her when it happened. It was . . ." His voice breaks and all I can hear is his sobbing. On the other end, Georgiana, his girlfriend comforts him, her whispers soft.

He was on the phone? *With Adalyn?*

"Why was she talking and driving? You should have known not to talk to her while she's driving."

"It was an Uber, man. The guy was texting and driving."

Fury. My nerves morph into pure rage, the strength inside me building and building to the point that my hand starts to shake.

"What the fuck!"

"She was heading to the game."

And just like that, my face blanches, the color in my skin drains and a cool chill takes over my body. She was coming to me. She was going to be with me.

And now . . . now she's in a hospital fighting for her life. *For their lives.*

"Fuck, Racer." Once again, the heartache of Adalyn in the hospital overwhelms me. I cry into the phone, neither of us saying anything but the occasional she's got to be okay. She's got to be okay.

Chris doesn't even bother with parking. He lets me out at the entrance, and I sprint up to the intensive care unit where I find Shannon and Logan in the waiting room, sitting closely together, their faces red and blotchy, the weariness in their eyes unsettling.

I pause, looking at their sullen faces, their hunched-over bodies, and the worst consumes me. On shaky legs, I propel myself forward and stand in front of them. When Logan looks up at the shadow above him, he stands, and we face off but instead of male pride getting in the way, there is a mutual understanding for each other.

"Wh-what do you know?" I stumble over my words, barely hanging on by a thread.

"I have no idea. All I could find out is she's been unresponsive."

My world comes crashing to a halt from that one fucking word. *Unresponsive.*

Trembling, my hands shaking, my legs ready to give out, I ask, "Is she breathing?"

Logan must sense my lack of control and helps me take a seat. "She's breathing, but if she's unresponsive, she could possibly have a head injury."

"And what does that mean for the baby?"

He shrugs, shaking his head. "I don't know, man. If there's internal bleeding, they'll remove the baby, especially if there was a rupture in the placenta. There are so many things that could have happened; I don't want to guess."

"No one has come out here to talk to anyone?"

Logan shakes his head, lips firmly pressed together. "No. Nothing."

After a few minutes, Chris joins us in the waiting room and holds on to Shannon, stroking her arm and occasionally kissing the top of her head. I know she's close to Adalyn, so getting the call at the game and then leaving to drive here on her own to the hospital must have been terrifying. Thank God Chris checked his phone before he drove all the way home so he was there for me. I wouldn't have been able to drive here. Other than the hustle and bustle of the hospital around us, the room is pretty silent, all four of us in our own heads.

Slouching in my chair, hands crossed on my stomach, I lean my head against the edge of my chair and close my eyes, praying to whoever wants to listen to please spare my girl and baby.

Please, please let her be okay. Please protect her and wake her up. Please let me see those beautiful brown eyes again, please let me see that smile, please let me feel her lips, taste her one more time. Please . . .

Please let me be able to meet my baby.

Pressing my fingers into my eyes, I let a few tears fall before wiping them away quickly.

"Hey, she'll be okay," Logan says next to me. "She's tough. She'll be okay." Clearing his throat, he adds, "And when she makes it through this, I want you to know, I won't be interfering anymore. You don't have to worry about me, man. She's all yours, she's always been yours."

Tilting my head to the side, I look Logan in the eyes. Man to man. *He loves her, but he's letting her go. For me.* He silently bows out, and I can't do anything but respect the fuck out of him, especially for saying it to my face. Lending my hand out, he grasps it and we do an awkward shake side hug, putting our grievances behind us.

Tragic events bring out the best in us at times, the pleading side of us, the forgiving side. I'm all three right now. But mostly begging and pleading to anyone who will listen.

After what seems like hours, a doctor comes through the door and calls out Adalyn's name. I press my hand against Logan's shoulder as I stand. Without even thinking twice, I say, "I'm her boyfriend and the baby's father."

I know the rules about giving information family only, boyfriends don't count, but the baby, that's a different story. He must see the desperation in my eyes, because he pulls me to the side and takes a deep breath.

"The baby is okay. We have a heart monitor hooked up right now, and we're keeping a close eye on him."

Him.

My world starts spiraling. We're having a baby boy. A son.

Tears spill from my eyes, and I make no attempt to wipe them away.

"There was some distress from the accident so that's why we're monitoring closely."

Swallowing hard, I say, "And Adalyn?"

Looking around, the doctor questions if he should tell me or not when I plead with him, my tears falling faster and harder. "Please," I choke on a sob. "Please just tell me."

Sighing, he leans forward and says, "She's in a coma. She suffered a traumatic brain injury when the car was hit. Her head slammed into the window . . . lost some blood . . . severe bruise . . . scar . . . broken wrist . . . cuts and scrapes."

She's in a coma. I have no idea what else he said. *My girl's in a coma.*

"A coma?" I swallow hard. "What does that mean?"

"It means, we're playing the waiting game now."

After a few more prolific medical terms thrown my way, he says he'll walk me to her room. Before I leave, I give everyone an update, and tell them to go home, but none of them move. Instead, they stay put and ask if I need anything.

It might not be the family I grew up with, or the friends I've known and loved for a very long time, but this little family of mine in California, it's more than I could ask for at this very moment.

The hospital staff doesn't seem to slow down as I walk past

them, and I can't help but remember what Adalyn told me when we were in New York. The stress of her job, the bad news she would have to hear the doctors deliver, the losses she experienced on a daily basis, how mentally tough her job was. I pray I'm not one of the loved ones a nurse has to see walk away, heartbroken and shattered.

When we reach the room, the doctor turns to me and says, "The only reason I'm letting you back here is because this is your baby, and because I know if you stay out there longer, people are going to start noticing *you*. For privacy, I'm allowing you to hide away, instead of being the talk of the waiting room." He grips my shoulder and reaches for the handle.

I stop him and sincerely say, "You don't know how much that means to me. Thank you, sir."

"You're welcome. And just so you know, we have a strict policy about patient confidentiality. You shouldn't hear about this in the papers tomorrow."

This guy and this hospital is getting one hell of a donation from me when this is all over, when Adalyn is back in my arms, healthy and smiling that beautiful smile once again.

The door opens to a dimly lit room, two beeping monitors flank the bed and in the middle, Adalyn lies silently on the bed. Her head is wrapped in gauze, her wrist is secured in white bandaging tape, and her face is swollen from small abrasions. *But she's alive.*

From behind, the doctor closes the door. With a heavy heart and lead feet, I make my way to the side of the bed and pull up a chair. Taking her hand in mine, I stroke her knuckles and brush the side of her cheek, avoiding any scrapes, not wanting to hurt her.

"Jesus, baby. Look at you." Tears spill out of my eyes. "Fuck, what I wouldn't give to trade places with you right now, to take away all this pain and make you the healthy one." Moving my hand to her belly where our baby grows, I lightly stroke the sheets covering her up. "This little one is so strong. This little guy." I choke on a sob. "He's strong just like you, not like his daddy who is a blubbering mess." Bending my head, I press a kiss against her stomach. "So strong."

Staring at her battered face where I can see bruises forming, I squeeze my eyes shut, hating seeing her like this. When you fall in love, you never consider moments like this, where you have to sit at your soulmate's bedside, and hope and pray they come back to you, wondering if you're going to be alone for the rest of your life, missing out on all the moments you could have shared with them.

I knew I couldn't live without Adalyn, I realized that the moment I had to move away from her, but I never thought living without her meant she would leave this earth.

Resting my head on her hand, trying to give her every ounce of strength I have in me, I say, "When you wake up from this, Adalyn, I'm going to make sure you never have to suffer again. This is it, baby, this is it for us. From here on out, it's you and me and the baby. No more dancing around, no more questions about our relationship, no more distance. I love you and will spend every minute until my dying day making sure you know that." I lift my head and kiss her knuckles. "Just get better, baby, just come back to me. Please come back to me . . ."

I hang up my phone and lean back in my chair, my eyes never leaving Adalyn. The Quakes have given me all the time I need off to be with Adalyn and the baby, making sure they're okay. What is unfair about my profession is no matter what, my decision will let someone down. My team, the fans, the front office. But my heart is in this hospital, and I'll be damned if I leave without it.

I might have fibbed a bit and said Adalyn was my fiancée, but to hell if that's not going to happen the minute she gets better. I'm proposing, I'm making everything right between us, and it starts with the beginning of the rest of our lives.

All last night, while holding Adalyn's hand, I researched comas and pregnancy. Let's just say, that was a bad idea. After a few terrifying articles, I put my phone away and talked to my son.

I told him all about my game, about the goals I scored, unsure of what to talk to him about. I told him about how one day, I'll be just like my father, strapped down in pillows and a helmet, blocking his shots at the goal. I told him he'll be so much better than I am at hockey, because not only will he have my talent, but he'll have his mommy's bravery. Over and over again, I kept telling him to hang in there, to keep growing and be healthy, because he's going to want to see how beautiful his mommy is. He's going to want to get to know her because she's one hell of a catch.

And when sleep finally captured me, I never left Adalyn's bedside. I held her hand the entire time, resting my head on the side of her bed, my other hand holding on to her stomach, trying to give my girl and son every last ounce of power inside me.

With a fresh cup of coffee in hand and a donut in the other—courtesy of Logan who told me to screw my diet—I watch over Adalyn, studying her beautiful features. I spoke to her mom on the phone this morning. The brigade is catching the earliest flights they can find to get out here. I offered to pay for them, but her mom graciously declined, telling me to keep my money for when I get to spoil our little guy.

My phone buzzes on my lap and I shove the rest of my donut in my mouth before answering it.

Racer: *How is she?*

Sighing, I text Racer back.

Hayden: *Still out.*

Racer: *Fuck, I was hoping she would snap out of it last night. The baby?*

Hayden: *He's still strong.*

Racer: *He?*

My throat closes up on me while I type.

Hayden: *Yeah, he.*

Racer: *Shit, congrats, man.*

Hayden: *Thank you. He's going to make it through this.*

She has to as well. There is no way I can do this without her. Raise our son by myself? No, I need her by my side, her laughing and teasing eyes playing with both of us. I need her challenges, her ribbing, her love. Fuck, do I need her love.

Racer: Keep thinking positively, man. Are you sure you don't need me to come out there?

What I wouldn't give to have Racer by my side right now, but I know he's still climbing out of debt and his schedule is jam-packed with his new construction company. There is no way I could ask him to come.

I'm about to text him back when something out of the corner of my eye catches my attention. Looking up, I watch Adalyn intently, wondering if my eyes are playing tricks on me, and when I think maybe they are, I see it again. Her finger twitches.

My heart stutters, a sharp chill running up my spine when I see it again. Setting my phone to the side, I slip my hand into hers and the smallest of squeezes comes from her hand.

"Baby," I cry. "Can you hear me? Adalyn, if you can hear me, squeeze my hand again." I pause, waiting and waiting until . . .

Her finger presses against me, and I split apart. *Wake up, beautiful.* She twitches again, and I smile.

She's going to be okay. My girl is going to be okay. At least I try to convince myself of that.

R esting my head on the bed, I dream. I dream of the day Adalyn and I welcome our baby boy into the world. I see it so clearly, her sweat-soaked hair in a ponytail, our little guy wrapped up in a blanket, pressed lovingly against Adalyn's chest. My arm is wrapped around her shoulders, and we're both looking at the human we created. It's beautiful. The smells, the clarity of the image, the feel of Adalyn stroking the thin strands of my hair . . . it feels so goddamn real.

"Hey."

"Hey," I reply. Her voice soft but clear.

"Are you awake?"

"Of course," I answer, wondering why she's asking me . . .

I jolt my head up, knocking away a hand from the short strands of my hair. Blinking rapidly, I make eye contact with those big, beautiful eyes once again. And in that second, I can feel it. My heart re-starting, beating for an entire different reason. It's beating for the woman in front of me.

Sitting up on her bed, I cup her cheeks gently and stroke her skin, almost in complete shock that she's awake.

"Adalyn." I search her eyes, back and forth, studying the heaviness of her lids. "Baby, you're awake."

"Mmm," she groans, placing her IV-covered hand on my arm. "You're here."

"Are you fucking kidding me? Of course I'm here."

"But the game." Her breaths are short. "I wasn't—"

"Stop. That doesn't matter; none of that matters. All I care about right now is that you're talking to me. Fuck . . ." Emotion takes over as I lean forward and press the softest kiss across her lips. "Adalyn, I thought . . . I thought I lost you . . . before I could fully have you."

Her eyes shut briefly and when they reopen, they are welling up in tears.

"Don't cry, please don't cry." I wipe away the droplets of water that fall. I press my forehead against hers. "I don't ever want to lose you again, Adalyn. Right here, this is what I want forever. You, the baby, and me. I love you, more than you will ever know."

Taking a second, she catches her breath and says, "I love you, Hayden."

Squeezing my eyes shut, a type of euphoria I've never experienced takes over my body, the type of euphoria I know a human can only experience once in a lifetime. *Now* is my time. For others, it might be when they meet their baby for the first time, or when they meet the love of their life for the first time. Not me, my time is right now.

"Goddamn it, I love you. I want you forever. No matter how hard it is, how difficult our lives might end up being with my profession, I want you to know, I will do everything in my power to make you happy, to make sure you're loved, and never have to worry about being lonely again. Till my dying day, I promise you this, Adalyn."

"Being with you will be all I need," she answers, her lips brushing a whisper of a kiss across my mouth.

What I wouldn't give to deepen that kiss, to let her know how serious I am, but I resist, not wanting to hurt her.

Sighing, I speak softly when I say, "The minute you're better, I'm claiming your mouth, because from this day forward, Adalyn, you're mine."

Leaning her head back on the bed, her eyes flutter shut, sleep taking over as she whispers, "I'm yours, Hayden, forever."

Forgetting all hospital protocol, I stretch my body across the small hospital bed and wrap my arm around her, bringing her against my chest, needing to be as close to her as possible. It's not going to be an easy road for us, but I know, from here on out, as long as we're together, we can get through anything.

EPILOGUE

HAYDEN

"I don't know. The blue is really speaking to me."

Giving Logan a very unhappy glare, he shrugs his shoulders and pats me on the back. "Sorry, man. We might get along now but my loyalty will always lie with Addie."

"So much for dicks before chicks," I mutter, causing Logan to laugh.

"Told you blue is the winner," Adalyn gloats while doing a very pregnant version of the running man, her large pregnant belly hanging over her grey sweatpants. She's in month nine and not giving a fuck about how much her belly is out in the open.

"Settle down there." I motion her to slow her dancing. "We don't need any water breaking when we don't have the nursery ready yet."

"Whose fault is that?" Adalyn taps her foot and eyes the two paint swatches on the wall. Red and blue.

"All of the baby books say babies can't see any colors but black, white, and red. Why not give him a room he can enjoy?"

"Because black, white, and red are not baby colors," Adalyn protests, hands on her hips.

"Says who? All the people who design all this baby crap? It's a mass market for suckers like you two. Oh look at this cute sailboat, or this dinosaur blanket . . . it's all about black, red, and white."

"And how convenient, that those colors just happen to go well with your hockey-themed room."

Casually, trying not to show my true colors, I say, "Hey, if it works out that way, it works out that way."

"What happened to wanting to keep me happy, huh?" Adalyn taps her foot, staring me down.

Logan's gaze bounces between the two of us for a split second before he shakes his head and says, "I'm out. You two are on your own." Giving the peace sign, he points at me and says, "Tickets for tomorrow's game?"

"In your fucking dreams after your betrayal."

Logan deflates but not for long because Adalyn walks up to him, gives him a hug and says, "Don't worry, I'll get them for you."

Betrayed, once again.

Ever since that awful fucking night in the hospital, Logan and I have been on good terms. We never spoke of our problems again. It was simply accepted we both love Adalyn and will do anything to keep her safe. And what's even better about this entire situation is that Logan has a girlfriend now, Mandy, and she's a good fucking time. They make for a good couple to hang out with. On off nights, we have them over with Chris and Shannon, to have game night. Adalyn and I lose to both couples every single time.

We keep blaming it on the baby, eating all of Adalyn's brain cells. Once the baby is born, it's game on.

Once Logan is gone, Adalyn turns toward me, her gaze intent. I've seen that look before. She's determined, not going to back down, and ready for ten rounds of arguing. She's about to get her way.

It's what happened when she moved into my apartment. *She* insisted on dating first, I insisted upon not letting her out of my sight. I won that round. Then when it came to the house we bought, she won with what house she wanted, not wanting anything too outlandish. Apparently an elevator in your house is "too much." I was voting for convenience. And now, with the nursery needing to be painted, I can see that look in her eyes.

This place is going to be blue.

Giving in before we can get into it, I say, "Can we at least agree upon on sailboats?"

"What is your beef with sailboats? They are a delightful nautical fixture."

"We aren't nautical people."

"We could be," she suggests, wrapping her arms around me, her belly bumping up against my stomach. "Want to buy a boat? Go sailing?"

"Not even a little." I chuckle, placing a soft kiss on her lips. "What about robots."

"What kind of message are we trying to send our kid if we decorate with robots?"

Brow pinches, mirth in my voice, I say, "Uh, I don't know, that they're cool. What kind of message is sailboats?"

Gesturing with her hand, she answers, "Come sail away with us, baby boy. Your dreams can reach as far as the ocean. Let your every dream set sail."

"Jesus Christ," I mutter, kissing her again. When I pull away, I whisper against her lips. "I'll give you the blue, but not the boats."

"Ugh, you hate me."

Laughing hard, I shake my head and drag her to the white glider she picked out from Pottery Barn. "On the contrary, I'm absolutely obsessed with you." I nuzzle her neck, kissing the soft column. "What about airplanes?"

She moves her neck to the side, giving me more access as my hands glide up over her stomach, to her full breasts. Pulling down the low cut of her tank top, I slip my hand into her bra and pinch her nipple, getting right to business. One thing I've learned from this pregnancy? Slow is not something she's interested in at the moment. She likes it hard and fast, and fuck do I come hard every time when she screams my name, begging for me to thrust harder.

"Airplanes?" she gasps and leans her back against my chest. "Mmm, I can do airplanes."

I slip my hand down the front of her sweatpants to find her wet already. "Fuck, Adalyn, why are you always ready for me?"

"Because, this is what you do to me, Hayden." She circles her hips against me, holding on to my neck while I work my fingers between her legs.

"I need you on all fours, baby. Now."

Helping her down, I take no time shedding our clothes and pressing inside her. So tight, so warm, so damn perfect.

"Yes." She arches her back, her ass pushing against me. "Yes," she chants.

Leaning over her, I roll one of her nipples in my finger, tugging and pulling, knowing in seconds she's going to combust.

Just like clockwork, while I fuck her hard from behind, my cock slipping and sliding in and out of her, her pussy convulses around my cock, pulling at me, dragging out my orgasm as hers takes over, spiraling both out of control.

I come hard, my dick pulsing, giving me sweet relief. Short and sweet, that's what we are right now, and I know once she has the baby, I will spend more time exploring her body, making love to her over and over again. But right now, my girl wants to be fucked, and I give my girl what she wants.

Falling to the floor, I tuck her into my shoulder and stroke the side of her hip, marveling in the softest skin I've ever felt.

"I don't care what you do with the nursery, Adalyn," I admit, knowing she's going to end up winning most of these fights.

She kisses my chest, her lips grazing past my nipple, sending a jolt straight to my dick. "I actually like airplanes. I think it's sweet. Who knows, maybe one day he'll be a fighter pilot."

I shake my head. "Nah, with a name like Connor Holmes, he's bound to be a hockey star."

"The poor kid, he's doomed from the beginning."

Chuckling, I kiss the top of her head. "As long as he's happy and you're happy, then I'm happy."

She kisses my chin and sighs, snuggling closely into me. "Good thing being married to you is all I ever needed to be happy."

"Damn right it is, Mrs. Holmes."

Lying on the floor of our son's room, I stare at the ceiling and realize how good I have it. I have my beautiful, feisty girl in my arms and a wonderful future ahead of us. A crazy, chaotic, but fulfilling future.

And all it took was a few punches. One punch to an asshole during the last game of a season. One punch to my heart when I met and fell in love with the person who became my everything. And then the final punch to my soul when she became my wife to have and to hold from this day forward. My dad's always told me *we don't solve problems with our fists.* Wise advice, although I may not have solved *problems*, but because of that first punch, I won the most important game of my life, and she's currently wrapped in my arms. Score one for the baby daddy.

THE END

Made in the USA
Las Vegas, NV
29 March 2023

69846279R00203